SMOKE AND STEEL

WILD WEST MC SERIES
BOOK 2

KRISTEN ASHLEY

This book is a work of fiction. Names, characters, places and incidents are a product of the author's imagination or are used fictitiously. Any resemblance to actual events, locales, or persons, living or dead, is coincidental.

Cover Art: Pixel Mischief Design

SMOKE AND STEEL

BY KRISTEN ASHLEY

"Sometimes you need a really crooked road to get your head straight."
– Unknown

AUTHOR'S NOTE

Author's Note about the Wild West MC Universe

The Wild West MC series are romance novels written about three motorcycle clubs: Aces High, Chaos and Resurrection.

The Chaos MC was introduced in my Dream Man series and had their own series that is now concluded. It spanned six books and three novellas.

Interspersed in this series will be a lot of lore that refers back to the stories of Tack and Tyra (*Motorcycle Man*), Tabby and Shy (*Own the Wind*), Hop and Lanie (*Fire Inside*), Joker and Carissa (*Ride Steady*), Millie and High (*Walk Through Fire*), Hound and Keely (*Wild Like the Wind*), Rush and Rebel (*Free*), Snapper and Rosalie (*Rough Ride*), Dutch and Georgie (*Wild Fire*) and Jagger and Archie (*Wild Wind*).

The Chaos series is set in Denver, Colorado.

Important to note, not only was the Chaos series a spinoff of my Dream Man Series, Dream Man was a spinoff of the Rock Chick Series.

The Aces High MC was introduced with Clara and Buck's story,

Still Standing. Buck's sister, Sheila, is the old lady of Dog, another member of the Chaos Motorcycle Club.

Aces High is situated in Phoenix, Arizona.

Resurrection, which was previously a motorcycle club called Bounty, was referred to in the Chaos series, but first took center stage in *Rough Ride*. Their decision to become Resurrection was explained in *Free*. That book also contains the love story of Beck and Janna.

Although Resurrection is based in Denver, they do their work anywhere it's needed.

The Wild West MC universe will bounce among these three clubs. *Smoke and Steel* is the first novel dedicated to the Resurrection MC.

I write this note because, as much as I might try to make each story a standalone for readers, in this particular series, there's so much that went on before, it's impossible not to refer to it. Not to mention, my loyal readers will expect the Easter eggs so they can see characters they spent time with in previous novels.

However, I'm well-aware that new readers might think, "Tack who?"

That said, I don't want to bog the narrative down with a lot of information about history that has spanned, essentially, over twenty books.

I hope new readers will go back and discover all of these stories.

But I didn't want to let you down with the one you have in your hands. I wanted you to know I've considered where you are with *this* story, and I did my utmost to keep it clipping along in a way you won't get lost, without covering you in information that doesn't have to do with the telling of Core and Hellen's story.

I hope it worked. Thank you for reading!

Rock on!

-Kristen

AUTHOR'S CAUTION

In a previous book in the Chaos series, an event occurred that framed who the Resurrection MC is today. All the brothers of that MC are struggling with past actions, specifically this event. These actions might be distressing for some readers. If you have issues around violence against women, I hope you find someone to provide help and support. But if you choose to read this book, I hope you view Core and his brothers with an open mind and an open heart as they work for redemption.

1

COOKIES

Hellen

I HEARD my front door open.

My first thought was, *Maybe the cookies were over the top.*

"Babe!" he called. "Cookies! Awesome!"

Or perhaps the cookies were just cruel.

I'd put on his second-favorite blouse (it could be his third, he didn't rank them, I just paid attention to him, unlike the other way around) and had my makeup two steps down from fuck-me-hard.

So I wasn't being *totally* in his face.

But my hair was loose, and although he didn't have the balls to claim it like he meant it (his tepid tugs were a bit of a turn off, and I'd learned to try to keep his hands out of my hair), still, he loved it down, mostly because I gave great hair.

And my ass in the jeans I was wearing sprung men on a glance.

He loved my cookies, all of them, no matter what variety I baked, because I'd perfected each version to the point most people told me to start my own shop.

Like I was going to waste my time on that.

Not a chance.

"What the...?" I heard him say.

He'd seen the box.

And here we go.

I turned to the doorway.

He wandered into my kitchen.

"Babe—" he began, wearing his remorseful face.

And I was glad.

Because that pissed me off.

And it did because, if he knew to be remorseful, he knew.

He knew.

I launched in.

"You don't have HBO Max. I have HBO Max. You asked to come—"

"Hell—"

"—over with your buds so you could watch some boxing thing, and I said yes. I was going out with my girls, but I said yes. All you had to do was tidy up after they left. I didn't ask you to vacuum and scrub the baseboards with a toothbrush. I asked you to tidy up. I came home to you passed out in my bed and beer bottles everywhere, left-over pizza congealing, a stain on my couch—"

"That's why I'm here now. I was going to—"

I wasn't listening, yet again, to what he was "going to" do.

"So when I left this morning, I asked you to take care of it before you left. You didn't. I came home to it. By then, every inch of my apartment smelled like stale beer and pizza."

"Like I was going to say," he stated with forced patience. "I'm here now to do it. You just did it before I could get to it."

I did a lot of things before he could get to them.

"It's *my* house, Bryan. And when I say you can hang here, and all I ask is you throw away some fucking bottles and put away some pizza, shove some plates in the dishwasher, toss some napkins in the trash, it's not a lot to ask. Hell, you're a grown man. I shouldn't *have* to ask. And I *wouldn't* ask if it didn't *mean something to me*."

He was giving me the "whoa" sign with his hand.

"Okay, I fucked up, but—"

"I woke up in the middle of the night to go to the bathroom."

He shut his mouth and tried not to let me see his smirk.

But I saw the smirk.

And, oh yeah.

Oh yeah.

Now I was *pissed.*

"Is something funny?" I asked quietly.

"No." He sounded choked because he was trying not to laugh, which meant he was lying.

"What's funny about me slamming my head into the cabinet door you left open over the toilet, even though I've asked you to close it probably thirty times, because last night wasn't the first time I slammed my head into it? Which means, I don't only want you to close it because cabinet doors should be closed. That's the reason the cabinet *has* a fucking door, so you can close it and not see all the crap inside. But also, because, when I slam my head into it, it hurts like fuck."

Me putting it that way, he looked remorseful again.

"Is it amusing to you to cause me pain?" I asked.

"Babe, I'm sorry. I'd had a few. I wasn't paying attention."

I let that go.

For now.

Instead, I pointed across the kitchen.

"Do you see that under-cupboard light that doesn't work?"

Bryan turned his head that way and made an "oh shit" face.

"Yeah," I agreed. "I mentioned it was out and I was going to email my apartment manager to fix it. You reminded me, if it isn't an emergency, it takes them a while to do something. You then said you'd do it. I said I thought that was great, if you did it, you could show me how and I wouldn't have to ask anyone again. That was a month ago. My apartment manager might not jump all over changing a lightbulb, but it'd be done in a few days. I've asked you five times. You keep telling me you're on it. I emailed them today. They're coming Monday."

He took a step toward me.

"Don't come closer," I warned.

He grinned, because he was good-looking and had a great smile, so just doing that allowed him to get away with a lot in the past—not by me, but others—and he kept coming.

"Bryan!" I snapped. "Do not come a step closer."

He was nearly to me.

"Dammit!" I shouted. "Do I need to call my brother-in-law to deal with your ass?"

He stopped, his face paling.

And I could not believe, while in the midst of this very conversation, I had to threaten him with Jagger in order for him to listen to me.

"That," I said softly. "That right there. That's why all your shit is in a box in the living room. Because you don't listen to me, and you don't respect me. You respect Jagger, because he's in an MC and he'd fuck you up, but you won't respect me, even though you've told me you love me."

"Hellen, babe," he cajoled. "None of this is a big deal. I'll go out now. Grab a bulb, show you how to fix it."

"No, I've waited on you to do that, and you didn't, so I took care of it myself."

"I'm good to do it now."

"I needed you to do it a month ago."

"It can be fixed in an hour."

"That's a month and an hour longer than I'm willing to wait for you to take care of it."

He started to lose patience. "Jesus, Hellen, none of this shit *matters*."

I crossed my arms on my chest.

"You see, this is the problem," I informed him. "None of this shit matters *to you*. When you use my washer and dryer, I ask you to get it done and leave them empty. Half the time you come over here to do your laundry, you leave your clothes in my machines for days, and by the time I wanna do my own, I have to deal with yours first, so I can do mine. Have I told you about this more than once?"

"Okay, I see this is a thing for you, so I'll be on it from now on."

"Why do I have to box all your stuff and be done with you before you agree to be on it, Bryan? Why can't words come out of my mouth, you take a second to listen, process, and if you have some issue, discuss, and if not, just be a decent partner?"

"Because it's just...fucking...*laundry*," he bit out.

"First, they're *my* machines, and I let you use them. And second, do you ever have to wait for me to clear my clothes out when you want to use them?" I didn't pause for him to answer. "No, because I get it done and clear them out even though they're *my* machines. Still, it's in my mind that you also use them. I'm doing you a favor, so maybe you could return that by not hanging up my machines."

He looked to his trainers, mumbling, "My God, this is fucked-up petty."

Okay.

Um...

No.

"Right. Just leave my key, grab your box and go."

He lifted his head, and his eyes were narrow. "Hang on a second. We're not over just because you're throwing a fit about your washing machine."

"Yes, Bryan." I uncrossed my arms and put my hands to my hips. "Yes, we are. Because it's become clear to me that you aren't getting this in a way you never will. I've put up with it for too long as it is."

"Put up with what?" He jerked his thumb at his chest. "Me?"

"Your disrespect for me."

"Oh, for fuck's sake," he blew out.

I stared at him.

Then I looked to the side, took a beat, and turned back to him.

"Hitting my head last night hurt a lot, Bryan."

His handsome face went soft. "Baby, I'm so sorry. It won't happen again."

"That's what you said the last time I hit my head."

"Okay, but I mean it this time. Seriously."

"I heard you laugh last night when I cried out. It woke you up, you called to ask if I was okay. I said I hit my head, and I heard you laugh."

His lips tipped. "When you're not being pissy, you gotta admit it *is* kinda funny. You're using the toilet, you get up and—"

I cut him off.

"It's not funny, Bryan."

His head jerked, possibly at my tone, which was firm but wounded.

I wanted to scream because it took me this long and cost me this many words and this much frustration, and I had to expose my hurt to finally get him to pay attention.

"And please listen to me when I explain all the reasons why it's not," I went on. "First, if I'd done something, even inadvertently, that made you feel pain, it would make *me* feel pain. I would not want pain for you. I especially would not want to be the cause of that pain. I'm not a frat buddy you're pulling a prank on. I'm your girlfriend, the woman you're supposed to love. How my pain could ever, *ever* translate to amusement to you, I have no idea. That's the first part."

"You're right, that was shitty," he muttered.

"It was, but as I've mentioned, it's happened before, even though I asked, not mean, not bitchy. Nicely. Courteously. Please keep that cabinet door shut, especially considering its position. You disregarded my request. More than once. What does that say about how you truly feel about me?"

"Baby, it's just me being a guy."

"No it isn't. Not every man on this planet does whatever the fuck they want, thinking they're...what? I don't know. So hot a woman will put up with it?"

Which, truth be told, he was incredibly hot.

But not that hot (in my estimation).

No one was that hot.

I carried on.

"Hoping they'll hook up with their mother who'll take care of their ass until they die? It isn't the cabinet. It's that and the light and the laundry and having to clean up after you and your friends. It's asking you to separate the cutlery when you put it in the dishwasher, that is, when you put anything in the dishwasher, because it's easier to put away, but you never bother. And requesting you recycle, and I find recyclables in my garbage."

His face was flushing.

"Okay, seriously, I know this is gonna make me sound like a dick, but I'm honestly not trying to be a dick when I say, if it means so much to you, and it doesn't to me, then you can do it yourself and not give me hassle, because it's not important to me."

"No, Bryan. See, *this* is the thing," I retorted. "I am not going to spend any more time, much less consider a long-term relationship, or I should say a *longer*-term one, and commit to a man who cannot perform minor considerations simply because he values the person he's spending time with. I'm asking you to *close a cabinet*. I'm asking you to *put a bottle in a different bin that is right beside the garbage bin.* I'm asking you to shove a fork in a certain slot. I'm asking you not to make insignificant promises, that are still promises, that you're not going to keep, and I have to deal with the consequences. That's all I'm asking. And you've demonstrated repeatedly you can't do these things. So we are done."

He lifted his hands in front of him in an "I give up," gesture.

"All right, baby, I get it. I see now how important this stuff is to you. I'll get on it. I mean that."

"And then what, Bryan? You'll be"—I did air quotation marks —"*good* for a while, and then we have this conversation again? We've been there before. It doesn't last. Or, because I made it clear your inaction has repercussions, you'll note these things, and do better, but then something else will come up, I'll share, you won't pay it any heed, and I'll have to get fed up to the point I need to do something extreme to get your attention, and only then I'll get your attention? Is this the cycle you want to land on me? Is this how you want me to live?"

He was stuck, considering that was where he'd put himself, so to that, he just screwed up his mouth and remained silent.

I didn't return that favor.

"Why do you get the girlfriend who folds your clothes when you leave them in my dryer, and rushes to court to bring you a new tie when you've spilled lunch on the one you were wearing? And looks after your dog when you're in Vegas with your buds? And bakes cookies for your boss's birthday to buy you points? Then I sit down to dinner with him and charm him when my family was having a get together and I wanted to be with them. But you were my guy, that was important to you, so I did my face and hair and put on an appropriate dress and sat at your side. And the man liked me so much, he told you to marry me and offered me a job. Why do you get that woman, and I get a man who doesn't listen to me until I feel the need to shout, either literally or figuratively? The man who thinks he can decide for the both of us what's important, and what's not, deeming my wishes unimportant, then deigning to acquiesce to them, still thinking they're petty, when they aren't? They're *my wishes*. So they *matter*."

The cookie timer went off.

I moved to the oven, peered in, then opened the door, took them out and put the tray on a hot pad on the counter.

I returned my attention to Bryan.

He was staring at the cookies.

What he wasn't doing was addressing my concerns in any real way.

"I'm sorry, Bryan, but I'm done talking, and I am because I've said all this before in one way or another, and you didn't bother to hear me. If you don't mind, I'd like to get on with my night. So if you could leave my key and then grab your box and go, I'd appreciate it."

His gaze darted from the cookies to me.

"That's it? We're together over a year, you decide we're done, you kick my ass out and we're done?"

And again, I wanted to scream.

I also wanted to cry.

Because he spoke truth. We'd been together for over a year.

I went there with him at first because he was good-looking.

I stuck around because he was funny, smart, interesting, and at the time, attentive.

He was also a mover and shaker.

He was an attorney, and his goal was to make full partner by the time he was thirty-five. It was a huge firm, which had been around for sixty years. The youngest they'd made someone a partner was at forty-two. It seemed an impossible goal, but he was going for it.

I liked a man with drive, ambition, because I was that kind of woman.

A woman with drive.

A woman with ambition.

He was also in killer student loan debt, and even though he made good money, he was living on the cheap because he wanted them out of his life. He could sacrifice. He could save. He could be responsible.

I was a woman who could sacrifice, save, be responsible.

He dressed great, and because he worked hard, he played harder. He didn't waste the small amount of downtime he had. He was busy and he was social, he had good taste in music and movies, and he made it a priority, being with me.

I had yet to have an excellent lover, and I knew that regardless of the fact I had yet to have one.

But he didn't suck in bed. He cared that I orgasmed, and he put effort into it, so that was a plus.

In the beginning, even though I was young, too young (in my estimation) to commit, (I was twenty-three), I thought there might be a possibility I'd found my man.

So I might know my own mind, and that mind was made up we were over, but this wasn't easy for me.

I just wasn't going to cry and moan and whine and beg in front of him.

I'd deal with those feelings when he left.

And this was another indication that he didn't get it.

Any of it.

"This isn't easy for me, Bryan," I told him.

"Could have fooled me, babe," he returned.

Okay, this had to end.

"You know, unless you clue in, yes, I'm going to say it, unless you grow up and make changes, one day, you're going to find a woman. And you're going to be able to hold on to her because she will love you more than she loves herself. And that is not a good thing, Bryan."

He stared at me.

I kept talking.

"Then, somewhere down the line, you're going to look at her and see the light is out in her eyes. She might find things to bicker with you about that make no sense, because they're not what really matters. She'll just be bitter she didn't stand up for herself, she didn't stop it before it was too late, and she's going to find ways to take that out on you. But what really mattered was that every day, in little ways, you showed her she was not important to you, and she put up with it. You did what you liked, and she sucked it up, because she'd asked and asked, and you didn't care enough to make the effort."

The flush was coming back to his face.

I kept going.

"Eventually, you treating her like she's not important will drive home the fact that she's not. She'll start believing it. And because she's not important, she needs you. Because...who else would have her? She's not worthy. She's going to be a shell of her former self, striking out at random, making your life miserable, and you're going to wonder what happened to the lively, awesome chick you first met, not understanding you buried her under your own shit. And it's highly likely from there, you'll scrape her off and find someone else you can smother with your neglect and self-absorption."

I watched him swallow, but he still didn't speak.

I wasn't holding high hopes for his bid to make partner if he couldn't even state his own damn case to his girlfriend.

But that was beside the point.

And I wasn't done.

"Or maybe you'll remember this conversation, and you'll realize the person you spend time with deserves for you to listen when they speak and give a damn about what they say. For you to take it into consideration. For you to make minor adjustments in your behavior to be a good partner and prove to the person you're sharing time with she means something to you. And I hope that happens for you, Bryan. But I'm not putting in any more work. Someone else is going to have to guide your way on that. I have my own life to live, and I'm not going to do it in clothes that smell like pizza and stale beer because the guy I like needs me to tutor him in how to give a shit about me."

He didn't say anything for long moments after I quit speaking, but I said no more since I'd stated my case.

Finally, he asserted, "I *can* do better, Hellen."

"This is the sad part for us both, Bryan. Because you've conditioned me not to believe that."

He dropped his head, tore his hand through his (very nice) hair (I'd miss pulling on that, and I did, like I meant it, and he'd loved it), lifted his head, and declared, "Shit, fuck, I'm in love with you. Honest to God, I can do better."

"I've made up my mind."

"Goddammit, Hellen!" he shouted.

That was when it happened, to my shame.

The tears hit my eyes.

Upon seeing my emotion, his expression warmed with hope.

"And even now, you're not listening to me," I whispered.

His face froze.

"This isn't *easy*, Bryan. But *I've made up my mind*."

"Okay, I'll go," he said quickly. "We'll give it some time. Take a break. I'll text you in a week."

"Please remember to leave the key," I replied.

His body jolted, and his face fell.

"Baby, you're killing me," he said raggedly.

I pressed my lips together and struggled to beat back the tears.

"I fucked up, I'm so fucking sorry," he went on, pulling his keys out of his pocket. "I'll give you some space. I'll take my stuff." He slid my key off his ring. "I'll text. We'll go out. Sit down and talk. I'll listen, and I'll hear. And we'll work this out." He set the key on the counter.

I didn't say that wasn't going to happen.

But that wasn't going to happen.

"Can I have a hug before I go?" he requested.

Translation: *If you hug me, then I know there's still a shot. I'll give you some space. I'll come back. Make a load of promises. Do better. Then backslide. But by then, I'll have sucked more of your time and chipped away more of your confidence. I'll have the chance to make you start wondering if you* are *being petty and then you'll just fold my laundry and it'll bug you, but you won't mention it. And by the time you've realized you've subjugated all your needs to me, you'll be menopausal and wondering what the fuck happened to your life.*

Fortunately for me, my translation of going to him and giving him a hug was different.

He held me close and tight. He was tall-ish, and I liked that. He felt good and smelled good. I liked that too.

He kissed my neck.

I liked that too, even though, under the circumstances, it was an asshole thing to do.

I pulled at his hold, and he let me go.

Then he looked me in the eyes and made a promise.

"I see a future for us, babe, and I'm going to make that happen.

Whatever you need. You matter to me. I hate that I didn't make that clear the way you need it. But I'll prove it to you."

I pitied the woman he trapped.

He gave me his cocky grin, which was a blow because I loved that grin, though I figured that wasn't why he gave it to me.

It was just who he was.

"Can I have a couple of cookies?" he requested.

I stepped away so I was nowhere near the tray of cookies, or him, and he frowned. He didn't like that.

But I flicked a hand at them, an indication he could help himself.

He took a handful, five stacked and cupped in his hand to be exact.

So not exactly "a couple."

But...whatever.

"Love you, Hellen," he said, putting a lot of feeling behind that, and it cut me because it was genuine.

"'Bye," I replied.

He didn't like that either.

But he left.

When I heard the door close, I followed him.

I stood at the door and waited, and when he was sure to be away, I turned the deadbolt and put on the chain.

I then went into the kitchen, sorted the cookies, put a lid on the dough, stashed it in the fridge, wandered back to my bedroom, curled up on my bed...

And I cried.

Core

Core was kicked back in his chair, boots up on the windowsill, bag of nacho cheese Doritos on his abs, a beer and a set of binoculars close at hand, when Pretty Boy left her apartment.

Normally, Core wouldn't register this too much, except to ignore the low-key way it annoyed him that the woman was with a dude like that.

Then again, it'd be more surprising she'd let a rough-trade biker into her bed.

Of course, Tack, Hop and High of the Chaos MC all had old ladies who wore tight skirts, stylin' blouses, high heels and carried those expensive purses.

But Core wasn't a high-maintenance-woman type of man.

That said, if the woman he was watching, Hellen Moynihan, Jagger's sister-in-law wasn't thirteen years younger than him, and if she gave him an opening, he wouldn't hesitate to give her a pop.

The way she worked that ass and the attitude that slithered off her wrapped around your dick and gave it a tug, he'd give her more than one.

All of these thoughts flashed through his mind, and then he was taking his boots off the sill, straightening in his chair, setting aside the Doritos and reaching for the binoculars.

He trained them on Pretty Boy and let out a low whistle.

After that, he chuckled.

Enjoying the show, Core kept his binocs on a very unhappy PB who was shoving a box, which looked like it was filled to overflowing with his stuff, into the trunk of his shitty sedan.

Core didn't know the story of that guy. He only knew he was twenty-nine, an attorney at some bigshot firm downtown, and he wasn't the focus of why Core's ass was right there.

He had no idea why Pretty Boy, who had to make big bucks, drove such a shit car.

Core just knew that she'd scraped him off.

He could have called it (that said, it was about time).

Woman like that wouldn't put up with a man who had his head up his ass, seeing as she'd expect her man to spend all his time kissing hers.

Still, it amused him to watch his walk of shame.

When he motored off in his crappy car, Core trained his binocs on her pad.

Lights on, probably going about her business, doing shit to her face and nails, preparing to lay waste to another man who she'd lead around by his dick.

Core might enjoy the novelty of that, if he had the shot of seeing her bowed before him, ass in his hands, taking his cock.

But he reckoned it'd get old fast.

He set the binoculars aside, sat back, grabbed his chips and scanned the street.

There was no sign of her.

That being, no sign of the woman who he was sitting right there, keeping an eye out for her to slither into town and make trouble for Hellen, or her mom, stepdad and sister. Like there hadn't been any sign of her for two weeks, even though they got word she was heading up from Phoenix.

He was beginning to wonder if the bitch they were looking for was even in Denver.

Nevertheless, he munched and kept his eye out, not knowing, soon, they'd all find out she very much was.

2

LIGHTNING BOLT

Hellen

"You're a man hater."

"Oh my God," Kyra muttered, her eyes going round.

Marcy pursed her lips in irritation.

I stared at Bree, who needed a reality check, and her girls, including me, were in the process of giving her one.

She just didn't want it.

And for some reason, in order to share that, she homed in on me.

"It's because your dad is such a jerk," she went on. "Now you hate all men. And we all have to suffer for it."

Okay, I'd been going softly-softly up to this point, we all had. Dancing around her feelings. Trying to get her to take a look at what was happening and come to the realization her boyfriend of only a few months was exhibiting signs he was a chronic user, because he was definitely using her.

It was important to note, my friend Bree wasn't stupid. She was buying his shit because he was gorgeous and talked a good game (even I, in the beginning, though he was very charming and ridiculously pretty, had thought he might be the real deal because he seemed genuinely into her, and I could understand that because she was my friend—but now, I didn't think that).

But her being bitchy because I loved her and was worried some guy was no good for her, I wasn't feeling it.

I also wasn't feeling like being singled out.

Which, of course, with me being me, meant it was time for me to lay it out.

"I don't hate all men," I replied. "I just hate predatory assholes like Christos."

"And what if I said something like that about Bryan?" she retorted hotly. "Oh wait. There is no Bryan. He didn't live up to your impossible standards so he's out."

I actually felt the tip of that arrow pierce my heart.

"Ouch," I whispered.

"Oh my God," Kyra repeated.

Marcy chimed in this time too. "You know that isn't right."

Bree looked contrite, but she didn't back down.

"Did she dump Bryan?" she asked the group. "Yes, she did," she answered before anyone could do it.

"And you were sitting right here a week ago with the rest of us, listening to her litany of woes about him, and agreeing, like we all did, that if he perpetuated some new thoughtless bullshit, he needed to sort his shit or take a hike," Marcy fired back. "And three days ago, after his buds coming over meant *she* had to head to the store for upholstery cleaner, she asked him to take a hike."

"Yeah, well if I had an issue with Christos...*which I don't*...then I'd expect you all to agree with me and take my back. But again, I don't have an issue with Christos. In fact, we're great." She did the thing with her nose that she did when she was being rebellious, something that was a big thing for her since, for the most part, she was a people pleaser. "He told me he's falling in love with me, and I'm thrilled he did, because I'm falling in love with him too."

Oh crap.

"Bree—" I started.

"No," she snapped. "I think you've said enough."

"Okay, seriously though, have you *not* seen *The Tinder Swindler*?" Kyra blurted.

Yikes.

She went right there.

Bree and Christos didn't meet on Tinder. They met on Bumble.

Kyra's delivery wasn't smooth, but it was a pertinent question.

Bree's face went red as a beet. "That's an awful thing to say!"

"It was all fun and games in the beginning," Marcy pointed out. "Now how many times has he asked you to bail him out?"

"And you've only been seeing him a couple of months," I reminded her.

"We're nearly to our three-month anniversary," she sniffed. "And I don't *bail him out*. I've given him a few loans. He's going to pay me back."

"And again, how many loans have you given him?" Marcy repeated.

Bree screwed up her face. "You all are ganging up on me."

"We're not," I said carefully. "We're just saying this is something to consider. In the beginning he's flashing cash, taking you to expensive restaurants, buying you things, and talking about Mediterranean cruises and flying you to see his homeland to meet his family. Now he's been in a lurch, not just once, and needs you to cover him, and you've only known the guy what amounts to a matter of weeks."

"We're not all freaks about our money like you. And we're not all uptight and controlling of our boyfriends…*like you*," Bree shot back.

The money part, she was right, in a way.

I could see how other people would think I was a freak about money.

Though, my opinion was, if they could, everyone should handle money like I did. They'd be a lot less stressed out.

You see, I'd gotten my first job at age fifteen, and from my very first paycheck, I'd religiously done what I still did today (with some minor tweaks).

Twenty-five percent saved for future use.

By "future use" I meant, if my stepdad Andy hadn't stepped up and paid for my education, I would have used it for that.

Since I didn't have to do that, it sat untouched until I needed to invest in myself (unless I had to move it around into higher interest-bearing accounts). Be that investment in the business I knew I was going to start one day (though I didn't know what that business was, until I did), or setting up my first apartment, or whatever.

Now that twenty-five percent went back into my business, my wardrobe or my home (like buying the kickass couch that Bryan or one of his friends stained with pizza sauce).

The next twenty-five percent was saved for a rainy day.

I'd since cut that back to ten percent because I had to feed myself, and, you know, do other grownup things like pay rent.

The next twenty-five (now ten) was untouchable, no excuses.

Unless I was about to starve or become homeless, that money was to sit until it was time for me to quit working so I could spend my days in Italy, eating and wandering on my Eat Tour (I just wanted to do that part, I didn't have a lot of interest in the pray part, and if love happened, great, if it didn't, I wasn't going to look for it) or whatever struck my fancy.

What didn't strike my fancy, when I finally allowed myself to chill out and just be (I was aiming at age sixty, but I kinda hoped it'd be fifty-five), was hurting for money when it happened.

The last twenty-five (now fifty-five) percent was for current use, rent, groceries, utilities, etc.

I had not been unemployed a single day since I was fifteen, including working when I was in university. And Mom and Andy refused to allow me to use my money for anything that had to do with college.

This meant I was sitting on some serious cash when I started my business while I was a junior at the University of Colorado. And even more cash when I graduated a year later and struck out on my own.

It was good I started early. Now I had more clients than I knew what to do with and had the happy problem of trying to decide if I wanted to work eighty hours a week rather than the sixty to seventy I was currently working, or hire someone.

I was leaning toward hiring someone.

So yes.

I could see Bree, who earned her money, paid her bills, then blew it on Gucci bags she bought retail (which was a crime, with so many resale websites out there—those were where I got my steals) would think I was a freak about money.

It was her comment about me being uptight and controlling about Bryan that was another shot to the heart.

"So you lied last week, and instead, you think I should have continued to put up with his shit?" I asked.

"I'm just saying your expectations are high," she replied. "They're *guys*. Guys are dufuses. He's not even thirty yet. He can be trained."

"And how much time do I invest in training him before it's time to give up. Another year? Two? Ten?" I asked.

"I don't know," she retorted. "I just know he's a catch and you didn't let him slip away, you unhooked him and threw him back, which is kinda crazy."

"I'm not looking for a fish," I stated. "If I spend time with someone, I expect to get some respect, or at the very least common courtesy."

Marcy butted in.

"I'm feeling a bit ill we're going through this again when we've known for a while that Bryan was oblivious the best of times, thoughtless the worst, and that was not okay."

"Well, I guess Hell bitching incessantly about Bryan," (Ugh! I didn't bitch incessantly!) "then he's gone, and now she's bitching about Christos, I...I..."

Bree trailed off and her attention did the same, wandering slowly across Fortnum's, a used bookstore on Broadway where we hung most Sunday afternoons, gabbed and drank coffee.

Marcy, Kyra and I turned to see what caught her gaze, and for the first time in my life, it happened.

You know that lightning bolt all the books said hit a woman when she saw a man she knew in an instant she wanted to jump?

That lightning bolt just hit me.

Dear God, he was fine.

Faded jeans. Black T-shirt. Biker boots. One of those wallets that was chained to his beltloop, the chain hanging down his hip and then looping up to his ass like the dip in a roller coaster you really wanted to ride.

He had dark, messy, overlong hair that had a lot of curl in it and a face you wanted to wake up to.

Tying the bow on the package that was him: he was tall, his shoulders were broad, and his ass was awe-inspiring.

I knew this because I was awed speechless and immobile, the only thoughts in my brain being how hot getting razor burn from his stubble would feel and how full my hands could get with that tush.

He was rough and I was ready.

As if he felt us staring at him, he turned our way.

When he did, I couldn't hold back letting out a small gasp, because I could see the striking light blue of his eyes from where we were sitting in the huddle of furniture by the window.

I was so engrossed by how amazing he was, I didn't realize until too late that he might have turned our way, but he'd done it to look right at me.

Ohmigod.

"Ugh, you just broke up with Bryan, did you not give a shit about him at all?" Bree asked loudly.

I watched the guy's lips twitch (and Lord have mercy, *what lips*), and he turned back to the line.

I turned back to our group in order to give squinty eyes to Bree.

"Oh my God," Kyra said in a whisper. "You just cock-blocked a sister."

"Uh, have you heard of a rebound?" Marcy was also whispering. "And that tall drink of water practically has 'rebound' tattooed on his forehead."

"Did you care about Bryan at all?" Bree ignored them and asked me.

"I looked at a guy, I didn't ask him to marry me," I replied. "But to answer your question, yes. I did. After I packed his box and put him out, when he was gone, I curled up in bed and cried until I was useless. I not only didn't finish baking the cookies I was making, I didn't eat them. Not a one."

Kyra gasped, such was the power of this revelation.

Yes, my cookies were that good.

But I hadn't shared the worst of it.

"I miss him. I pick up my phone half a dozen times a day to text something to him. I don't want to clean my sheets because they still kind of smell like him. And he's going to get in touch in a few days after giving me space, and he's going to ask to talk, to work it out, and it's going to gut me all over again because I know he isn't right for me. He isn't good for me. He won't make me happy, which means I won't make him happy. So I might ghost him, though that's unlikely, because what we had means he doesn't deserve that. So I'll call him to set a time to sit down and share what he wants is not what I want. This will be nearly impossible to do. So then I'll probably cry myself useless again."

"I didn't know you cried like that," Marcy said quietly.

"I broke up with my boyfriend," I pointed out.

"You should have called," she returned.

I shrugged.

Marcy was still speaking quietly when she noted, "You know, you're allowed to be human and lean on people when the occasion merits it. We can be there for you like you're there for us when we need you. You don't have to be strong for everybody all the time, like you had to be when your mom left your dad."

That meant a lot, and I hoped the look on my face shared that it did.

Marcy's answering smile, which was full of sympathy, said I succeeded.

"Never go through a breakup alone is my motto," Kyra put in, her gaze kind and worried and resting on me.

"You're not a cynical loner like Hellen," Bree stated.

Everyone's eyes cut to her.

"There's a girlfriend line," Marcy snapped. "And, sister, you just jumped over it like you're Carl fucking Lewis."

Bree stood, picking up the Dior saddle bag she paid five thousand dollars for, when she just had to wait a season and she could buy it for twelve hundred dollars less.

She tossed it over her shoulder, tossed her strawberry blonde hair, then declared. "I'm in a bad mood and being bitchy. I need to go home to Ben and Jerry's." She settled her gaze on me. "I'll think about what you said. But really, Christos is very sweet. I mean a lot to him. You can't imagine how embarrassed he was to ask for my help. He's Greek. They're macho. I could see how upset it made him. But it's a temporary situation. He's cash poor. He promised me, it'll turn around. Still, it didn't feel good to watch a guy I'm falling in love with grovel like that, then you guys piling on didn't help."

We'd hardly "piled on." Not until she got bitchy.

I didn't get a chance to refute it, she kept talking.

"It'd also be good you think on what I said, not the bitchy way I said it. I got mad because you all don't really know Christos, but it also doesn't feel good you kinda think I'm an idiot."

"We don't think you're an idiot," Kyra cut in.

"It feels that way."

Well...

Shit.

"That wasn't what was intended," I said.

"And I didn't intend to be bitchy, but I was, and I'm sorry. Now I need some Phish Food."

Pure Bree, when she was done, she was done.

She did an air kiss and took off.

The bell over the door rang. When we first started coming there, Fortnum's was so popular, it rang all the time and drove me batty.

I didn't even hear it anymore.

She waved to us through the window.

We waved back.

When we lost sight of her, I asked, "Either of you know how much he's into her for?"

She'd shared she gave him another loan, she just hadn't shared how much.

"First time, she gave him five hundred," Kyra gave it up immediately. "This time, it was seventeen."

Whoa.

"Seventeen hundred dollars?" Marcy asked, her neat, black, arched brows nearly hitting her tall, soft Afro.

Kyra nodded glumly.

A short, sharp whistle rent the air.

We turned toward the door.

Tall, Dark, Rough and Ready was there, carrying a to-go coffee in his long-fingered hand.

The minute he caught my eye, he winked at me, his white teeth showing in a brash, sexy-as-hell Hollywood smile.

Then he slid his mirrored aviators on his nose, the bell over the door chimed, and he strolled out.

"I don't know whether to think that was completely gross, or a total turn on," Kyra said.

I knew.

It was door number two, thank you.

"A man whistles at me like a dog, he immediately occupies another universe, one that I'm not in," Marcy put her vote in.

The whistle was cocky AF.

But it was also hot AF.

And he was gone, so it wasn't like I was ever going to see him again. Thus, I could think that.

If he hadn't taken off, and instead he approached and presented a pickup line, *that* would be gross.

The way it went down, fortunately, I had someone else to think about, since I'd be using my vibrator a lot more considering Bryan was out of the picture.

I wondered if Tall, Dark, Rough and Ready knew how to pull hair.

"We probably didn't handle it all that well with Bree, but still, I'm not certain about Christos," Marcy declared.

"Me either," I agreed. "Three months and twenty-two hundred dollars do not add up."

"How do you get cash poor?" Kyra asked. "If you need cash, don't spend the cash you have."

"Yup." Marcy ended that with a pop.

We could just say, Kyra and Marcy shopped on the resale sites, like me. They also had moving and shaking to do, like me.

We'd all met at college. Bree and I were roommates our freshman year. We'd hooked up with Marcy, who was a year ahead of us, then Kyra, who was a year behind. Starting my sophomore year, we'd all lived together when we could, and now Kyra and Marcy were roommates again.

This meant I'd spent four years living with Bree, studying with Bree, partying with Bree, taking road trips with Bree, grocery shopping and cooking with Bree.

And she was still a huge part of my life because I loved Bree.

That said, if someone put a gun to my head, I'd have to admit I'd migrated my bestest best friend to Marcy because we were the same person, except she was Black and I was white.

I still loved Bree like crazy.

So that whole scene didn't feel great.

Kyra took off next because she had a date she needed to get ready for, and Marcy and I ordered fresh coffees and tucked ourselves back into the couch in front of the window.

"Are you feeling it?" she asked.

I didn't have to request she explain.

"I'm feeling it," I told her.

"Okay then, how would you feel about some recon?"

Now I was lost.

"What?"

"Follow Christos around. Get the goods on him. Evidence. Show Bree before she talks her parents into remortgaging their house because some diamond mafia is after him or something."

We'd all watched *The Tinder Swindler*, and clearly, we'd all taken mental notes.

"That's extreme, Marce."

"He's a scam artist, Hell. She works as a PA in a marketing firm, she's been with him three months, and she's handed over two months' rent. This is a situation."

She was right.

This was a situation.

Because we both knew Bree. And she might have a nest egg, but it probably wasn't that much.

Seventeen hundred dollars was a weird number. Which meant it was likely all she had left in her savings.

"You brought this up after Kyra took off because...?" I prompted.

"Because Kyra still buys stuffed animals...for herself. We have two cats, but if I let her, we'd have eleven. She's got more friends than anyone I know because she collects strays of all kinds. She's a sweetheart. Made of gold. But she is not street smart. It scares the hell out of me, but she's even worse than Bree. She'd be a nightmare on an operation like this."

An operation?

"Maybe you should tell me what you're thinking," I suggested.

"I'm thinking of following him and seeing what he's up to," she repeated.

Hmm.

"Do you know where he lives or works?" I asked, skeptical of this plan, but not entirely against it.

"I know where he lives, I dropped Bree off there once. I don't know what he does for a living, and that says something, don't you think?"

I did think.

Oh boy.

"You know what would stop the Tinder swindler?" she asked.

I knew.

"Marce—"

"A friend or a favorite auntie or someone saying, 'stop giving that jerk your money.' Someone doing a deep dive into his shit and finding out he's full of it. I know that Tinder guy on the documentary had a real racket going, but...come on."

I didn't want to judge a sister, especially not those who'd fallen for that man's shit. Truth, he had the con down to an art.

But yeah, someone injecting a little common sense or doing a little leg work, and maybe a lot of heartbreak and debt would have been saved.

Or better, that guy would have been caught a lot earlier.

Good news: part of what she said, I could do.

"Right, I'll do a deep dive," I told her. "We'll reconvene to share what I find and decide from there."

"I think we should tail him because, my guess, Bree's small potatoes. He's gotta have other bitches he's fleecing. She says he works a lot. At what, she's vague about, but I'll press. And she and Kyra are tight. Maybe Kyra knows. Another guess, he's working and taking other women's money."

I would have that same guess.

"Let's start with the online stuff first. Okay?" I suggested.

She seemed disappointed, sucked down some of her cold brew and plopped back on the couch.

But she nodded.

I thought about Bree. I thought about Christos. I thought about Tall, Dark, Rough and Ready.

And I thought about Bryan.

I thought about him because he'd failed me, but he was smart and sharp and knew the law. I could have told him about Christos, and he'd have good advice. He would also help look after Bree.

But Bryan was out.

So someone had to save Bree.

And she was ours.

So that was going to be Marcy and me.

3

SHITSHOW

Core

"WHAT THE FUCK are these bitches doing?"

Core asked that question to the windshield of his truck.

It didn't answer, and apparently it was go time for Hellen Moynihan and her friend to perpetrate some fucked-up shit that Core was going to have to get involved in.

It figured.

This was his last night on Hellen detail.

Weeks ago, Rush, the president of the Chaos Motorcycle Club, had gotten the intel about the issue coming up from Phoenix, and the possibility it could take a direct line to Jagger's in-laws, Jagger Black being one of Rush's brothers in Chaos.

Considering what that issue was, and how she'd behaved in the past, it could manifest itself as a niggle of annoyance, or Armageddon.

Jagger loved his wife and dug his in-laws. Consequently, he was super hip on helping them avoid Armageddon, and he wasn't real excited about them being annoyed either.

Rush decided the best course of action was to cut it off at the pass and send it home.

The Chaos MC was a club that'd had a rough go of it for around thirty years or so.

But they were now good. Brothers happy. Most of them married and making babies. Businesses raking in a shit load of money. Everyone fat and sassy.

They dipped their wick in things every once in a while, just to keep sharp.

But Rush didn't want his brother, Jagger, worried, and Core got that. Jagger worried would mean his blood brother, Dutch, would get worried, which in turn would mean their stepdad, Hound, would get worried.

Jagger and Dutch could make a man who could look after himself stand up and take notice.

But no one in Denver, or maybe the whole Rocky Mountain region, wanted Hound worried.

Dustin "Hardcore" Cutler could handle himself, but the thought of Hound pissed off and pushed into protection mode gave even Core a shiver.

His entire club had learned that the hard way.

So Rush called Beck, the president of Core's club, the Resurrection MC, and asked them to take point on lookout.

Even though this had been a total waste of a shit ton of time, it was an unwritten but unbreakable rule that Resurrection owed Chaos, and they would until all the members who did the base, shitty thing they did to a member of the Chaos family, were dead.

Core was one of those men who did that thing.

That meant now, anything Chaos asked, if it was within their power, they did it.

So Beck had offered the assistance of the Resurrection MC.

Now it had been weeks, and that trouble from Phoenix hadn't showed. They all had things to do. So Beck and Rush had a chat and they decided, since the brothers were already planning on it, one more night, and then they were going to back off.

He wasn't the only one from his club on Hellen. He shared her detail with Eight, Muzzle and Rainman, so that meant it was his luck he'd be on tonight when she got up to some dumb shit.

It started a couple of hours ago when he was kicked back with a brew and a bag of Bugles, it was getting dark, and she exited her place wearing all black, including enormous black shades, and the sun was almost down.

Plus, she had on sensible shoes.

The woman never wore sensible shoes.

Shit, even lounging at Fortnum's two Sundays ago, she'd been wearing a sexy pair of those tall wedges.

She also had her hair up in one of those big buns at the top of her head.

Last, she was not carrying her ever-present designer bag.

She was carrying a pair of binoculars.

All this said to Core that whatever she was up to, she meant business, and not the right kind.

She headed to her car.

He tossed the Bugles aside, grabbed his keys and hauled ass to his truck.

He followed her as she picked up her friend.

Then he followed them to some house in Littleton.

After that, he sat on his ass and watched them watch a house from their car.

Incidentally, she didn't make him following her, and he didn't try too hard to hide it.

He had no idea why she dressed like a cat burglar to do this. Both of them were shit at surveillance, and they didn't leave her car. The only time they made any attempt to hide was when they ducked after some dude came out of the house.

Core got a good look at him and noticed he was so pretty, it made Hellen's castoff seem looks-challenged.

The man got into a shiny BMW and took off.

Obviously, they weren't after him, because once he was gone, they stopped ducking but continued to sit and watch the house.

Core was getting fed up with it, he was about to jump out of his truck, go knock on her window and ask what she was doing, when both doors to her car opened and the women got out.

This was what made him talk to his windshield.

The friend crossed the road, head turning this way and that, keeping an eye.

Core felt it in his dick, though, witnessing how Hellen crossed the road.

She did it not only like she lived in that neighborhood and belonged there, but also like she owned it and all of Denver.

Jesus, that bitch was something.

They approached the house, and things went south immediately, at least they did for Core, because they didn't walk to the front door and press the bell.

They headed toward the side hedge and disappeared down it, toward the back.

"God fucking dammit," he muttered, threw open his door and angled out.

He was a noticeable dude, especially in a nice neighborhood like this, so he didn't fuck around getting to the hedge.

It was now dark, and he kept to the shadows as he followed the hedge to the back of the house.

The friend was nowhere to be seen.

But Hellen was standing to the side of a big window, her back flush to the house, up on her toes, peering over her shoulder in the window.

He could hear music coming from inside, but he wasn't sure if it was loud enough to drown out sound from outside, so he got close to her.

And it didn't escape him he got right up into her space, and she had no idea he was there.

He could be stealthy, what his club was about, it was essential.

But she was even shit at this part of whatever the fuck she was doing.

If you were somewhere you weren't supposed to be, you kept your senses sharp for any threat. You didn't stand there and let a man, who was six inches taller than you and had at least fifty pounds on you, get right up in your shit.

But once there, he didn't dick around.

He asked low, "What the fuck are you doing?"

She made a peep, jumped, whirled, took a step away, but then froze and stared up at him, her pretty lips parted, the whole surprise gig.

So, she could be cute.

That didn't help how she affected his dick.

"You..." She didn't finish, she just went back to staring at him.

"Text your friend to head back to the car," he ordered.

"Who are you?"

"Text your friend to head back to the car," he repeated.

Her brows drew down over her eyes. "Do you know Christos?"

He looked in the window.

There were three guys in there, sitting around a kitchen table. Two had their heads close, looking at the same phone. One was doing something on a laptop. They were all of the same ethnicity, maybe Italian. They were all dressed like Neiman Marcus threw up on them. And they were each one better looking than the next.

He returned his attention to Hellen.

"We can stand here and chat, they could hear us or one of them look out the window and see us, or you can text your friend and we can *talk at your car*."

When she hesitated, he reached out, grabbed her hand and pulled her to the hedge.

She came with him, and when he looked back, he saw her walking, hand in his, no struggle, head down, phone illuminated in her other hand. She was texting her friend.

He was surprised at this, first because he was a stranger. As far as he knew, she'd seen him once at Fortnum's.

Second, because she seemed like the kind of woman to put up a fight, even when it would be stupid to do it, just to make a point.

Last, because he was how he was, and she was how she was.

Sure, Jagger was a part of her family, and anyone who was family of a brother of Chaos was Chaos family. So she clearly had experience being around bikers.

But he'd had thirty-six years of people like her thinking people like him were someone you feared or looked down on and avoided.

The fact she walked hand in hand with him and did what he told her to do, for some reason trusting him right off the bat, did something to his dick too.

Also something was happening in his chest.

Like the rest, even though this was harder, Core ignored it.

He didn't take her to her car.

His truck was a few car lengths down from hers, farther from the house.

He took her there.

They stopped on the sidewalk by the passenger door, and he let her hand go, which kinda sucked, but it would seem weird if he held on to her.

Then he repeated himself. "Now, tell me what the fuck you're doing."

"Who are you?" she demanded.

"Hardcore. Resurrection MC."

Another wave of surprise hit her, then he could tell she thought she knew something.

"Oh my God, does Jagger know what Christos is up to?" she asked.

This Christos thing again.

"Who's Christos?" he asked in return.

The friend jogged up but took the last five steps with her torso shifting back, her eyes locked to Core.

She stopped next to Hellen and demanded, "Have you been holding out on me?"

"No," Hellen answered, flipping a hand at Core. "I'm as surprised as you are. He just showed up."

Both women looked at him.

Core sought patience, not his biggest strength.

"What. Are you two women. *Doing here?*" he clipped.

"What are *you* doing here?" Hellen retorted.

"Keeping an eye on you," he told her.

"Why?" she shot back.

He debated whether or not to tell her.

Straight up, he'd wondered why they hadn't gone to the family in the first place. That part wasn't communicated to him, and once Beck showed him a picture of Hellen, he didn't ask.

But now, he had to make a decision.

It wasn't like they'd bugged her house and Core knew everything about her. That said, he'd been watching her on and off for weeks, leaving for work, getting home from work, grocery shopping, hanging with her chicks, her family, going out with her man.

And everything he'd noticed when it came to Hellen Moynihan said the woman had her shit together.

"There are concerns your cousin is up to something," he shared.

It took a beat for her to get pissed.

Yeah, she knew what he was talking about.

"She's *such* a disaster," she bitched.

"Who?" the friend asked.

Hellen turned to her. "My cousin, or my second cousin, Eleanor. She lives in Phoenix. She's my dad's uncle's daughter. She's bad news." Her attention returned to Core. "What's she up to?"

"We don't know. Rush just wasn't taking any chances."

Another look came over her face, and fuck him, he liked that one too.

"He's so sweet," Hellen muttered.

"So, you're her phantom bodyguard who shows up during coffee time, whistles and winks? Is that part of the invisible bodyguard playbook?" the friend asked.

"A woman stares at a man like she wants to climb him like a tree, he's gotta throw her something, and if you got a dick, that's definitely in the playbook." Core replied.

"Valid," the friend said under her breath.

Hellen wasn't thinking sweet thoughts anymore.

Not even close.

"I didn't stare at you like that," she snapped.

"You totally did," he returned.

The friend remained silent because Hellen totally did.

"I was admiring your wallet," Hellen kept at it.

"You were panting after my ass," he corrected.

"Hardly," she dismissed.

"Tell yourself that," he muttered.

"Okay, you are officially the worst bodyguard ever," she announced.

"Oh yeah?" he asked, then he laid it out. "First, I tailed you from your house, and you didn't make me. Second, I snuck up on you, got in your space, you didn't even know I was there. What if I was one of those dudes in the house? You wanna be dragged in there to explain to three guys why you're dressed like Catwoman on a casual day and snooping in their shit?"

"He has a point there," the friend said. "Including the 'Catwoman on a casual day' comment, which I'll also note is funny."

The friend was wearing army green joggers, hot pink trainers and a lighter green sleeveless top with a V front edged in a ruffle.

It said a lot about her she could make that top seem edgy.

"Name?" he asked the friend.

"Marcy." She offered her hand. "How you doin'?"

He took it, gave it a firm squeeze, let go and said, "Core. And I'd be doin' great if one of you told me why the fuck we're all standing here."

"Maybe we should go somewhere else and talk," Marcy suggested.

"Maybe you and me should do that and discuss what's next and he can go back to phantom bodyguarding," Hellen parried, aiming this at Marcy.

"I'm in," Core said, also to Marcy, immediately after Hellen stopped speaking. Then he made the plan. "We'll meet at Moynihan's."

After he said that, he left them standing on the sidewalk, rounded his hood, got in his truck and started it up.

He waited behind the wheel, his vehicle humming, going into staredown with Hellen, and this lasted so long, he started chuckling.

She couldn't hear it, but she saw it, and it made her madder.

Which made him start laughing.

Marcy dragged her to her car.

He followed them to Hellen's apartment.

He parked and his long legs got him close fast, so he followed them into her pad.

Her complex wasn't the greatest, it wasn't the worst. A bunch of fake adobe with different floor plans for the studio, one- and two-bedroom townhome units.

He knew this because he'd dated a woman who lived there and then later partied with some friends who also lived there.

Resurrection had made a deal with the apartment manager (which meant cash had exchanged hands) so they could hang in an empty apartment across from Hellen's to keep an eye on her. They'd lucked out with this scenario. It was a lot easier to get made, day in and day out, sitting in a vehicle staring at an apartment.

When she let them in, even though he could see some of it through her windows, getting the full view, he was mildly surprised at what he saw.

She was young, but she had her shit tight.

It wasn't a big place, it wasn't full of stuff, it wasn't in-your-face chick either. All of which he approved of.

Whites. Blacks. Grays. Browns. There was space. Room to move. Room to add to what she had. Comfort.

And style.

He liked it.

It was her.

"You want a beer?" Marcy asked as Hellen was turning on some lights.

"Yeah," he answered at the same time Hellen said, "Don't get him a beer. He isn't staying that long."

In response to that, Core sat his ass on her gray-white couch and stretched his legs out in front of him.

She glared at him.

He smiled at her.

She rolled her eyes.

He smiled bigger.

Marcy came back with beers for all of them.

She handed them around and made a point to park her ass in a brown-leather butterfly chair, which meant Hellen's only choice was to hit the couch with him.

She looked like she smelled rotten eggs while she did it.

He burst out laughing.

"What's funny?" she demanded through it.

"You are so into me," he teased, still laughing.

"And you are so full of yourself," she shot back.

"All right, kids, you two can hammer this out later, when I'm not here," Marcy butted in. She then added in Core's direction, "I hope you brought condoms."

Core busted out laughing again.

He also decided he liked Marcy.

"Oh my God, Marce!" Hellen snapped.

"Moving on," Marcy decided, her attention going back to Core. "The deal is, we have a friend who's dating some guy she met on Bumble. She thinks she's falling in love with him. In the beginning, he gave her the full treatment. Fancy car. Fancy restaurants. Flowers.

Gifts. A weekend away. Promises of more good times to come. Now he's bumming money off her."

Well, hell.

Core took a drag off his beer as Marcy continued.

"So Hellen did an online dive into him, and on the surface, he seems legit. He has social media. He's got friends. He's posting pictures of him with Bree, or just Bree, and he seems really into her. He's a partner at a firm that has a website. You call the number and ask for him, they say he's not in, but they'll take a message for you."

"But you don't buy it," Core surmised.

"We don't buy it," Marcy agreed.

"What tweaks you?" Core asked.

"Well, now it's the fact he lives at a house of quintuplets, him being one of them," Hellen said. "So, if he's a hotshot venture capitalist with tons of money to hand out to aspiring entrepreneurs, why does he share a three-bedroom house in Littleton with four other guys?"

"Pertinent question," he grunted.

"Four other guys Bree doesn't know he lives with. She thinks he lives in that house alone. She thinks this because she never mentioned any roommates, and she's been to that house more than once. Did those men look like they were hanging at a friend's house, that friend right now out on a date with his girl Bree?" Hellen went on.

Core wasn't feeling this situation, because no, they didn't.

They were making themselves at home because they were home.

"But all this started because he's supposedly in a partnership that invests millions of dollars in startups." Hellen kept at it. "And if that's the case, why would he be cash poor and need to borrow what would amount to chump change to him, but it's two months' rent for his girl?"

Jesus.

"Another pertinent question," he replied.

"Oh, and by the way," she carried on, "he's been seeing that girl for all of three months. He drives a BMW, and he wears a Patek Phillipe that could be knock-off, and is, I'm guessing at this juncture. And so are the Chanel earrings he gave her for their first month anniversary."

"I got a question for you," Core said.

She gave him a *let's have it* chin jut.

"What's a Patek Phillipe?"

"A really expensive watch."

"And another question," he continued.

She sent him another jut.

"Why didn't you call Jag in on this?"

"What?" she asked.

"Why didn't you tell Jagger about this and ask him to handle it?"

"Why would I do that?" She seemed sincerely bewildered.

"I don't know," he returned. "Because he's your brother-in-law and because he's also Chaos. Chaos has had a charter in this city for six decades at least. They know everybody. If they don't know somebody, they know someone who can find out, and then they can take care of business on the other end."

"But...we can and *are* taking care of business on *our* end," she asserted.

He didn't know what to say to that. Or at least he didn't know what to say that wouldn't completely offend her.

So he kept quiet.

"He's just a Tinder swindler," she declared. "Marcy and I get some evidence, show it to Bree, Bree demands her money back and ends it with him. Done."

Should he tell her?

She looked to Marcy. "I think he's got more than one social media profile. Probably working with different names and pictures with his other victims. But I don't know how to find them. I don't remember any of those guys showing as friends of his, and I would have remembered them. I'm not sure what's up with that house, but we need to get inside. We're gonna have to figure out how to do that. I think damsel in distress, maybe a flat tire. You engage the guys with fixing the tire on your car, I'll sneak inside and figure out how he pulls off the lives-alone thing when Bree is there."

That answered that.

Fuck yeah, he was going to tell her.

But first...

"You are not fuckin' doing *any of that,*" he declared.

He got both of their attention when he said that.

"Sorry?" Hellen asked calmly, but fire was flashing in her eyes.

"This isn't a little scam, baby, this is a big one. This dude isn't doing this to your girl and some others. *All* those guys are scamming chicks."

Hellen's eyes got big, and yeah, there it was again.

Cute.

She turned those eyes to Marcy. "Holy shit. I didn't think of that."

"I didn't either," Marcy replied, looking equally shocked. "Whoa. But it makes total sense."

"Your problem is," Core kept speaking and regained their attention, "you don't know if this is a contained thing, or if this is a bigger deal. Guys like this can lay waste to only so many women before they have to move along. They're too pretty not to be noticed. And there are a certain number of hours in each day, so they all might have several women on the go at once, but to keep them believing, they can't throw them a bone every once in a while. This means there's a limited amount they can handle at one time. You gotta put the effort in, and this kind of effort takes time. In the end, though, there's only so much blood you can get from each stone, and once they're tapped out, these guys are vapor."

Both women didn't take their gaze off him.

Core kept talking.

"They might be genius at this shit, willing to go the extra mile and invest some of their take in infrastructure to support the con. Better explanation, they bump a percentage to someone higher up on the food chain, someone who recruited and trained them for this deal. That someone builds websites and sets up receptionists that take messages and provides them with BMWs, expensive watches, and good-enough-to-fool-them knockoffs to give out as gifts. Or that gift is the real thing, they just scammed it off some other poor woman who fell for their shit."

Neither of them said anything, but both of their eyes were even bigger.

Core got to the important stuff.

"In other words, you're not gonna do dick to get on the radar of these assholes. You tell your girl what you know, *minus* the part where you saw his buds at his house, and strongly suggest she scrape him off. If she gets scammed from there, that's her deal and at least you tried."

"Okay, no," Hellen refuted. "That's not what friends do. She needs to know it all."

"Sweetheart, I guarantee you this guy gives exceptional head. He's so good at it, he might be even better at it than me," he told her.

Color came up in her cheeks that belied her sharp tone. "Why would you say that?"

"Because you can get hooked to the car and the restaurants and the gifts. But if you start giving your money to some schmuck you've known a couple of months and think you're in love, I don't care how good-looking he is, you're getting laid in a way you like a whole fuckin' lot."

"This is no lie. Remember that guy I dated, Hell? The one I got head from, and it was so good, if he asked, I would have given him a month's rent. Wouldn't even blink. Fortunately for me, he didn't ask," Marcy put in. "Unfortunately for me, that was all he did well. Still, I considered hanging on, just for the good part."

Hellen didn't pipe up, which made Core look to his lap while he did a slow grin, because he knew then she'd never been gone down on that good.

"You're impossible," Hellen hissed.

He turned his grin to her.

She did an eye roll ending on a side-eye with such perfection, he wanted to reward her with a kiss.

Instead, he took a pull off his beer.

"I think you have more explaining to do," Hellen pushed.

He swallowed and said, "Right. This is how it's gonna go. He's going to have an answer for everything she throws at him. You need to prepare because she's going to believe him. But the reason you don't tell her this is a larger sting is because she's going to be so into him, she's going to tell him everything you say. That means he'll know *you* know. And that won't make him happy. Because those boys aren't done in Denver, and they're not gonna have some bitches messing up their paydays. You with me?"

Slowly, Hellen turned her head to Marcy, who was already staring at Hellen, and he knew they were with him.

Neither of these two were stupid, that was clear.

Hellen looked back to him.

"We can't let him take any more of her money."

"There is no 'we,'" he returned. "As of now, *you* are out of it. You tell her what you know, you've done your duty. If she lets him clean her out, that's on her."

"But we don't know anything damning except his partners in crime," Hellen fired back. "We can't say, 'Hey, Bree, you need to dump Christos because we looked into him, and everything checks out, but we continue to have a bad feeling about him.' We've already told her we thought things were fishy."

"How'd she respond?"

"She got really mad."

"That's because you're trying to come between her and her orgasms," Core concluded.

"Oh my God. Stop talking about sex," she snapped.

Core and Marcy exchanged a glance.

Marcy made an "eek" face.

In other words, Hellen also hadn't been properly laid.

Yet.

Core chuckled.

"I kinda hate both of you right now," Hellen stated.

"Just trying to lighten the atmosphere, sis," Marcy said conciliatorily. "It's getting heavy because everything Core is saying makes sense. This is a bigger bad than we knew, and we're stuck. Also, Bree is too if she doesn't get her head out of her ass about Christos."

Hellen plopped back into her couch and took a long drag off her beer.

This was silent speak, meaning she agreed with her friend, but she didn't like it.

"I say we wait it out," Marcy suggested. "If she tells us she's given him more money or something weird comes up, we give her the three strikes, he should be out talk."

"And if she doesn't listen?" Hellen asked.

"We'll make sure her parents don't remortgage their house for this guy," Marcy answered.

Core butted in. "Say what?"

"*The Tinder Swindler*, it's a documentary. Have you watched it?" Marcy asked.

He shook his head.

Marcy explained.

"Same thing, except, and I hate it that these words are coming out of my mouth, that man was masterful. We're talking yachts and private planes. And his bitches weren't rolling in it. They were opening credit cards and taking cash out of them for his ass. He'd woo one with the money he got fleecing another. He left them hundreds of thousands in debt."

"Fuckin' hell," Core grunted.

"Exactly," Marcy agreed.

"What happened to the guy?" Core asked.

"He got a little bit of jail time and now he's putting up pictures of himself in his garage full of Lamborghinis because, whatever his new angle is, he's got one and it's working for him just fine," Marcy told him.

"Fuckin' hell," Core growled.

It occurred to him then that Hellen was quiet, so he looked to her to see she was slouched in the corner of the couch, sipping beer and moping.

"You put your ass on the line for your friend, which is really cool, babe, whether she listens to you or not," he reminded her.

It was then she said something he really wished she hadn't.

But she did.

She said, "Life sucks all around. You're born into it being a shitshow. You gain coherent thought and learn what a shitshow is, and you're in the thick of it. And then you live it, with each day that passes, understanding how huge of a shitshow it actually is."

After she said that, she sucked back more beer.

But when she was done, she looked tired, sad...

And beaten.

Which was why Core made the decision he made in that moment.

And, fuck him, it was crazy.

She might be uppity and high maintenance, but there was definitely something about her that got to him.

So he made it.

And like any time he made a decision, he wasn't going to change his mind.

He was all in.

4

BINGO

Hellen

I SAT at the desk in my office, irritably tapping the end of my pen against my blotter.

I was irritable because a man I only knew by the biker name Core had strolled into my evening plans, dropped the bomb that Eleanor was up to no good (as usual), horned in on our investigation of Christos, pointed out it was much worse than we thought so our hands were tied, helped himself to my beer (or, to be fair, didn't say no when offered one) and looked far too good sprawled on my couch...

And then, after I bitched about how life was a pain in the ass, he'd looked at me with this expression on his face like he'd beat down an entire army with just his fists if they threatened to do me harm.

I'd seen that look before. On occasion, Andy, my stepdad, wore it. These occasions included when my birth father was dicking with my mother, me, my sister, Liane, or anyone was messing with us or his kids from his first marriage, Archie and Elijah.

Also, Jagger had watched Archie the entirety of their wedding ceremony with that look on his face. And before him, his brother Dutch had done the same with his bride, Georgie.

Still, I'd been stricken by that look on Core's face because no one had ever looked at me like that.

Stricken and moved.

Something velvet glided through me as we locked eyes, and it was a feeling I'd never felt in my entire life.

It was akin to how it felt to have Andy in our family.

But it was much stronger.

It was exquisitely beautiful.

And after that...

Nothing.

He downed his beer, ordered me and Marcy to stay out of trouble, then waltzed out my apartment.

Did he leave his number?

No.

Did he tell us his real name?

No.

Did he suggest he'd see us (namely me) again?

No.

Just walked out like he walked in.

Smoke.

Of course, I could text Jagger and ask how to get in touch with Core, but that would mean Jagger would ask questions.

And why would I need to get in touch with Core?

I hadn't thanked him for looking after me because of whatever Eleanor was up to, but I hadn't asked him to do that, so that was a lame excuse.

Anyway, he made Bryan's level of cocky, which I thought was off the charts, look amateur.

"What am I thinking?" I muttered to myself, forcing my laptop screen to come into focus, meaning I forced Core out of my mind, and the first thing I saw was the Google tab I hadn't closed down that was for Christos's firm.

As much as it irked me, the operation was done. As sick as it was, we had to wait until Christos screwed Bree some more to try to talk some sense into her, but other than that, unless we wanted to court trouble, we had to let it go.

We weren't supersleuths, PIs, cops or FBI agents, and five extortionately hot guys living together and running cons was bad business I didn't need in my life more than it already was through Christos running one such con on my friend Bree.

He was going to take Bree for a ride, and I hated that.

But there was nothing I could do.

And I hated that more.

I lifted my gaze and saw the full layout of my office.

I wished I'd had the idea, and the money, to do something like this.

It was inspired.

It was a new-concept, shared-space business rental. An entire floor, gutted then built with window offices around the circumference, the corner ones bigger (and more expensive to rent). It wasn't enormous (there were fourteen offices), but it looked bigger with the open plan in the middle, and the offices all having walls of glass facing the inner space.

The middle held handsome furniture, which included low cabinets that provided storage that you could also lease, as well as a waiting area with modern, streamlined furniture and current magazines arranged on the tables.

Further, there were four cubbies in a square, again, that you could rent to seat your PA or staff member (two were taken, and if I hired someone, I'd put her there). There was a copier and fax station, and a cache of office supplies that if we partook were billed to us, but at least we didn't have to dash out to Target if we needed something, like paper.

And there was a receptionist who dealt with scheduling the conference room we all had access to (the only non-office space on the circumference, and it was kitted out with AV and internet, and white, high-backed swivel chairs, so it looked bomb). She also did the monthly billing, and you could pay extra to have her answer your phones, take messages and handle your schedule.

I did not utilize that service.

All the offices were taken, save a corner one, and I had my eye on it.

But for now, I needed to focus on growing my bottom line so I felt less vulnerable to any client movement, and then I could shift focus to growth.

I was a social media manager.

I started doing this for a friend in college my sophomore year. She filmed videos to show how to do hair because she was really good at it.

Her how-tos were great, but her editing was dire.

I told her I'd show her how to do it better, and somehow, she engineered it so I was doing the editing, not teaching her, and this taught me my first major lesson in business: time and knowledge had value, and I shouldn't give either away for free.

Her followers escalated, she was raking in freebies and getting offered appearances for money, and when I asked her to pay me, she told me she couldn't possibly because she was a starving student.

A starving student selling to her fellow students expensive shampoo, conditioner, combs, brushes, pins, hair dryers and all the rest that were given to her in exchange for promotion. In other words, with zero overhead.

I decided screw that and screw her and stopped doing her editing, by which time two other people had approached me, and you better believe I charged them.

She lost followers because suddenly the professional look of her content took a nosedive, and in the end she had to hire someone to do it (she'd asked me to come back first, and I didn't care what it said about me, it felt good to say no). I looked into the person she hired, and they charged more than I did at that time, by, like, *a lot*.

Karma.

I found I wasn't only good at editing, I was fascinated by social media, and I knew I could monetize it on the back end.

So I did.

By day, I went to school to earn my business degree.

By night, I studied and then read everything I could about the social media revolution. The good, the bad, and the terrifying.

I followed everyone who was good at it, and some who weren't to know what to avoid: actors, singers, authors, artists, reality stars, influencers, bloggers, people who were just funny or creative with content, not to mention scrolling indiscriminately and going off on tangents to find new creators to follow.

I spent hours figuring out how to advertise and monetize. I studied trends and hashtags, taking notes, making charts for how long they lasted, more charts examining the rise (and fall) of the followers of various creators, and notes on my speculations as to why these things happened.

My two clients became four, and that rose to nine by the time I graduated.

By then, I wasn't only editing, I was creating all kinds of content to adhere to social media strategies I devised for my customers.

Now, I was managing the social media of thirty-one clients, and I created and scheduled their content, monitored it, boosted it, reported on it, tweaked it, and recommended adjustments if needed.

It was an interesting job. In an ever-changing landscape it kept me on my toes, as new social media outlets sprang up, geared (or just used) by different generations or ideologies, what worked where, the wax and wane of popularity, and the never-ending possibilities of content.

Social media wasn't going away, but I needed to expand services because I knew I'd get bored, and no niche business like this would ever make the impact to an income sheet I intended to make.

At that moment, what I offered was limited, and as my clients' presence expanded, they'd outgrow me.

So I was going full-force into branding, marketing and advertising.

I'd taken tons of marketing classes in college, and since I graduated, I'd done two online graphic design courses, three website programming courses and one newsletter design course.

I wanted to provide the full experience of everything a potential customer/follower would see online and make it work for them full-spectrum.

As such, when I had a meeting with a potential client, I needed them to come to a place like this, not meet me at a coffee shop.

This location looked high-end and professional. There were compliance rules in what furniture you had in your office and how you could decorate so you could have your own vibe, but it fit an overall one that made the entire space coalesce.

And now I needed a PA who could deal with calls, scheduling, reporting, and posting content so I could stay on top of trends, create that content and strategize my expansion of services, then roll it out.

This would not only free up some of my time, having an employee would also give the impression I was established in my business.

Right then, I needed to scroll TikTok, Twitter, Insta, Reddit and Facebook. I needed to recheck my numbers to be absolutely certain I could employ someone, offer benefits, and keep them employed into the future (I was pretty certain I could, but this was a big step, it involved someone else who would count on me, and I was nervous about it).

And all I could do was stare at that tab for what I knew was Christos's bogus business.

On this thought, my phone rang.

I looked down, trepidation hitting me because I worried it was Bryan, who had started texting to discuss getting together to work things out.

Luckily, I saw it was Mom and took the call.

"Hey, what's up?" I greeted.

"Hey, sweetie," she replied.

Damn.

I knew immediately by her tone that something was not good.

And I knew that tone so well, I further knew whatever it was, it was about Dad.

He hadn't reared his head in a while. Not a surprise after he called to ask about tickets to my graduation, and I told him only people who invested in my future got to go, and anyone who felt entitled to go even though they didn't earn that privilege could go fuck themselves.

He had a few choice words to say to me, and I did not hold back on my retorts.

This had the effect of him barraging my sister, Li, with his bullshit, some of that landing on Mom, but in the end it had the desired effect for us all.

He faded away, and unlike the other times he took a vacation from being a father for whatever reason he had, he stayed away (these reasons were mostly work, and believe you me, my mother, sister and I had learned the hard way that any addiction affected the ones you loved, even insidious ones like being addicted to earning status and money).

Now, though, I knew he was back.

"You okay?" I asked.

"Can you come over for dinner tonight? Or tomorrow?" she asked in return.

She didn't want to mess up my day by talking about this on the phone.

I was happy to go to dinner, anytime. Mom was a great mom as well as a great cook, I loved Andy to bits, and Li and I were close.

That said, I wasn't a procrastinator.

So I queried, "What's Dad done?"

"I think we should talk face-to-face."

Holy shit.

"Is he...okay?"

"He's fine. It's your grandfather."

All right then.

Zero interest.

None.

Zilch.

Dad was Dad because Granddad was Granddad.

Not to mention Grandma was Grandma, but in female solidarity, I had to note she lived in a different time, and it took a lot of strength to fight the fusillade of mental abuse and control a malignant narcissist unleashed.

But that was as fair as I got because she was bitchy, vindictive and bitter, she wallowed in all of it, and spread it around with glee.

"I care about this because...?" I prompted.

"Honey, he's your grandfather and he's your father's father. It's always hard to lose your dad."

"I'm not sure when that time comes for me it'll be very hard."

"Hellen," she said softly, disappointment in her tone.

That wasn't the daughter she raised.

On the other hand, it *was* the daughter Dad created.

"He reached out to me," Mom told me. "He misses you girls."

Bullshit, I thought.

I said nothing, but I made a mental note of how deeply I was not a fan of him reaching out to Mom at all for anything.

"This is tough on him," she pushed.

Mom, heart of gold. He'd done her dirty, he'd done us all dirty, and she didn't put up with it forever, she didn't lose herself to it, she got free and fought for herself and her daughters.

But she had a kind soul.

"Maybe he's learned something these past couple of years he's been out of your and Liane's lives," she suggested.

This idea was hopeful, yet ludicrous.

"We'll talk at dinner. I'll come over tomorrow if that's cool."

"Okay, sweetie."

"You and Andy good?"

"Yes, honey. Just plugging along."

There was something to be said about a low-key life. Work. Home shared with the man you loved. Two healthy daughters. TV and cooking and looking forward to a couple of vacations a year, planning what you'd do on holidays and looking forward to retirement.

That wasn't the life I wanted, but it was the life Mom did, and I was glad she had it.

"Right, see you tomorrow," I told her.

"Can't wait. Love you."

"Love you too, and my love to Andy and Li."

We disconnected, and I realized I didn't mention Eleanor or ask if she told Liane about Dad/Granddad.

Both could wait until dinner tomorrow.

But Dad getting in touch increased my irritation to vexation, and I homed in on Christos's webpage tab.

I then clicked on the tab.

Whoever created it went full bore with a "history and about us page," "what we're looking for," "projects we're working on," and "how to submit" pages, and their content was lucid and thorough.

There was also a "contact us" page with email, phone number, fax number and an address.

I stared at the address.

I opened another tab, typed in the address, and Google showed me the front of a building, offered me the option to go to a website or get directions, etc.

I clicked directions.

The address was real. It was a place, maybe a five-minute drive from my office.

I went back and hit the button for website.

It took me to Christos's firm's page.

I then opened another tab and typed in, *How do you find out if a business is registered.*

I clicked go and then followed through by checking the state registry.

I was feeling nothing would come of it since they covered their tracks so well, they'd surely register their company, even if it was bogus.

I sat up straighter when I saw they did not.

I did a deeper dive in how to find out if a company was registered and went to the national database. They'd only register nationally if there was some need, and they weren't.

I then typed in, *Can you do business in a state if you're not registered.*

At that, I learned you could, but only if you were like me, a small, one-woman show.

However, I was registered, and Christos's gig was not a one-person show.

"Bingo, motherfucker. Gotcha," I said to my laptop, closed it, grabbed my phone and my bag, and I took off.

5

LUNCH

Hellen

When I drove by Christos's office building, I was unsurprised it looked vacant.

I found a place to park on the street a couple of buildings down, fed the meter, and experienced whiplash in the form of total surprise when I walked back to the location, and Core was standing at the front doors. He was leaning a shoulder against the glass, biker boots crossed at the ankle, arms crossed on his wide chest.

He had on his mirrored aviators, and they were trained on my approach.

I was experiencing the heretofore undiscovered sensation of weak knees, something I didn't like, and a corresponding tingle at my clit, though that felt nice, obviously, just not why I was feeling it.

"What'd I say?" he asked when I stopped two feet from him.

Oh, hell no.

"Were you waiting for me to come here?" I demanded. "Or are you still following me?"

"Neither. Just had the luck to be checking it out when I saw your stupid-ass car drive by with you in it."

Oh my God!

I drove a white Mini-Cooper with black racing stripes.

It was awesome, the deal I swung on it used was even more awesome, though the mileage on it stunk.

Fortunately, my brother-in-law knew everything about cars, so if it ever gave me problems (and, so far, it hadn't), I knew where to go.

"My car isn't stupid."

"There's only one car more stupid than yours," he announced.

He didn't elucidate, so my brows acted against my better judgment, and they lifted in question.

"Sorry, I was wrong," he stated. "Your car is the stupidest car there is."

Okay then, minor pining for him that morning cured.

He was a jerk.

"Why are we talking about this?" I asked.

"You get in an accident at high speeds, you're toast." He added to that by clicking his teeth and drawing a line across his neck.

"It's good I'm a safe driver then," I retorted.

"You need something bigger, with better driver visibility. Taller, sturdier."

"I'll be buying an electric car as soon as that expenditure comes up on rotation."

"And when's that?"

"Two years, if fortune favors me, three if I'm still saving."

"That's a long time to take your life in your hands driving that shit car."

Such a jerk.

"Can we stop talking about my car?"

He shrugged a single broad shoulder. "Sure."

"What are you doing here?" I asked.

"Same thing you're doing here, I reckon."

I took him in top to toe and buried the fact I liked what I saw.

Instead, I noted, "You're leaning against the door, so I assume some budding entrepreneur won't soon be arriving to open it."

"Smoked glass, hard to see in, still,"—he adjusted from his position, turned, shoved the sunglasses up into his hair and cupped the sides of his face as he looked in—"they furnished it, or maybe rented it furnished," he said to the window. He turned back to me. "But no one has been in there for a long time."

I approached, shoved my own glasses into my hair and did the cupped-face thing.

Furnished, even art on the walls, but deserted.

I looked back to him. "How do you know no one's been here for a while?"

He stepped aside, pointed to a mail slot his body had been hiding, and even though the glass was smoked, you could see the small mountain of fliers and junk mail on the floor underneath it.

"They forgot a detail," he remarked.

They sure did.

"I checked the state's registry for companies, they aren't on it," I informed him.

"Mm-hmm," he hummed.

"Not on the national one either," I added.

"Reckon not," he replied.

I looked to the doors, to him, to the doors and him again. "How did you know to come here? I don't remember telling you what Christos's firm's name was."

"Got a friend who can get me info, asked him about that Littleton house. He tracked down the owner and got a name on the rental agreement. It isn't Christos, but looking at Facebook, it is the guy at the laptop in the kitchen last night. And"—he jerked a thumb at the doors—"according to his Facebook page, he works here."

And there it was, my avenue to find out more about these guys. I hadn't even thought of searching based on the company.

"So it's official, it's a ring of scammers," I muttered to his T-shirt that stated he was a Def Leppard fan.

"Babe," he called.

I lifted my gaze to his.

"I asked you a question."

Was I so deep in the awful thought a swindler ring was preying on the females of Denver, I hadn't heard him when he was standing only two feet away?

"Sorry. What?"

"What'd I say?"

"I don't know, I missed it."

"You did not miss I told you last night to leave this shit alone. And here you are"—he flung a hand my way—"not leaving this shit alone."

Ugh!

"I'm not sure when my world shifted on its axis and you became the boss of me," I drawled.

"I didn't tell you to stand down to be an asshole, I told you to stand down to protect you."

"I get that," I returned. "I also was pretty certain no one would be here, so I didn't think it was dangerous. And if someone was, I could walk on by, and no one would notice. But once I checked the registry, I came here to be sure. And now we have *real* evidence to go to Bree with."

"Yeah, and I been thinking about that."

Him thinking about this situation might mean he'd been thinking about me, and this thought caused another clit tingle.

I reminded myself he was a jerk and inquired, "What have you been thinking?"

"She isn't listening to you, maybe she'll listen to me."

Holy cow.

Why hadn't I thought of that?

It wasn't that he was a guy, and it wasn't that he was the guy he was, in other words, at a glance you knew he was streetwise and had been around the block (though, the truth of it was, when it came to Bree, all of this, including the fact he was male, would be meaningful).

It was that, sometimes when those closest to you see something you don't, if you want that something, you can find ways to disregard it, telling yourself they're being overprotective or jealous, or you have daddy issues (bluh). But when someone objective outside your group says it, you take note.

I mean, it was worth a shot.

"Text her, and your girl Marcy, set a meet. Soon. 'Cause, see, if we get to her, she dumps him but doesn't expose you, he might know the jig is up and relay that to his buds, and they'll consider cutting ties and moving on."

It was annoying because this was a great idea.

I didn't tell him that.

I pulled out my phone and sent Marcy a very long text about all I'd discovered, and what Core was offering to do.

When I lifted my head from doing this, he said, "Let's get lunch. I'll drive."

And before I could agree to this, or not, just like last night, he strolled to his truck.

I stood there watching him, and once he was in, I walked to the passenger side and stared at him through the window.

It whirred down and he said, "It's open."

"I'm hungry, Hellen, are you? Wanna grab some lunch with me?" I intoned. "That's how it's done when you ask someone to lunch, or a version of it."

He smiled. "Just get in the truck."

"I know you know you're all that, and I'm not stupid enough to try to convince you that you aren't, because you are. But I've been around a lot of men who think they're all that, and as such, I'm immune to your bullshit."

"You hungry?" he asked.

I was actually starving.

"That's beside the point."

"I'm going to Las Delicias," he declared.

I climbed in his truck.

He was chuckling when he pulled into traffic.

My phone emitted a selection of recorder notes from *The Mandalorian.*

That meant I had a text.

"What the fuck? Core asked.

"Text," I answered then read Marcy's reply. *You've talked to Core!?* Which was followed by a big-eyes red-cheeks emoji, and that was followed by a tongue-out yum emoji and then a drooling emoji.

God.

I texted a reiteration we needed a sit-down with Bree and avoided her response.

I shifted my gaze to the windshield and asked, "What's your real name?"

"Come again?"

"What's your given name?"

"Why do you ask?"

"Just making conversation."

"Dustin."

Interesting.

"You don't seem like a Dustin."

He sounded amused when he inquired, "What do I seem like?"

"Butch. Blade. Chuck."

He burst out laughing, and I remembered what I'd discovered the night before.

He had a great laugh. Robust. Uninhibited.

Real.

Bryan had a variety of laughs depending on who he was with and what version of himself he was trying to be. He had a laugh for his boss, which I knew was fake. He had a laugh he laughed with his buds, and it made him sound like a deviant frat boy.

I liked to think when I made him laugh, it was real.

But if you put out a different you for the different people in your life, how could you be real at all?

Not so with this man.

Core was Core.

The end.

And I was already attracted to him but understanding that just made me more so.

By a lot.

Even if he was a jerk.

Fabulous.

"Chuck?" he asked, his voice trembling because he was still laughing.

That, too, was attractive.

I was *so* glad I decided to go to lunch with him.

Shit.

"You give off Chuck vibes," I lied.

He let loose laughing again.

I sighed.

When he quit, he shared, "No one has called me Dustin for fifteen years."

This begged the question how old he was.

My guess, mid-thirties.

I didn't ask though.

"Not even your mom?"

"Nope."

I looked to him. "She calls you Core?"

"She's dead," he told the road, his usually expressive voice completely flat. "So she doesn't call me anything."

Oh no.

"Shit, I'm sorry," I said softly.

His aviators swung my way, then back to the road, and he was talking softly too when he replied, "You didn't know, baby."

"Still, I'm sorry."

"It's cool," he muttered.

It wasn't, though it was nice he tried to tell me it was.

I faced forward and decided to shut up.

"What'd Marcy say?" he asked.

I gazed down at my phone.

No new texts.

"Nothing, so far. She just expressed surprise I've talked to you."

"Right."

We made it to Las Delicias, and that ended the conversation. Core found a parking spot, we walked in, were seated in a booth, and I found something else to like him about.

He didn't touch his menu.

Neither did I.

In other words, we were both LD regulars.

"Were you born in Denver?" I asked.

"Yup," he answered. "You?"

I nodded.

The waitress came with waters, chips and salsa, we ordered, and she took off.

He spread out, both arms along the back of the booth, the better to stake his manly claim on new territory, at the same time display his wide chest for my and the restaurant's admiration, both of which I should have found gross, but instead, my vagina did an involuntary spasm.

He leveled his light-blue eyes on me.

"Why'd you dump him?"

I nearly choked on a chip, managed to swallow it, and asked, "What?"

"Your boyfriend. Keeping an eye on you, saw him walk out with a box of his shit. Why'd you give him the boot?"

This was absolutely not his business.

However, it'd be interesting to see his reaction to why that happened.

"I have a cabinet over the toilet. He had a habit of not shutting the door to said cabinet. Obviously, this means I cracked my head on it anytime I didn't notice to shut it before I used the facilities. I asked him repeatedly to close it, he kept forgetting. I cracked my head in the middle of the night, he heard me cry out in pain, asked me if I was okay, then laughed when I told him what happened."

Core was now frowning, and it had to be said, it was kinda scary.

"There was more, like not recycling even though I asked, and not cleaning up after he and his buds used my place to watch some boxing match, even though I asked him to do that too. It's little stuff, petty." I reached for my water, sipped, put it back. "But it adds up and I have more to do in my life than try to train some guy who doesn't think things that matter to me are important."

I wasn't sure Core heard the second part, considering once I was done speaking, he asked, "He heard you crack your head and he laughed?"

I scooped a chip, mumbling, "Yeah, that was the one I got stuck on too."

"So you ended it, and he just took his box and left?"

"He's putting out feelers for a chat."

"You gonna go there?"

It dawned on me only then that this was a conversation.

It wasn't an exploration.

He was curious, and it wasn't because he was interested in me.

Not in that way. The way I was trying, and failing, not to be interested in him.

In other words, he wasn't into me.

In fact, his good looks, the confident, assertive man he was, he wasn't wearing a wedding band, but that didn't mean he didn't have a woman. All he was, he probably did.

Sure, he teased me about wanting to climb him like a tree, but I saw now he was just messing with me.

Not, as I'd thought, flirting with me.

I'd read it wrong. It'd seemed that way before.

But a woman knew.

There was a distance in that booth between us.

Sure, we were chatting, it was easy, friendly, but I felt it.

We were getting to know each other, but we weren't *getting to know each other*.

A new wound opened, and how I could spend a year with a man I liked very much and hurt when it was over, but the hurt I felt right then seemed more acute and like it dug a whole lot deeper, I didn't know.

I gave it all to push past it.

So he wasn't into me. I barely knew him, and he was probably taken. This wasn't the end of the world.

Furthermore, I was guessing I was younger than him in a way some men weren't into. I was mature for my age, but I was still at least a decade younger than him.

I knew bikers liked what they liked, because Jag was all biker, but Archie wasn't a biker babe. And their wedding, as well as Dutch and Georgie's (Georgie also wasn't a biker babe), had been chockful of bikers, and not every woman there was wearing the stereotypical halter top and bandana wrapped around her head. Not even close.

So maybe it was because I was younger than him.

Or maybe he had a woman in his life.

Or maybe it was because I just wasn't his thing.

Okay, yeah, as much as I told myself he was a jerk, truth was, he was hot, he'd demonstrated the capacity to give a shit about me (and Marcy), and our banter was fun. Not a lot of guys had the balls to shovel it back at me. It was a massive turn on.

So I wasn't his thing, but he was mine.

Um, yeah.

That hurt.

"Hellen," he prompted.

"Sorry." I shook my head. "Yeah, no. I'm not going to go there with Bryan."

"Good," he murmured, took his arm from the booth and reached for a chip.

I didn't ask why this was his response when he'd never met Bryan, and not only because I didn't get the chance.

My phone rang, this time the actual *Mandalorian* theme.

Core's brows tugged down when he heard it.

I glanced at my phone, and then blew out a breath when I saw Marcy was calling me.

She rarely called. We texted, and we saw each other all the time, so we didn't need to chat on the phone.

She was just being nosy about Core.

"Marcy," I told him.

He jerked up his chin.

I took the call. "Hey."

"Okay, *wild* but get this," she began. "I was in the middle of texting you back when Bree called."

I sat straighter and felt Core come alert.

"Okay," I said.

"At first it was weird, then she started crying, and after that she told me she thinks Christos stole from her."

My gaze flew to Core's.

This time, his brows shifted up.

"Stole what?"

And the way they drew back down, mm-hmm.

That was definitely scary.

"She was missing some pearl earrings her grandma gave her, but she thought she just misplaced them, and she'd eventually find them. She just hasn't had the time to go searching. But this morning, she couldn't find the diamond pendant her mom and dad gave her when she graduated. It means a lot and it's worth a lot, so she says she'd never misplace it. When she takes it off, she puts it on her necklace tree, no exceptions. She wore it last night, and distinctly remembers putting it on the tree before she brushed her teeth. It was gone this morning, and the only person who's been in her place outside her is him, including last night, when he spent the night. He left before her and kissed her goodbye, and she knows he took that necklace with him."

"Holy crap," I breathed.

"So she says she believes us now. He's a grifter, and she's both really hurt and really ticked."

"Well, I guess we don't have to sit down with her and Core."

Core tipped his head to the side.

The waitress came with our food.

"She wants us to come over tonight," Marcy informed me.

"Okay, I don't have plans. I can be there."

"Me too. I need to text Kyra."

"Cool."

"Her grandma died last year, remember?"

I had my phone between my shoulder and ear and was unrolling my napkin from my cutlery when this stopped me dead.

"She tore apart her place this morning after she saw the necklace was gone," Marcy went on. "Those pearls aren't anywhere to be found. Her grandma gave her those for her sixteenth birthday. They were pearl studs, so maybe they wouldn't pay off her student loans. But they'd been given to her by her dead grandma."

I was feeling sick.

"Has she talked with Christos yet?" I queried.

"Nope."

"Can you call her back? Tell her not to?"

"I can, but why would I do that?"

"Because we have to figure out how to get those back."

"You don't think the Greek Bumble Syndicate hasn't already pawned them?"

Good point.

"Right. I just don't...let me talk to Core. Fill him in. I just don't think it's strategic to let him know she has his number yet."

"Talk to Core?" she asked leadingly.

"I'll be in touch."

"Wait!"

I disconnected.

"Spill," Core ordered before I could even put the phone down.

I gave him the skinny.

When I was done, he forked some burrito in his mouth, chewed, swallowed and looked at me.

"Marcy's right, she's gotta kiss that stuff goodbye."

"This guy can't get away with this shit," I snapped.

"He won't."

His tone struck me.

"What?"

"He won't."

"Are you saying she should call the cops?"

"No."

I studied him.

Then I admitted, "Okay, I'm not following."

"Eat your lunch."

And again with the boss.

"Core," I bit out.

He gave me a gentle look. "Just eat your lunch, baby, go about your day, give support to your friend tonight, and don't worry about it."

I wished he wouldn't call me baby.

It sounded nice.

But it wasn't real.

"I can't worry about something I don't know what it is."

"There you go," he replied.

I glared at him.

He winked at me.

And then he resumed eating.

6

SUCKER

Core

THE CALL CAME as he was walking from his bike to the clubhouse.

He pulled his phone out of his back pocket and saw her picture on the screen with MOYNIHAN over it.

At lunch, when he'd tossed her his cell and told her to program herself in, he'd taken hers and done the same thing.

When he got his back, he'd snapped a photo of her after she told him not to, which meant he caught her with a grumpy, scrunchy face.

It was fucking adorable.

"Yo, Catwoman."

"Ohmigod, can you be more annoying?" she asked.

He was grinning when he opened the door and entered the clubhouse.

A few years ago, when the club was in turmoil, and before, when they were wannabe badasses and fucking shit up, their homebase wasn't all that much to brag about.

Now, after they bought their first dispensary as a crew (then bought the next four), cleaned up a variety of messes and kept the spoils, it was pimp.

Two pool tables. Jukebox. Kickass bar. Leather furniture that was smooth as a sweet piece's ass.

Each brother didn't have a private room, like Chaos's clubhouse (this was something they were going to see to with a huge-ass addition when Rainman said they had enough money to do it and do it right), so if a party turned into a private party, you had to stay sober enough to drive the bitch to your house, or hers.

But their meet room was even more awesome than the common room. They had a large, fully stocked weight room. They had a big kitchen with all the top-of-the-line appliances.

And their fortified artillery vault was the shit.

He caught a couple eyes, sent out a couple chin lifts, headed to the bar and asked Hellen, "Why you calling, sweetheart?"

"Eleanor."

"What?"

"My cousin," she reminded him. "My dad's picked this stellar time to come back into my life, so we're having a family dinner tomorrow to talk about it. I need to know what's up with Eleanor so I can share with Mom."

Her dad wasn't in her life?

He knew she was Archie's stepsister, so they weren't blood.

But beyond that, he didn't know dick about her.

And he didn't like this news.

"Where's your dad been?" he asked, deciding against grabbing a beer and instead leaning into an elbow at the bar to focus on listening to her.

"I don't know. Just not around me. And that was my preferred state of our relationship. But apparently my granddad is sick, and he misses me and my sister. Though don't believe that. I don't. He called Mom to get her to extend an olive branch. By the way, I love my mom, but I'm heading to dinner tomorrow with a lighter."

Fuck, she was funny.

He started chuckling.

"Wild stab with all this info, you don't get along with your old man," he joked.

It was the way of some people's worlds, like Core's.

His dad was an asshole, deadbeat, alcoholic bum. He embodied everything a man shouldn't be. He was a total piece of shit.

So Core got where she was coming from.

What he forgot, in having her in his ear, having her reach out to him, call, connect, and how good that felt when it shouldn't, was the fact she was not him.

She was Hellen.

And evidence was suggesting she was getting under his skin.

"He treated my mom like shit. He treated my sister like shit. He treated me like shit. Fortunately, he wasn't around much to be that way with us. Unfortunately, when he was around, he doubled down to make up for lost time. He accepted the challenge when Mom divorced him, and he made every day they were apart a nightmare too. Fortunately, she found Andy, and he cushioned these blows so much for Mom, Dad lost the power to deliver them. So at least that part was good."

"But he kept landing them on you." His voice was rough and pissed, and he didn't have it in him to hide it.

That was how big of a sucker he was becoming for her.

"He's pathologically self-absorbed and a control freak. This is not a good mix. So yeah, until I told him to fuck off when I graduated from college, he managed to ruin a few of my days."

Core wanted to ask his name and address.

He didn't.

He gave advice.

"Don't give in to his shit."

He heard it himself, his words coming out like a threat, so she couldn't miss it, which was probably why she didn't start gabbing again.

"Your life. Your family. Your dad," he grunted. "Not for me to say. I just got some experience with shitty fathers and the sooner you excise them out of your life, the better."

"Your dad was shitty too?" she asked quietly.

She had a rich mass of dark hair.

She had tawny green eyes.

She had a beautiful mouth.

And he'd put money down the skin on her ass felt better than those fucking couches.

She was also smart, funny, loyal, she didn't take any shit, but it was fun as fuck to shovel it at her.

But this was no longer about the fact she wasn't his type.

Having spent time with her, it was about the fact he was tainted, had been since birth, that part not his fault, but he had committed his own sins that were irredeemable.

She was too good for him.

He was gonna take care of her friend's problem and then he was gonna exit her life.

All this meant he wasn't going to share about his old man.

"It's an epidemic," he said.

"Sadly, yes. The good ones are hard to find."

Having a bad one, and being a bad one, he knew that better than her.

"Sorry to unload on you," she apologized.

"Don't mind, baby," he murmured. "So Eleanor, who I know as Nails."

"Nails?"

"Don't ask."

"Ulk," she gulped audibly, guessing why her cousin was given that name.

He needed to keep their boundaries tight, but that still made him smile.

Beck, their president, walked in. He did a scan of the room and caught sight of Core.

They exchanged nonverbal greetings, and Beck moved Core's way.

"The intel on her was spotty," he continued. "She caused some trouble with a club we got an alliance with down in Phoenix, the Aces High MC. They got heavier shit they're dealing with, and word is, as retaliation, she reached out to the people who were causing the heavy shit. These people are not good people and the trouble they could cause is intense. Other than that, we don't know what she's up to. We don't even know if she made some deal with that crew."

"Okay, so should I say anything to my mom at all?"

"I wouldn't."

There was a beat of silence, and then she asked in a careful way that wasn't like her, "Is Chaos involved in this too?"

"Yup," he confirmed. "We're indirect, Chaos is direct. One of the Chaos brother's old lady is sister to the president of Aces High."

Hearing this, she reminded him, "She's dad's cousin, Core. They aren't close, and she took a different path in life, but they're cut from the same cloth. Dad's whole side explores dysfunctional in a myriad of ways."

Well, hell.

Now he was realizing why they covered Hellen, Haley, Andy and Liane, and not the dad, even though Nails was blood with him.

Because Rush knew the dad was not close to his daughters, so he didn't bother to ask for that manpower. So, if Nails fucked with his life or dragged him into shit, Rush didn't care.

"You think she might have gone to your dad?" he asked.

"I just think it's weird I don't hear from him for two years, you show up on the lookout for her, then Dad calls about Granddad being sick. Granddad is her uncle. And I've been accused of being cynical because I am, but Dad hates Andy. And Andy's daughter is married to a Chaos brother."

If what she was alluding to was true, this was next level asshole.

"Would your dad play you like that?"

"I want to say no. I want to think he's unhealthy for me because he's messed up, though bottom line, there's love there somewhere. But..."

She let that hang.

This meant she wasn't in the clear.

She was out there.

Which meant this meeting he called needed to happen pronto.

"Okay, babe, I'm at my clubhouse now. We're having a meeting. I'll tell the men. But we'll be looking into this."

"Okay."

He was about to end their chat when she called his name.

"Yeah?" he said.

"I don't know, just, uh...thanks, I guess."

"Best expression of appreciation I've ever gotten, babe," he teased.

"It's a talent of mine," she retorted.

He started laughing, even as he made a special effort to ignore he'd been doing that a lot lately, all around her. Laughing more than he had in twenty years, even when Kiki was in his bed, and Kiki was damned funny.

"Talk to you later," she said.

"Later, sweetheart."

They disconnected.

Beck was watching him closely.

"What was that?" he asked.

"Hellen. Shit's going down, brother," Core told him.

"I was guessing that when you told everybody to haul their asses in for a meeting," Beck replied. He looked to Core's phone then back to his face. "Knew you had to come out for her last night, but now you two are pals?"

He shrugged. "She's edgy. She's hilarious. And she's a ballbuster."

"Just your type," Beck muttered.

Yeah, in heels with designer bags.

Fuck.

"We need to do this meeting, Beck. Shit's going down."

Beck nodded and turned to the brothers hanging around the pool table.

"Let's do it," he called.

No hesitation, Beck made the order, the men were on the move.

Some of them got fresh beers, and Core tagged his own.

They went to the meet room, grabbed their cuts off the pegs on the wall and shrugged them on.

Some of the members were already in there, sitting the table, drinking a brew and shooting the shit, so there were some greetings with fist-bump hand clasps that ended in a forearm hit, the unofficial handshake of Resurrection.

And then they all took their seats.

Beck's reign couldn't have been more different than their last president, Spiderweb.

Web was still with them; he was now chaplain.

But Web's reign was chaotic and led to them going down a path they nearly couldn't pull themselves away from.

It wasn't entirely Web's fault. They all participated. And they had a couple of snakes in their garden that poisoned the crew, both of whom had now long been excised.

That had been when they were called Bounty, and they'd been so fucked-up, they'd lost their charter.

With Beck's guidance, they rose from those ashes.

Now, Resurrection had order. Their bylaws were long and thorough. And there was a lot of shit you could do that was considered so out of line, you were out, no chance to defend yourself, your patch was stripped.

Gone.

These things included breaking the law (unless that activity was club mandated), touching your old lady or any woman in anger, ditto kids, consuming narcotics that weren't legal, and hitting a piece that wasn't in a condition to consent (and this went so far as non-consent of any kind might lead to them having a chat with one of their LEO associates).

There was shit you could get called out for in a way you didn't want it, and that included not going to scheduled training, not attending mandatory meetings, not pulling your weight during missions, same with not doing your part to make sure the brotherhood's business interests ran smoothly.

And then there were things that really set Resurrection apart from other clubs.

For instance, most men sought out MCs because of the culture, the brotherhood, the order, but also because the life was a good life and not a lot of questions were asked. There were rules and boundaries. There were also parties and women, booze and drugs, and outside those rules and boundaries, anything went. The club, brotherhood and your bike were more important than anything, in some cases more important than your woman or even your kids.

The ROs, or Resurrection Originals, had voted unanimously that wasn't the way they were going to roll.

Not exactly.

You cheated on your woman, that was yours to own and yours to deal with. If it ended up requiring legal fees, you paid that. The club didn't take your back.

And if you didn't pay child support, that was another reason your patch would be stripped.

You started to drink too much, and it became a habit, you could count on Web or Spartan sitting you down to talk about what was fucking you up. If that didn't work, the whole club would take you up to their woods in the mountains. Then all the brothers would be pitching tents and starting a campfire, and they wouldn't come back down until your shit was right, and you were committed to doing what you needed to do to keep it that way.

They partied. They got rowdy. But they did not fight. Not physically. Not among themselves, not out in the world.

It showed a lack of control, a lack of focus, a lack of honor, all things they'd suffered from in the past. Doing it might not get you cast out, but you'd face your brothers and need to explain yourself, and if you didn't have a good explanation, things in the club would get dicey for you.

Further, their clubhouse and club activities were not open to all. Any biker bunny who was looking for a good time wasn't allowed to wander in when she heard a party was happening at Resurrection. If they were at a rally, their campsite was closed to people they didn't know. You had an invite from a brother, or his old lady, one who'd been accepted as an extension of their family by the men, you were in.

Otherwise, you got yourself an invitation, or you were out.

They weren't strictly insular, women came and went, brothers had friends outside the brotherhood who were welcome, allies were too, extended family was considered Resurrection family.

But they weren't sociable, and if they didn't know you, they weren't welcoming.

Last, most clubs proudly wore their cuts, or the leather jackets or vests that had their patches sewn on them, and they wore them everywhere.

The overriding mission of Resurrection needed to be covert. Because of that, unless it was an organized ride or a rally with other clubs, they never wore their cuts outside the meet room.

Resurrection was known to their own: The MC community.

They did not advertise themselves beyond that.

But they put their cuts on for meetings.

And yeah, all of this was written down and if you pledged, you memorized that shit, demonstrated while you were prospect that you could live it, and only then were you let in as a member.

Once that happened, you wrote your name in your own blood on their charter.

People not in the life didn't understand that most motorcycle clubs were highly ordered, from full charter down through the local clubs. They had rules. They had elections. They had officers. They were democratically run. They had missions. And punishments were doled out when a member fucked up.

Resurrection took that to extremes.

Beck's club was so organized, they even had assigned seating at the table.

Beck, as president, at the head. And incidentally, he'd earned the name "Washington" or for short "Wash" because he'd disavowed his old club name, and since he was the first president of Resurrection, that was what he'd earned. That said, due to history, all the ROs called him Beck.

Web, as chaplain, sat at the foot.

Core, as vice president, was at Beck's right. Muzzle, as sergeant at arms, at his left.

Eightball, their enforcer, was at Web's right, Spartan, their secretary at his left, and Rainman, their treasurer, next to Spartan.

This was the original crew, the ROs, or the men that were in Bounty when Core joined. They lost Griller supporting Chaos in a war Chaos eventually won, but Griller bit it on the path to that victory. And they scraped off Pacino and Digger because they were pieces of shit.

Since then, they got two new members, Shimmy and Brain, who sat in the only remaining seats.

Not in the room were their prospects, Speed and Linus.

But all the full members were there, so Beck called them to order.

He then looked at Core and announced, "Core brought you here, he's got shit to say."

Core looked down the shiny, kickass table that they'd spent a small fortune on, and took in his brothers.

He then laid it out about the scam going down with Hellen's friend, and after that, shared that Nails might have gone to Hellen's father, and was using that angle to fuck with Archie's family, and as such, Jagger and Chaos.

He finished with, "We promised Chaos we'd be on the lookout for her, and we need to be thorough in doing that, so we gotta look into the dad and that branch of the family. And I wanna call a vote to investigate this scam these assholes are pulling, and if we agree, put it down."

"We got Chaos's back on the Nails situation, so Muzzle, Shimmy, rope in Speed and Linus, look into that," Beck ordered and turned to Core. "Can you get us details on them?"

He nodded. "I'll call Hellen."

Beck took a beat to study him before he turned to the table.

"Now we gotta vote on these Greeks. In favor of putting a stop to their shit, say aye."

Every hand went up and every man said, "Aye."

That was easy.

It was also expected.

Core smiled because his brothers were the fucking best.

"You're point on that," Beck declared, eyes to Core.

Core nodded again.

Beck's attention was back to the table at large when he said, "That's that, anyone else got anything while we're here?"

There were some nopes, nos and nahs.

Beck hit the gavel, declaring, "Great, then. Janna's holding supper for me. We're done." And again to Core. "But we're talking."

"Right," he agreed, kept his seat, but called out, "Eight, don't leave. Want to brief you on what I'm thinking on the Greeks and get this ball rolling."

"Fuckin' A," Eight replied and ducked out after the rest, needing to do that ducking because the bastard was seriously tall.

Core and Beck were left alone.

Beck didn't beat around the bush.

"You gonna go there with Jagger's sister-in-law?"

Core shook his head. "No, man. She's somethin' else, but not my type."

"Sounds like your type."

"Well, she isn't."

"Right then, what's your type?" Beck asked.

Core was thrown by the question.

"Say what?"

"Kiki was a long time ago, brother," Beck pointed out, and Core felt the back of his neck get hot at the mention of his ex. "You get your fair share of pussy, but nothing serious since her. So what's your type?"

"Not Hellen."

Beck sat back in his fancy-ass, black leather swivel chair, one of eleven around the table.

He then said low. "You're allowed to be happy."

Core wasn't doing this shit. "I gotta talk to Eight."

"Me, more than you, had reason to go dark after what we did. Then I met Janna. I'll never wash completely clean. I still have nightmares, brother. I still stop in the middle of what I'm doing and feel the rush of filth flow through me. But Janna reminds me every day I'm not that man anymore. I gotta live with what I did, *we* did, but I'm not that man anymore. Rosie's moved on. Snap's moved on. Chaos has moved on. We share we never forget by taking their backs. But straight up, Rosie's the one who has to give it to us, and she has. That was another lifetime...for all of us. So what's fucking with you?"

"Nothing's fucking with me, Beck," he lied.

"We all put some serious shit out there in those woods, brother. So I know Eight isn't settling because I figure he's going for the gold to beat out Gene Simmons on how many women he can fuck before he finds the one that's gonna do it for him. Muzzle keeps jacking shit up because he's got shit taste and attracts bitches, but he also hasn't yet learned how to treat a woman for a long haul. What's your deal?"

Core was done with this.

"I don't have a deal," he clipped. "She's just not my gig."

"You brought her friend's shit to our club and asked us to deal with it."

"I caught her putting her ass on the line to extricate her friend from a bad situation. She's loyal. We value that, am I wrong?" Core bit out.

Beck's eyes narrowed. "Why you pissed at me?"

"Because you're acting like I'm fuckin' fifteen with a crush and straight up, brother, this is none of your business."

"I love you, brother, and I want you happy, so fuck you, it is," Beck shot back.

Goddammit.

What did you say to that?

Core said nothing.

"Janna worries," Beck said, toning it down. "She thinks the world of you. She says it's a waste no woman is getting what you got to give."

"I just haven't found one yet. For fuck's sake, are you my brother, my president, my friend or my dating advisor?"

Beck put his hands to the arms of his chair and stood.

He looked down at Core and finished it, "All right, I'll let it go."

Thank fuck.

He then walked to the door as Core rose out of his seat too.

But Core made no other move because Beck stopped at the door and looked back at him.

"Your dad was scum, you fucked up, there's a difference," he stated. "Punish yourself for what you did, I get it. I'm right there with you. But don't punish yourself for the man he was. Because you are not that man."

And after delivering that successful parting shot, Beck walked out of Resurrection's meet room.

7

SHE SHED

Hellen

I WAS SHUTTING down to leave the office in order to go to Mom and Andy's for dinner, when *The Mandalorian* theme came from my bag.

I was feeling anxious because I'd made a decision, called a staffing agency and scheduled a meeting to discuss finding an assistant.

I hadn't pulled the trigger, but I'd taken the next step, and it was freaking me out.

And last night's scene with Bree hadn't been a blast.

She was upset on so many levels, I lost track, but felt for her on all of them.

Earrings that meant something to her, gone. Same with the necklace. Her money probably gone too.

I was right, she couldn't afford it. He'd not only cleaned out her savings, she'd admitted to us she'd amassed some not insubstantial credit card debt because she'd been paying for them to go out for the last few weeks due to his "money problems." And we could just say

Christos wasn't a Las Delicias kind of guy, he also wasn't a home-cooking kind of guy, so they'd been going out a lot.

He'd played with her emotions. He made her question her judgment. He put her in a situation where she felt she had to confront her friends in defense of him.

On top of that, she was heartbroken, because she really was into him.

I barely slept because she was a mess, she was my friend, I was pissed as all hell at Christos, asshole men in general who fucked with women, and I was worried about Bree.

Topping that, Core had reached out via text to get details about Dad, my grandparents, and my other family that was in town who Eleanor might approach.

They were the first texts we'd exchanged, and maybe he wasn't a big text person, because not two hours before, we had a phone conversation where he was warm and teasing and all I knew of Core (so far), and through the text he was short and all business.

Maybe it meant he was home with his girlfriend, and he couldn't be friendly/flirty texting some chick where she might see (or maybe she was one of those women who checked their partner's phones).

If that was true, that meant Core was that guy. The friendly/flirty guy who wasn't that way all the time and hid it around his woman.

And that would suck.

So, yeah, barely any sleep last night.

And as such, I was tired and really all I wanted to do was go home and curl up in my couch with a thriller in my hand and a good glass of wine.

It didn't get better when I pulled out my phone and saw who was calling.

My gaze shifted to the glass vase filled with a velvety red dome of roses, at least a hundred of them, which meant it had to cost a fortune.

They'd been delivered a couple of hours ago.

The card said, DINNER? PLEASE? -B

They were from Bryan.

As was the call.

I didn't want to take it, but procrastination was not my thing. A lot had happened in the few short weeks since we'd been broken up, so much on my mind, I couldn't say I was suffering for his loss as much as in the beginning.

That didn't mean the hurt wouldn't come back when that door was reopened.

The sooner I dealt with it, though, the sooner I could get on with my life.

And I cared about him enough to stop him from doing something that I knew he'd eventually regret, like spending that kind of money on roses for a woman he had no future with.

"Hey, Bryan," I greeted.

"You picked up." He sounded relieved.

Instantly, I compared his voice to Core's.

Bryan was a litigator, and as such, needed to convince judges and juries he knew what he was saying, and they should go along with it. I'd sat in court and watched him. I'd been impressed. He had a smooth, nice, confident but average voice and a great vocabulary.

Core's voice had texture. Just the sound of it told a story. It was lower, deeper, kind of gritty, and a lot more manly.

Easy winner (number two).

Okay...

What was I doing?

It didn't matter.

Bryan was no longer in my life (mostly), and Core was making it clear he was not going to be in my life in that way.

This was a waste of headspace.

"Yes," I pointed out the obvious to Bryan's remark.

"Did you get the flowers?"

"I did."

"Did you like them?"

"They're gorgeous."

"Did you see the note?"

"Yes, Bryan."

"Baby," he whispered.

Another man I wished wouldn't call me baby, but for a different reason.

"I have to go to dinner at Mom and Andy's," I told him. "I can't do this now."

"Quick then, can we meet for coffee?"

"Bryan—"

"Just so I can see you. I miss you, Hellen. I'll buy you a cup to go, we'll get on with our days and sit down sometime later to talk things through."

Talk things through.

Like that was a given.

I was just too tired to do this now.

"Okay, listen," I began. "Bree's boyfriend is scamming her, and it's upsetting all of us. And my dad wants to mend fences, which just upsets me. I understand where you're at, but I honestly can't do this now."

"That Christos guy is scamming Bree?"

Why did I say anything?

And how could I forget he *just didn't listen to me*?

"Bryan, I can't do this now," I stated in a firm voice.

"Right, right, right," he muttered like he was talking to himself. "Though I gotta say, I'm more worried about your father. What's he up to?"

Bryan knew all about my dad.

Bryan had never met my dad.

Bryan hated my dad because Bryan didn't like he'd hurt me.

I felt a warmth hit my belly it wasn't his to give me anymore, and I fought the urge to throw my phone at the four-hundred-dollar arrangement of roses on my desk.

"Okay," Bryan read my non-response for what it was (finally!). "I'll let you go, but will you fill me in over coffee? The

Cliff Notes version if that's all the time you have, so I don't worry."

"All right," I gave in.

"Saturday?"

This guy.

Saturday meant neither of us would have to rush back to work, stripping away an excuse I could latch onto in order to get away from him fast.

Did he think I was an idiot?

But coffee and then it'd be over?

"Fine," I agreed.

"Ten? Fortnum's? Or do you want to go somewhere else?"

"That works."

"Awesome, baby. See you then."

"Then" was the day after tomorrow.

And then we'd be done.

"See you then."

"Love you, Hellen."

"'Bye, Bryan."

I rang off, hating to do it, leaving his sentiment hanging. I knew it hurt him, so it didn't feel nice. I'd already done it once, and it, along with all the rest, sent me to bed on a crying jag that put me off cookies. Even though I'd never outright told him I loved him, because I wasn't sure I was there, and then became sure I wasn't going to get there, a curt "'Bye, Bryan" wasn't the way I used to roll.

But...onward!

I tossed my phone in my bag, checked everything was good for me to leave, then I took off.

I had the urge to phone Core on the way to my parents', coming up with a variety of reasons why I needed to talk to him.

Fortunately, they were all lame, so I managed to stop myself and hit Mom and Andy's.

I parked, got out and headed in.

"Mom? Andy? I'm here!" I called after I walked inside.

Mom came out of the kitchen, took one look at me, and said, "Oh, honey. Didn't you have time to go home and change into something comfy?"

She was approaching me with arms out.

I opened mine, and we hugged.

"Waste of gas money when I can do this," I remarked and kicked my pumps off.

She watched, grinned at me, patted my face, and replied, "Always so smart with your money. That's my girl." She turned and headed back to the kitchen. "Come, I'm putting the finishing touches on dinner."

I tossed my bag on the couch and followed her. "Where's Andy and Li?"

"Outside, doing something with the bunch of lumber that Andy dragged home from Lowe's last weekend. I'm not allowed to look. The final unveiling is going to be a surprise. They're giving me a girl shed."

"She shed," I corrected.

"What?" she asked, opening the oven and pulling out a roasting chicken.

"Nothing. Sweet of Andy to do."

Her smile was beautiful and private when she told the chicken, "Andy's sweet."

I studied my mother.

Did I want that look one day?

Or was all that was going on a lesson to me that I enjoyed my life, my friends, my space, my business, so I was good?

I didn't mind going into the office early or working late. I didn't even notice it. I loved what I did.

Further, I didn't mind living alone. I had to admit that it'd been kind of a relief that Bryan wasn't around anymore, everything was as I wanted it. I didn't have bathroom towels to pick up from the floor or whiskers to rinse out of the sink or plastics and beer bottles to fish out of the garbage to recycle.

I also didn't mind going to bed alone.

Bryan had never moved in, but he slept over a lot because his apartment was a pit, and he had a roommate. He snored. I was a light sleeper. It drove me crazy. I might miss his hands and mouth on me. The intimacy of having a man in your bed. The further intimacy of knowing him and his body and what he liked, and him knowing the same about you. The boost you felt that a man wanted you in that way.

But I'd just talked to him, and outside of him slightly irritating me, I'd had no reaction.

I was seeing now I'd missed him for a while, like a habit I enjoyed but it wasn't healthy for me. So I quit it, it wasn't altogether easy, but I was able to get on with my life, and right then, I was realizing I could live without him just fine.

"Hellen?" Mom called.

I focused on her.

She was basting the chicken.

"Sorry, miles away," I said.

"Are you thinking about your dad?" she asked gently.

"I was thinking about Bryan."

"Oh, sweetie," she cooed.

"No, I was thinking about the fact I'm over him."

She blinked.

The sliding glass door to the backyard opened and Andy and Li trooped in.

"Yo, bitch!" Liane greeted.

I grinned at my sister.

She was wearing a T-shirt that said, F*** THE PATRIARCHY!, cutoff shorts, her skin was tan, her long hair was in a sloppy knot on top of her head, she had not a swipe of makeup on her face, bare feet, and they were filthy, and I could see dirt under her short fingernails.

She'd earned a useless degree in Women's Studies and Political Science and now worked for a nursery that also did landscaping.

She used to be a lot more sensitive, more like Mom, wanting

everyone to be happy and get along. But somewhere in the latter part of her college career (around the time my discussion with Dad meant he vamoosed), she'd started to come away from being a Haley Harmon Mini-Me and came into herself.

Now, she made crap money, lived with her parents, got high a lot, dated men with longer hair than mine, and was living her best life.

"Hey, hon, gonna wash my hands real quick," Andy greeted, getting into my space, kissing my cheek, then heading to the kitchen sink while saying to Mom, "Damn, baby, that smells *amazing*."

Mom had roasted approximately two thousand chickens for Andy in their time together.

But to Andy, every one of them smelled *amazing*.

Liane horned in beside Andy so they could use the same water, but she looked over her shoulder at me.

"I mean, Dad. Bummer."

There you had it.

Dad.

Bummer.

I was blaming the sleep deprivation, but part of me wanted to dissolve into tears because they were so normal, this felt so safe, it never changed and it never failed to prop me up, even when I wasn't feeling down.

But now, I was feeling down.

So now, it felt beautiful to be with these people I loved.

"Good idea, Li-Li," Andy declared, glanced back at me, then returned his attention to his hands, still talking. "Let's get this out of the way so we can enjoy the rest of the night without him looming over us. Now, before your mother says her piece, I'm going to preface it by sharing, it's your choice and we'll support you no matter what."

"Andy!" Mom snapped.

"What?" Andy asked, reaching for a dish towel to dry his hands.

"You essentially just told them it's okay for them to keep shutting their father out of their lives," Mom explained.

"Well, it is," Andy said simply.

I wanted to laugh, but laughing might screw with my ability to fully witness this byplay (I loved Mom and Andy's byplay), so I didn't.

Mom looked to Li and me in turn, speaking. "Just to say, he's right. It is. Though I'll also share that you only have one father."

"Agreed," I cut in and pointed at Andy. "He's standing right there."

What happened next was unexpected.

Andy went rigid. Mom froze too. Liane's mouth was hanging open.

They were all staring at me.

"What?" I asked.

"I didn't—" Andy cleared his throat. "I didn't know you felt that way, honey."

"I..." Oh shit. "I mean, is that okay?"

All of a sudden, Mom burst out crying.

What on earth?

Liane went to her, a massive grin on her face.

Andy came to me and pulled me into a big hug.

"It is absolutely, one thousand percent okay," he said into my ear.

His voice was kind of croaky.

I held on to him and replied, "I thought you knew I felt that way."

He didn't let me go even as he pulled slightly away to look at me. "I did know. We'll just say it's nice to hear the words."

"God, I'm sorry I didn't say them before," I mumbled to his throat.

"Hellen, look at me."

I looked at him.

"Promise. That's one thing you can say that's never too early, and it's never too late."

I smiled at him.

He dipped in and whispered in my ear, "And in case you didn't get this, I fully support you telling your father to fuck off again."

"Andy!" Mom cried. "I heard that."

Andy moved to my side, his arm over my shoulders, so I kept mine along his waist.

We'd stood this way before. He'd stood this way with Liane. And Archie. And, obviously, Mom.

It was what you did with your dad.

I took note of it then because I'd just realized he *was* my dad.

I was still tired, but suddenly I felt tons better.

"Do you want me to lie to your daughter?" Andy asked my mother.

"*Our* daughter, obviously," she fired back.

Oh *man.*

Again, I had to fight back crying.

"And no, but she should do the right thing," Mom concluded.

"Well, I say the *fair* thing is me calling him because it's my turn to tell him to fuck off," Liane announced.

That made me snicker.

"Your mouth, my darling girl," Mom warned. "It isn't even okay for Andy to say that word."

"Whatevs." Li blew it off, went to the salad Mom had made, and popped a cherry tomato in her mouth.

I nearly gagged.

I hated tomatoes.

"Right, this is my official piece," Mom declared after she shoved the chicken back in the oven. She took us all in with her hands on her hips and went on, "It's true. Your father hasn't done much to earn your time or your affection. But you two are young. God willing, you have a *long* life yet to live. Not giving him this last shot, not giving your grandfather another shot, not seeing your grandfather in what might be his dying days, not opening your heart, taking the high road, when it's all said and done, you'll have many years to regret it."

After Mom finished, Liane literally collapsed in a heap to the floor and bemoaned to the ceiling, "Why did we get Glinda the Good Witch as our mother? Why, why, why? Why couldn't we be spawned of Elphaba?"

"Stop being dramatic and get up from that floor," Mom ordered.

"Your unerring moral compass *can* be inconvenient, Mom," I noted.

Andy chuckled.

"Though, I, for one, am glad my skin isn't green," I finished.

That was when Mom laughed.

"Brownnose," Li said, picking herself up.

"Girls, set the table. Andy, open some wine. I have potatoes to mash," Mom bossed.

We all got to it.

Because that was how it worked in our family.

"It looks like Dolly Parton decorated this place. It's everything. She's gonna love it," I remarked as I looked around the she shed that was far from a pile of lumber. It appeared complete.

It was after dinner and Liane was giving me a tour.

Li arranged herself on the wicker sofa that had thick pads in a bright floral, and she did this so she was upside down, legs thrown ever the back, head dangling close to the ground.

"I know, right?" she agreed.

I sat in a wicker chair that was lousy with tassels.

I then offered, "I'll call him."

She dug into her pocket and produced a vape.

She offered.

It wasn't nicotine, it was cannabis.

I still declined.

She puffed.

She then said, "It's my turn."

"I—"

"H, you can't protect me all my life. I'm a grownup. I have an awesome but slacker job. You're attempting to rule the world. I've got more time than you do. I can call our father and arrange for us to sit down and talk."

The grownup part, considering her attire and position, could be debatable.

But it wasn't.

Li, like me, knew who she was.

And who she was, was a woman who wanted to work to play. She liked clothes but wasn't into makeup. She liked to travel, but she preferred camping to saving up for a five-star. Her goal was to fix up one of those snazzy, boho vans, find a man who'd put up with living in it, a dog and a cat who got along, and then go out to explore the world, stopping to make money when they needed it.

It wasn't my thing, but I hoped she got what she wanted.

"Any plans I should know about?" she asked after the scheduling.

"Not Saturday morning. I'm having coffee with Bryan."

She whipped around to sitting. "You are?"

I nodded.

"Why?"

"He thinks we can work through it. Me breaking up came as a total surprise to him. It maybe shouldn't have, but it did. Now, he's had time to let it sink in, and I need to show him the respect of sitting down and sharing it's truly over."

"Babe, don't let him talk you into giving him a second chance."

As if.

Still, I was surprised my sister said that.

"I thought you liked him," I noted.

Her shoulders went up and down. "He's likeable. He's not difficult to look at. And he works real hard to make everyone think he's a cool dude. Maybe part of that is because he's a cool dude. Though, I think most of it is because he's a salesman. I don't know why he is, but he wants everyone to like him. That's like...not possible. And it could get kinda cringey."

I couldn't say she was wrong.

"That said," she continued. "The worst part about it was that he wanted so bad for everyone to think he's a good guy, to fit in everywhere he went, and then, essentially at home, he doesn't bother paying attention to your needs. I mean, if he loved you and wanted to spend time with you, looking at that as a possible commitment thing, you should be the one he worked hardest to make think he was a good guy. That's weird. And a total red flag, taking you for granted that way."

She wasn't wrong about that either.

But four of her words stuck with me.

Taking you for granted.

My eyes were aimed, unfocused, on the hot pink table with the bright floral arrangement on top that sat in the corner as I thought this through.

"I still liked him, though, H. Because he actually is a good guy. He just wasn't perfect. No one is," Liane said.

I focused on her. "I don't think I want to get married."

"To Bryan?"

"To anyone."

A huge grin spread across her face, and she started laughing when she said, "I wonder what Mom's going to think about this whole take-the-high-road thing with Dad, considering he's the reason neither of us is gonna go the traditional route with that malarkey."

"I don't know if it was Dad," I replied. "I mean, yeah, it probably was. Part of it. But we also had a long time with her and Andy, and they work." I considered it and finished, "I think it was Bryan."

Her expression grew concerned. "Were things worse than what you said?"

Obviously, I shared with my sister.

We were complete opposites, but I told her everything. She returned that.

We'd had a time in our lives where it was essential we bonded. You did that when you had a parent whose love wasn't quite healthy. Then Mom had to work after we left Dad, and as latchkey kids, Li and I spent a lot of time together.

We created our bond, and even when things got better when Mom left Dad, and then when Andy came, we kept it strong.

In other words, she knew all about Bryan.

"How much worse did they have to get?" I asked. "And that's the first question you had. But he didn't apologize or start to take me seriously until he realized how serious I was about ending us. I have my own home, my own business, things to do with my life, but he got to a place he didn't even thank me for drying and folding his laundry and having it ready for him to take home. It's the conventional way people look at relationships. He said my concerns were petty. He said this because I'm not only expected, as a woman, to adapt, I'm simply expected to take on this stuff. He's a great guy if he rushes to my place after work to clean up after his buds, even if they were *his* buds who made the mess, I asked him to do it the day before and I have to live with it, not him. Why is he great for cleaning up after his own damned self?"

"Good question, and he isn't," Liane agreed.

"No. But if he did it when I asked, he'd expect me to thank him. Like he's doing me a favor. I get that men are programmed like that, they see it at home. Growing up, the mom takes on the lion's share of the day to day, the dad mows the lawn, kicks back and watches football. It blew his mind that the stuff he thought was petty would end us. He still doesn't believe we're over. I don't want any part of legally binding myself to that kind of life contract."

Li was grinning again. "Preach it, sister."

Oh yes.

I was preaching.

And I wasn't finished.

"I read this article written by this woman who had a job and kids, and her husband wanted to do something special for her birthday. He thought he was being awesome. But after making her breakfast in bed and him baking a cake with the kids and wrapping her present, she got up to a kitchen that was a disaster, and she had to clean it up. She went to the closet to get dressed, saw he'd wrapped her present in there and left all the shit on the floor for her to put away. When she complained about this to him, he was upset she wasn't appreciative of all he'd done. When 'all he'd done' meant she ate a breakfast she didn't have to cook for once and spent five seconds opening a present she didn't have to wrap, but she had to do all the shit work on the back end. And he threw her a guilt trip because she wasn't grateful."

"We shouldn't use wrapping paper," Li remarked. "It's an unnecessary depletion of natural resources."

I couldn't argue that.

But it wasn't the point.

"I know there are women who love doing that kind of thing. And good for them. But I don't want to get stuck in that."

"H, if you're trying to talk yourself into understanding your right to let Bryan go, you could have stopped five minutes ago," Liane affirmed. "What you feel is right. It's right, no matter the reasons. Though all of what you're saying are exceptional reasons. I will say, I'm unsurprised, because it's all kinds of ballsy that you don't want to bind yourself to something that might morph into that bullshit, and that's who you are. All kinds of ballsy. If it was easier for us to walk away when men walk all over us, things would be a lot different in this world."

"Damn straight."

"Though, I do think there are guys who aren't like that." Another grin. "Or I hope so, since I intend to find one."

"I hope so too," I muttered.

For her and for me.

"We should have brought the wine. I'll go get it," she offered.

"We should go back in and hang with Mom and Andy."

Upon me saying this, Mom shouted from the house, "Your phone is ringing, Hellen!"

I pushed up, Liane came with me, and we slid out of the door in a way Mom couldn't see inside the shed if she was watching.

She wasn't.

We went inside, I nabbed my phone, and it said I had a missed call from Marcy.

As I was reading that, I got a text.

I saw some of what it said on the notification and swiftly opened it.

Mayday! Mayday! Bree's gone from wrecked to pissed and she's decided payback. There's no talking her out of it. I've tried.

YOU ARE NEEDED ASAP!

Well, it seemed I wasn't going to enjoy one last glass of wine with my family, drive home and crawl into bed early to catch up on some sleep.

Shit.

8

GONE

Core

The call came when he was seasoning his steak to slap it on the grill.

It was Eight, who was supposed to be in Littleton staking out the house or picking one of the grifters to follow to get a further sense of what they were dealing with.

Core had spent the day following one himself.

They could go in hard on these guys, teach them a lesson, run them out of town, but if they were part of a larger operation, that could buy the club heat that was always annoying to have to expend the effort to cool down.

First, they needed to track the players, note MOs, discover the extent of the operation, and instead of tearing the leaves off the weed, yank it out by its root.

At this juncture and that hour, there was no good reason for Eight to phone, so Core abandoned his steak and took the call.

"Yo," he greeted.

"I think you need to be here, considering a carload of bitches just showed. One got out and stabbed one of her own tires with a knife. The other one walked up to the house where the Greeks are staying. And the one who walked up to the house is yours."

Core fought the buzzing in his head because he knew "yours" meant Hellen.

"Fuck," Eight bit out. "I think I saw another one jump the fence at the back. Gotta go."

Eight disconnected.

Core looked down at Nanook, his malamute.

He was salivating and staring at the counter.

"Let's go," Core said.

Nanook barked and Core left the steak on the counter as he prowled out to his truck.

He opened the driver's side door, Nanook jumped in, then sat on Core's passenger seat panting as Core swung in, started up the truck and took off.

He opened Nanook's window.

Nanook stuck his head out and smiled.

Core was not smiling.

Halfway to the house, he got a text.

He glanced at it.

It was an address from Eight.

Stopped at a light, Core loaded it into his satnav.

When he arrived at the Walgreens parking lot, Eight was standing outside his truck with three women, one was Marcy, another one was one of the women he saw at Fortnum's.

The last one was Hellen in a pleated pink skirt, a white blouse, and shiny beige pumps with very high stiletto heels.

Red encroached at the sides of his vision.

He parked, grunted, "Stay," and Nanook woofed. He threw open his door, got out and stalked to the huddle.

"Core—" Hellen tried.

She was safe.

All was good.

Even so.

He got in her face and roared, "*What did I say?*"

She shut her mouth and began to look pissed.

"These guys are not good guys, Hellen," he reminded her.

"Let me—"

"We have no idea how big this is. We have no idea the men we're dealing with. We have no idea the lengths they'll go to protect their scam. What the fuck were you doing?"

"Taking a friend's back," she returned, cool as a cucumber.

"In four-inch heels?" he demanded.

She now appeared uncomfortable. "I will admit, my shoes could have been a hindrance. But I didn't have time to change them. Things were underway."

"What fucking things?" he ground out.

"It was my fault," the new girl said.

He turned to her.

She quailed.

"Speak," he grunted.

"Well, uh..."

That was all she could get out.

"So," Marcy took over, "in *The Tinder Swindler*, one of the chicks he swindled took a load of his stuff and sold it on eBay in order to pay back some of the debt she got into because of him. It pissed him off. Like, deep-end ticked. But there was nothing he could do. The swindler got swindled. Christos decks out in labels. Bree decided she wanted to look for her necklace, and while she was in their house, grab some of his stuff she could sell to get back her money. Obviously, for her to go in, we had to get the other guys out."

It wasn't a bad idea, and it was fucking moronic.

Core turned his attention to Eight.

"I pretended I was her old man," he explained to Core's unspoken question, jerking a thumb to Marcy. "When they came out, told the dudes the women called me before they went to the house, but I wasn't able to get there quick, so they were looking for someone to help. But I finally showed to change the tire. Then I stuck the spare with my blade, told the guys they'd lured out of the house we'd have to come back to fix the flat, rounded those two up, shoved them in my truck and they texted the other one. We swung around to get her and now we're here."

"I don't know why you didn't just change the tire," Marcy noted.

"Because if he did, he couldn't haul all your asses here so I could fucking *lay you out*," Core bit off. "Marcy? You? Seriously? What the absolute fuck?"

She did a head-tilt shrug. "I tried, bro. There was no talking her down."

He turned to the new girl. "So you fall for some guy's line, he takes you for a ride, your friends look after you, and you pay them back by dragging them deeper into your shit?"

Her eyes grew huge, and her face got red. Marcy sucked in her lips, but Core wasn't sure that wasn't to hide a smile.

Hellen shifted closer to him and murmured, "Core."

He looked down at her.

She was so close he could smell her perfume. He didn't know what it was, he just knew he liked it.

Fuck.

Him.

"No, baby," he growled. "You, all of you, could have been jacked up because of this chick's choices. I'm not gonna keep my mouth shut so I won't hurt her feelings. She's gotta start *thinking*."

"Can we talk privately?" she requested.

He wanted to talk *very* privately with her.

He wanted to take her to his house, bend her over his knee, throw up that pretty skirt of hers, and spank her until she couldn't sit for a week without remembering his hand smacking her ass.

Then he'd fuck some sense into her.

That was out, so he debated the merits of being semi-private with her now.

He blew out a breath and moved to his truck.

When he stopped and turned to her, she asked, eyes on Nanook. "You have a dog?"

"You're beautiful and you know it," he said, putting effort into it coming out evenly.

Her gaze swung to him, and her lips parted in surprise.

"You can be cute, and you know it. You got spunk, and you know that too. You know a man is going to get a load of you, open his fly and offer you his dick as your lead. Warning, Hellen, I am not that kind of man."

Now her cheeks were pink, and he wasn't sure it was all anger.

"What are you ta—?" she started.

"Yes, I have a dog. Yes, he's fuckin' awesome. Right now is not about my dog. Right now is about you letting your girl lead you to making seriously stupid-as-fuck decisions that put your ass on the line."

"Don't talk to me like I'm a child," she snapped.

"You act like a child, I'll talk to you like a child." He lifted his arm and jabbed a finger over her head in the direction of the Littleton house. "That's teenage-girl bullshit and you know that too."

"You're aware, I don't have to stand here listening to you lecture me."

"We're on this. Resurrection has taken this on. Do you know what that means?"

"I don't know if I care," she huffed.

"Jag tell you about our club?"

"I've heard you mentioned, I can't say I paid a lot of attention."

"We're called the Angels of Death."

Her eyes widened.

He got closer and dropped his voice lower. "Yeah, baby. We're called the Angels of Vengeance too. You see, we got on a dark path a few years ago and did some seriously ugly shit. When we pulled ourselves out, as a club, we agreed our mission would be our penance. Nothing could make up for what we did, but we committed ourselves to a lifetime of seeking redemption. That means, if good was getting fucked over by bad, we go after the bad, and we fuck them good. You with me?"

She was holding her own, her eyes not leaving his, keeping her space even though he was in it, but she swallowed, and her voice held a thread of alarm when she said, "Yes. I'm with you."

"So those fucks dick with your friend, it bothers you, I see that, you're like all the other women we help. Your friend is too. And it's without a doubt they're fucking with more of you. I take it to my brothers, they vote, we take on her shit. I took it to my brothers. We voted. Reason Eight was there tonight is that we...are...taking...on... her...*shit*. Did I tell you they weren't going to get away with it?"

"Yes," she admitted.

"Well, it makes it harder now, because Eight's been seen. And he's a big man, but he's got skills and he's never been made on a stake-out, a shadow or a tail. So that's a loss to our cause. I was on the side-walk having a conversation with you the other night, and newsflash, if they saw me, which they could have, they also saw you and Marcy, and this made what you did tonight not only crazy risky, but straight-up dumb. So I might be out. We only got so many brothers to get this done, and we're not just gonna suggest they pack up and leave town. We're dealing with this, *all of it*, no matter how big it is. You and your girls doin' stupid shit is gonna fuck our intention to get your friend justice, and anyone else they're dicking over."

"You weren't clear this was your intention," she returned.

"Lesson, baby, I say don't worry, *you don't worry*. I say don't worry, it means *I'm fucking handling it*."

"What are you going to do to them?" she asked.

"Good question, because this gives you practice. *Don't worry* about what we're gonna do."

She was getting pissed again, or more pissed.

"Are you aware at all of how big of an asshole you're being right now?"

"Entirely aware. But I'm happy to ramp that up if it means my message gets through your head."

Her nose scrunched up, her eyes squinted down, and he knew she was off-the-charts pissed.

"Are we finished?" she asked.

"Is my message through your head?"

"Yes, Core, it got through, loud and clear. Now, can your friend take us to Bree's? We need to call AAA to deal with Marcy's car."

He twisted to Eight, put his lip to his teeth and whistled.

Eight nodded and moved to the women who were huddled off to the side, watching Core and Hellen.

He turned back to Hellen and ordered, "Get in the truck. I'm taking you home."

Her chin listed into her neck in surprise.

"No, you're not."

"Yeah, I am."

She moved to step around him.

He got in her space.

She stopped, tipped her head back and glared up at him. "I'm not playing this game, Core. Let me pass."

"Get in the truck."

"Let me pass."

"Get your ass in the truck."

She tried to step around him again. He cut her off. She made an angry noise that was cute and hot, but he was still ticked at her, so this time it didn't register, and when he heard Eight's engine catch, he twisted to look.

Both her friends were staring out the windows at them as Eight drove away.

The new girl looked terrified.

Marcy gave them a finger wave.

Okay, that almost made him smile.

"Fucking Marcy," Hellen muttered irately.

Core looked back to see she was pulling her phone out of her purse.

He swiped it out of her hand.

Her head snapped back. "Core!"

"Get in the truck."

"I'm not getting in your *fucking truck*."

She went for her phone, he pulled it out of her reach.

"*Fine!*" she shouted, started to stomp around him toward the drugstore, but he caught her by the back of her neck, curled her into him, then tangled his fingers in her hair.

Thick. Soft.

Goddamn.

She was tits crushed to his chest, belly to his cock, soft breaths coming from her lips whispering against his lips.

And yeah, the perfume did a number on him, but all the rest, it was practically impossible not to get hard.

He could kiss her, and she'd kiss him back. He knew it. She knew it.

And with them both this ticked, it'd be hot as fuck.

He knew it.

She knew it too.

"You gonna get in my truck?" he asked softly.

"Yes," she whispered.

His dick stirred.

He let her go to take her hand and lead her to the passenger seat.

Nanook read the situation and jumped in the back.

He opened her door and stood behind her as she climbed up. He slammed the door, rounded the hood and folded in.

He started the truck and pulled out.

Nanook shoved his head between them and panted at the windshield.

Core gave himself a minute to calm down, giving her one too.

After that minute, he said, "My boy's name is Nanook."

She didn't reply.

He glanced at her.

She was looking out the side window.

He drew in a deep breath and let it out as a heavy sigh.

"You know I like you," he said.

She didn't speak.

"Seeing as I like you, not big on the idea of something happening to you."

She remained silent.

He gave it another minute, then two, and tried again.

"You eaten?"

She made no reply.

"I haven't eaten."

She still said nothing.

Right then.

At the next light, Core changed directions.

She lived east of Colorado Boulevard.

He lived south, close to Englewood.

Instead of going to her place, he headed home.

She was so busy pouting, she didn't notice.

He knew when she did because she straightened in her seat.

Nanook took that opportunity to sniff her then try to lick her.

Core opened his mouth to command his dog to stop, but Hellen didn't rear away.

She buried her pink-tipped fingers in his fur and scratched.

Nanook licked her again.

Core decided he needed to keep his eyes on the road.

She said nothing, even when he pulled into his garage.

He got out.

Nanook, not dumb by any stretch of the imagination, hopped down behind Hellen.

Core walked toward the door to the house, hit the garage door button, it started trundling down, and he opened the way to the house, sweeping his arm to invite her inside.

She went in.

She strutted through his laundry room and stopped in his kitchen.

She glanced at the steak, but otherwise didn't look around.

Nanook's head swung between the two of them as they went into a stare off. Then, with a groan, he hedged his bets and sank down to his belly between them.

She finally spoke.

Lifting her hand in front of her, palm up, she asked, "May I have my phone now?"

"How pissed at me are you?"

"There is no quantity yet invented to measure the intensity of how pissed I am at you."

"Say they were onto you."

She shook her head. "It doesn't excuse—"

"You in a skirt and high heels. Maybe five of them in that house. You and Marcy nabbed first, your friend comes over the back fence thinking she's good, they get her next. What do fucks like that do to women who are not toeing their line?"

He saw her jaw bulge as she ground her teeth.

But she stopped doing that to say, "Christos wasn't there, obviously. We knew that. He knows Marcy and me."

"So four on three. Four men, three women. They still got you and you know it."

She glared at him.

She knew it.

He kept at her.

"To answer my question, they teach them how to toe the line, and sweetheart, they do it in a way you never forget. Eight called me, that was all that was in my head. I have spent five years cleaning up the trail of misery left behind from women who have been used by men like that. If they realized what you women were up to, you become someone else. The you standing here, pissed at me, is gone. *That* was why I was so fucking furious."

"I can cogitate, Core. I figured that out when you shouted in my face."

"It was an honest reaction."

She nodded sarcastically, and yeah, she could do that because he didn't miss the sarcasm.

"It was something."

"Tables are turned, I do something jacked, you telling me you wouldn't be that pissed at me?"

She ground her teeth again.

She'd be that pissed at him.

"Shout in my face? Make your anger clear? And then when it's done," he tossed both hands to his sides, "get me someplace good to work it out?"

"Is that what we're doing? Working it out?"

"I'm gonna grill a steak. I'm gonna grill you one too if you haven't eaten. We're gonna have some beers. You're gonna tell me what a dick I am, I'm gonna admit I was a dick, because I was serious pissed, but I recognize I went over the top. Then I'm gonna take you to your car and follow you so I know you're safe home."

He said something there, something that penetrated, because her head ticked and the feel of her eyes on him changed from hot as lasers to hot as weaker lasers.

But she said, "I'd rather call an Uber."

He shook his head. "Those aren't safe for a woman alone, baby. Are you nuts?"

That was when it happened. Something clicked for her then, he saw it. This wasn't a minor thing. The way she was watching him completely changed.

Then she said, "It's late. I've already eaten."

"I haven't."

"Well then,"—she indicated the steak on the counter—"eat."

He wanted to smile, but he didn't.

"You still mad?"

"Yes. Very."

He opened his arms. "Wanna come here and hug it out?"

She took a step back, and a little bit of his sassy Hellen could be heard in her, "No. Thank you."

That was when he smiled and finally went back to his steak.

He dug her phone out of his pocket, put it on the counter and invited, "Help yourself to beer."

"Is that your way of saying you want me to get you a beer?"

He turned his head her way. "I got opposable thumbs. When I'm ready for a beer, I can get my own. You're offering to pop one for me, knock yourself out. But I'm doing something right now so I can't drink it. In other words, no, that was my way of saying, if you want one, grab a beer."

Now she was studying him like he was an alien.

"What?" he asked.

"Nothing," she murmured and headed to his fridge.

Meat was involved, so Nanook got up and sat by Core's leg while he finished seasoning.

He gave up on the grill and decided to pan fry.

"So you help women?" she asked.

He turned from the skillet he'd dropped butter into and saw she was at his back window, staring at his yard.

"Women. Men. Kids. Mostly women and kids."

"And to be the Angels of Death, that entails?"

"You know much about MCs?"

She turned to him and shook her head.

He laid it on her gently.

"Brother business is brother business, sweetheart. There might be men who share with their old ladies, but only if their old ladies are woven into the fabric of the club and dig that they never open their mouths, not ever to anyone, even other brothers, about the club business they know."

"Mm," she hummed, took a sip from her beer, and looked back out the window.

He was going to bake some tots to go with his steak, but instead, after he put the meat into the sizzling butter, he pulled out some chips.

That was when he got himself a beer.

He'd just flipped the filet when she asked, "You brought me here, to your place, does that mean you don't have a girlfriend?"

Well, shit.

A woman asked that question for one reason.

So now they were here.

"Nope," he answered.

It was then he needed to say that wasn't what this was. He needed to share that he was definitely into her, but they weren't going to go there. He was seeing at that juncture that taking her to his house might have been making a statement he didn't want to make.

Strike that, he did want it.

He just wasn't going to allow it.

On top of all that, he needed to try to explain why he lost his shit about her putting herself in danger when they weren't going to go there.

She was attracted to him, he knew.

She was sucking him deep, he knew that too.

He cared about her, a lot. That night, he'd made that clear.

She cared about him too. No woman put up with a man being that deeply in her shit if he didn't matter to her.

It was time to build the wall to keep her safe.

But Core didn't say any of that, and he didn't lay that first brick of the wall she needed him to build.

Because he was a sucker for her.

Because she made him laugh.

Because there was something about her standing in his kitchen, even still ticked at him, that felt so right, he'd never felt that rightness in his life, except the time he'd signed Resurrection's charter with his own blood.

"I forgot your dinner with your folks. Did you decide what to do about your dad?"

"We're meeting with him," she told the window.

Not smart.

He kept that to himself.

But worry hit his gut, because he knew very little about her father, but he also knew that was not going to go well, and he didn't want that for her.

"My mom prefers her daughters take the high road, even when it's rocky," she explained. "She's worried we'll regret it if we don't. Sadly, she's correct."

"Right," he muttered, slapping his steak on a plate, thinking her mom was right, at the same time she was wrong.

He dumped some cheddar Ruffles beside it and took it to the counter.

Nanook dogged his heels.

Hellen didn't move from the window.

He pulled out a fork and knife, cut off a good strip, and dropped it to Nanook.

His boy caught it with an audible chomp and swallowed it whole.

Core grinned.

He had a hunk in his own mouth and was chewing when she finally looked at him.

"We're done, aren't we?"

His throat closed and he almost spit out the steak.

He forced it down, opened his mouth...

But she got there first.

"You aren't looking after me because of Eleanor anymore. You'll be dealing with Bree's thing, just you and your brothers. So there's no reason we need to be in each other's lives anymore, is there?"

"Baby," he said conciliatorily, "I know you're ticked—"

"It's not that I'm ticked. It's that, regardless you give quite a few mixed signals, you've made it clear we're not going to go there. You have your life, I have mine, and it's actually dumb luck, the dumb part being me, we met at all."

"You're not dumb," he said.

She tipped her head. "I'm not?"

He'd earned that.

"It was a dumb thing to do. But you're not dumb. And I get you felt the need to stick by your girl. If she was determined to carry that out, much better you and Marcy were there. So mostly, I was pissed as shit at her, but I don't know her. So I took it out on you. That said," he made sure to add, "I was also pissed at you."

"What is this, Core?" she demanded.

"What's what?" he asked.

She turned fully to him and lifted a hand, flapping it between them. "*This*. What's *this*?"

God fucking dammit.

Now, it was the time.

He just hated that it was.

He was going to go gentle again, he opened his mouth...

And again, she got there before him.

"You don't have to say it." She spoke quietly. "I know. So after this, I promise I'm not going to let Bree do anything stupid, but I figure she's already made that promise to herself. This means you won't have to save us again, neither will any of your friends. So we're done."

It was like taking the steak knife and cutting himself from gullet to gut, having to say, "Yeah, baby. You're right. We're done."

She lifted her chin a smidge. "Can I please have my phone to call an Uber?"

"I'm sorry, sweetheart, please do not make me put you in a car with a stranger."

He saw the sheen of tears before she looked out the window again.

Core finished his steak fast, ate a few chips, swilled it back with some beer, and called softly, "Ready?"

She immediately set her beer on his kitchen table and walked to him. He handed over her phone as she walked right past him toward his garage door, not even glancing up at him.

Not giving him those pretty green eyes or what was in them, he'd even take her hurt, that was how deep he was sinking into her.

Jesus.

Yup.

Gutted.

Nanook started to come with, and her voice was throaty when, for some reason, she begged, "Not the dog. Please. Can he stay at home by himself?"

"Sit. Stay, Nanook."

Nanook sat and didn't move.

They hit the garage.

He opened her door on the truck.

She avoided looking at him as she climbed in.

He got in beside her, pulled out and drove her home.

He was idling at her curb when he turned to her.

"Hellen—"

"'Bye, Dustin," she whispered, already opening her door.

She leaped out and slammed the door without looking back.

Running on her toes up the walk, she was closed into her apartment before he could release his breath.

And she was gone.

9

WHAT MATTERS

Core

IT WAS ten to midnight the next night.

Friday.

Core was standing a few feet from his bike, his back resting against the brick of a building.

He was in an alley behind a restaurant in downtown Denver, and he had his phone to his ear.

The voice that came over the line was either altered, or someone was typing out the words and the reading was automated. He didn't know which.

The brothers had discussions about it. Core was in the camp it was automated because, he reckoned, that was the only way The Nerd rolled.

"Your assignment has been accepted," the voice said. "Research will commence at zero hundred hours Saturday." In other words, in ten minutes. "Expect a report at eighteen hundred hours on Sunday."

After that, there was a disconnect.

But it was good news.

The Nerd was going to do the online footwork on the Greeks.

Resurrection had other geeks they could go to for that kind of thing, but none of them were anywhere near as good as The Nerd.

Because of that, the brothers had more discussions about whether The Nerd was a one-man operation, or it was a coalition of computer geeks who worked together. Results were always thorough and swift, and when they went to one of their other assets for this kind of thing (even Brody, who was the best in Denver), they couldn't produce those results in that short of a time.

The Nerd referred to itself as The Nerd, but Core was convinced identifying as being singular was one of many tactics they used to throw people off.

The Nerd was underground. The Nerd didn't charge. The only thing you had to do to keep in the good graces of The Nerd was to keep your mouth shut about them, and you accepted that they worked for you when they wanted to. You told no one about them. You submitted your assignments, and they accepted them, or they didn't, and you didn't push it.

The Nerd had introduced itself to Resurrection when the club was working with a mom who was a friend of a friend of Rainman's old lady.

Shit had been real with her daughter—behavior changes, mood deteriorating rapidly and alarmingly. All of this defying explanation, nurture and therapy.

Then it happened. The mom came home and found her girl in her car in the garage. The car was on. The garage door was down.

She didn't die, but she'd been in that garage long enough with oxygen not getting where it needed to go, the mom would be taking care of her girl forever.

The dad was an asshole, checked out, no help.

And eventually, when she went through all her daughter's stuff to try to find answers, the mom discovered her sixteen-year-old daughter was caught in a cyber-sexploitation gig. Journals she kept shared she was terrified, and so ashamed, she didn't tell anyone, not even any of her friends, that some perverted piece of shit was making her life torture.

The cops wanted nothing to do with it. Cyber-crimes weren't easy to solve, and the victim was as good as dead. They took it on, but their tepid attempts to make headway were not lost on the girl's mother.

This was when she asked Resurrection to wade in.

She wanted justice and she wanted this guy stopped.

They could do both, but they didn't have the skills to find the guy who did it.

They got their geeks on it, but the perpetrator was talented. It was taking forever, and then, somehow The Nerd learned what they were doing. They waded in, got Resurrection what they needed, all of it, which was deeper and broader than any of them knew.

In the end, The Nerd discovered it involved eleven girls.

At that point, it was Resurrection's turn.

And now the perp would never do that again to another girl.

Core wasn't surprised The Nerd took on the Greeks. That sitch was right up their alley.

Then again, there weren't many Resurrection assignments The Nerd turned down.

He shoved his phone in his pocket as the back door opened and the kid came out.

He was a busboy at an expensive steak restaurant.

He hustled to Core.

"Got it?" Core asked.

The kid nodded and held out his phone.

Core took it. It had been engaged and was open to pictures on his camera.

Core slid through them.

There were five pics of Christos wining some chick. Lots of smiles. Lots of touching. A bottle of Dom in a bucket. Him using his credit card to pay the bill.

He emailed the pics to Resurrection's account and handed the kid back his phone. He then pulled out his wallet, opened it, yanked out a C-note and gave it to the kid.

"Thanks," he muttered, returning his wallet.

"Anytime," the kid said, pocketing the bill.

Core jumped on his bike and rolled out.

He'd been on the case all day, and it was business as usual with the Greeks. If they were tweaked by Hellen and Marcy's antics, they didn't let on. Eight had been replaced by Muzzle. They were still in recon mode.

The Nerd would get them what they needed to get rolling in a serious way.

But Core wasn't feeling those guys just getting on with it after what happened the night before. If they told Christos and described the women who showed, he'd know.

It didn't seem like it was even a blip for him, seeing those pics with him out on the town with another chick.

So either they felt untouchable, even if they'd been made by one of their marks, or Eight's explanation flew for the other guys, and it was just some women with a flat tire, a man was involved, so it wasn't worth giving it any more of their time.

He had to hope one of those was the case.

But Core put it out of his mind. There was no more he could do on it that night. It was late. He was wiped.

And thinking about it meant he couldn't escape thinking about Hellen.

Though, it didn't much matter what he tried because Hellen was constantly on his mind.

He remembered his dad in one of his few good times saying, "You know right away. You just know. When you meet her, there's no question." He'd then snuggled up to Core's mom, kissed her neck, held her close, and shot Core another smile, all appearances of a man who had everything he wanted.

But from that, what Core remembered the most was the stiff way his mom held her body and the fake smile on her face.

They'd divorced shortly after.

But to Core's memory, his mother had never had reason to smile genuinely, except for one glorious period of time, and his father had never truly been out of their lives, except for that glorious period of time.

It had fucked him up the first night he met Kiki—which was also the first time they fucked—when he woke up the next day with her in his bed, and he knew.

He just knew, right away.

She was it.

No question.

He'd been happy as hell. She was the shit. They fit. They were perfect.

And it fucked with his head, scared the piss out of him.

But he drove Kiki away.

Now it was happening again.

He knew who Hellen was.

No question.

And he needed to keep her away or she'd find out what he was.

It wasn't a good sign Eight was leaning his ass on the seat of his bike in Core's driveway when Core got home.

He rode up next to him and shut his bike down.

For obvious reasons, Eight was no longer on the Greeks. He was ferreting out Nails if she was in Denver and dicking with Hellen's family. So Core was thinking this wasn't going to be a late-night beer with his bud, but instead, bad news.

"All cool?" he asked, swinging off his bike.

"We gotta talk."

Core studied him, but he shouldn't have bothered. Unless he wanted to, Eight didn't give much away.

He nodded, let them in, then walked Eight through his house after giving Nanook's head a quick rubdown.

He let his dog out the back, stepped out with him, and Eight followed.

Core bought his house two years ago when they opened their first dispensary, money started pouring in, the club had maintained their righteous path for three years, and Core finally felt like he had a solid foundation under his feet.

Since he bought it, though, he hadn't done dick to it, outside buying furniture.

Except the back patio.

He'd laid some attractive pavers, built a wood-burning fireplace and a built-in grill with a sink, a fridge and a high bar for eating. He'd installed some decorative brick around the base of the pillars that held up the roof that covered it and dropped a load on some pimp, comfortable furniture. He took care of his yard and planted some awesome greenery.

The fence needed to be updated, and that was his next project, but he liked being out there. Every inch of it was his hard work and it looked nice.

He should get on with the house, but he had no clue where to start with that.

The bones were there since it had been flipped.

Though he could do a backyard, home décor was not his gig.

Nanook went to his personal bathroom space at the side of the house, Core went to the seating area.

He took a load off and watched his brother do the same across from him.

"Want a beer?" he asked.

"Nah, bro, not gonna stay long. Got pussy waiting for me at home."

That was Eight. He had pussy waiting for him everywhere.

"What's up?" Core prompted.

"Marcy came into one of the dispensaries with a message."

Core sat up straight.

"She talked to Brain," Eight went on. "Brain talked to me."

"Is Hellen okay?" Core asked swiftly.

Eight gave him a look.

Fuck, fuck, *fuck*.

"Listen, brother—" he tried to pedal it back.

"Marcy wants you to know, Hellen's meeting with some dude named Bryan tomorrow at ten. Bryan wants to talk things through."

Core felt the back of his neck start burning.

Eight kept his eyes trained on his brother. After several beats, he asked, "Got nothin' on that?"

"Not my business," Core pushed out.

"Right," Eight said disbelievingly. Then kept at him. "She's got some meet set with her pops Wednesday night."

Fuck, Core needed a beer.

He said nothing.

"Marcy also told Brain a story."

Goddammit.

"This isn't mine to have," he informed his bud. "We're not that."

"When she was a kid, Hellen had a dog."

Core grew very still.

"She loved that dog. It was her best bud. She fed it and it slept with her. Then one day, her pops comes home from one of the many business trips he was always on, and for some reason, he's pissed about something. So the dude just gets home to his family, and in the middle of a lot of screaming and crying and begging, not only Hellen, but her mom and sister too, he takes her dog, leaves and comes back...without the dog."

Core's fingers curled around the arms of his chair.

"Never brought the dog back," Eight went on. "She never saw that dog again. No clue what he did with it. Also never had another pet because she never got over losing her bud. When he was taken away, she was six."

Jesus Christ.

Like he knew what was being discussed, Nanook jogged in, alternately panting and sniffing the ground. He went to Eight to say hello and get a head scratch.

Then he came to his dad.

He sat beside Core's chair, and Core buried his fingers in his boy's thick ruff.

"Apparently, Nanook triggered her," Eight continued. "Marcy said Hellen isn't doin' too good."

Core looked away.

"You're triggered too."

When Eight said that, Core looked back.

"And it's no fuckin' surprise, brother," Eight carried on.

"We're not going here. I'm wiped. You gotta get home. And Hellen is not a thing."

Eight ignored him.

"When we did what we did to Rosie, it tore Beck apart. The reason was easy to fathom. But you, Christ, I watched you that night. You got your licks in. I got mine. I stepped back, took a look at you, and my gut went sour. Almost puked. You were watching the brothers fucking her up, and you looked haunted. It was then I woke the fuck up. It was then I got out of the fog that was my own damage and realized I'd just bought my ticket to hell, and I was never clawing my way back. But there was something else happening for you. It wouldn't be until later, when you gave it to me, I knew what that was."

"Did you hear when I said we're not going here?"

"Yep."

"Then why you pushing this shit?"

"'Cause someone's got to get your head out of your ass, and I've decided that's gonna be me."

"My head has been in my ass a lot of my life, Eight, but with this, I got it straight."

"You are so full of shit."

Fuck it.

Enough.

He pounded his chest. "You think I'd be good for her?"

"You bought your ticket to hell right alongside me, brother. So you got work to do on this earth, and giving a woman good is part of that work."

"And you think I got that in me."

"I was around when Kiki was around," he reminded Core.

"Don't need the reminder."

"Kiki was awesome, and you gave her good, but no one had ever taken away her dog."

Core felt a muscle jump in his cheek.

"Shit happens for a reason," Eight kept at it. "I would never, not ever, repeat my part of what we did to Rosalie. I would never, not ever, stand aside and let anyone else do it either. But it cannot be denied that a bunch of fucked-up motherfuckers saw the light after we pulled that shit on her. Kiki was not meant for you, because your path had to be clear for who was."

"And you've decided that's Hellen."

Eight shook his head. "Man, I shoulda filmed you with her last night. You get serious about business, you go stone-cold. When it's time to take care of shit, you're the coldest motherfucker I've ever met. It's perfect for what we do. So imagine my fuckin' surprise seeing you that hot. You're up in her shit, she does not walk away. She stands her ground, eye to eye, and we drove off. But we idled, bro. I knew you were good, but her bitches needed to see it too. We all saw her walk hand in hand with you to your truck. Now tell me, what else am I gonna fuckin' decide after watchin' that show?"

"You know this is bullshit and you know why it is."

He did know.

This was why Eight leaned forward and did it deep, his face hard, his eyes locked on Core.

"Say it to me," he ordered low.

"Fuck you," Core growled.

"Say it to me," Eight repeated.

"Fuck you," Core clipped.

"Get it out."

"Fuck you, Eight."

"Okay, I'll say it. Your dad was a drunk. He was a wife-beater. He was a user. He was fucked up. And one night, he got so fucked up, he came to his ex-wife's house, beat your mother to death, surfaced from the haze of booze and insanity enough to see what he'd done, and ate a bullet."

Core didn't move a muscle.

"You were sixteen, out with your friends, and you came home to that shit."

"You know, I can't forget this, so I'm not sure why you're reminding me."

"Because you are your own man, Core. You're thirty-six. You're not going to repeat his mistakes."

"Ask Rosie if she feels the same way."

Eight sat back.

"Yeah," Core said, knowing without a doubt he'd scored that point.

"You know, Rosalie was Beck's woman, and he was right there with us. I gotta tell you, I marveled at the fact he did that to his own woman, and he was able to move on. It didn't hit me until later that he never did. He just knew Janna needed someone to love her, to look out for her, to make her feel safe, to be at her side. She was in love with him, he fell in love with her, so he gave her that. I know for a fact, because he's told me, and you were sitting right there, bro, you heard him say it. So we both know that he knows he's not good enough for her. But she thinks he is. And what she thinks, what she wants, *that* is what matters. What does Hellen want?"

"Goddamn fuck you," Core bit.

"What's she want, Hardcore?"

"Fuck you, Eightball."

Eight gave him a good, long look.

Then he stood and said, "Think I made my points. I'll let myself out."

Nanook followed him to the door to the house but stayed outside with Core when Eight closed it.

Core didn't move.

He tried not to think.

He failed spectacularly at this.

Not the dog. Please. Can he stay at home by himself?

When he was taken away, she was six.

What does Hellen want?

Nanook took him out of his thoughts by jumping up to rest on his paws on Core's lap.

He felt the vibe and he was worried about his dad.

"It's okay, boy," Core muttered, giving him another rub down.

Nanook jumped off and Core watched him trace back and forth from Core and the door.

He wanted them inside. He wanted his dad to let the day go.

He wanted him safe.

Core knew that.

So Core got up and gave his pup what he wanted.

10

GRENADES

Hellen

THERE WAS NEVER a time when I wished I was a little less me.

Walking into Fortnum's, seeing Bryan at a table with two drinks, one of them for me, I wished I was a little less me.

This was because his eyes moved over my body with appreciation and eagerness.

In order to help communicate what was going to happen during our chat, I tried to dress down, I really did.

But I'd ended up in red shorts, a red-and-white print blouse and a pair of open-toed, zebra-print, wedge sandals with ribbons that tied around my ankles.

I should have worn some joggers, but I never wore joggers outside the house unless I was taking a walk on a chilly day.

And I didn't do it then, not only because it was late August in Denver, and it wasn't a chilly day.

Because I couldn't be anything else but me.

I approached Bryan.

He got up and moved in.

I tilted my head so he only got his lips on my cheek.

He schooled his face not to appear disappointed when I pulled away.

"Hey," he greeted. "You look great."

"Hey," I replied.

I didn't tell him he looked great, but he did. Dark hair styled with product. Khakis rolled and cuffed at the ankle. Button down that was such a light pink, it was almost white, but on his feet were pure white, leather sneakers.

He hadn't shaved that day, like he did every day when he went to office or into court, and I knew he didn't because he knew I liked scruff.

And he smelled good. Expensive. Not an outlay he'd make on himself, it was the cologne his mom bought him every birthday and for Christmas.

We sat.

He pushed my drink my way. "Got you covered."

"Thanks," I murmured, picking it up and sipping from it.

Minor score for him, he'd ordered me my favorite: a vanilla mocha skinny.

"Doing okay?" he asked.

No.

I was not.

I had this thing with him right now, for one.

I had a thing with my dad on Wednesday, for another.

Core had a beautiful dog.

Core lost his ever-loving mind at the very thought I might be in danger.

Being pressed to Core's long, hard body was heaven, even if he wasn't kissing me.

And Core knew how to take ownership of a woman's hair.

Last, Core did not want me.

I was just one of the women he and his buds helped.

I was just another thing they did.

Granted, this last seemed at odds with him losing his shit about what Marcy, Bree and I did, and even more at odds with him containing me by pressing me to his body.

But the man was so protective of women, he looked in actual pain at the thought of allowing me to get into a freaking Uber, for goodness' sakes.

I didn't know what his deal was.

I just knew I'd never find out.

"Things have been better," I answered Bryan.

At these words, he looked both concerned and hopeful.

The hope was hard to see.

I wasn't going to lay my woes on him. I wasn't going to lean on him. He wasn't going to get the chance to make me feel better.

But he didn't know that yet.

Okay, time to get this done.

I scootched closer to the table in my chair and sat up straighter in preparation to give it to him.

"I don't like not being around for you to talk to," Bryan announced before I could say anything.

I pressed my lips together.

"These last few days, knowing you were going through stuff, it fucked with my head."

"Bryan—"

"I want you to marry me."

I lurched with surprise in my chair.

"I get it," he said. "I've been a fucking idiot. But I get it now."

"You get what?" I asked hesitantly.

"We were together for a while. We didn't discuss moving forward. Me moving in. Our future."

I opened my mouth.

"You were going to worry," he stated. "Of course you were. I told you I loved you, but I wasn't clear about where we were heading."

Where we were heading.

Like he got to steer that course on his own.

I sat back, shifted my coffee cup this way and that. It was difficult. I'd spent time with this man. I liked him. I knew he loved me, and I wasn't so over him that it didn't hurt knowing that and knowing what was about to come for him.

Even so, I let him dig his own grave.

Or...dig it deeper.

Because seriously, even now, he was demonstrating he just... didn't...*listen to me*.

"So let me be clear," he stated in his important, listen-to-this summation voice. "I took a look at my finances. There's not much I can cut back on, unless we move in together, in order that I can save faster to buy you the ring I want you to have."

I want you to have.

"Though, I do think we should move in together," he continued. "It's time. It's time for us to make that commitment. It'll be a crunch, both of us in your place, but your rent is cheaper than mine, it'll help me get closer to buying your ring, and we won't be there forever. Just a few years. And I promise, Hellen, I'll be a better partner."

He stretched his arm across the table, pulled my cup from my fingers and held my hand.

"Also, baby, I promise it's leading to something." He gave me his big, white smile. "You'll get what you want. I'll pop the question when I can do it right. Then you'll get that future you want. We. *We'll* get the future we want. You just have to stick with me. Three, four more years, I'll be out from under the brunt of the debt, and we can move on."

When it seemed he was finished talking, I said, "You want."

"Sorry?"

"*You* want," I reiterated. "You're talking about the future *you* want. I've shared with you the future I want. I've shared with you about my business and where I want it to go. I don't have very many plans after that because it's my main focus in the now. So, if you listened, you'd know what I want for my immediate future. But I've never mentioned any of the things you're talking about. So I honestly don't wish to sound awful, but I have to point out, you're talking about the future *you* want."

Gently, I pulled my hand from his.

Bryan frowned.

"And since we're here, you need to know, I don't want to get married, Bryan."

His expression cleared and he nodded swiftly. "Okay, agreed. It's time we talk about the recycling."

And...

Damn.

He'd led with the marriage thing because that was what he thought I was angling for. That was what he'd convinced himself I was doing. He thought I was pitching a fit because he wasn't committing.

Honestly?

I didn't blame him.

For centuries, men and women had been conditioned to think that was what was in the cards for both of them. It was what they were supposed to strive for. The white dress and the cake were supposed to be the woman's overarching dream.

Then, he was supposed to strive and build and venture and earn and rise.

But she didn't get to dream beyond that day of flowers and dancing.

Her role was to take care of everything, including the children they made together, so he could build and earn and rise.

Sure, she could have her job or her career. But she still needed to take care of everything so he could build and earn and rise. In most cases, he got paid more. To him, that made sense. To some, it made sense to her as well.

If something came around, say a once-in-a-century pandemic, and shit got real and kids needed to be taken care of because they couldn't go to school, her job or career was lost.

So he could continue to rise.

This was because she wasn't conditioned to dream that what came next was her choice. That what came next for her was a priority. That she could compete. That she could expect to get paid as much as him, or more if it was merited.

She wasn't conditioned to dream of rising.

She wasn't conditioned to dream of *anything*.

Anything except that white dress.

And now that I had Bryan over a barrel in his mind, and apparently (according to him), we were negotiating the entirety of our future, he was willing to talk about the little things that meant something to me.

Like recycling.

Not my career.

Not the future I truly wanted.

"I care about you," I said.

He smiled again.

"But this is not a play for a proposal. This is not about the recycling. This is...it's..."

I got opposable thumbs. When I'm ready for a beer, I can get my own.

"It's?" Bryan prompted.

I shook thoughts of Core off.

"It's..."

You're gonna tell me what a dick I am, I'm gonna admit I was a dick, because I was serious pissed, but I recognize I went over the top.

"Hellen?"

I'm gonna admit I was a dick, because I was serious pissed, but I recognize I went over the top.

I'm gonna admit I was a dick.

I looked down to my lap.

"Hey, hey," Bryan called. "Baby, look at me."

I lifted my gaze to Bryan.

"I'm so sorry," I whispered. "I'm not in love with you."

He sat back like he'd been shot.

"I'm so sorry," I repeated.

"You were with me for a year," he said, voice small, wounded.

"I cared about you a lot. I thought I—"

He cut me off before I could finish. "You thought what?"

I watched him closely because I wasn't real thrilled with the sudden shift of his mood.

"You thought what, Hellen?" he pushed.

When I didn't immediately reply, he did it for me.

"You thought you'd hooked yourself to an attorney, good money, good times, but he drives a shit car because he's responsible and he doesn't want a life burdened with debt, and that wasn't what you'd signed on for?"

Okay.

No.

I mean, how fucking important to my life did he convince himself he was?

Did he pay attention to me *at all*?

Good God, how many men thought this way? How many men thought it was all about them, and the only purpose a woman had in her life was to land the man who would provide for her the way she wanted?

How many men were so convinced of their own self-importance, they couldn't see what was sitting right in front of them.

I stood.

"We're done."

He stood too.

"Fuck that, Hellen. You and all your bitches are about the life. I'm totally not surprised Bree got scammed by that asshole. He was so suave, it was creepy. But she thought he was her path to a lifetime of Tiffany and Chanel, so she was blind to everything else."

Maybe there was a hint of truth in that when it came to Bree.

But only a hint.

And "all my bitches" worked hard for what we had, and we didn't ask anyone to give it to us.

Like I had never asked Bryan for one thing.

Not one fucking thing.

"I think if that's how you feel, we should leave this where it is, and both get on with our lives," I suggested.

"You don't think you owe me an explanation for why you wasted a year of my life?"

"I don't owe you anything, Bryan," I stated coldly. "I didn't ask for anything. I didn't expect anything, except for you to be a decent person and treat me with respect. I ended it with you because you didn't offer the latter. I'm finalizing it now because you're proving you're not the former either."

"Don't pretend that wasn't your game," he scoffed.

I secured my bag over my shoulder. "If you need to tell yourself that."

I started to move away.

I didn't finish because Bryan took hold on my arm.

Firm hold.

His fingers pressed in, and it hurt.

I looked at him, right in the eyes, because with my wedges, he was only an inch taller than me.

Core would be three.

"Take your hand off me."

His face twisted, he opened his mouth...

And then...

"Yo."

It came quietly.

We both turned our heads to see the big man who was the barista at Fortnum's standing close, his eyes glued to Bryan. He had a lot of hair and a very bushy, long beard.

He was always low-key scary because he never seemed in a good mood, and a lot of the time, he was really loud.

But he made insanely delicious coffee.

Right now, though, there was nothing low-key about his scary.

And part of that was him being quiet.

"You can take your hand off her, or I can throw you through the window. Your choice. One second," he threatened.

The threat was real, we both knew it, Bryan especially, because he didn't take that second.

Though I knew that wasn't the only reason he did it.

No way in hell would Bryan make a scene. He cared too much about what people thought of him, even strangers.

He let me go.

"Good," the barista said. "Now get the fuck out of here, and I better never see you again, and by that I mean in here or *anywhere*."

Bryan scowled at him, scowled at me.

He then moved to grab his coffee, but the barista grunted, "*Hup*."

Bryan left the coffees on the table and stalked out.

The bell rang like a signal that was all over.

After that scene, sadly, I felt no relief.

"Like I'd let him take my coffee with him," the barista muttered, openly offended.

I turned to the big man.

"Thanks."

"You good?" he asked.

"I'm kind of bummed I had a yearlong relationship with that guy, but other than that, I'm okay."

"Right. Just sayin', next time you and your girls go on a righteous crusade, you call me."

I blinked.

He grabbed my cup, slid a black Sharpie from behind his ear, took the cap off with his teeth and scrawled a phone number on it.

He put the cup down, recapped the marker, shoved it back into the mass of hair beside his head and refocused on me.

Then he said, "I got grenades."

And with that, he returned to the espresso counter.

The redhead, who I was pretty sure was the owner, sidled closer.

"Um," she started. "Tex kinda has an ear to all the goings-on in Denver."

"You don't say," I replied.

She grinned.

Then she said, "He's serious about calling him, and, well, the grenades."

I blinked at her too.

How did these people know these things?

She winked at me.

Then she, too, walked away.

11

SOMEONE ELSE'S FUCKED-UP LIFE

Hellen

"I'M NEVER TAKING Mom's advice, not ever again."

Liane was fidgeting.

"Don't be nervous," I advised. "If he acts like an ass, we agreed, we'll just walk away."

"I just...this was a mistake."

I stopped twisting the stem of my wineglass on the table and scanning the swanky restaurant Dad and Li agreed for us to meet in (this was totally a Dad pick, she just decided not to fight a battle that wasn't worth her energy) and looked to my sister.

She was a wreck.

I was shocked.

"Li," I said softly.

"I never, you know, thanked you," she blurted.

I was confused.

"For what?" I asked.

"We left him. Then Mom had to work full-time. And you grew up,"—she lifted her hand and snapped—"like that."

I rolled my eyes and teased, "I was always grown up. I was born fifty."

"You were not," she said quietly.

At her continued tone, I got serious.

She kept speaking.

"You played with Barbies. Okay, so you were the boss of them, and they all had high-powered jobs, I think one was the President, and one was the CEO of Microsoft, but you played. You ate big bowls of cereal and watched cartoons in your jammies with me. You'd wrestle with Tigger."

I looked away when she mentioned our dog.

"You were a kid, Hellen. And then you had to be something else, for Mom, for me, so you became that, and you never got to go back."

I returned my gaze to her. "It was who I was meant to be anyway. So maybe I got there earlier. It was where I was going, so it's no big deal."

"Still, thank you."

"We're family."

"Just shut up and let me be grateful."

I gave her an irritated side eye.

She grinned at me.

"Girls."

We both looked up at Dad.

But only I sucked in a quiet breath.

Because...fucking hell.

How hadn't I seen it before?

Product in his hair. Carefully-crafted stubble. Pink button down under a blazer. Dark wash jeans.

Bryan was my father.

"Whoa," Li said under her breath.

She saw it too.

She slid out of the booth, I came out with her, and we'll just say the hugs were tortuously awkward.

We slid back in, Dad opposite us.

He looked down at his menu. "You two pick what you want to eat?"

Ummmmmmmmm...

I glanced at Li.

She was glancing at me.

We were both surprised at this opener.

She turned to him first. "Yeah, Dad."

"Place has a magnificent surf and turf," he muttered, surveying the room. He found what he was looking for and jerked up his chin in demand of attention.

Right, did Liane and I spend two years out of his company because we were fed up with his shit?

Or had I been in a fugue when we all enjoyed a movie together last weekend so us meeting up for dinner was no big whoop?

The server came.

Dad asked for a Jack and Coke.

After that, he demanded to know where the bread basket was and why it wasn't yet at the table, explaining to her his history with this restaurant and how that had *never* happened before. This was delivered in the manner he was a neurosurgeon, and she was his surgical nurse, and her incompetence had cost his patient their life.

He finished berating our server by ordering oysters on the half shell as an appetizer.

Man, I forgot how mortifying it was to be around him when he had someone he thought was lower than him to treat like shit.

Now, I was remembering.

"You girls want anything to start?" he queried magnanimously, still going for the "nothing to see here, just a dad with his daughters" look.

So, was he nervous?

Or was he crazy?

"I'm good," I said.

"Those mozzarella things," Li ordered.

The server smiled tightly, promised the bread basket would be there soon and walked away.

Dad looked at us.

And then his lips turned down.

"Really, Liane, this is a nice place."

My back shot straight.

"You couldn't put on some mascara?" he inquired.

Liane made a noise.

Now, I hadn't forgotten that.

No, I had not.

Dad needing to be in control of every nuance about us. What we wore. Our grades being better (I was all As, Liane was an athlete and never slipped off the honor roll either, so what he expected was unknown, and when you're a kid and a teen, doing very well, and someone expects more, it was immensely and harmfully baffling). Harking back to Li's sports, lecturing her about her performance in a game he might catch if she was unlucky, and he'd never played lacrosse in his life. Lecturing to me about practicing my flute (I used to love playing, he made me hate it, and as such, I hadn't picked up my flute in two years), and he'd never played any instrument.

Us being painstakingly appropriate for every occasion because we were a reflection on him.

That last being what he expected right now.

"Seriously?" I asked.

Dad's attention cut to me, he took in my expression, lifted both hands and pressed down.

"You're right. You're right." His eyes moved between us. "I have two beautiful girls. Makeup or not. That wasn't the way to start."

"No, it wasn't," I confirmed.

Dad shot me a look I also remembered very well.

I was annoying him.

He buried that and declared, "It means a lot you agreed to tonight. I've missed you. Your grandmother really misses you. Your grandfather is in a bad place, and we all want to mend the rift in this family."

I took a sip of my wine, put the glass back to the table, began twisting it back and forth again, then asked, "What did you miss about us, Dad?"

His lips thinned before he pointed out, "Being like that won't help, Hellen."

"I'm sorry, but I feel the question is valid."

"You're my daughters," he returned. "I haven't seen you in years. I wasn't invited to your graduations—"

"Because you told me, and I quote, 'A woman of your intellect should be an attorney, you need to study pre-law. I'm not going to throw money away on you studying something nebulous, like business.' And then you threw not one cent away on me studying business."

So, maybe that wasn't a direct quote. But it was the gist.

His gaze moved over me, and he forced out, "I see I was wrong about that. You look like you're doing well. I hope you are. Though your mother says you're seeing a lawyer?"

Not, *I've missed out, tell me, what do you do for a living?*

Not, *Do you enjoy what you do? And by the way, what is it that you do?*

But, *You're seeing a lawyer?*

"He didn't pay for my blouse, or my earrings, or my haircut, or my Tom Ford foundation. I did. And we broke up."

The busboy came with the bread right before the server showed with Dad's drink.

They left and Dad looked at me. "Your attitude is not enhancing our dinner."

Liane squeezed my thigh under the table.

I shut up.

"Tell us about Granddad," Liane urged.

Dad was returning his glass to the table after drinking from it.

"He's not in good shape."

"Is he ill?" I asked.

"He's old. He didn't take care of himself. He's reaping those rewards."

Well then.

That was the very definition of encapsulation.

"Uh, Mom said that things were pretty bad," Li noted.

"He's got diabetes. He didn't manage that, so his feet are messed up. He has to go for dialysis. He's got arthritis, so he's constantly in pain. He's recently stopped eating most everything, so he's very thin. I think he's just done. If I were him, I would be too."

"Do you want us to go see him?" Li asked.

Dad leveled his gaze on her. "Since you're his granddaughters, and you cut him out like you did me, before he dies, that would be nice."

Even though that was a dickish response, I decided to make an effort.

I mean, he'd never showed he cared a lot for his father, but it *was* his father, and it sounded like Granddad wasn't long for this world.

"Maybe we three should take this time to try to understand where we've been, and where we wish to be as a family," I suggested.

"It would have been nice if you started with that," Dad admonished.

Okay, I was done with my effort.

"It would have been nice if you started with telling us you missed us, we looked beautiful, healthy, and you were so glad to see that. Then you could have moved on to sharing you were delighted and so very relieved we agreed to sit down to break bread with you. After that, you could have asked us to catch you up with our lives. Who are we now? What do we do? Are we happy? Then you could have shared about your own. Instead, you asked if we knew what we were going to eat, made sure you'd ordered your drink and appetizer, informed our server she'd made the unforgiveable mistake of failing with the bread basket delivery, and made Li think she was something less because she didn't put on mascara. In other words, par for the course of my twenty-three years with you."

I'd hit a nerve with all of that, I was oh-so-unsurprised to see.

"You would think you'd sit across from me in a very nice restaurant, drinking a glass of wine I will eventually be paying for, eating an excellent meal I'll also be paying for, and showing your father some goddamned respect for once," he retorted.

But it felt like a dozen arrows shot through me.

Because...because...

Because I'd just realized he was the reason I was like I was with money.

The part about wanting a lot of it, but also the part about being mildly obsessed with it.

Dad was a workaholic.

And so was I (maybe?).

"It isn't about who's buying the meal, Dad," Li said tersely. "Not everything comes down to money."

"It's always about that. How many times did your mother threaten not to let you come for visitations because she wanted money?" he demanded.

Not this again.

And yes, it was again. He *always* brought this up.

"Because you were making a hundred and sixty thousand a year, and she was making thirty-five, and *you didn't pay child support*," I returned. "She didn't want money. She was demanding you pay what the court ordered. Oh, and then there were all of our games and concerts you didn't show up for, she would get ticked about that. Oh, and of course all the visitations *you* couldn't make because you were away on business. And I remember a lot of those, Dad. You were gone more often than you were home, we never saw you. Before the divorce and after. But oh boy, when you were ready to spend time with us, the world needed to stop spinning until you got what you wanted."

He drew his glass to his mouth, murmuring loudly, "She sure handled her money problem, finding that painter to take you all on."

To take us all on?

In all of that, the only thing he could focus on was Mom handling her "money problem" by marrying Andy?

I turned to Li.

"Out," I ordered.

She was already exiting the booth.

"What—?" he began.

"My turn," Liane said. Then to Dad. "Fuck you, Dad."

His face started getting red.

The server was approaching with his oysters and Li's mozzarella things, but she peeled off the other way.

"We'll discuss, and if we decide it will be best, we'll contact Grandma about maybe going to visit Granddad," I told him. "But don't hold your breath. Throughout our lives, they showed us as much love and care as you did. So outside of proving Mom and *Andy* raised us right, I'm not sure they earned us showing that in return."

His eyes were darting around the restaurant, even though no one gave one shit about us, and none of us knew any of these people nor would we ever see them again. And even if we did, who the fuck cared?

But he was worried about what people were thinking.

So.

Very.

Dad.

And so very Bryan.

Last, and most importantly, his daughters were about to walk away from him again, and that was what was on his mind.

"Sit down," he hissed.

Right.

This was my father.

And because it was, before it was done, he got one more thing.

"Heads up, Eleanor might be coming to town to start some problems."

He blinked rapidly, both confusion at what I said in the context of where we were and also probably despair, because Eleanor was a pain in the ass.

Time to conclude.

"It isn't that hard," I shared. "All we needed was love from you. Not money. We needed time. Attention. Love. That was all we needed. And I know it isn't that hard because Andy gave it to us, and watching him do it, it seemed like the easiest thing in the world."

His face drained of color.

Maybe it was my words, maybe it was the finality of my tone.

I didn't pause to decipher which.

I took Liane's hand and dragged her out of there.

We both got in my Mini and sat there, silent.

Then Liane screamed at my windshield, "*He's a fucking fucker!*"

"Honey," I whispered.

She jerked my way. "God! I hate him!"

"We tried. Okay? It's good we tried. Yes?"

"Stop being Mom," she grumbled.

I painted on a smile.

"And stop fake smiling. It's freaking me out. You look like a Stepford. That was lunacy." She faced forward and mumbled, "Fucking fucker."

"Mom's going to be worried, Andy too. Let's get you home."

She said nothing.

I started up the car.

We were on the road when my sister's voice cracked as she repeated, "Fucking fucker."

I found her hand.

She held tight.

Oh yes.

She was right.

Fucking fucker.

I DROVE TO MY APARTMENT.

Summing up the evening:

Mom was distressed she'd advised us to do something that upset us so much.

Andy was so livid, he eventually went to the garage, and all we heard was him banging on something (Mom said he was making bird feeders to mount around her she shed, and this made sense, since she was a birdwatcher).

Liane bitched and moaned and vowed never to do that with Dad again.

I stayed calm, sipped the wine Andy poured for us before he went off to hammer things, and made absolutely certain my sister had talked it out, my mother knew we were okay, then I headed home.

I parked in the drive I shared with the unit above me.

And I was walking to my apartment when movement caught my eye.

I looked that way and there was Core, wearing a white tee with a black skull design on the front, faded jeans and his black biker boots. He was sauntering my way, his truck parked on the curb behind him, his eyes on me.

His dog was trotting at his side.

Swear to God, he could be a commercial for just about anything —trucks, faded jeans, dog food, crack—and I'd buy it.

When Nanook saw me, he dashed to me.

I was having trouble breathing, but I bent, thankfully my hair falling forward to hide my face while my mind scrambled to find a reason Core was there, and I scratched Nanook behind his ears.

I continued to do this even as I felt Core stop beside us.

I saw his boots right there, close to me.

He let me avoid the fact he was there for a while.

Then he asked, "How'd it go?"

Somehow, he knew tonight was dinner with Dad.

And there he was.

That was when, for the first time in my entire life, I completely came apart.

I wasn't so far gone I didn't feel his arms around me or him taking my purse or Nanook snuffling and pressing at me.

He got my keys out of my bag and let us in.

He took me to the couch and sat me on it.

Nanook jumped up and shoved his nose in my face and neck while I sat there sobbing.

"Boy, get off the couch," Core said quietly.

Nanook moved to do as told but I twisted violently, wrapped my arms around him, and cried, "*No!*"

Core said no more. I cried into thick fur, then I heard fingers snapping, lost the fur, but got strong arms around me and a T-shirt covered chest.

Core shoved a wad of tissues in my hand.

I cried, then I cried some more, I did some hitched breathing that made Core's arms tighten, then I cried some more.

Through this, I wiped my eyes and blew my nose and threw the used tissues on the floor, only for Core to shove clean ones in my hand the minute it was empty.

I petered out and was essentially sniffling and keeping my face tucked to his chest because I knew my makeup was a disaster.

"So, it didn't go too good," Core drawled.

I let out a loud snicker, shook my head and thought, *fuck it.*

I pushed away from his chest, swiping my eyes one last time with a tissue, and I looked at him.

"We're officially done with our father."

His blue eyes were moving over my face, but his lips only hummed, "Mm."

"Am I a mess?" I asked.

His gaze rested on mine. "Totally."

"Awesome," I mumbled, looking away.

He caught my jaw in his hand and made me look back.

I started having trouble breathing again.

"Been waiting for you to get home," he murmured, those blue eyes dropping to my mouth.

Okay.

Okayokayokay.

What was happening with him *now*?

"Sat outside in my truck for the last two hours."

Two hours?

Oh my God.

"Core."

His thumb slipped along my lower lip.

I stopped breathing altogether.

His eyes lifted to mine.

"I'm not sure I can deal with your mixed signals tonight," I admitted.

"Am I sending mixed signals?"

"One hundred percent yes."

His thumb slipped back over my lip. "Right now, am I sending mixed signals, baby?"

I quit breathing again.

Because the answer to that was...no, he was not.

"I'm not good for you, and I know it," he informed me, (uh... what?). "We're gonna talk about that because you gotta make a decision having all the information. That's not happening now. Not when you're vulnerable. But I knew tonight would be bad, and I tried to keep my distance, but I couldn't. I had to be here for you. So for now, let this just be what it is. Okay?"

I nodded. "Okay."

Another thumb swipe and then he dropped his forehead to mine.

He closed his eyes.

There was something poignant about that, deep and meaningful.

To fully feel it, I closed my eyes too.

Yes.

I still didn't know what it was, but whatever, it was beautifully deep and truly meaningful.

And having that feeling, having him right there, I could wait for him to share the meaning with me.

He shifted, running his nose along my jaw, then he slid his fingers in my hair and tucked my head back to his chest, his other arm still around me.

"What does it for you?" he asked. "Ice cream? Tequila? Soppy movies?"

He didn't offer making out or sex, which was disappointing, or alternatively an indication of how much of a mess my makeup was.

"Soppy movies?" I ribbed.

"Is that your choice?"

"God no."

He chuckled and held me.

"He hadn't seen us in two years, and one of the first things he did was give Li shit about not wearing mascara," I whispered.

Core sat back and curled me deeper into him, stretching his legs out in front of him and crossing them at the ankles.

At first, this just felt nice.

And then I realized he was settling us in so he could listen to me.

I nearly started crying again.

I didn't.

I told him about my dad, about that night, and more.

Not all of it, but more.

When I was done, he pulled us both off the couch, bringing us to our feet, and a sheer wave of panic struck me because I thought he was leaving.

"Get comfy," he ordered. "I'll raid the kitchen."

I relaxed.

He strolled into the kitchen.

I watched.

Nanook watched.

Nanook then looked to me.

He appeared undecided.

"Go on," I urged.

It was his dad, and it was a kitchen, so Nanook loped after Core.

I went to my room and put on a pair of drawstring pajama shorts, a bralette and a cami. I avoided looking at my face, but definitely washed it. I put on some moisturizer.

I came out to Core stream-surfing the TV, the used Kleenexes having disappeared and everything in my snack cabinet on my coffee table along with two opened beers.

It was at that juncture I was reminded I hadn't had dinner.

I thought of this rather than thinking about Core cleaning up my snotty Kleenexes, not only because that was gross, but because I'd had a rough night. I didn't have it in me to process him being a man who would tidy up used Kleenexes.

"Documentary about someone else's fucked-up life?" he asked.

"Absolutely," I answered, plopping down beside him.

At that point, I was getting friend vibes, so I was also feeling weird, a little annoyed, and a little worried I'd read it wrong yet again.

But how could Core talking about not being good for me (and what was that about?) and me making an informed decision be getting it wrong?

Friends could be not good for you, sure.

But they sure didn't swipe your lip with their thumb or run their nose along your jaw. At least not any of the friends I'd had.

So him sitting there and me sitting there when ten minutes before we were cuddling, yeah.

It felt weird.

That was, it did until Core tagged my neck, pulled me to the side, shifting his long body while he did it.

We both ended lying on the couch, me tucked in front of him.

He pressed into me as he reached for a bag of honey-barbecue Fritos.

I reached for a beer, took a sip, then grabbed the Lesser Evil popcorn.

Core hit go on the remote to start a four-part doc on the whole sorry, creepy Warren Jeffs situation.

I sipped, munched, relaxed and enjoyed the fact that if I dropped some corn to the floor, I didn't have to worry about having to clean it up later. Nanook did it for me.

Eventually, Core was finished with the Fritos, and he draped his arm along my waist.

I'd carried a lot of weight in my life, but that felt nothing but good.

Not too long after that, I fought it, because I didn't want to lose all I had right then.

But it had been a tough few days.

So I lost the fight.

And, pressed back to Core's front, his arm around me, I fell asleep on my couch in the curve of his arm, never having felt so comfortable.

Or so safe.

12

PURPLE PEN

Hellen

I WOKE up in my bed alone.

I hadn't slept in it alone.

Somewhere along the line of Jeffs's pedophilic misdeeds, Core'd had enough. He'd roused me by turning off the TV. He'd woken me by picking me up.

I was too tired to marvel at this feat.

"I can walk," I mumbled.

I could, but after he put me on my feet, with the way I was listing, he spotted me all the way to bed.

I collapsed in it, and fortunately before I had to try to find the energy to say, "Don't go," he slid in with me.

He pulled me close. I fell back asleep.

In the middle of the night, he let go of me and turned.

I fitted myself to his back, my arm around him.

His fingers found mine and tucked them tighter to his body.

After that, I fell asleep again.

And now was now.

I got up on a hand in bed, looking around.

"Core?" I called tentatively.

Nothing.

No Nanook bopping in to say good morning.

I turned to my nightstand to see what time it was, and along with noting my alarm clock said it was five forty-three, I saw a piece of paper that had been torn from my grocery pad in the kitchen.

It was printed with pink lines and there were pink curlicues in the corners.

There were words on it in a bold scrawl in purple ink (which was the pen I had in the kitchen, and the only color pen I had in the house, save for pink, that said, the grocery pad was not something I'd purchase, too girlie, Mom put it in my Christmas stocking last year, along with the pink pens—I could do purple, but I wasn't a pink kind of woman).

It said:

Babe,

Oh my God.

Pure melt.

Yes, he'd called me babe before but something about it on a nightstand note made it *awesome.*

Had to go deal with the Greeks. We need to brief about that.

Call me.

X

So he was gone.

He was also a man who left a note.

And more melt, he was a man who signed it with a kiss.

Needless to say, I got out of bed, started my morning gig, went to the kitchen to make coffee, went in search of my bag (I found it in the butterfly chair where Core obviously put it) and pulled out my phone.

It seriously needed a charge.

But I saw I had three texts from Marcy, and one each from Kyra and Bree.

They were wondering about the dinner with Dad.

I made coffee, grabbed one of my charge cords, took it to my bedroom and plugged it in by my vanity.

I then hopped in the shower.

I had my hair done and was putting on makeup when *The Mandalorian* theme sounded.

I looked down to my phone and the screen said the call was from Core.

A flutter moved through my belly.

But...

Whoa.

Heretofore I had not been a flutter girl.

But that was definitely a flutter.

I took the call and put Core on speaker so I could continue dealing with my eye shadow.

"Hey," I greeted.

"You're awake," he pointed out the obvious.

"I am indeed," I confirmed.

"So why didn't you call me?"

"Uhhhhh..." I didn't quite reply.

So his *Call me* meant immediately upon waking?

I wasn't sure how I felt about that.

"You were a mess last night, babe," he went on. "You doing okay?"

Oh.

Well then.

His *Call me* meant he was worried about me and wanted to know that I woke up and was fighting fit to face the day.

Shit, there went another flutter.

"I have puffy eyes, but other than that, I'm good," I shared.

"Good," he grunted.

"You used my purple pen," I told him something he knew, and did it with a smile that could be heard in my voice, because Core and a color purple didn't go together.

Add the piece of paper with curlicues in the corner, it was borderline hilarious.

"I searched for ten minutes for something else, and I couldn't find anything but pink. And my hand might turn into a gnarled claw if I wrote in a pink pen so I had to do the job in purple."

I started laughing.

"And she laughs," he said softly, and I could hear the relief.

My laughter faded.

Yes.

Last night had been emotional and he'd been worried about me.

You never wanted anyone to worry about you, still, it felt nice.

"I'm a lot better this morning, Core. Thanks for taking care of me last night."

"That's why I showed," he replied, then put that behind us by asking, "You free tonight? Wanna take you to dinner."

Okay.

All right.

Okay.

Was he asking me out on a date?

"Dinner like, just you know...dinner? Or dinner like...*dinner*?" I went about ascertaining.

His voice was lower when he answered, "Definitely *dinner*."

That caused a wave of flutters.

So weird, but even so, they felt great.

"I'm totally free."

"Awesome. I got no idea where the day is gonna take me, but I'll keep in touch. I'll try to be done around six. Work for you?"

"Works for me. Is everything good with the Greeks?"

"I'll fill you in over dinner, but yeah. It is. We should close that out soon."

I was surprised because that seemed fast to me.

I didn't get into that since we'd be getting into it at dinner.

On our first date.

Instead, I said, "Fantastic."

"Gotta go, baby. Have a good day."

"You too."

"Later."

"'Bye."

My screen went blank and it took everything I had not to pull it from its charge cord, hug it to my chest and dance around my bedroom with it like Belle with a book.

Suffice it to say, I was into Dustin "Core" Whatever His Last Name Was.

And I was beside myself we had a date.

After I finished getting ready, I spent some time typing out a long message to a group text with the girls, sharing about Dad, but also about Core, before I got in my Mini and went to the office.

The date was obviously the priority thing on my mind all the way to work, which of course took me to the fact that I had no idea what to wear out to dinner with a biker.

Fortunately, my stepsister could help me.

When I got to the office and started everything up, I had ten texts in reply to mine.

I decided to deal with those before I texted Archie.

Ohmigod! Core showed? Marcy

I cannot believe your dad played dinner that way. Kyra

Yeah. Your dad is awful. But Core! Yippee! Bree

I knew he was into you! Marcy

We need details. Also Marcy

Soon. Bree

Friday cocktails at Marcy's and mine. Kyra

Perfect. Marcy

I'm in. Bree

Yay! Kyra

I'm in too, I replied.

I was about to go to my text string with Archie so I could ask about biker dating protocol, when my phone rang in my hand.

I sat still and stared at it because it said the call was from Bryan.

"What on earth?" I muttered, continuing to stare at it, not about to pick it up.

I went to my group text string.

Bryan is calling right now, I texted.

What!?!?! Kyra

WHY?!?!?! Marcy

I don't know. I'm not picking up. Me

Good! He can kiss your ass! Marcy

Oh my God! What's he up to now? Bree entered the conversation.

The ringing had stopped and it wasn't long before it said he left a voicemail.

Shit, he's left a voicemail, I told them.

Listen to it! Bree

Report back! Marcy

I went to voicemail and played it.

"Hellen. It's Bryan. I.... Okay, just, I'm sorry. That wasn't me. The way I behaved...what I did at Fortnum's. My feelings were hurt, what you said was unexpected, and I don't know what came over me. I haven't been sleeping. It's all I think about. Christ, Hell. I'm so sorry. I really am so sorry. I get we're done, but I hate that's the last thing I gave you to remember about me. You'll always be my first love, and I'll always be that clingy, selfish dick who put his hand on you in anger. I can't handle that. You don't have to respond to this. I just want you to know I'm sorry."

That was it.

I was stunned.

He sounded ragged. Undone.

God, poor Bryan.

He apologized. He's not sleeping. He hates what he did. He told me I don't have to call back, he just wants me to know he's sorry. I told the girls.

Three texts came in quick succession.

Well...that's sweet????? Kyra

Good for him. Bree

Fuck him. No excuse. Marcy

I could have called all of those.

Are you going to call him? Bree

I don't know. Me

Concentrate on Core. Don't think about this now. Marcy

What Marce said. Kyra

I'm going to do that. I replied. Then I sent, *And I'll think about accepting his apology.*

That's the right thing to do. Bree

Marcy nor Kyra agreed in text, but I knew this was because they disagreed. They'd been pretty pissed when I told them what happened with Bryan. Bree had too, just not as much as Marcy and Kyra.

I sensed Bree thought I shouldered some of the blame for the breakup in that I was being too hard on Bryan. She might seem excited Core had asked me to dinner, but she'd always liked Bryan quite a bit.

And it had to be said—though, nothing wrong with it, not only was it programmed into her, but I could see the allure—Bree was one of those women who dreamed of the white dress.

I had a feeling she saw me in that white dress with Bryan.

My email was up, and when I glanced at it, I noted I had one from the staffing agency.

I opened it. It was details about prospects for my PA job.

I was keen to see what they had for me, so I moved on from the girls and Bryan, into reading applications and resumes.

And as usual, I got so engrossed in work, I totally forgot I was going to text Archie.

13

BACONATOR

Hellen

I WAS DEEPLY INVOLVED in editing some content that would go up on TikTok for Alaia, a curvy content creator who did the trifecta: clothes, makeup and hair, and had over five million followers, when the recorder notes sounded on my phone.

I looked down at it and saw I had a text from Core.

I picked it up, opened it and read, *Finished. Swinging by my place to shower and let Nanook out. Should be at yours in an hour. Cool?*

I glanced at the time on my computer.

It was five twenty-three.

Shit!

I still didn't know what to wear and I lived twenty minutes from my office (traffic willing), so if I finished what I was doing, closed down and took off, I'd only have twenty or thirty minutes left to get ready for our date.

I did not want to push it back, not even a minute.

I had the feeling bikers weren't all that picky about appropriate date apparel and further, Core wouldn't take me on a chartered flight to eat dinner at the Ritz in Paris, so I didn't need to suddenly produce an LBD worthy of the Ritz.

Fortunately, Denver was an anything-goes fashion city, but like the jean shirt was called a Canadian tuxedo, jeans could just be considered tuxedo in the Mile High City if you styled them right.

So I texted, *Cool. See you soon.*

I didn't send it though. Instead, I wondered if I should sign off like I normally did with people I cared about.

I didn't wonder long.

I typed in *xx* and sent the text.

Then I shook a leg.

An hour (and three minutes) later, when my doorbell rang, I was in my bedroom, wishing I'd taken one single minute to text Archie for advice, because this feat ended up being harder than I expected.

I'd been through four outfits and it was becoming clear I didn't really have what I would consider biker babe garb.

Currently, I was wearing a pair of seriously faded crop jeans with a slight tear in one knee and a sleek white tube top, its hem reaching low, providing full midriff coverage and tucking into my jeans. I'd put on my zebra wedges with ankle ribbons.

I'd also spent time giving my hair more fluff and adding a bit of makeup, nothing extreme, but it definitely said "night out."

Last, I'd carefully done my lips in one of my several versions of very red lipstick.

It was time, so I'd have to do.

I quickly grabbed the perfume I'd put on that morning (Jo Malone Wood Sage and Sea Salt), spritzed minimally for a refresh, then I moved out of my room.

I checked the peephole and instantly started salivating.

I then opened the door.

And there stood Core in another pair of faded jeans, not as faded as mine or what he wore the day before, but still faded.

Up top was a crisp, black button down, which made his chest seem to need its own zip code.

His hair was still wet from his shower, curling more than it normally did when it was dry, specifically around his ears.

I needed to know his last name.

I needed to know why on earth he didn't think he was good for me.

I needed to get my fingers in that hair.

I needed him to fuck me.

My gaze shifted from his curls to his eyes.

And automatically, I took a step back.

Instantly, he took a step in.

I took another step back.

He did another forward step and shut the door with such force, it slammed, and I jumped.

He suddenly stepped wide and to the side, so I had to do a half pivot to keep him in front of me.

He stopped moving.

I stood in front of him, unable to move.

We stared at each other.

At the look on his face, I was close to hyperventilating.

My panties were drenched.

And my back was to the short hall that led to the tiny powder room and the hallway closet that stored the washer and dryer.

Oh, and my bedroom.

The reason for his wide sidestep.

He was positioning me.

His blue gaze burned into my tube top.

"Core," I breathed.

It raced to my face.

I was sensing I picked the right outfit.

"It's gotta be you," he growled.

I knew exactly what he meant.

No problems with that.

I walked to him.

When I arrived, his arms closed around me with such force, my breath huffed out. He leaned in, bending me over those arms.

Nice.

And his mouth was on mine.

Our first kiss.

I slid my fingers into his soft, damp hair and held him to me, opening my mouth at the same time he slipped his tongue inside.

Okay, this...

This was how a woman needed to be kissed.

Hot and wild and hungry and demanding.

The perfect first kiss.

No.

More.

It was the perfect first kiss of the rest of your lives.

I felt that thought and that kiss in my belly. It melted, and my hold on him tightened.

He started walking forward and I had no issue walking back.

We kissed the whole way, his arms separating, one of his hands going up into my hair, one down to my ass. We only stopped when I felt my bed against the back of my legs.

He lifted his head.

Losing his mouth, I emitted a mew of displeasure and opened my eyes.

He had my lipstick smeared all over his lips and into the whiskers around them.

The red was so striking, violent and lurid, it defined the kiss we just shared to the extent it looked pornographic.

It was a total turn on.

"You have my lipstick everywhere," I whispered.

"I don't give a fuck," he replied.

I pressed into him.

"We going there?" he asked.

"Yes," I answered. "Absolutely."

And then I was down on the bed.

There was a lot more kissing, it was better, hotter. There was groping, which was part of why the kissing was hotter, but it was just good on its own. And it seemed we had a hair pulling contest (he won).

Then my tube top was down and Core left a red smear across my chest before he sucked in a nipple, going for it, and there was serious power behind that delicious pull.

I arched into the feeling and the man giving it to me.

I felt him release the button on my jeans, the zip went down, his hand went in at the front, then frustratingly slid around the side to the back.

He cupped my ass over my panties and pulled me into his hard crotch.

Okay, that was *awesome*.

I whimpered at the feel of what I was doing to him and maybe my nails sunk into his scalp (not maybe, they did).

Core growled in approval at that and switched nipples as he trailed the waistband of my panties inside my jeans, stopping at the front just above my mound.

"If you don't dive in, I'm going to—"

He dove in.

I gasped.

Now *that* was how it was done.

No effort. Core knew where a clit was and just what to do with it.

He lifted his head as I rocked against his fingers.

I forced my eyes open, and it was then I saw the savage look on his face.

I read it immediately. I knew what it meant.

He wanted more. He wanted it faster. He wanted it now.

He wanted me.

"Don't hold back," I panted.

"Baby."

"I need it too."

That did it.

He slid his hand out of my jeans and took his feet.

"Give me a hand," he ordered, gaze on my tube top.

He didn't need to ask twice, I grabbed hold of it at the sides, pulled it over my head, and tossed it away.

By the time I looked back at him, he had his wallet out and was retrieving a condom.

I sat up so I could touch him.

"Lay back. Don't move."

Bossy.

I liked it.

I laid back.

Eyes never leaving me, he flipped the condom to the bed, bent to cup the back of my ankle in his hand, and he tugged the ribbon.

I suddenly had a deeper appreciation of those ribbons, the feel of that tug on the sensitive skin of my ankle sent a surge wet between my legs.

Off went one shoe. Then the next.

After that, he yanked at my jeans so hard, I nearly came off the bed, and I felt my vagina ripple. Without any other option, my panties went with them.

Once I was free, he chucked them to the floor, pulled off his shirt, I spied some tattoos I was in no shape to study in that moment, then he went after his own jeans.

After those were gone, he bent to grasp my hips. He dragged me fully back into the bed as he joined me.

He grabbed the condom.

I opened for him, he fell through, and I rounded him with my legs.

I felt him working between them, then I felt his tip.

This was happening.

We held eyes.

He slid in an inch, but before he went further, he caught my jaw like he did last night—a touch so poignant, so right in that moment, my breath caught at the wonder of it.

And in a smooth glide, he was inside me.

I had him.

He was big, and it took me a second to physically accommodate him, but it might have been the best second of my life.

"Yeah?" he grunted.

"Oh yeah," I confirmed.

He cupped my breast, squeezed hard, slid out and thrust, his eyes locked to mine.

Keeping claim on my breast, he pinched my nipple with thumb and forefinger, and the blaze that tore through me drove my hips up into his.

"Damn, baby," he purred.

"You're holding back," I accused.

"You can't take it how I need it right now."

"Try me."

"Babe."

"Core."

"Hellen."

I latched onto his hair, pulled myself up to his face, and demanded, "Fuck me."

His eyes caught fire even if I heard amusement mingled in the heat of his tone when he murmured, "Well, all right."

And then he fucked me.

Even with no clit action, it was so spectacular I came within a few strokes. As I did, I gasped and whinnied and held on like I was on a mechanical bull and the prize was a million dollars.

It.

Was.

Phenomenal.

"Fuck, you're something," he groaned, tugging my hair back, arching my neck. "Yeah," he grunted, bucking into me.

But at the hair tug, a second orgasm rolled over the first.

I was panting and clasping him with everything available to me when he shoved his face in my neck, planted his cock to the root and groaned deeply into my skin.

His body trembled on top of mine as he pumped inside a few times when he was coming down.

And then it was me in my bed with Core in me, and that was it.

That was my world.

Last night, I'd never felt safer.

In that moment, I never felt more right.

I didn't question this, any of it.

From the arrogant whistle and wink, to Core being real and himself no matter the good or bad of it—no games, no acting—to his overprotective streak, sense of humor and tender side.

If I gave myself a minute to consider it...

If life hadn't been kinda crazy the last few weeks...

I would have known he was something special, the guy for me at that first wink.

Lazily, I twisted my fingers in his loose curls.

He kissed my neck, behind my ear and lifted his head to look down at me.

"You got lipstick all over you, babe."

"I don't give a fuck," I whispered.

He shot me his Hollywood grin, rolled, twisted, adjusted, and pulled us both up so he was shoulders on my pillows and I was draped down his side, my head on his shoulder.

We lay that way for a while, fully recovering, though I did it with a close-up view of the swells of his pecs, so I had a feeling I enjoyed that time more than he did even if I was too close to decipher the ink that was there.

Eventually, he muttered, "Gotta get rid of this rubber."

"Cool," I replied.

He kissed the top of my head, angled out of bed and walked to the bathroom.

I rolled the other way, dashed to my vanity and nabbed my makeup wipes.

I looked into the mirror and nearly burst out laughing.

My hair was a sexy mess. I was seeing now my smoky makeup definitely said, "fuck me now!" a demand Core didn't miss. And the red around my mouth, my cheeks, my neck, down my chest and highlighting my nipples was obscene, yet somehow chic. I looked like a layout in Maxim.

The toilet flushed, and I bounced back to bed with such enthusiasm, it was almost a skip.

I was also not a woman who bounced, and I definitely didn't skip.

But in that moment, I bounced.

I was sitting cross-legged, one of my pillows pressed to my chest and lap, when he came back, and I saw why he felt big inside, because he was impressively endowed semi-hard.

Core's chuckle brought my eyes up to his face.

"You gotta let it take a breath before you call it back to attention, baby."

I smiled at him.

When I did, he was bent forward, arm out, one knee raised, about to climb back into bed from the foot, when he arrested, watching me smile.

"Intense orgasms and big dicks make me happy," I explained.

He exploded with laughter, crawled up the bed, I appreciated the show, then he tugged the pillow away from me and yanked me on top of him.

"Though," I went on like I hadn't been interrupted by his mirth and movements. "This is the first time I've experienced either. So thank you. I finally have something juicy to write in my journal."

He smiled at me, cupped my ass and gave it a squeeze, but he said no words.

I still liked his reply a whole lot.

"I grabbed my makeup wipes," I shared.

"Hit me," he ordered.

I twisted to reach for them, yanked one out of the pouch, and, arched against his chest to give myself clearance, I swiped at his face.

It wasn't designed to deal with whiskers, it snagged and tore, but I didn't give up because I got off on the intimacy of wiping me from Core's lips.

When I was done, I tossed it to the nightstand.

"Give me the thing," he ordered, hand up, four fingers moving in sync in a "gimme" gesture, so I handed him the pouch.

He pulled out a wipe and went to town on my mouth and cheeks, then threw the wipe on top of the other one.

"You missed some," I said.

"Nope. Those are my marks. Sexy as fuck. You're sleeping in those."

My clit quivered.

"I like you naked and happy and thoroughly fucked," he shared. "But I'm hungry."

I frowned.

He smiled again.

"I could rustle up some grub," I offered hopefully. "I have skills in the kitchen."

My ploy with offering this suggestion was that we wouldn't be far from bed and he wouldn't have to put many clothes on, because I might have been stuck on his cock a while ago, but his chest, abs and thighs might be my new religion, and I needed some time to become acquainted with his tats.

He tucked some hair behind my ear and said in a quiet voice, "I wanted to take you to dinner, baby."

Core.

Great in bed.

Great in a crisis.

Great during a breakdown.

Great with used Kleenex removal.

And sweet.

"Would drive-thru at Wendy's work?"

He shook his head, lips again curled up, but asked, "You a Baconator girl?"

"Have you seen my ass?"

He squeezed it again, and said low, "Oh yeah."

"So. What do you say?" I pressed.

"Sweetheart,"—he pulled me up his chest so we were face-to-face —"I wanted our first date to be special."

Okay then.

Correction.

He could be *very* sweet.

"I don't know what you consider special, but a man I like who I'm glad likes me taking one look at my outfit and making it clear he's struggling not to caveman me to bed, then he semi-cavemans me to bed and gives me the best orgasm of my life, is a *very* special date in my books. And we're not even an hour into it."

His brows went up. "Semi-cavemans?"

"You backed me into my bedroom doing this down an entire hall all while kissing me."

"Your hall isn't that long."

"Just let me be impressed."

His body was shaking. "Have at it."

"But if you want to get dressed and eat *inside* Wendy's, I'm game."

"You need to have Wendy's now, don't you?"

"Kinda, yeah," I admitted.

"What's a full caveman?"

"Dragging me by my hair, which I don't advise, or carrying me over your shoulder, which I also don't advise. Though it'd be hot, you couldn't use your hips like you did if you have a hernia."

"You're not heavy," he murmured.

I rolled my eyes.

"You're a lot of things, Hellen, but too heavy in any way those words can mean, I already know, will never be one of them."

What could I do after he said that?

I kissed him.

When I was done, I wasn't on top of him, he was on top of me.

He lifted his head and said, "Let's go get you a Baconator."

"So, the Greeks," I prompted before biting into my Baconator.

We were in a booth at Wendy's.

And I had taken a moment to consider the state of the world when I walked up to order, bright lipstick smears across my chest above my tube top, and the girl taking our order didn't even blink.

"Yeah, like I thought, a bigger operation," he shared before biting into his.

I chewed, swallowed and asked, "Wow. How big?"

"There's five guys here. There's six working in LA. Three in San Francisco. And there's twelve in Vegas."

"How am I not surprised Vegas is a hot spot?"

"Yeah," he agreed through a smile.

"So how'd you find this out?"

"We have some resources that can get us deep dive intel. Now we gotta pull together an operation. It looks like headquarters are in LA. We gotta take that out simultaneously with the locals. This means we'll have to pull in favors from other MCs."

I munched a fry then asked, "Is that a problem?"

"We like to keep things tight to our crew. Makes it more manageable and other MCs sometimes don't have the discipline we do."

I was equal measures curious, impressed and concerned by this.

"Does that make things dangerous for you?"

He took a bite of his sandwich and chewed while studying me.

"Me being a cry baby last night is not my norm," I assured him. "I'm a big girl. You can be honest with me."

And I need that from you, I didn't say, but with the way he continued to watch me for a beat, I knew he was weighing my unspoken words, especially at this juncture in our relationship.

He made a decision, one which relieved me, because it was the right one.

"We'll send one of our guys to each location to call the shots," he said carefully. "Which means, yes. If the MC we're working with goes off script, or is too gung-ho, or dicks something up, our guy there will be put in a spot."

Not awesome.

"Where will you be?" I asked quietly.

"LA. It's my op. So I'm on the command center."

His op.

Now I was more curious and concerned than impressed.

"Okay," I mumbled, dunking a fry in ketchup.

"We do a lot of this stuff, babe," he assured, and that did nothing to alleviate my curiosity. "And sometimes it's bigger than us. So we got practice with guys who might fuck shit up."

"Okay," I repeated, and popped the fry into my mouth. After I chewed and swallowed, I asked, "When is this going to happen?"

"It's looking like early next week."

"Hmm," I hummed, bummed out by that, foremost because I didn't want him working with some rogue, disorderly bikers that might put him in a spot.

Onward from that, I was still puzzled by his role in this at all, though it didn't take much brain power to read between the lines. That said, he was not a cop, a PI or a special agent either, so the matter-of-fact, experienced manner he spoke of this stuff was troubling.

Last, this was our first date. I was guessing with how much he was smiling and how hard he came we'd have another one, then more, and it wasn't easy to date and have sex with a guy who was off to LA to deal with bad dudes.

"It'll be an in and out, Hellen. I'll be gone two days, three tops."

There was that matter-of-fact experience.

I was in too good of a mood to push anything heavy right then, therefore I nodded to him.

"So, just a few more days of women getting screwed," I remarked.

"About that."

With the way he said those two words, I grew alert.

"We been taking pics of these assholes out on dates, or in bed fucking, or whatever we can nab that paints the picture that they're not just hanging with a female friend. Then we email them to the other women each particular guy is fleecing."

I felt my eyes get big, because that was epic.

"Yeah," he agreed on a semi-smirk.

"How do you know their emails?"

"Our resource has a lot of skills."

"So they're losing the women?"

He did a quick shake of his head. "Some of them are backing off. Some are sticking."

"Doesn't that mean Christos and the others know someone is onto them?"

"Yup. Which is why we can't fuck around taking them down. They know something's fishy. They're doing their own investigation, and the local crew is making plans to pull out of Denver. Bree wasn't a big mark, they got women with a lot more money and a lot more stuff, some of them married, so there's also extortion going on. This is actually the gig that brings in the big bucks, because these women aren't hip on their husbands finding out they fucked around on them or having videos they didn't know were filmed out on social media, and they're willing to pay to make sure that doesn't happen."

"Holy crap," I breathed at this news.

"Yeah, these guys are motherfuckers," he muttered before carrying on with the briefing. "Still, they'll take what they can get, as long as a woman buys their shit, lets them in her bed so they can get off and she's got something they can scam off her. But now, they're winding things up with the women who didn't scrape them off so they can move to a new city. This means we gotta act fast."

This bent in conversation obviously begged my next question.

I kept my voice low when I asked, "So when you do whatever it is you're going to do, do you turn them into the cops?"

"Looked it up," he began. "The guy from the documentary you talk about served five months of a fifteen-month sentence."

With that asshole's path of heartbreak and destruction, that wasn't fair.

But Core's response also wasn't promising.

"Is that a no?" I queried.

He put his burger down, sucked back some pop, put that down, and focused on me.

"They won't do it again. That's all I can say for now. You can ask, and maybe we'll get there one day, baby, and if we do, I can tell you. But right now, that's all I got to give. Bottom line, though, is they won't do it again. And that's a guarantee."

A guarantee.

I thought about this.

I thought this wasn't a promising response either, because I could read between the vigilante lines.

I still had questions about why his club got involved with this kind of thing.

Even so, I then thought about Christos making off with Bree's earrings from her grandma. I thought about how petty that was for him in regards to something that meant the world to her.

I got it. It was a small grab to feel out if she noticed so he could go bigger. When she didn't notice, he went bigger and she lost something even more precious to her.

I thought about the fact that our justice system was fucked, so if they used the money they stole from women to get themselves a good attorney, it was unlikely they'd pay. And if they did, they'd get out in no time at all, just like *The Tinder Swindler*, and go their merry way setting up shop again.

But Bree would never get her things back. She was going to question herself and her read on people, maybe for the rest of her life. She was never going to forget that she not only slept with the enemy, she let him in her house to take her precious things and defended him to her friends. And that was never going to sit comfortably.

After thinking all this, I went back to eating my hamburger.

"From the minute I laid eyes on you, I knew you were the shit," Core said softly.

That felt really nice.

I smiled through chewing.

"You should know, Nails surfaced," he told me.

My eyebrows shot up as I swiped my mouth with my napkin. "Whoa. Really? Where?"

"She's back in Phoenix. And it seems she didn't make a deal with the bad guys down there."

"Did she come up here?"

"Yeah. Made contact with her dad. He wasn't fired up his biker bunny daughter showed. She didn't stay long. We got this from a source close to her down in Phoenix. We've had no contact with him, so we don't know why she came up, but we can guess."

"What's your guess?"

"She was bragging around Phoenix she had an in with this crew. We know now she was talking smack, but we didn't when Rush set Resurrection on your family. Told you, they're bad news. She's also bad news. They weren't feeling an association with her in reality or in rumor. They sent someone to shut her up. She left town because, how they'd shut her up, she wouldn't like. Since she's back, she probably got word to them she'll quit running her mouth."

"Sounds like Eleanor," I muttered, dunking another fry.

"What's her story?" Core asked.

I dropped the fry in my mouth, chewed and shrugged.

Then I answered, "I don't know her very well. It won't surprise you she didn't come to a lot of family gatherings, then, after I got older and could decide where I wanted to be, I didn't either. But stories of her antics are a favorite pastime for that side. Her dad is the baby of the family. He had three kids. She was the middle. What he knew of how to raise kids, he did with his own and spoiled the baby. Apple of his eye. Golden girl. Eleanor acted out to get attention, at least that's what Mom says. When this attention wasn't enough attention, she went off the rails, and please do not feel me guilty by association, I hope you know my immediate family is biker friendly."

His eyes twinkled.

I liked it.

He confirmed verbally too.

"I know that, sweetheart."

I nodded. "But my dad's family, they're not. When she started hanging with that crowd, it didn't go well for her. I don't know if she's officially disowned, but it doesn't surprise me Uncle David wasn't super welcoming. The reason she's in Phoenix at all is because she wasn't wanted here, and no one really hid it."

"Then that tracks with info she's unsuccessfully dealing with a chip on her shoulder."

"Yes."

We kept eating, and when Core reached for his Frosty, I said, "So Eleanor's in Arizona, and the Greeks are going to be dealt with, now what are we going to do for excitement?"

The twinkle was awesome.

But the look in his eyes right then was far superior.

"I got a few ideas."

"I sense I'll like them."

"I know you will."

"Cocky."

"Baby, you had an out-of-body experience when you came. It was so huge, your out-of-body body came too."

I started laughing.

And not only because he was kind of right.

Because he was funny.

And because I had a Baconator and a Frosty on standby, and I had them because I wanted them, and Core made sure I got them.

Also because he was beautiful to look at across the booth in Wendy's from me.

But mostly because this was the best date I'd ever had.

And I knew that in a way I'd never forget it.

14

THE END OF A FRIEND

Hellen

I WAS WOKEN by a squeeze on the hip and the prickle of whiskers accompanied by the soft swipe of lips on my jaw.

I opened my eyes and saw it was still dark. We were fast approaching autumn, but it was still summer, days were long and morning sun came early.

Therefore, sleepy and surprised, I looked through the shadows to see a fully-dressed Core bending over me.

"I gotta get to my pup, baby. He's probably been crossing his legs for the last few hours and that's not cool."

My God, I'd forgotten about Nanook.

He was right, that wasn't cool.

He pressed his lips hard against mine and pulled away.

"Got plans tonight?" he asked.

He wanted to see me again.

Right away.

I almost said, no, I did not have plans, because I wanted to see him too.

Then I remembered cocktails with the girls.

"Yeah. I'm having drinks with my friends."

"'Kay. Call me. I want you Saturday night."

That was *so* happening.

I smiled at him.

He touched his mouth to my smile and then he walked away.

I SAT at my desk in my office.

I'd selected four candidates to interview, and as such, next week would be busier than normal because of those appointments. This meant, to keep on top of things, I had to work this weekend.

Not unusual.

Along with that, the fact I'd decided to take this next step had me nervous, so I felt the need to score a few more clients. With an additional staff member, I'd have time to see to them, but mostly I wanted more money flowing in to cover the additional going out.

This was because I didn't want to be one of those employers who fucked over their employees.

Whoever I chose, I wanted her to have an excellent experience working with me. I wanted to pay a salary that wasn't just competitive, it told her I valued her as a human and wanted her to be able to afford to live a decent life. I wanted to contribute to her 401K. I wanted her to have proper time off so she could live a full life and refresh, which in turn I hoped would keep her sharp and loyal. And I wanted her to think outside of being a PA and pay for courses she could take should she wish to expand her knowledge and skills base.

I could do this now by the skin of my teeth.

But I wasn't a fan of living by the skin of my teeth, so I needed to expand.

For the most part, I got clients through word of mouth.

But I had my own social media accounts for my business, and

part of my contract with my clients included the fact I could use my work for them to score some more.

I needed to get on that.

Before I did, I had to do something else.

I picked up my phone and texted Core.

You and Nanook want to come over for dinner on Saturday?

It was maybe five minutes later and I was jotting down some thoughts on how to push out a new client call when Core responded.

No. I'm feeding you. My place. Five too early?

I was smiling when I replied, *No. That's perfect. Can't wait. xx*

See you then, baby. Bring clean panties, he sent back.

Translation: we're fucking and you're spending the night.

I had no argument with that.

As I stared at his text, feeling the excitement at all that was happening with Core, I made a decision.

I'd moved on, and it was only fair that Bryan was free to move on too.

Decision made, I called him and wasn't surprised I went to voicemail.

To ratchet up his billable hours in his bid for partner, he made my sixty to seventy hours a week look like I was a slacker. He was probably neck-deep in motions or sitting beside a client in court, and without a doubt, he was not going out for drinks with his buds tonight. Or if he was, he'd show up at around nine.

I realized then, it was not only one of the reasons why it took so long for me to understand he wasn't the one for me, it was one of the reasons we worked well together for so long.

He didn't give me shit about the time I spent on my business. I did the same for him.

But in reality, what this meant was that we hadn't spent a lot of time together.

Bryan would stay the night a lot. We'd meet up for lunch here and there. We'd make plans to share an entire Sunday together every once in a while. We'd make "special dates," which were dates where we made an effort to carve out time to go out for nice dinner or to a movie. On weekends, we sat beside each other on my couch with our laptops, in each other's presence, but in our own worlds, working.

In other words, we slotted each other in when we could.

It was on that thought that I knew what I felt for Bryan had completely faded away.

When we were together, I knew his schedule. I knew when he'd be in court. In an abstract way that didn't break confidentiality, he talked about his cases, and I enjoyed listening. His work was fascinating.

But right then, not knowing if he was in the office or in court didn't bother me.

So yes, for me, it was over and this had nothing to do with starting things with Core.

"Hello, this is Bryan Thomason. I'm afraid I can't take your call right now. Leave a message and I'll get back to you as soon as I can. If this is urgent, phone my assistant, Joelle, at..."

He gave her number, and then there was the beep.

"Bryan, it's Hellen. I wanted you to know I got your call. I appreciate you giving that to me. It means a lot. I'm glad to have the man who made that call to remember when I think about you. I'm sorry it didn't work out between us, but you're a great guy, and I know you'll find someone who will make you happy. I wish that for you. Our time together had meaning for me. Thank you for that. Take care."

I ended the call and continued to stare at my phone, reaching for some feeling.

I cared about him enough to be sorry he hurt because we were over.

But for me...

Well, there was nothing.

I KNOCKED on the door of Marcy and Kyra's apartment that evening, it swung open, and Kyra nearly gave me whiplash after she latched on and dragged me in.

"Drop a cocktail on her," she ordered Marcy, who was standing at their kickass brass and glass bar cart, a piece of furniture they had that I envied.

However, not only was a bar cart low priority on my build-my-life list, I didn't have room for it in my small pad.

I had to admit, whenever I saw their setup, I wondered about going back to the roommate days. Sharing rent and utilities, they were able to live in a newer development that had a pool and a clubhouse. They had the needed two bedrooms, but they also had an open plan that featured space for a dining table and a bigger kitchen and living room than mine.

I could get a one-bedroom in their complex that would give me four-hundred extra square feet.

It'd also cost five hundred extra dollars.

So, yeah...

Their setup might be rad, but a-little-goes-a-long-way-because-you-work-a-lot-and-you-play-when-you-aren't-working-so-you-don't-need-more was the way for me.

For now.

"Sock it to us," Kyra demanded as she shoved me into their plush couch. "Don't leave anything out."

Marcy plonked a fancy glass in my hand (I hadn't gotten to the full set of fancy glasses yet in my build-a-life plan either, though I had pretty wineglasses).

Marcy was our appointed mixologist and had been since my sophomore year.

I looked at the yellow concoction in my glass then up at her in question.

"I don't know what I call it," she answered. "It has pineapple juice and rum and some passionfruit puree with soda water to cut it. It's tart and it's sweet. It tastes like a tropical Starburst. I'm undecided if it's a keeper, since, I'll warn you, it isn't my best effort," she judged herself honestly.

I sipped.

No, it wasn't her best effort, true, but it was tasty.

"It has my approval," I shared.

She smiled.

"Okay, *hellllloooo*," Bree called. "Details on the date with the biker Jax Teller threw out of the Sons of Anarchy because he was *way* hotter than Jax," she prompted.

This sounded impossible, but it was true.

Core was *way* hotter than Jax Teller.

"We had dinner at Wendy's."

Bree and Kyra both looked sick, and Marcy made a noise like she was in pain.

I started laughing.

Then I gave them the details.

When I was done, no one looked sick anymore.

"I am *never* going to be able to drive by a Wendy's again without my heart beating a little faster," Kyra declared. "I mean, it takes some chops to make Wendy's romantic, but Lord, that man did it."

He sure did.

"I get it, with all that talk about the Baconator, now I need one," Marcy said.

I started chuckling, such was the power of the Baconator.

I stopped laughing when I saw how Bree was looking at me.

"What?" I asked.

"This isn't a rebound," she remarked.

No, it was not.

Or, at least I hoped it wasn't.

"No," I confirmed.

"You know, B," Marcy cut in, her tone mildly peeved. "You can start drifting out of a relationship while you're in said relationship. It wasn't like everything was going perfectly, they had a big blowup, Hell ended it, and now she's just moving on. Bryan wasn't right from the start, it just took her a while to get to that understanding."

"I called him and thanked him for calling me," I put in, just in case Bree was worried I hadn't done the right thing by Bryan and that was why she looked so weird.

"That's nice," she said before sipping, though it sounded like she didn't mean it.

"What's your deal?" Kyra asked.

Yes, I wasn't the only person who read she didn't mean it.

"Okay, don't get all mad at me,"—she visibly braced in her seat —"but I mean, this sounds like it's the start of something. Not just some fun you're having after a long-term relationship ended. That means you're trading an attorney for a biker. I know that sounds bad, but Marcy,"—she turned to Marcy—"you told me his club makes their money by selling marijuana. I mean, am I the only one who thinks this might not be a great idea?"

The air in the room had turned chilly, and it wasn't only coming from me.

"You know," I began, "my brother-in-law is a biker, and he's a really great guy. He loves Archie like crazy. He's a blast during family dinners because he's hilarious. He puts up with Elijah." Elijah was my stepbrother, and although, after a big blow up a few years ago, things had improved, I still held a mild grudge because he'd treated my mom like shit for a long time. "All of his biker brothers and their women are cool. You've been to one of their hog roasts. You know they're awesome."

"It's just..."

She didn't finish that.

"It's just what?" Marcy snapped.

Bree's face got hard. "I can see you're all pissed at me, but someone has to say it."

She took a big breath.

Then she said it.

"It's a step down."

Right.

Someone *didn't* have to say it, though after she did, we were all silent because we all didn't know how to respond in the face of her bullshit.

Unsurprisingly, it was Marcy who broke the silence.

"I really can't have you in my house right now."

"Marce!" Bree exclaimed. "Be real. Bryan's going to make partner in a few years and he's going to be rich as shit." She shifted her attention to me. "That's who you are. That's what you want. You told me you were going to live the five-star life. Do you think this biker is going to give that to you?"

Another reason why women kept getting typecast in this role?

There were too many other women who did their best to keep them there.

"Core gave me a Baconator," I reminded her.

She made a scoffing noise.

"Since I haven't made things clear in the years I've known you, I'll do it now," I began, openly impatient because I was tired of having this fucking conversation. "I *am* going to have the five-star life. But I'm going to get it for myself."

"How's it going to look, you strolling into a Waldorf Astoria with Core?" she asked.

"I don't know," I retorted. "I also don't give a fuck. I'll be paying a whack to stay there, so they can keep their opinions to themselves. Then again, I don't care where I am or who I'm around, someone has one, they can keep their unwanted opinions to themselves."

She didn't miss my point and her head moved like I'd smacked her.

But...

Seriously?

"As for Core," I continued, "he's probably rolling in money. Marijuana sales are *huge*. But even if they weren't, my point about the Baconator was, early indications are that he's happy if I'm happy. So if the Waldorf isn't his thing, I think he'll be able to suck it up. Then again, not many people have an issue with enjoying the amenities at a Waldorf Astoria property. Even, and this is just a guess, bikers."

"I can't believe I'm sitting in my own house, listening to someone I love defend the person she's attracted to and wants to spend time with," Marcy butted in.

That made Bree really mad and she didn't hesitate to share why.

"Excuse me? Were you not part of the gang up on me about Christos?"

"Bitch, he was *scamming you*," Marcy shot back. "Tell you what, I thought that guy was too smooth from the start. He wasn't my thing. But he was yours. I didn't say, 'Listen, babe, he's too pretty and perfect. It freaks me out.' *I* wasn't sleeping with him. It wasn't my choice and my opinion didn't matter. It was only when he started stealing from you that I spoke up. Do you not see the difference?"

Bree opened her mouth.

But our sweet Kyra got there first.

"Marce already said she isn't comfortable with you being here right now, it's my place too, and I feel the same. So before you make it worse, maybe you should go and think about what you said to Hellen, but more, what you said about Core. I mean, not only is that not even close to cool, he's going after Christos and his gang for you. I'm blown away you have so little respect and gratitude. It really stinks."

"I cannot believe you two are kicking me out." Bree's tone was as shocked as her expression.

"We need some space from you." Marcy affirmed that was where they were at.

Bree glared at her, then Kyra, and for some reason, her longest, most heated glare was at me.

Then she slammed down her fancy glass so hard, I thought she'd break it. She snatched up her purse, walked to the small foyer space and turned on us.

"You all have a lot of thinking to do too," she informed us.

I had no idea what she expected us to think about, *we* hadn't just exposed the bigot within.

But with that, she stormed out.

"Oh my God, that sucked so huge," Kyra breathed.

"Fuck her. I need a Baconator. Is Wendy's on DoorDash?" Marcy asked, pushing out of the couch and heading for her phone on the kitchen counter.

I watched Marcy closely.

She had a tough outer shell, but a gooey inner core. She was making a good show of hiding it, but I could still see she was shaken by what just happened and didn't like it.

"Yes," Kyra answered. "But Hell had Wendy's last night."

I pulled out my own phone. "I'm sure I'll find something."

I did, and Marcy was so upset, she deserted the mixologist duties she never shirked and opened a bottle of wine.

We all went on with our evening, pretending that didn't happen.

But it happened.

And we didn't talk about it (then), but I figured we all had the same worry.

Because that scene was so gross, it might have meant the end of a friend.

I WAS NOT one of those chicks who got belly flutters or bounced.

I was also not one of those chicks who grappled with the dating game and agonized over what was the right play to make in any given situation.

In other words, when I got home earlier than I normally would after cocktails with my friends (because, let's face it, we weren't in the mood), the normal me would not hesitate to call Core because I wanted to hear his voice.

This new belly-fluttering, bouncing me wondered if he'd think I was being too keen if I called him.

Furthermore, I wanted to talk out Bree's bullshit, and since it had been about him, and she hadn't been nice about him, I couldn't share that.

Still, I wanted to hear his voice.

"Fuck it," I muttered, curled into my couch and touched go on my phone.

It only rang a couple of times before he answered, "Yo, babe. All cool?"

No.

Though him sounding normal and happy to hear from me and not reticent and wondering why I was phoning when we had plans the next night so I needed to back off did make me feel a little better.

"Yes."

"You home?"

"Yes."

"Good night?"

No.

"We all had a fight with Bree."

"What?"

"Bree was being...uncool and it pissed us all off. So much, Marcy and Kyra kicked her out. And I'll share that isn't our normal MO. We usually get along really well. And for sure no one has ever kicked anyone out."

"It happens," he said.

"What happens?"

"You grow out of people."

For a second, I was stunned at his simple wisdom.

"Especially at your age," he continued. "You start to get stuck into life. See what's important, what's not. What the road ahead of you looks like. And who you want on it."

"Uh, do you know my age?"

"Yup."

"How old are you?"

"Thirty-six."

Just as I suspected.

"Does the age difference concern you at all?" I asked hesitantly.

"If it did, my dick wouldn't have been in you twice last night."

That made me start laughing, partly due to relief.

It also made me think of our second go around after we got back from Wendy's, which of course produced a flutter.

"Does it concern you?" he asked.

"Not if you're going to lay wisdom on me to make me feel better about the fact I'm understanding that I'm drifting away from a person who's been an important part of my life for six years."

"Glad I could give you that," he murmured warmly.

"It's not thrilling I'm losing a friend, though."

"What happened?"

I couldn't tell him that.

I boiled it down to, "She's got different priorities in life." With the theme of that, it seemed time to feel him out a little bit. "Tonight, she exposed that she thinks finding a man to give her the life she wants is where we all should be."

"Think her getting wound up in that Greek exposed that, baby."

Yes, it did.

"That's not me, you know. If I want it, I'll earn it," I told him. Then I gave him the rest of it. "And I want a lot, so I'm willing to work hard to get it."

"Watched you for a while, babe, and it isn't lost on me you got goals."

He seemed entirely unconcerned.

Good.

"What's your last name?" I asked.

He chuckled and muttered, "She's fucked me and she doesn't know my last name."

"Core," I snapped.

"It's Cutler, baby, and I don't give that first fuck you took my cock before you learned my name," he teased.

"You're kind of annoying," I told him.

"Don't care you think that, as long as you keep taking my cock."

I couldn't help it.

I started laughing.

When I was done, with genuine feeling coating the words, he said, "Sorry you had a shit night with your girl."

Man, he was good at this.

"Me too."

It hung there between us.

We both got tired of it hanging at the same time. I knew when he asked, "Want company?" while I asked, "Wanna come over?"

I followed through with a semi-breathy, "Yes."

"Gotta bring Nanook," he warned.

"I'm totally okay with that."

"Right, I'll be there in half an hour."

"Okay. Cool."

"See you in a bit," he replied.

"Core?"

"Yeah?"

"Thanks."

A second passed.

Then another one.

After that, he said gently, "Sweetheart, I'm into you. Which means I want this from you. Your bad nights and your good ones and you wanting me with you. You got nothing to thank me for."

"Okay then, thank you for that too."

"Shut up." That came through a chuckle. "See you in a few."

"Yeah, see you."

Core was head and shoulders to my headboard, the rest of him slouched in my bed, and I was sitting on his big dick.

But I wasn't allowed to move, by Core's verbal command and the fact he had both hands clamped to the juncture of my thighs, holding me filled full of him.

It was excruciating, partly because his big dick felt good inside, but mostly because he also had a thumb to my clit, his beautiful eyes were on me, and both were doing things to me that made me need to *move.*

"Honey," I begged.

His voice was deeper, rougher, amazing-er when he replied, "Unh-unh, baby, be good."

I'd never been told to "be good" by a man.

It was torture.

And it fucking rocked.

I could feel my pussy rippling against his cock, he could too, which was why he sunk his teeth in his lip.

That was so sexy, with all the rest, I was done.

I didn't know how he knew it, but he did.

Which was why he grunted, "Pop."

Given permission, immediately, I started bouncing uncontrollably as I exploded magnificently.

He gave me that for a few strokes and then he pulled me off his dick, put me on knees, positioned behind me, placed a hand in the middle of my back and pressed me down to genuflecting in front of him.

And it was definitely genuflecting, and coming at the same time being on offer for him absolutely rocked too.

He claimed my hips in both hands and drove in.

I bucked back, still coming.

He squeezed my ass cheeks, growling, "Fuck, this beautiful ass. Been wanting this ass in my hands for fucking *weeks.*"

He then shoved his thumb inside.

No one had ever done that to me.

It felt great, having him inside both places.

I whimpered, shifting up to my hands so I could put more power into surging back into his dick.

"Down," he ordered.

I dropped down.

"Good, baby."

Oh God.

He stroked my cunt and my ass and I wasn't certain what was happening to me.

I'd orgasmed but now...

Now, it was so big, coming back again so fast, it was too much.

"Core."

He smacked my ass with his free hand.

No one had done that to me before either.

The sweet sting, his big dick, his dominance.

I came undone.

"Baby, baby, baby," I panted, coming and coming, and oh my fucking God, *coming*.

He slid his thumb out, clasped my hips again and slammed me into his cock.

"Milk me with that pussy, fuck yeah," he groaned, thrust in and grunted repeatedly, loudly, unashamedly, uninhibitedly.

He was a man coming hard, and he didn't care if every neighbor I had knew it.

I loved that sound so much, I felt every muscle between my legs contract tightly listening to it, feeling it, and he grunted again, gripped my ass hard, and growled, "Yeah, baby."

He took me through his orgasm and he took me while we both came down.

Then he slid out, gently rolled me to my back and lowered his weight to me.

With the back of his fingers, he pulled the hair out of my face.

"All right?" he asked.

"Yes," I puffed out.

In a hazy way, I saw him grin.

"You're a goddamn knockout lay."

"I aim to please."

"Your pussy does shit I've never felt in my life. It fuckin' rocks."

"My pussy thanks you for the compliment."

His body shook with laughter, he touched his mouth to mine, slid his lips to my ear and said, "Back in a sec."

He rolled off me, yanked the covers from under me and twitched them over me.

I turned to my side and curled up, watching the bathroom doorway so I didn't miss him returning.

He came to the side of the bed this time, lifted the covers and slid in beside me.

He tangled our legs and held me in his arms.

"I'm glad you came over," I said.

"I didn't miss that," he teased.

I shoved my face in his throat and smiled.

"Gonna see to Nanook in a sec and shut the house down. You ready to sleep?"

I couldn't move, so it wasn't like I was ready, it was that I wasn't good for anything else.

Still, sleep was necessary to any living being, and he'd been up super early.

So I said, "Yes."

"Right," he muttered, kissed the top of my head and slid out of bed again.

It wasn't long before he came back, and I not only got him, but heard Nanook's doggie groan as he settled in on the floor on Core's side.

"I love that sound," I told him, cuddling into him front to front.

"What sound?"

"A dog settling in close."

He tightened his arms around me, and for some reason, he did this super strong.

It took him a second to relax.

When I felt him settle in, I mumbled, "'Night, Mr. Cutler."

His body shook again with soft laughter before he replied, "'Night, Moynihan."

I pressed closer and not long later, I fell asleep.

15

A LIFE INCOMPLETE

Hellen

THE NEXT EVENING, I knocked on Core's door.

There was a woof from inside, a second one, a few moments passed, then he opened it.

His eyes slid over me, he grinned big, hooked me with an arm around my waist and bent me over it, laying a huge wet one on me while Nanook brushed against our legs excitedly.

I was a big fan of his hello.

When he allowed me to surface, he didn't let me go as he said, "You just kick ass being you."

Okay.

Wow.

That might have been the best compliment anyone ever gave me.

No.

It just was.

And again, indication I'd chosen well with my outfit.

Casual dinner at his house, I'd picked another pair of crop jeans, these with a ragged hem. I added a cute, floral, blousy cami top that dipped in the front and gave a hint of cleavage. On my feet were flat, gold sandals that showed a lot of skin, seeing as they were mostly thin straps, including ones that wrapped around my ankle.

I'd gone for loose curls in my hair and light, summery makeup.

I also brought my big Fendi tote because extra panties were not all I needed. I needed my toothbrush, face wash and moisturizer, some PJs—because we'd been sleeping nude, but that wasn't normally my thing—a selection of makeup in case we decided to get brunch tomorrow, and a different top to wear.

"Say hi to my dog before he loses it," he ordered, letting me go, but instantly taking hold of the guitar strap to my Fendi and sliding it down my arm.

He walked in.

I bent to Nanook, who was indeed very excited to see me, and gave pets as we followed him in.

"This stuff for the bedroom?" he asked after the tote.

"Yes," I answered.

He disappeared down a hall.

I kept petting Nanook as I looked around.

There wasn't much there. Big TV. Three-piece furniture set in a contemporary design and neutral color (gray) that was so basic, it veritably screamed for toss pillows and throw blankets. And tables dotted around that made it look like he bought the arrangement from a showroom floor and that was that.

It was much the same as what I'd seen of his kitchen, which looked new and sleek with gray cabinets, white quartz countertops and clear, light-gray glass subway tile backsplashes.

But outside a steak left out on the counter and some jars of seasonings sitting around it, there was nothing there and it was clear this house had been flipped, or he'd done a complete overhaul of it (at least the parts I'd seen), but he hadn't really done anything to make it his.

He might be so busy with his club, their marijuana concerns and his vigilante activities that he hadn't gotten down to buying a blender and some art for his walls.

But there seemed something wrong about this.

Like a life incomplete.

He came back, threw his arm around my shoulders and led me into the kitchen, asking, "You hungry or you wanna kick back with a drink first?"

"I could wait to eat."

"Perfect," he muttered.

He let me go to open the fridge. "Got soda. Got waters. Got a couple of bottles of wine for you. Got beer."

"What kind of wine?"

He pulled out a bottle and studied it. "Sauvignon blanc." He reached in to shift the other one around so he could read the label. "Viognier." His gaze came to me. "The dude at the store said they were good."

"I'll try the viognier."

"Gotcha," he replied.

I leaned a hip against the counter, Nanook leaned against me, and together we watched Core open the bottle then pour it into a surprisingly stylish wineglass.

He handed it to me, and I quipped, "You have good taste in glassware."

His lips curled. "I bought them today after I bought you wine and realized I couldn't serve it in a Solo cup."

I frowned. "Please tell me you don't use Solo cups, meaning your good time will last two hundred years on this earth."

"Baby, I drink beer from a bottle, so the earth is safe with me."

I laughed, sipped the wine, it was delicious, and the three of us went out to his back patio.

Okay, this space said he lived there and wasn't renting a poorly decorated Airbnb.

Although I'd add some toss pillows, decorative lanterns and other accoutrement, he had a great rug that brought the space together.

There was a handsome couch out there, he took us to it, and then we were down, Core in a corner, me tucked to his side, Nanook seated by his dad's knee.

"Have a good day?" he asked.

It was only then I realized his day included buying me wine then going to get a pretty glass for me to drink it from.

"I worked all day," I answered, sounding subdued, because his gesture meant a lot.

"That sucks."

"No, I like working."

"Then it doesn't suck."

I laughed softly and sipped wine.

"This space is fantastic," I told him.

"Did it myself," he replied.

"Color me impressed." I put feeling into that, because I was.

He said nothing, but his arm around my shoulders gave me a squeeze.

"How long have you been here?"

"In this house?"

"Yes."

"Couple of years."

That was enough time to own a blender.

"Hmm..." I hummed.

"Hmm what?" he asked.

"Nothing," I muttered and took another sip.

"Got something on your mind, say it," he urged.

I stopped staring at the wide-seated, comfortable chairs across from us and twisted my neck to look up at him.

"No shade, your house is awesome, though it looks like you just moved in."

He smiled at me, gave me another squeeze, then said, "I can lay the shit out of flagstone, but got no clue when it comes to lamps and pictures and all the rest."

This information led me to another belated realization.

He not only was single, but if he'd lived there a couple of years and it looked like it did, he had been for some time.

Which, with all things Core, seemed impossible.

"Now what's in your head?" he queried.

"You cleaned up my tissues."

A shock of surprised laughter and, "What?"

"When I had my crying jag. You cleaned up my tissues. You put away the chip bags. You took me out for a Baconator. And just now, you grabbed my tote and took it to the bedroom for me."

"Is it my turn to remind you of shit that happened the last couple of days?" he joked. "Warning, my list is probably gonna be indecent."

I had to laugh, because that was funny.

Then I said, "No, I just..." I shrugged and looked away, bringing the wine to my lips. "You're a rare breed."

I took a sip.

"Babe."

I turned back to him.

"Her name was Kiki. We lived together for three years. I loved her. We ended. So it's her you got to thank for training me."

Not your sadly deceased mother?

I didn't ask that. I'd put my foot in it with a mention of his mom once. I was going to let him take us there if it came up again.

And anyway, the mention of a woman with the kickass name of *Kiki* and "I loved her" was enough to focus on, thank you.

I lifted my wineglass and said cautiously, "Here's to Kiki."

He read the caution. "It was a while ago, Hellen. And it ended in a way it was a definite end."

"But you loved her?" I asked quietly.

"She was great."

Oh boy.

He dipped his face closer to me. "It's over. I've run into her once or twice since we were done. She's got someone new,"—his eyes twinkled—"I've had some fun. Now, in case you missed it, I'm about seeing where things are gonna go with you."

"I'm about that too."

"Good we're on the same page."

"Though, my turn to give a warning, if I'm going to hang at your house, a trip to HomeGoods might be essential."

He assumed a mock offended expression. "What, fancy-assed wineglasses aren't enough for you?"

"You need toss pillows."

He burst out laughing.

I watched.

He was really handsome, totally gorgeous.

But when he laughed, his face clear of anything but humor?

He was beautiful.

Still doing it, he dipped in again, this time to kiss me, pulled back and asked, "You get all your work done?"

"Why?"

"Because I leave for LA on Monday, and I want you here when I get back, so I better get on those toss pillows, and I sure as fuck ain't gonna pick them."

Not a fan of the LA trip.

However...

The other part.

Score!

I twisted toward him excitedly, which had the unfortunate result of dislodging his arm, but he just tangled his fingers in my hair, and that worked for me.

"Okay, first, while you're away, can I take care of Nanook?"

"Absolutely," he murmured, a softness coming to his gaze.

"And second, I do have my work done so we can totally go shopping tomorrow."

"Sounds like we got a plan," he agreed and took a pull from his beer.

I leaned over his thighs to where Nanook was now lying on Core's rug, head up, eyes closed, tongue out, panting, in Happy Zen Doggie Land.

"Nanook," I called.

He swung his head to me.

"Did you hear that? I get to take care of you when daddy's away, and tomorrow, we get to go shopping."

Sensing my vibe, he woofed excitedly.

"I'm not taking my dog shopping, babe."

I looked to Core. "If I've had to put up with all those fucking poodles and mops in strollers when I'm trying on shoes, now that I have access to a canine, I'm getting mine back."

Humor lit his eyes as he remarked, "I see this is a thing for you. But unless it's a service animal, no dog should be out in public like that. It's not about the public. It isn't cool for the dog. You can know to your bones how your dog will behave, but you can't begin to guess what shit people will pull. Anything can happen. They got instincts. They'll react. It isn't okay to put them in that position."

I sat back away from him and pouted.

"We can take him for a walk in the park later," he offered.

I grinned huge.

The humor fled from his face, something else replaced it, and he ordered, "C'm 'ere right fucking now."

With nipples all of a sudden tingling, I went there, right fucking then.

I might have spilled a bit of wine before he was done with me, but I was okay with that.

When he tucked me back in his side, I asked, "What's for dinner?"

"Grilled barbeque chicken, grilled asparagus, sweet corn on the cob and cornbread."

I tipped my head back to stare at him.

"So you cook?"

"Yeah."

I was thinking I had Kiki to thank for that too.

Until he went on.

"My mom taught me that. Her cornbread is the best."

I loved knowing that about him.

I loved his back patio.

I loved his dog.

And I loved that he bought me wineglasses.

I CLIMAXED SO HARD, for a second, I literally blacked out.

No joke.

First it was seeing stars, and then I was blissfully floating in a cosmos of nothing.

I came back to the room to feel Core using his tongue to clean up after the explosion he set off between my legs, and that was not better, but it still was the best I'd ever had.

Finally, he pulled himself over me.

"Take my money," I said the second I caught his eyes. "All of it. And just so you know, some of it I've been saving since I was fifteen."

No hesitation, he tipped his handsome head back and roared with laughter.

I watched.

And no, it wasn't better than getting head from Dustin "Core" Cutler.

But it was close.

IN HIS TRUCK on the way to HomeGoods the next day (as suspected, bringing a cache of makeup came in handy, also as suspected, showering with Core was otherworldly), I asked, "Okay, so what's the budget?"

"No clue," Core replied. "Five, six thousand dollars. What do you think?"

Slowly, I turned his way.

"Five or six thousand dollars?"

"Not enough?" he asked the road.

I looked to the road as well. "We need to go to the mall too."

"We do?"

"And Target."

"Hellen."

My name trembled with amusement and maybe a little bit of unease.

"Shh, honey, I'm making a game plan."

His laughter filled the cab.

"I take it the marijuana business is booming," I remarked.

"Uh...yeah."

That was good, because I wasn't sure the vigilante business paid all that well.

"So you know about that?" he asked.

"About what?" I asked back.

"That the club sells pot."

"Yes. Marcy told me."

Like my sister, Marcy imbibed, so did Kyra, so she knew.

He made no reply and that felt strange so I looked at him.

"I don't have an issue with weed, Core."

"I don't want to fuck your girl over."

Now I was confused.

"Sorry?"

"But it turned out right."

"What are you talking about?"

"She came to a store. After I tried not to go there with you, she tried to light a fire under me. She came to one of our dispensaries and got a message to me that you were meeting your ex, also your dad, and then, babe, she shared about how your dad took away your dog."

With the specter of Tigger invoked, automatically, I looked out the side window.

Though, that explained how he knew I was having dinner with dad. I just assumed Andy had told Archie, Archie had shared with

Jagger, and in the course of biker communion, Jagger had let it slip directly or indirectly, and the info found its way to Core.

"Don't be pissed at her, Hellen. I would have found some reason to come back to you, but she gave me the opening."

I said nothing.

"She knew we were into each other and she just wanted to get my head out of my ass."

Now we were here.

Good, because I wanted to be here.

"Why was your head in your ass?"

It was his turn to say nothing.

I looked to him.

"Core?"

"Later, babe. This is good. We have a day planned. I leave tomorrow. We'll get into it later."

"Is it because I'm younger than you?"

"We already had that conversation."

"Is it because you're a biker and I'm...not?"

His lips tipped up at that. "No."

"Is it—?"

He glanced at me, reached out, took my hand and held it firmly before looking at the road and saying even more firmly and maybe a bit irritably, "*Later.*"

I considered pulling my hand away and pushing it.

Something wasn't right and I didn't want to wait until later to discuss it.

But I thought about barbeque chicken last night, and how Core wasn't wrong, his mother's cornbread was the bomb.

I then thought about loading Nanook up and taking him for a walk in a park, and how that was a fun thing to do after dinner.

I also thought about learning that maybe some public places weren't out of the question for pups, because after the walk, we got ice cream, sat outside and ate it, and Nanook got a pup cup.

I thought about Core's bedroom, which was just as personalityless as the rest of his house, but his king-size bed was super comfy and the spring in his mattress gave a new meaning to life.

And Core going down on me was just life.

I thought about watching Nanook when Core was out of town and him wanting me there when he got back.

I thought about the fact that everything he'd said and done shared what he'd asserted yesterday evening.

That he wanted to see where things could go with me.

I wanted the same.

So today wasn't our last day together until the end of time, and today didn't need to be about putting him on the spot to share what he didn't want to share right now.

We were new.

We had a lot to learn about each other.

We had time.

I could let it go and wait.

And I would blissfully go on for quite a while, falling in love with a man not realizing how bad a decision that would turn out to be.

16

HE WAS HOME

Core

The house was huge, a modern structure, lots of windows, on a steep hill overlooking the lights of LA.

It was also a tactical nightmare, especially considering its security system set a wide perimeter, which meant Core and the men with him were hunkered down in some scrub seventy yards from the structure, and once they knew they were a go, they'd have a steep climb.

There were five guys inside, the whole LA crew, which was a boon.

Core had seven men with him.

The lights flickered in the house. Easily, this could be misinterpreted as a glitch from those inside.

It was not a glitch.

It was the first indication they were good to go.

He had his earbuds in his ears and was waiting for confirmation from The Nerd of what the flicker actually was, the security system was down, when one of the men with him bolted out of the brush toward the house and right into the security perimeter.

This would alert the men inside if it was not yet deactivated.

Terrific.

So these motherfuckers were gung ho.

Core cursed under his breath as the others took that cue and headed up the slope.

He went after them as the automated voice in his ear said, "You're a go."

At least there was that.

He ate the distance with his long legs, passing everyone who took off before him.

The guy who went prematurely hit their rendezvous point at the corner of the house, one of the only areas that didn't have windows, and as they'd planned, he stopped.

Core got to him, lifted an elbow and slammed it full force into his sternum.

The man grunted, flew back and nearly went down.

After he righted himself, Core got in his face.

"When I said I was point, it wasn't a fucking suggestion," he snarled.

The man stared at him, fear in his eyes, a bonus to being known as an Angel of Death.

Core didn't waste any more time.

He led them to a back door, slid it open, then they were inside.

"We're in," he whispered to The Nerd, though The Nerd knew this considering they were tracking heat signatures.

Proof of that: the automated voice came back.

"Leader in office. Two in the basement playing a videogame. One in bedroom three, apparently asleep. Out."

He heard the disconnect.

He took the earbuds out of his ears, shoved them in his pocket and looked to the men.

He pointed at three of them, gave them two fingers, then pointed to the floor, after which he made motions with his hands like he had a game controller.

They moved out.

He pointed at two more, then up, giving them one finger then three, to indicate one man in bedroom three.

They took off.

The other two he gave a nod, extended his forefinger upwards to indicate they were dealing with one man, then he moved with them following him.

They hit the ground floor office swiftly and with zero hesitation, Core first.

The man behind the desk took one look at the three coming in and reached for a gun lying close at hand.

But Core was already there. He'd pulled his knife out of the scabbard at his belt and rammed it through the man's hand, pinning it to the wood of the desk.

One of his crew had already positioned behind the guy, so he had a rag shoved in his mouth to muffle the scream.

He also held the guy down in his chair.

Not that he was going anywhere with his hand stuck to the desk.

The last guy took the bungee cords looped around his shoulder and made light work of tying the guy to the chair.

Good.

So these fuckers might be gung ho, but when shit needed to get done, they were on it.

Calmly, Core moved to one of the chairs angled in front of the desk.

He folded in, rested against the back, and looked into the man's eyes.

And then, quietly, he said, "Right. This is how it's gonna go."

THE THUMB he was pressing to the sensor turned it from blue to green.

He dropped the thumb, and the hand, arm and body attached to it thudded to the ground.

He shoved the gadget into the port at the side of the keypad. The light on it showed red, then green.

"Hit it," he said.

His earbuds were back in.

The Nerd got on it.

The keypad above the sensor lit up, then scrambled. It went dark with only the number one illuminated, another scramble, then number six, and this went on through numbers eight, nine, five, a repeat of five, and last, seven.

A click was heard.

"You're in," the voice said in his ear.

Core pulled down the latch, opened the door and triggered a light that came on inside.

That was when he saw the room wasn't big, but the space had been fully utilized.

He walked in, the seven men behind him holding position outside the vault.

He was quick, but he was thorough as he made his selections of the inventory. He put what he chose in a black velvet jewelry bag he'd had stowed in his back pocket. He took enough from the piles of cash to cover what the club had agreed was theirs.

After that, Core walked out of the vault, stepping over the inert body on the floor, and muttered, "It's yours."

The men swarmed in.

Core jogged up the stairs and spoke to The Nerd, "Your turn."

There was a beat of silence.

Then, "It's done," and a disconnect.

That meant accounts were emptied, and tech was wiped, including computers and phones.

No more incriminating videos and pictures.

And the rest of their financial assets were gone.

Core took the earbuds out of his ears and sauntered out of the house.

Core was mildly disappointed when he hit the garage door opener on the approach to his house and didn't see Hellen's ridiculous car in the garage.

He'd texted her when he'd gotten in his truck at the airport, telling her he was home, and she'd said she'd meet him at his house.

She was probably tied up at work, where she'd been taking Nanook every day for the last three days to hang with her.

And if the pictures she texted of his happy boy curled in a dog bed in the corner of her office were any indication, Nanook liked to go to work.

Core drove in, parked and got out, going to the back of the cab to shoulder his duffel. He walked into the house, not bothering to close the garage since she'd be driving into it soon.

Monday morning, he'd given her a key, a garage door opener and his dog.

She'd given him a smile he'd never forget his entire life.

It might have been about the key.

Though he knew it was mostly about the dog.

He dropped the duffel in the laundry area, hit his kitchen and tossed his keys on the island.

He then halted and let what she'd done to his kitchen wash over him again.

She'd dragged him through Denver last Sunday, not attempting to hide her glee.

When she was done, he'd dragged in all the shit she bought (but he paid for), and unless she needed him to assist, he stretched out on the couch, smoking a joint and enjoying watching her unpack and place stuff in his house.

His kitchen now had a black blender, a black coffeemaker, a

white crock that had all his utensils sticking out of it, a thick, wooden, countertop butcher block upended against the backsplash, a black olive oil bottle (filled), a black soap dispenser at his sink and a two-tier wire thing on the island.

It had been empty when he took off on Monday.

Now it had bananas in the top and fruit at the bottom, the bright colors of the fruit stark in the monochrome of the space.

He felt his lips quirk and turned to the living room.

He then stopped dead.

She'd bought some pillows for the furniture and a blanket she tossed over a chair. He'd set up the lamp that arched over the couch and the other one that had a tripod base she told him to put in the corner. She'd added the lamp on the table at one side of the couch. It looked like two black rods at right angles to each other (she said it was all about rugs and lighting, and when she'd switched on that rod light when it got dark, and it cast a soft glow on one side of the couch, he saw she wasn't wrong).

Last, there was a gray rug that had black lines running through it, for which they had to move the furniture to roll it out over his bare hardwood floors.

She'd also bought some small frames you'd set out on tables. She said she had to think on what to do with them. And she'd added some pillows to his bed and two lamps for the nightstands in his bedroom.

But that had been the totality of her Sunday haul.

Now, however, the wall behind the couch was wallpapered in what looked like black crocodile, and mounted on it was a huge rectangular picture in a chrome frame. On it, there was a black skull on white positioned to the left. It looked like it was in motion or disintegrating because there were dots to the right that grew thicker the closer they got to the skull.

The wall and print changed the entire room and it was fucking fantastic.

He walked in to get a closer look and stopped again, because his TV was now set into a dark gray media unit that had glass front cupboards at the bottom and shelves on the sides and above the TV.

He got closer and saw she'd taken the books that he had stacked in one of the bedrooms, because he didn't have anywhere to put them, and set them in those shelves. One of the frames she'd bought had a picture of Nanook being a good boy, sitting and smiling up at her behind the camera. Holding the books in place were simple, black bookends, but there was a chrome mudflap girl leaning back into one hand to hold up one line of books.

Though she wasn't a traditional mudflap girl. She had the tits and legs, but she had a ponytail in her hair, was wearing a skirt and had one hand up, reading a book.

Last, alone on a shelf, there was a big square book that said *100 Years* at the top and had the orange Harley Davidson logo in the middle.

Core moved to it, grabbed it and flipped it open to see text and pictures of the story of Harley Davidson Motorcycles.

His throat was fucked-up when he put it back and did a turn to take it all in again.

He'd grown up in a trailer, and when his mom left his dad, they'd moved to another trailer. They had the basics, and not much more, and those were purchased at Goodwill, the Salvation Army or thrift stores, and these included his clothes and hers.

His mom had two jobs for as long as Core was able to understand the concept, one was as a waitress in a truck stop and the other was as a bartender in a seedy bar, so she was hardly raking it in at either.

Didn't matter she didn't make much, they had even less when his dad rode up against a tough time, which was a lot since the man never bothered to hold down a job.

In those times, he'd come over and demand what was in her wallet.

He'd then beat her to shit or sweet talk her into going with him to her bedroom, something that also happened a lot, not because she wanted it, but because she didn't want him to beat her to shit.

Core had learned to take off when they were back there because he didn't want to hear his mom and dad fuck. Or, what he understood later was happening, his dad coercing his mother into nonviolent rape.

Though when he got older, and more importantly bigger, the night happened where he made it plain he wasn't going to put up with his father's visits again.

He'd had some practice fighting by then, but his old man was an easy win, being a man wasted by booze who could only make himself feel like a man by beating a woman and intimidating her into taking his dick.

After that, all that shit stopped for nearly a year.

It had been a golden time for him and his mom. The only one they'd ever had. He'd gotten a job helping one of his bud's dad's roofing business during the summer, and with his first check, he'd bought her a brand-new dress.

When he went back to school, it was the first time she bought him new jeans, shirts and sneakers.

It was also the first time girls gave a shit about him, and he didn't have to beat bloody anyone who gave him crap about being poor as dirt and living in a trailer. Though he'd spent years making that message clear, there was always some fuck who needed it told to him.

That golden time ended when his father came back for one last epic round, doing it at a time when Core wasn't there, and Core knew he planned that shit.

After that, it was over forever.

Kiki had some skills with making a house a home, but she was into a more country-type vibe and Core didn't like it. He never said anything because he didn't really give that much of a fuck. He was just happy to have a good woman and a home to go to.

He couldn't say this was his thing either, exactly, probably because he never took time to figure what his thing was.

And still, it kicked ass.

From what he could see, it had Hellen written all over it, since she decorated in all grays and blacks and whites at her place too.

But the truth of it was, it was her and it was him. It took the invitation to stay awhile of his furniture, her pillows and his TV and added a style that was hers, but it was also just him.

He'd been living in that house for two years.

But he'd never come home to it.

He'd just come home.

He heard her car in the garage, and outside turning to face where he'd first see her when she came in, he didn't move.

Nanook showed first, racing toward him and jumping up on his hind feet with his front paws to Core to show the love.

Christ, yeah.

He was home.

He gave his dog a rubdown and caught Hellen rounding the wall that housed the laundry area and hid the kitchen that was open to a dining table space he hadn't bothered to fill since he never threw dinner parties.

She stopped moving and started talking the minute his eyes hit her.

"Okay, the wallpaper is removable and everything else is returnable. I kept the receipts. It's just that I told Kyra about our Sunday, and she works for an interior design firm. She got all excited because she's never done anything for a man, much less a biker. She kept sending me these ideas, and they were so cool, I couldn't stop myself. Full disclosure, she and Marcy came over one night to help."

He needed to tell her.

He needed to tell her about the trailer. About how gentle and loving and broken and used his mother was. About how brutal and sleazy and detestable and foul his father was.

He needed to tell her about finding them, the smashed-up furniture, the blood, the gore, the clear indication his mother knew this time it was different and the last thing she did on this earth was put up one helluva fight.

He needed to tell her about going into the foster system after that, and how dicked up that was.

He needed to tell her he got in trouble delivering beat downs and doing stupid shit even before his father killed his mother. And how he lived with the shame he put his mom through that and the guilt that ate at him because she died maybe thinking she'd created another man like his dad.

He needed to tell her he hoped in her final moments she remembered that golden time, when they were good, safe, and he bought her a dress, which made her face light up and showed him for the first time how beautiful she'd been before his old man stole everything from her.

He needed to tell her how all this meant he needed somewhere to belong where he knew he was around men who got him.

He needed to tell her he found that in Bounty, but it was fucked-up because they all had a story that drove them there, but they not only let it fester, they fed off it and it took them where none of them ever wanted to be.

He needed to tell her he got so wound up in that life, it led him to participating in a gang beat-down of a defenseless woman.

And he needed to tell her all that came after in what would be a lifetime of all of them making amends.

He needed to give Hellen the information that was necessary for her to make the decision if she wanted to sleep next to that man, take his cock, and buy a cool-as-all-fuck picture to mount over his couch.

He wasn't going to tell her.

Not now.

Not while she stood there in her tan slacks and her short-sleeved silky mocha tee and her shiny beige pumps, watching him closely, openly worried she'd stepped over a line.

He couldn't do it.

It was fucked-up. Selfish. Wrong.

But that was who he was at his base.

He was fucked-up.

Selfish.

Wrong.

"You hate it," she murmured, disappointed and still worried.

"I'll pay you what it cost because it's the absolute shit."

Her face lit up.

Just like his mom's did when she got that dress.

And that was why he was selfish. That was why he was an asshole.

Hellen liked him. She trusted him. She enjoyed being with him.

She wanted him.

And for the life of him, he couldn't take that away from her.

Not now.

Not yet.

He wasn't kidding himself. He knew that was selfish too.

He still was going to give her time, them time, he wasn't going to waste too much of hers, and then he'd give her what she needed to decide.

But now he was going to give her what she wanted.

For a while.

She started moving to him. "Did everything go okay?"

"It's done."

"Good."

She stopped moving when he announced, "I'm gonna fuck you in a second."

Heat hit her gaze and he felt it drive through his dick.

"I'm gonna do it hard and I'm gonna try not to scare you while I do it," he warned. "It gets too intense for you, you say, 'skull,' and I'll back off. That's gonna mean I'm gonna leave you and finish myself off. But if you walk right now to my bedroom, that's what's gonna happen."

She didn't even take a second to think about it.

With a smirk on her lips and heat still in her eyes, she walked right by him, dumping her purse in the armchair as she went.

Core took three deep breaths.

Then he turned on his boot and followed.

SHE WAS LEGS WIDE, belly to the bed, moaning into his comforter as she took his cock.

Her dark hair was all over, she'd curled her fingers into the material at her sides to hold on, and she was egging him on with her cunt.

He was almost there, it was gonna be huge, and this time, he wasn't going to blow in a condom.

So he pulled out, rolled her over, straddled her, slid the condom off and took himself in hand so he could come on her skin.

She watched for a second then moaned, "No," wrapped her fingers around his at his dick and tugged it toward her face.

He followed her lead, she shifted under him, he positioned and thrust into her mouth.

Fucking Christ.

Wet heat.

Her nails went into the flesh of his ass as she took his face fucking, sucking when she could, licking when she got the chance, and *damn*, she was too much, with a grunt then a long, low groan, he shot down her throat.

He glided as she sucked at him before he started losing the hard.

Only then did Core slide out.

He rolled to his back.

He got a couple of breaths in and then her face was over his, her hair curtaining them.

Before she could open her mouth, he ordered, "There's a shiny black bag in my duffel in the laundry room. Go get it."

More bright eyes from Hellen and then she raced off.

He had no idea what she thought her present from LA was going to be, he just hoped she liked it. Then again, when he'd given her a version of it before, she'd gone wild, so he was betting she would.

He was on his side, up on an elbow when she came back.

He'd been looking at the ceiling when she left, so he hadn't noticed her pull on his tee.

He frowned.

She bounced on the bed, settling on her knees, ass to calves, holding the shiny bag that had been crunched in his duffel.

"Can I open it?" she asked.

"Yup."

She pulled the box out, threw the bag to the side, then opened the box.

She'd just drained his dick, but it still stirred at the noise she made when she saw what was inside.

Pink tinged her cheeks as slowly, her eyes came to his.

"You want it?" he asked.

She nodded.

"C'm 'ere, baby," he called gently.

She came to him as he sat up, but twisted and reached to his nightstand.

He got what he needed, took the box from her, took care of business with the tube of lube, then laid back and touched a finger to his mouth before he murmured, "Lose the tee and climb on."

She did as told, and while she rode his face, he slipped her new plug up her ass.

That sound came back when she took it and she rode his face harder.

He held her to him with one hand, reached with the other to grab her tit and squeeze her nipple. He'd fucked her ready, so it didn't take long before she got wild and drenched and came in his mouth.

He held her there to lick her clean while she whimpered, then he dragged her down his body and took her weight, her breaths still sharp against the skin of his neck.

"Good?" he asked.

"Yes," she breathed.

"Missed you," he murmured, giving her a squeeze with his arms.

"I could tell," she replied.

Core smiled at the ceiling.

"I got you something else while I was in LA," he told her. "But you preempted that by giving me crocodile wallpaper, which, warning, if you and your girls have any more plans for surprises, means you'll earn getting fucked, plugged and eaten out."

Her body on his trembled with her laughter.

"And here I am marveling at my newfound knowledge of what a unique gift giver you are," she joked.

"Smartass," he muttered.

She got serious. "I'm not complaining about what you got me."

"Noticed that," he replied, running a hand down her back to her ass, which she tipped just that little bit for him when he got there, something else that stirred his cock.

He touched the cool jewel at the end, the reason for his pick. It was purple.

He was looking forward to seeing that winking at him.

She pressed her face in his throat and whispered, "Are you gonna fuck me there?"

"Want it?"

"I think so."

"Never had it?"

"No."

"We'll try, see how you like it."

"Okay."

He gave the plug a little twist.

She twitched on him and licked his throat.

She was going to like it.

"Ready again?" he asked.

"Had enough of a breather?"

"Is that a challenge?"

She lifted her head and looked down at him.

"Yes."

He surged up.

An hour later, when he got back from the bathroom, he saw his woman sprawled on his bed on her belly, plug winking, eyes closed, passed out.

He smiled to himself, shoving down the unease that rode his every moment with her.

Because at least he bested her challenge.

It was the next morning when she was in her underwear, leaning into the mirror in his bathroom, putting on makeup to get ready for work, when he came in and gave her the other present.

He put the boxes on the basin beside her.

She glanced down at them. "What's this?"

"Your not-sex-related presents from LA."

"I cannot believe you're a man who remembers to pick up gifts on a business trip," she mumbled to herself, but there was his girl, she didn't hide her excitement or hesitate going for the boxes.

But he nearly laughed out loud at the "business trip" thing.

He didn't when he saw her notice the gold lettering on the burgundy box, times two.

So the reason they cost a whack was real. Baccarat meant something.

She opened one, gasped, then opened the other, and gasped at that one too.

"Saw 'em in a shop window and they reminded me of you," he muttered, suddenly feeling super fucking uncomfortable.

Her gaze rose to his and there was no bright excitement and happiness there.

What was there was way fucking bigger than excitement and happiness, he knew that even though he'd never seen that look in his life.

"They're just glass butterflies," he said.

"Crystal," she corrected softly.

"Whatever."

"I love them."

"That was the goal."

She came to him, pressed close, slid her fingers in his hair and pulled him down to get her kiss.

When she finished with his mouth, she whispered, "Thank you."

He needed to break this mood. "I prefer the other gift."

His plan backfired.

She collapsed against him in laughter, and that wasn't better than what he'd seen on her face a minute ago.

But it was a close second.

When she moved away, he went to his back pockets and put the jewelry pouch and a stack of cash wrapped in a paper band on the basin.

"For your friend," he said. "I don't know if any of those are hers, but I grabbed everything that fit the description of what was taken."

Her eyes were huge as she stared at the black velvet and the bills.

"And three grand, bit more than she gave, but whatever. Maybe it'll help with the credit cards."

She looked back to him.

"If none of that jewelry is hers, she can either replace what was taken from her, or she can give you back that pouch. But she only replaces what was taken, she gives the rest back. There's four pairs of pearl studs in there and seven diamond pendants. They had a thing about sitting on shit they stole before they fenced it, and everything everyone got went to the central vault, probably because, if they needed to gift it back out to a mark, they'd have it. So hopefully, not enough time had passed for them to hock her shit before I got my hands on it."

"When you said it's done, you really did it right," she said with a voice and a face full of wonder.

"Resurrection doesn't fuck around, babe," he replied.

Then he left her to get ready for her day.

THAT SATURDAY, after three days of dinner together every night, then sleeping beside her and waking up with her, Core found Hellen lounged on his couch under his skull print with his dog, her feet resting on the back and her laptop open on his coffee table, when he returned from a workout at the clubhouse.

However, she was not, as she told him she was going to do, working.

Both she and Nanook were looking at her phone.

Or she was looking at her phone, Nanook was lying down her side in the curve of her arm and panting.

Core didn't miss that when he showed, Nanook's welcome was not physical, just a pup smile.

His dog didn't leave their woman.

She tipped her head back to take him in, her mass of hair spilling down the side of the couch.

He started instantly to get hard.

"Nanook and I have decided he needs a TikTok," she announced.

"Get to my room and get naked. I'm not going to shower twice."

Her expression changed, then in the next beat she was tossing the phone aside, grabbing Nanook's head, giving him a kiss on it, then she rolled to her feet and strutted down the hall to Core's room.

She didn't hurry.

Even so, when Core followed, to get his shit under some kind of control, he moved a lot slower.

"THIS ONE?" she asked.

They were finished, still in bed, him on his back, her at his side, as well as at his tats.

She was sliding a finger along the ink that trailed under his collarbone that said *Iustitia, Tribus, Honoris, Fidelitas.*

"Justice. Clan. Honor. Allegiance. Resurrection's motto in Latin."

"Cool," she mumbled, then went down to his right rib cage, where he had the head of a roaring bear inked in his skin. "This one?"

"I like bears."

She smiled at him.

He felt his abs contract and his chest get heavy when she slid her finger over the mermaid with a mess of hair floating up, down and all around her, so much of it, some of it covered her naked chest. Her graceful tail curled under her. Her beautiful face was nearly hidden by her hair and the arm she had curled over her head.

It covered his left pec.

It covered his heart.

He knew Hellen would get there eventually.

And he knew what he had to give her when she did.

"This one?"

"My mom loved mermaids."

He heard the tone in his voice, and she didn't miss it either, her gaze racing to his, her hand flattening on the mermaid.

Her hand there, warm and light…

Christ.

"We don't have to talk about it," she said quickly.

"She died an ugly death."

"Okay," she whispered.

"She'd like you. She'd respect you. She'd admire your strength. She let a man break her, and by the time she could do something about it, she was too broken to fix."

Hellen was struggling with that information, so much, she tried to hide it but couldn't.

"Your dad?" she asked carefully.

She was asking if his dad broke his mom.

"Yes," he said clearly.

"Again, we don't have to—"

"He beat her and he took her money. Never knew him to work. Did know him to drink until he was sloppy and mean. He was pure shit. Pure evil and pure shit."

Her expression was startled, he knew, not only at his words, but the fierceness of his tone.

"My God, Core."

It was time.

At least for some of it.

And knowing it was, he was both tense and relieved.

"I got him in me."

She didn't know what she was talking about, and still, her face grew stubborn and she snapped, "You don't."

"I absolutely do."

"Okay, so I have my dad in me too. He's all about money. Working hard and earning. He lost his marriage to it. He lost his family to it. Trying to use it as control, he lost his daughters to it more than once. I started work when I was fifteen and it's been about money since then for me too. I'm borderline obsessed with it. And since we had dinner with him, I've been worried something I admired about myself, maybe wasn't such a good thing."

"There's hustle and there's greed, babe. You want a good life, you work for it, even if that work is long and hard," he returned. "You just want, that being *want*, plain and simple, you let the things that matter suffer so you can feed your need. You're the first, he's the last."

"Yes, there's your wisdom again," she pointed out. "Was your dad wise?"

Point scored for Hellen.

He clenched his teeth.

"You are not shit," she bit off. "And you are *not* evil."

The forcefulness of her tone punched him in the throat.

"I hate that you had a dad like that," she went on. "What happened to him?"

"He's dead too."

She didn't say it, but her face said, *Good.*

"Baby," he started gruffly, not knowing how to lay it out for her, "I've lived some life."

"No shit?" she asked. "You're an Angel of Death, Core. You

started us with a version of 'don't ask, don't tell' about what clearly is your club's bent toward vigilantism. My guess is, to take care of the Greeks, you didn't operate fully within the law. You also didn't sit down with them for a counseling session to show them the error of their ways."

He was drowning here and she was cracking jokes.

Funny jokes, but fuck.

To get his head above water, he pushed up in bed to rest against his headboard and pulled her over him so she was straddling his lap.

"And how do you feel about that?" he asked.

"Preferably, I wouldn't want my boyfriend possibly to be arrested for taking down a multi-state swindling scheme. I was worried when you were gone. I'm afraid to learn how often this happens and how dangerous these operations are. Fortunately for you, my brother-in-law is Chaos, and I watched that documentary about them, so I kinda get it. Though, I'm a victim of seriously conflicting emotions, because what you did for Bree was totally fucking awesome. But it also freaks me way the hell out."

"We're good at what we do," he assured. "We got experience. We train. We've been doing this for—"

"God!" she exclaimed, tipping her head to look at the ceiling. "I don't want to know how long you've been putting yourself in danger!"

With that, she tried to swing off him.

He grabbed her hips and kept her where she was.

"We're not done," he growled.

"What do you want me to say?" she demanded.

"We do what we do because it's who we are. It's never going to change, babe. And it fucks me up, because I dig you a fuckuva lot, but I gotta say, if you can't deal with it, I can't get out of it. Because I can't and because I won't. I made a vow I am not gonna break. What we do is the man I am now, it's the man every brother in my club is, and if you can't hack it, then we can't be."

Her face paled.

"Are you breaking up with me?" she breathed.

"Are you breaking up with me?" he shot back.

Her eyes slitted. "So I can't communicate I'm worried about the fact *you're a fucking vigilante* without you threatening to break up with me?"

"I didn't threaten to break up with you," he clipped.

"Then what does 'then we can't be' mean?" she demanded.

"It doesn't mean I'm threatening to break up with you."

"It means exactly that!" she shouted.

"I was laying it out for you!" he shouted back. "I wasn't fucking breaking up with you!"

"An ultimatum," she bit. "Same thing."

"An ultimatum is a choice, Hellen, it's not the same fuckin' thing. Your choice. Decide."

Her brows arched up. "Right now?"

"Right fucking now," he growled.

She glared at him.

He scowled at her.

She didn't move.

He didn't release the hold he had on her hips.

She was still pissed but he didn't miss the look behind her eyes when she pointed out, "You're hard again."

"Ride it," he grunted.

No hesitation, she reached between them, took hold of his cock and positioned him.

They'd had the conversation that week. She was on the pill, he hadn't fucked anybody since he met her, wasn't going to fuck anybody but her, she promised the same, they were both vaccinated against HPV, and they both carved out time to hit a clinic and came up clean.

So now it was ungloved.

So now her tight heat was also wet, and the minute she sunk down on him, he needed to thrust.

Core tried to move them, but she clamped on to his hair and his throat and snarled, "No."

That was such a huge turn on, he settled, and she rode him fast and hard, glaring into his eyes, pissed as shit and working it out in a way he was never going to argue.

She undulated on top of him, her hair swaying, her tits bouncing, her pussy milking, and he got too close.

"You gotta get there," he gritted.

"Blow," she ordered.

Oh fuck no.

Not before her, not unless he made that decision because he had a plan.

He clenched the flesh of her hips trying to control her flow as he moved in with his finger. "Get there."

She went faster. "Blow, baby."

He was at her clit but she wasn't there.

Fuck.

He yanked her off. She cried out in fury. He put her where he wanted her, on her knees facing the headboard. He got her ass tipped by pulling her hair to arch her back. Then he positioned and drove into her pussy, one hand going for her clit, the other after her tit.

"Not fair," she panted, hands to the headboard to brace for his fucking.

"Get there," he grunted in her ear as he fucked her harder than she could him.

It didn't take long before she whimpered, bucked, shivered in his hold and spasmed around his dick.

Thank, Christ.

He moved to hold her by the back of her neck and watch his wet dick take her below the swells of her sweet ass.

Only then did he blow.

Hard.

Once he came down, he impaled her and rounded her with his arms.

"We're not breaking up," she wheezed.

He grinned, then closed his eyes and rested his forehead against her shoulder.

She had more.

She didn't have it all.

But she had more.

And that was where she landed.

"Your choice, baby."

"You're a fucking dick," she said to the headboard.

He buried his face in the side of her neck and agreed, "Mm-hmm."

"Don't agree with me when I'm still pissed at you."

"Okay, I'm not a dick," he said. "I'm the best boyfriend ever."

He sucked her ear lobe.

She shivered against him.

He slid a hand down her belly and cupped her mound, feeling him still inside, the other hand he used to cup her breast.

"I guess I'll have to put up with you being a fucking vigilante," she groused.

That was cute.

And the relief it washed through him was immense.

But he was dead serious when he promised in her ear, "I'll make it worth it."

"Whatever," she mumbled. "I'm losing you and you shot a huge load, *again*," she accused, like it was his fault she was such a great fuck. "I can already feel it leaking."

He'd never come so hard than with her. Kiki was hot in bed, but Hellen was off the goddamn charts.

He pulled out, kissed her neck, then dropped to his ass, back to the headboard.

She flounced off the bed, and he watched as she flounced to the bathroom, her ass making him rethink his decision that there was no God.

The covers were fucked-up from both their goes. He found an

end and pulled it over his lower half, but the way it was, it left a leg exposed.

She flounced back, and probably to irritate him, he liked her naked, she went to his dresser and pulled out a tee.

She tugged it on and told his exposed foot, "I'm getting water. Do you want water?"

"Come here, Hellen."

She stopped and glowered at his face. "I'll come back after I get water."

"Come here."

She rolled her eyes, flounced to him, and he beat back his smile just as he reached long when she got close, tagged the front of his tee and pulled her into the bed on her knees beside him.

"Okay, Cutler, I'm here," she pointed out the obvious.

"We're new, but you're important to me," he said gently.

She rubbed her lips together, not ready to let it go.

"And they're my brothers. Mom dead, they're the only family I have. Truth, they're the only real family I ever had. And each and every one of them, baby, they'd die for me."

Her mood cracked, he saw it and felt it.

"Something for you to think on," he told her. "With that, it's never a you-or-them thing. If we get there, it will be an us thing. They'd die for you too. Are you getting me?"

"I probably should meet them, you know, just in case one day the impossible happens and they have to do something that dramatic for me."

He felt his lips twitch.

But he agreed, "Yeah, you should."

"I'm glad you have that family, Core."

She meant it.

Still, she said it like a threat because she was holding on to being ticked.

His lips twitched again before he ordered, "Stop being pissed at me."

She turned her head and gave him the side-eye.

He moved fast, tackled her to her back, pulled his tee up to her tits and kissed her exposed belly.

He then loomed over her and said, "I'll get our water," before he laid a wet one on her.

When he was done, she didn't look pissed anymore.

Once he saw that, Core rolled off her, the bed, and it felt like his body weighed less as he went to get them some water.

Even so, there was still heavy.

But at least he'd given her more.

And she didn't leave.

17

OH BIKER GURU

Hellen

The next day, Sunday, the bell over the door rang, and Core and I strode in tucked tight together by Core's arm slung over my shoulder.

The instant we did, we heard bellowed, "*Now that's what I'm talkin' about! ALL RIGHT!*"

I looked to the espresso counter at Fortnum's to see Tex turned to the side and pumping his arm, at the end of which was a clenched fist holding a portafilter.

He stopped, swung the portafilter in our direction, and the patrons in front of the counter stepped aside in a practiced dance as the wet espresso grounds in the filter gave up their fight to adhere to the safety of the filter and went flying. They landed with a splat on the other side of the counter.

"Traded up, girl! I approve!" he shouted. "Free coffee for you!"

"For the last time, Tex!" the redhead added her own shout. "Stop giving away coffee at your whim and *stop throwing coffee grounds.*"

Tex completely ignored her (then again, I'd heard her shout at him "for the last time" more than once, and we could see the results of that).

All the patrons ignored this too.

This meant they were regulars.

I looked up at Core. "Does he know you?"

A short nod. "Everyone knows Tex."

Okay then.

Time for me to ignore *that*, considering Tex had grenades.

Though, perhaps an explanation about how Tex knew of my girls' and my shenanigans.

Core steered us toward the comfortable furniture in front of the window.

Marcy was there, watching us with approval. Kyra was there, watching us with a dreamy look in her eyes.

And shit.

Ambush.

My sister was there, staring at Core with speculation.

Noticeably absent?

Bree.

We'd told her we were going to meet up and asked her to come.

She had not deigned to reply.

Core stopped us and said to Kyra. "Thanks for the crocodile wallpaper."

God, he was just *awesome.*

She bounced in the couch. "You like?"

"It's the shit."

She beamed.

"You know about Kyra, and essentially introduced yourself, but this is my sister, Liane," I introduced.

The twinge of nerves I had when I saw her there faded away when Core didn't blink. He just let me go to reach out a hand to her.

"Liane," he greeted.

She didn't reach out a hand.

Apparently, she'd turned into a biker bitch since I saw her last.

I thought this because she reached out a fist for a bump, saying, "Yo, bro."

Yo, bro?

He gave her the bump, but then she tried to do some complicated handshake with him that he didn't know. Core was game, but it went on so long, eventually he caught her hand in both of his and said, "Cool to meet you."

Marcy snickered.

I ordered my sister, "Stop being a dork."

Li ignored me.

"Crooked Road is my favorite dispensary in all of Denver," my sister complimented my guy about his business.

"Glad to hear it."

"Just, you know, for future reference," she went on. "Do you give family discounts?"

Marcy snickered again. Kyra giggled.

I snapped, "Liane!"

But Core chuckled and said, "We do now."

I curled into his side and put my hand to his flat abs.

When he tipped his head down to look at me, I advised, "Ignore her."

"No," he replied simply, bent and touched his lips to mine, then turned to the group. "Enjoy girl time." Back to me. "Call me when you're done." Another quick kiss and he sauntered out, the bell ringing as his goodbye.

The redhead handed me a coffee. "On the house, I guess."

"I'll pay," I said quietly so Tex wouldn't hear me.

"Not a problem. Seriously, I'm more ticked about the coffee grounds that *I* have to clean up *again*."

She then took off to clean them up.

I settled in an armchair.

No one said anything for a moment.

Then Kyra cried excitedly, "You're so loved-up, *I could die*."

"He's hot," Liane decreed.

I took a sip and glanced at Marcy.

She said nothing.

But she was smiling.

THE NEXT SATURDAY, I was on the couch on Core's back patio, my laptop resting on my crossed legs.

I heard the French door open.

Nanook, who was lying on the rug in front of me, let out a mini-howl of greeting.

Core, who was hanging out the door, called, "You need anything?"

I didn't answer him.

Instead, I said, "I'll be done in a little while."

"That wasn't my question," he pointed out.

My lips curled up. "No, I don't need anything."

"Cool, baby," he said, nonchalantly lifted up his chin then disappeared from the door, and it closed.

I stared at it for a second.

I heard Nanook settle in.

Then I got back to work.

A WEEK and three days later, I was sitting in my office with Xanthia sitting across from me.

Xanthia was my new PA.

She was great.

"A conference," she said.

"Sorry?" I asked.

"Invite your clients to a conference. Somewhere cool, not Vegas or Orlando. Some quiet spa retreat in Big Sur, or wine, foodie place in Monterrey, or desert oasis in Sedona. Someplace I can get us discounts on rooms and services. We figure out a cost that isn't crazy that they have to pay, but cover some of it so it seems like a bene of service from you. We do classes, panels, maybe spring for an expert, a whole share-the-knowledge and brainstorm-the-future and create-the-next-trend thing. But not too much so they can get massages. It needs to seem like a vacation that's a write-off. And while they're there, you announce your new slate of client features. They'll be lulled by the surroundings to understand your awesomeness, and they'll sign on."

And there it was.

Xanthia was great.

"That's an insanely good idea," I replied.

She looked pleased.

"Can you add to your tasks, doing some research to find a venue? Not urgent. I need to tweak the new menu and look at the financials, so there's time."

Now she looked excited. "Totally can do that."

My new-client call brought in five new customers, and I'd mentioned to two I already had I was going to be offering full-spectrum services, and they'd shifted up a level so I could oversee their websites and affiliate links. This was an indication that there might be others who had grown so much, they were ready to outsource those kinds of tasks. Not to mention, Xanthia was still learning the ropes.

So there was a lot of work to be done.

But I had no doubt she totally could do that.

Yes, she was great.

And yes, the decision to hire her was the right one.

I wasn't only relieved.

I was exhilarated and ready for what came next.

Mom and I had margaritas.

We also had eye candy.

This was in the form of Core, Beck, Eight, Muzzle and Andy carefully erecting a new fence behind the shrubbery at the edge of Core's yard.

They did this with Nanook's constant supervision.

Apparently, it was sweaty work.

Hmm...

I'd used the new-fence ploy to sneak a meet-the-parents in that wouldn't seem overly wrought and would give Andy the excuse to do something Andy, for some reason, loved to do.

Manual labor.

My ploy was a wild success.

By the way, Liane wasn't there because she was working. And Archie and Jagger weren't there because apparently Archie and Jagger were taking advantage of the waning throes of summer and were on an extended trip somewhere on his bike. It involved a yurt. After I heard that word, I quit listening. Still, I hoped they were having fun.

Elijah wasn't there because I didn't invite him (I really needed to get over that).

I hadn't understood why Core wanted to tear down that fence, but now that the new one was going up, I saw it. It completed his backyard vision.

Well, that, and the toss pillows and smattering of lanterns I'd gotten, and the rusted, reclaimed steel wall sculpture of a motorcycle Kyra had found and Core had mounted over the fireplace.

Core might argue my contribution was part of that backyard completion, but he didn't complain when he rested his head on a toss pillow as he was stretched with me on his couch and we were kicking back with the fire going.

I got a text from Kyra. It was a picture with the words, *For the dining room.*

I pulled up the picture.

Straight up, she had this down.

I showed Mom.

She disapproved.

"Honey, he really needs a dining room table."

"He has a kitchen table."

She gave me a, *think of your future* look.

I was.

And I liked my thoughts.

I got up and strolled to where the men were working.

Core was the only one who stopped what he was doing to watch me.

I didn't mind the sweat one bit and communicated this by leaning in to give him a kiss.

"You guys need water?" I asked.

"That'd be good," he answered.

I showed him my phone. "Kyra's suggestion for the dining room."

His lips curled up. "Get it."

I knew he'd love it.

That was when my lips curled up.

I walked back to the house, hearing Mom sigh as I set my margarita down before I went in to get the men some water.

She knew.

Okay, so the way it was going, one day, Core and I might discuss hosting a Thanksgiving or something, and for that, we'd need a dining room table.

But that day was not today.

I delayed hydrating the guys to tell Kyra to order the gray pool table with black felt for Core's dining room.

Then I took care of my dad, my man and his friends.

THAT EVENING, Beck, Eight and Muzzle were gone, Liane had come over after work and she was playing Frisbee with Nanook in the yard, and Mom was with Core at his bar, fussing with some food preparation while he made us dinner.

Andy and I were hanging on the couch.

I had eyes to Mom and Core.

We'd been together every night since he got home from LA.

It wasn't a decision thing, as in, "Hey, wanna come over?"

It was simply our thing, as in, before I left in the mornings, Core asked if I had any preferences for dinner because he knew we'd be sharing it. And if I had an answer, I'd give him that answer because I knew the same.

He cooked. It was his thing. We'd go out on occasion. I'd rustle something up on occasion.

But for the most part, he fed me. He liked doing it, I liked eating it because he was good at it, but there was something more there for him. Part of his protection mode, definitely his provider instinct.

And, I sensed, his mom taught him more than just how to make cornbread.

So it was his way to be with her memory.

At first, I thought Mom butting in would mess with his mojo.

I shouldn't have worried.

He was gentle, respectful, gave over space to her as a mom who needed to do these kinds of things like she needed to breathe.

They worked great together.

And there was something beautiful, watching Core with Mom. He wasn't young enough for her to be a mother figure to him, but there was a version of the care and respect he gave to me that was gorgeous to see.

"I like him," Andy said low.

I turned my attention to him, my heart tripping.

"He's solid," Andy continued. "Knows how to work with his hands. Isn't afraid of hard work. And he thinks the world of you."

Andy's approval meant everything.

He pulled me into him with an arm around my shoulders.

"Who woulda thunk, two of my girls with bikers. I like it."

I did too.

Oh yes.

I liked it too.

My car rang, and it was Core.

I took the call by saying, "I'll be there in a jiffy. I'm just going to give her a shot to look over the stuff and get out of there."

"I don't like this," he replied.

This wasn't the first time he'd said that.

Quick catch up:

It was now late September. We'd been together a month and a half.

Everything with Core was awesome.

Actually, everything was just awesome.

My family loved Core. My friends loved Core.

Nanook loved me.

I was constantly sexed up in a happy way.

Work was good.

Life was good.

Now, although I'd met Beck, Muzzle and Eight (obviously), also Web (Beck and Web were who hired me to do the social media for the dispensaries), I hadn't been introduced to the rest of the club.

It was a thing to get everyone together for a full Resurrection shindig. It took time.

The time was now.

It was happening this afternoon, with Marcy and Kyra coming to a party they were having at the clubhouse (Li couldn't make it, she was working again).

This was a big thing, not only Core bringing me to meet his brothers, the men inviting my girls too.

"It's a closed clubhouse, babe," he told me. "We don't let everybody in."

I could tell, even though the words were simple, the meaning was not.

I was a bit nervous, but mostly excited.

I was excited because it was happening. I knew it, though I'd never done it.

Still, I recognized it.

I was falling in love.

Our big blowout about Core's club's activities was behind us. I got why he thought he wasn't good for me (with that and his issues about his dad).

We were beyond that now.

It wasn't lost on me it was intense and going fast. We each had our lives, but when the time came, we didn't like to be apart. I was rarely at home anymore. I had a ton of stuff at Core's—in his bathroom, his closet, his dresser.

We were practically living together.

And it worked.

It didn't just work.

It was right.

And the only time we fought outside that Saturday afternoon that seemed forever ago, was when he tried to pay me back for the things I did to his living room (he won).

And the disagreement we were now having about Bree.

In other words, the only pall during this time was that Bree was giving us the silent treatment. No texts, no calls.

I didn't know what to think about this except it was bullshit. I hadn't said whacked things, she had.

I'd been trying to contact her for weeks, telling her I had what Core got from the Greeks. And the operative words were, Core put his ass on the line to get them from the Greeks.

Still no go.

I didn't know what to do, because I wanted her to have her things back if what I had contained what she lost, but I couldn't leave them outside her door.

Incidentally, this unnerved Kyra, but it pissed off Core and Marcy.

Which led to now, me heading to his after spending some time in the office and hitting my place to get ready to meet Core's brothers, but I was going to pop by her apartment to give her the stuff.

Core was adamantly against a drop by. He didn't want me around her unless I knew how she would receive me, and however she did wouldn't upset me.

But what was I supposed to do?

"It's going to be fine," I assured. "If she's bitchy, I'll leave the jewelry with her and tell her to call me when she's gone through it. Then I'll swing around and pick it up."

"Don't want you leaving thousands of bucks of jewelry with that woman."

Bree had become "that woman" to Core because, a) she was jacking me around and he could tell it hurt me, and b) she was jacking Marcy and Kyra around, he liked them and it hurt them too.

"Okay, then if she's bitchy, I'll just give her the money and tell her I might have her necklace and earrings, but if she can't be civil, we'll wait until she can and try again."

"Don't even give her the money. If she's a bitch, leave."

I was not going to do this. It was her nest egg. I was her friend. Sure, we were in a rough patch that might end with us drifting away from each other, but she needed it. I had it. Core put his ass on the line to get it for her. I was going to give it to her.

"Okay," I lied.

"And she lies to me," he muttered.

Eerie how well he knew me already.

Totally going fast and being intense.

I was pulling up on the curb outside Bree's house, so I said, "I'm here. And I'll be at yours in half an hour. Tops."

"Better be," he grunted. "Love you. Later."

And he hung up.

I sat in my idling car, frozen.

Love you. Later.

Was that throwaway?

He'd never said it before.

Oh my God and what the fuck!

I was going to *kill him* for dropping that on me when I was about to confront Bree. Of course he'd know I would hear that and want to get to him ASAP.

Hot, sexy-as-fuck, biker *schemer*.

Argh!

I switched off the ignition, grabbed my purse, which had the jewelry pouch and money in it, got out of my car and headed up to her apartment.

I considered covering the peephole after I hit her doorbell so I had a better chance of her opening it to me if she didn't actually see it was me, but I didn't.

Surprisingly, the door opened quickly.

My heart lifted.

Then it fell right to my feet.

"Yeah, I want mayo," Bryan called over his shoulder, not looking my way.

Then he looked my way, his face lost all color, and he grew statue still.

"Pringles?" Bree yelled from somewhere in her house (obviously, the kitchen) and then, "Who is it?"

Bryan moved out, right into me, so I had no choice but to move back.

This nearly made me fall over the step that led up to Bree's door, and he reached out and caught me.

I tore my arm away from his hold and took another step back, this time carefully.

He shut the door behind him, not taking his eyes off me.

"Hellen."

My name was strangled. Agonized. And that was when I knew this wasn't just a friendly thing. Such as, they knew each other and regardless of our breakup, they liked each other enough to hang out together.

I knew it even before I read in his eyes the guilt and shame and love and regret, and so many awful, ugly things, all of them washing over me, it felt like I was about to be swept away by them.

At that juncture, the door opened and Bree came out.

She had her mouth open to speak as she rounded Bryan and saw me, then she, too, went pale and still.

"Go inside," Bryan ordered Bree.

She didn't even twitch, just stood there gaping at me.

And there was guilt there too. And shame and love and regret.

Fucking hell.

I hated it when Core was right.

"Go inside!" he snapped.

She jolted, shaking her head. Slowly it swung toward Bryan, but he was on the move again.

To me.

"Okay, okay, Hellen," he started, coming forward, and I was again going back. "It's not what it seems."

I peeked around him to see Bree staring at his back like he'd plunged a knife in her chest.

It was what Bree thought it seemed to be.

Oh my God.

Could this get worse?

"She reached out after we had that issue at Fortnum's. It just happened. It's not a thing."

Bree made a choking noise from behind him.

She reached out after Fortnum's.

She, that being my friend of six years, my once roommate, my sometimes partner in crime, one of my four ride or dies (Li being the OG), *Bree* reached out to Bryan, my ex.

That was weeks ago.

Was it before or after she gave me shit about downgrading to Core?

I stopped retreating.

Bryan stopped too.

"It's just...God...*fuck!*" he exploded, tearing his hand through his hair.

I took a step away from his emotion.

He lifted a hand to me. "No. I wouldn't hurt you. That isn't me. I wouldn't touch you like that again, Hellen. This is just dicked up. This isn't what it seems. You...to me, what you are to me..."—he sucked in a huge breath—"This is just dicked up."

"It is that," I agreed quietly.

"God, can we..." He looked back to Bree, then to me and got minutely closer as he made his choice. "Can we go somewhere and talk?"

There it was.

It could get worse.

"You fucker," I heard Bree whisper.

He turned to her.

"We'll talk too."

"Oh yeah? We will?" she demanded, beginning to lose it.

I wanted nothing to do with this.

Sure, at the time they got together, things were over for Bryan and me.

However, maybe one of my best friends could wait until he finished all his laundry and washed away my perfume before she jumped at her chance.

I dug in my purse, took out the money and extended it to Bryan.

"Here, it's what Christos stole from her. It's been retrieved."

Mutely, he took it.

I leaned to the side to catch her eyes. "Like I said when I tried to get ahold of you, I also have some earrings and necklaces, and yours might be among them." I flapped a hand between them. "But I'm gonna let you two work this out. I'll give them to Kyra. You can contact her to make a time to look at them and see."

I turned to walk away and Bryan called urgently, "Hellen!"

I turned back. "You know, you...you were free." His face fell. "But still, going there with my friend that close to our breakup, uncool." I leaned to the side and jabbed a finger at Bree. "But *you, you* know what you did."

She knew.

I knew it when she got so defensive, she shrieked, "*You were with another guy!*"

I shook my head and said, "You know."

And then I left them both to be dicks to each other and not to me, got in my car and drove away.

"WHAT'D I TELL YOU?"

God, he could be so annoying.

"I said I didn't like it," he reminded me.

We were in Core's truck even though I wanted to be on his bike, but he didn't want us to be on his bike because he couldn't say I told you so if we were on his bike (which was why I wanted to be on his bike, incidentally, that and I loved being on the back of his bike with him, (that part of Archie and Jagger's weeks-long sojourn totally made sense to me)).

"You're done with her, yeah?" he asked.

"Of course," I answered.

"Him?" he pushed.

I looked to him and saw how he was scowling at the street.

"We're over, honey."

"I know you're over. You sucked my dick this morning like you wanted to swallow it. I might have to put a bit in your mouth when you go down on me to slow you down so I don't lose it. Woman gives a man head like that, she's not into her ex."

God!

He could be *so annoying*!

"I could stop giving you head," I suggested fake sweetly.

He made a scoffing noise.

That made me mad.

"I can live without your cock, Cutler."

"You can, baby?" he taunted.

Okay, maybe I couldn't.

I turned to Nanook who was snuffling at the open window in the back.

Since we took the truck, I insisted on Nanook coming with.

"At least you're never annoying," I cooed.

He knew my cooing voice, loved my cooing voice, stopped snuffling and woofed, "I love you," at me.

"I love you too."

"Babe," Core growled.

"I'm done with them, all right? Both of them," I snapped. "Yeesh. You were right. I shouldn't have dropped by. Obviously, the silent treatment was hiding something, oh wise soul. Oh biker guru. I should have listened to you."

"You are so getting spanked tonight," he muttered.

I rolled my eyes. "Like that's a threat."

"Catwoman, we've played, but we haven't gotten as serious as I can get, and I promise you, your claws are no match for me."

Wow.

That sounded promising.

I smirked at the windshield. "We'll see."

"Yeah, we will," he purred.

Man, he could cause a clit spasm even when he was being exasperating.

Whatever.

We made it to the clubhouse without him further vexing me, and the nerves came back, more than ever.

This wasn't going to be just the brothers. Their old ladies were going to be there too, and I hadn't met any of them yet.

This was like Core having to meet a dozen Andys *and* Moms *and* Lianes all at once.

He parked and turned to me.

"They're gonna love you."

"How do you know?"

"Because I love you."

He dropped that bomb, threw open his door and knifed out.

I threw mine open too and dropped down, Nanook coming with me.

Core was strolling around the hood of the truck like he hadn't just rocked my world.

I was staring at him in shock.

He took my hand and started dragging me to the doors of his clubhouse.

I planted my feet, skidded a bit, he stopped and looked back at me.

"Don't think you can lay that on me and then just take me to a party," I informed him.

He moved into me, held my hand tight, cupped my jaw and dropped his face to mine.

"You have that. You give it back when and if you feel it. But until that time, you know you have it from me. And now, can I go get a beer?"

"I've never been in love," I told him.

His gaze grew guarded. "All right."

"Still, I know I feel that for you."

His gaze became something else.

And then he said, "Thanks for that, though I knew it with the way you suck my dick."

I felt my eyes get huge, I pushed his chest with my free hand and stepped back.

He started laughing, yanked on my arm, I collided with him, and he bent me over his arm and laid a long, wet one on me.

We made out for a while in front of his clubhouse, and when we finally surfaced, he asked, "Now can I have a beer?"

I rolled my eyes.

He shot me his Hollywood smile, whistled for Nanook, who was exploring, and pulled me in to meet his family, his dog following.

Once inside, my eyes became adjusted only for me to become surprised, because it was *lit*. Pool tables and awesome leather furniture and an amazing bar.

I didn't know what I was expecting, maybe something worn in and a little dodgy but in a cool way, like the Chaos Compound.

This was not that at all.

People were looking at us.

I clocked Marcy and Kyra already at seats at the bar, Beck behind it, talking to them, and I was about to pull Core that way to start my meet and greet easy when Core called out to my friends, "Bryan and Bree are fucking."

My chest collapsed.

What was he doing?

He knew Marcy!

Marcy's eyes got so big in her head, I thought they'd pop out.

Kyra looked sick.

Then Marcy screeched, "*What!?*"

Core took us that way, explaining (loudly), "Hellen dropped by to give her the stuff we retrieved, and Bryan opened the door."

"Oh my fucking *God!*" Marcy shouted.

I darted my eyes around.

We totally had onlookers, and those onlookers, it appeared, were every breathing being in the place.

Including Nanook.

"Marce, calm down," I mumbled.

"Calm down?" she asked. "Are you shitting me?"

"This can't be," Kyra said in a small voice.

Marcy's head swung to her, and that was when she blew her stack (no, the other shouting wasn't Marcy blowing her stack, as would prove true in five seconds).

She hopped off the barstool, stabbing at her phone.

I pulled my hand free from Core's, shooting him a scorching glare that should have made his hair catch fire, and moved to Marcy.

She was pacing with the phone to her ear.

"Marce—" I tried.

"Yeah, bitch," she snapped, took the phone from her ear, and stabbed it again. "You better believe I'm calling."

"I can't do this right now. It's been a shitty day," Bree whined over the speaker.

"No shit? Your girl comes over to *hand you the cash that was stolen from you and her man put himself out there to get back for you* and she finds out you're banging her ex who's been her ex for like...*a day*?"

"It hasn't been *a day*," Bree returned.

"No, no, no, no, no," Marcy chanted. "Sister Book states quite clearly that the statute of limitations to move in on a woman's ex is at least a year, two if you're going for sister sainthood, and you're fucking him *now*?" Marcy looked to a woman who was sitting in a man's lap, smiling at her, and she asked, "Am I right?"

"Girl, you so are!" the woman shouted gleefully.

"You hear that?" Marcy asked.

"Where are you?" Bree asked back.

Marcy didn't answer her.

She said, "Hellen is tough. She's over him and doesn't give a shit. But Kyra thought more of you. You hurt her with this. You hurt her, Bree."

"Well, I'm not with him anymore. We broke up. He flipped out Hellen caught us. He's still in love with her. Like, *right in front of me* he *chose her*. So you all can be happy."

Core made a scary noise behind me, and I dropped my head.

Needless to say, I kinda skirted that part in my retelling of the situation.

Kyra walked up at that juncture and took the phone from Marcy.

"You're not nice," she said into it, hit a button and handed it back to Marce. "She's stupid. This is stupid. Aren't we supposed to be at a party?"

"Damn straight, darlin'," a man I'd gauge was at least a decade older than Core called.

I felt Core's heat behind me.

"You got something to share?" he asked.

I whipped around. "It wasn't necessary information."

His brows shot up. "How could he choose you?"

"He just"—I flicked my hands out at the sides—"asked me if we could go somewhere and talk when she was right there. That's it. Obviously, I didn't go anywhere to talk with him."

"Why didn't you share this with me?"

"I don't know," I noted sarcastically. "I mean, what I did share got you telling me I told you so and gloating about how much I love your cock. So leaving them to their damage so I could get to you when Bryan made it clear he wasn't over me, what would that get me?"

Core scowled down at me.

I glared up at him.

An arm caught me around my chest and yanked me backward into a solid body as a man shouted, "I vote she's in!"

I looked up to see Eight had hold of me.

"All in favor," he yelled.

There was a chorus of, "Ayes!"

Well, at least that happened.

"We're claiming her friends too," the woman on the couch called.

I looked toward Marcy and Kyra. Kyra looked shy and pleased. Marcy smiled slowly at me.

A very pretty woman got close, hooked her arm with mine, pulled me away from Eight and toward the bar, saying, "Hi. I'm Janna. I'm Beck's. And I think you need a drink."

No truer words had ever been spoken.

I went with her, glaring over my shoulder at Core.

But he was over it.

I knew with the soft look on his face, the tenderness in his eyes.

He knew I loved him.

And he loved me back.

So okay.

I was over it too.

18

PAST SINS AND ALL

Core

Core sat at the bar.

Muzzle was next to him, back to the bar, elbows on it.

Both of them had heads turned toward the pool table where Spartan was absolutely murdering Hellen at a game of pool.

She was terrible.

It was hilarious.

Marcy, who they'd learned that night knew her way around a stick, thought this was as funny as Core did, and she was alternately giving Hellen shit and trying to teach her how to play.

Spartan wasn't holding back on giving her shit either.

But there was his woman, she didn't get pissed they were ribbing her. She was shoveling it right back.

Peanut and Rainman were taking her back, both of them trying to break Spartan's concentration.

But the man had probably played five thousand games of pool in his life. Core knew through experience he could wipe the floor with you in his sleep.

As shit as she was at it, she had no chance.

Still, in the thick of this, there she was, fancy cream sweater tucked in just at the button of her jeans, strutting around the table in her high-heeled booties, wearing fuck-me makeup and having get-on-your-knees hair, total style and still looking born to be in the clubhouse of an MC.

Core knew it would be like that.

And he knew the crew would dig her.

Kyra and Janna were curled up together in a couch, half watching what was happening at the pool table, half bonding.

"Seems that crew might even out, they take on Janna," Muzzle noted.

It was true.

Two outgoing women who called them as they saw them, two women who were good to show their soft side.

Maybe that was why Bree didn't fit. She didn't sound like she was the first, she also wasn't the last.

Odd man out never felt good, but she sure as fuck found a shit way to cut herself loose.

Janna was like Kyra, and then some. Janna was shy, quiet, could sometimes be straitlaced. She hadn't slotted into the old lady role easily. Beck had his work cut out for him to make her feel part of the family.

He put that work in, she got there.

That said, Janna was no Queen Bee.

She wasn't like Tyra had been during Tack's tenure as President of the Chaos MC. And she wasn't like Rebel was now that Rush was prez.

For Resurrection, when that role needed someone to fill it, that fell to Peanut, Rainman's woman.

No, Janna loved to look after her old man and the two kids they'd made. She loved her family, all of it, and they loved her. But she liked to fade into the background, and since that was what she needed, that was what they gave her.

And anyway, Peanut, Ducks (Web's woman) and Choppy (Spartan's old lady) more than represented the ballsy biker bitch contingent of the Resurrection MC.

When they were Bounty, he couldn't remember those women being much more than watchful, unless they got drunk, which gave them permission to get wild.

But shit, they flourished when the brothers pulled their heads out of their asses.

It was a lesson for all the men, but especially the single ones, Eight, Muzzle and Core.

And when they were on their mountain, they made sure to impart this wisdom to the new brothers, Shimmy and Brain (who was already taken), and they'd give it to Speed and Linus when it was their time to patch in.

That lesson being, when you were so under the shit that buried you, you could lose sight of the fact, if someone was tied to you, you'd bury them in that shit right along with you.

Rosalie knew that even before they did what they did.

Same with Pea, Chop and Ducks, they knew it too.

It was just the men who had to get their shit tight, something they did.

Now, it was good.

Nope.

Watching Hellen and her girls, for Core, it was awesome.

And he wanted to feel the fullness of that.

But he couldn't.

"Janna could use a posse," Muzzle noted.

He was right. Pea, Ducks and Chop were great women, but not only were they polar opposites in terms of personalities, they were older than Janna.

She never seemed lonely, she was in so deep for Beck and their kids.

But she sure as shit looked content where she was right then, gabbing with Kyra.

"Up to Hellen," Core grunted. "It's her crew."

Muzzle turned to him. "Yeah." Then he changed the subject. "We're a team this week out on rounds."

"I know."

"Might have a sitch. Beck didn't want to get into it with this going down tonight, he'll brief us tomorrow."

Great.

Muzzle studied him a beat then said, "Not sure why you look like someone ran over your puppy. She's the shit. Everyone loves her."

"I haven't told her."

Muzzle knew exactly what Core was saying, that was why his lips thinned.

"I know." Core looked down at his beer and muttered, "Fuck."

"You gotta tell her, brother."

He looked to Muzz. "No shit?"

Muzzle turned fully to him. "I noticed, and I don't sleep with her, so I figure you noticed too that she's in deep for you, man."

"Told me she loves me," Core murmured.

"Okay then," Muzzle said. "You love someone, you love them, past sins and all."

Core was getting pissed. "Yeah? Where's your old lady again? Since, when you had to do this, it went so well for you."

At that, Muzz got pissed.

"We're not talking Janna here," Core continued. "And that's no shade on her, but Hellen broke up with her last man because he didn't put plastics in the recycling bin."

Muzzle's brows shot up. "No shit?"

Core shook his head. "It was more. He was a lazy ass and a dick. Kiki got up in my shit about that kind of thing when we were together. It's no skin. It's important to her, you recycle, for fuck's sake."

Muzzle had been the youngest of them back in the day, now the new men were younger than him. Even so, to Core, sometimes it felt like he was still the baby of the bunch.

And Muzzle had yet to have a long-term relationship, or at least one that lasted more than a year.

In that moment, Muzzle appeared to be filing this away for future reference, which might explain why Muzz, every once in a while, as he waded through the bitches he seemed to attract, he would find a decent one, and then he'd do some stupid shit and lose her.

Muzzle absorbing that knowledge almost made Core smile.

But he didn't.

He knew Muzzle was going to give it to him before he did it, so Core braced.

"What I said earlier is true. She doesn't love you if she doesn't love you, past sins and all. You know I'm not making light of our history. I'm just saying, you are not that man anymore. You put a lot of work into not being that man. And if she doesn't know it, then she's not the right woman."

Hearing those last words spoken, he loved Muzz, but it took a lot not to land a fist in his face.

He didn't.

He took a long pull of his beer.

"Think about that, because I'm right and you know it," Muzzle told his profile. "And then tell her, because the longer you wait, brother, the shittier it is you waited. And that will be all on you."

Core knew he spoke true.

About all of it.

"She's heading this way, Core, and the woman is skipping."

Instantly, Core turned his head so he could watch that.

Hellen wasn't exactly skipping. She led with only her left foot, so it was more like galloping.

It was still cute as all fuck, which meant when she got to him, he'd turned on his stool to face her, and he was grinning.

She collapsed between his spread legs, pressed to his crotch and abs, her hands flat on his chest, her head tipped back.

Christ, she was something.

And she loved him.

Said it straight.

I love you too.

He curled an arm around her.

"So, according to Choppy, I need a club name," she declared.

She then raised her brows like he could lay one on her right then.

"Foxy," Muzzle decreed.

She turned her head in Muzz's direction and shouted, "Ohmigod! *I love that.*"

Shit, she was drunk.

And Core loved *that* because it meant she was having a good time, not to mention it was going to make things even more fun when they got home.

She arched into him, pressing against his dick like his last thought was a promise she was giving, as she called, "Muzzle just named me Foxy!"

"Ohmigod!" Marcy yelled. "I love that!"

"Second that emotion," Choppy shouted.

"Yee ha!" Peanut hollered.

Hellen came back to him. "I think that's going to stick."

"Reckon it is, baby," he murmured, smiling down at her.

"I suck at pool," she announced.

"Noticed that."

She pressed into him again, lifting up on her toes, and stage-whispered, "I think they like me."

He heard Muzzle chuckle.

"Told you," he replied.

She rolled her eyes.

Core wondered how long they had to stay.

He needed her home.

He needed to be inside her.

And he needed to figure out the words to use when he gave it to her, past sins and all.

On the whole, in bed (or in the shower, or on the couch, or against the kitchen counter), they tended to get nasty.

Core liked to fuck, obviously.

Hellen liked to get fucked, down and dirty.

She let loose and she gave over.

She was her own woman in the world.

She let him own her in bed.

That night, though, even if she was slightly inebriated, he didn't go there.

Missionary, her legs wrapped around his ass, her eyes holding his through the dark, their fingers laced, he moved inside her, slow and easy, and watched her take it, watched her feel it.

Watched her understand what he was saying.

He knew when it was building, because he started going faster. She lifted her hips to meet his thrusts, her heels digging in to pull her up, her fingers tightening in his, stretching the webbing to the point it stung, her other arm sliding around him and holding close.

"Love you," he rumbled.

"Love you too," she whispered.

He smiled down at her beautiful face, feeling her pussy grip him tightly, like she wanted him inside always and didn't want to let go.

Anytime he was inside her, he wanted that too.

It was the way of nature when it was right.

And for them, it was right.

So it started happening, and he had no choice but to go at her faster, harder. She took it, met it, coaxed it.

And then she gave it.

Once she did, he gave his too.

When it was done, he rolled so she was on top.

She kissed his skin, nuzzled him, she did this awhile before she settled, her cheek to his collarbone.

Core loved every touch.

At the same time it scared the shit out of him, because he knew he could lose it.

"Okay, that answers that question. Sex is more profound when you love the person inside you, and you know they love you too," she whispered against his skin.

Core arched his neck, shut his eyes tight, and felt his chest seize.

Fuck, he had to tell her.

He didn't tell her.

He righted himself and shared, "Gonna be late a couple of times this week."

She lifted to look down at him and didn't ask questions, didn't demand answers, didn't give him even a modicum of shit, because she loved him and took him as he was.

She just didn't know all he was.

"You want me to stay at mine?" she asked.

"No. Unless you want me to go there when I'm done."

Her lips curled up. "I'll text where I'm at and you can go wherever."

"Right."

She kissed him, pulled away and said, "Gonna clean up."

"'Kay, baby," he murmured. "Be fast. Want you right back."

"I will," she promised, kissed him again and slid off him.

He watched through the shadows as she walked to the bathroom. He also watched as Nanook got up from lying beside the bed so he could follow her.

He needed to tell her.

And he would.

Soon.

It was overkill and corny as fuck, but since it seemed to work, when the dude showed in his kitchen and switched on the light, Core was leaning in the doorway that led to the man's living room, making a play of cleaning his fingernails with the tip of his knife.

Muzzle sat at the kitchen table, drumming fingers on it that shone with the steel of some brass knuckles.

"So," Core said casually. "Yeah, it's been a minute since we checked in."

The guy stood stock still, and no fucking joke, right there, he wet himself.

Indication this fuck knew he broke the rules.

Considering the bent of that indication, Core wondered why he did.

But they weren't there to ask questions.

They were there to repeat a message.

"Usually," Core went on, "we don't have to deliver a message twice."

"I'll—" the guy began.

Core flipped his knife in front of him and caught it by the hilt. Another shit move he'd never normally do, but he'd practiced it after he did it in the course of a situation that was happening, and the dude they were seeing to loosened his bowels just watching him do it.

So Core added it to his catalog.

This guy watched Core's work with the knife and made moves to make a getaway.

"Dude, you know we'll catch you." Muzzle entered the conversation. "And this already should be an unnecessary stop for us. It's put me in a bad mood. I'm thinking you putting me in a worse mood won't go too good for you."

The guy stopped.

"Now, what did we say about you and teenage girls?" Core asked.

"She's a neighbor," the man said on a rush. "We were just talking. I can't be rude to my neighbor."

"I'm thinking we covered that," Core returned. "Neighbor. Stranger. Girl you walk past on the street. Unless she's behind the counter at Burger King and it's her job to deal with you, she doesn't exist for you."

"It was just a conversation."

"Yeah, and you flirting with the girls you were coaching, which included smacking their asses and taking ones you liked the best out for coffee and fucking with their heads and touching them in ways they thought were creepy because you were twenty years older than them and married, all that was innocent too, yeah?" Core asked. "They were freaked about it, but they wanted to play, and if they didn't have *conversations* with you, you'd bench them. So for a long time, they kept their mouths shut. And I know we went over this before, but let's talk about that hole you drilled with a direct line to their shower."

The guy lost it.

"*How do you fucks know this shit?*" he cried.

Muzzle stood.

The man's body jolted in terror.

"We will never, *never* not know when you fuck up," Muzzle said low. "Remember that after we leave. Your life will get a fuckuva lot easier."

Core sheathed his knife.

Muzzle advanced.

Core pulled his gloves from his back pocket.

This was something new for him, but he wasn't going to Hellen with split knuckles.

It didn't take them long to repeat their message.

They left him on the kitchen floor, and being environmentally conscious and all, they turned out the lights before they closed his door behind them.

Core slid beside Hellen in her bed and fitted himself to her back.

She dug her ass in his crotch.

His dick started to get hard.

Fuck.

It was late.

"Baby?" he called.

"You're home," she slurred.

Sleepy.

He pulled her closer. "Yeah."

"Mm..."

And she was out.

Core curled deeper into her.

Then he was out too.

A couple weeks later, Core was behind the counter at Crooked Road's Englewood store with Shim when she walked in with Li.

It was Saturday. For once, she wasn't working. She was spending the day with her sis.

"I want that and I want that and I want that," Li was chanting it out, pointing at all the jars of weed on display.

Core started chuckling.

Shim was checking Li out.

Core stopped chuckling and said low, "Brother."

Shim shot him a grin.

Hellen made it to them at the counter.

"Pot to her is Saks shoe department to me," she shared unnecessarily.

But it piqued his interest because his baby had some shoes that did serious things to him.

"You been shoe shopping?"

She shook her head, not quite hiding her disappointment.

He knew why.

She was being careful with money because she had Xanthia, and until she was ready to roll out more services and rake in more income, she was living lean.

They needed to talk about moving in together. They spent all their time together already, it was plain dumb she was paying rent.

He didn't have a mortgage, and even if she insisted on paying half of the utilities (which she would), with no rent, she'd be tanking her monthly expenses, so she might be able to buy herself some new shoes.

And he wanted her to have what she wanted.

They also needed to talk about other things.

But he wasn't finding it in himself to get around to that either.

Suddenly, a phone was in his face with the picture of a sexy-as-all hell black pump with a killer heel and a red sole on it.

"She wants these, but they don't have any on her resale sites, so she won't buy them," Li told him.

Core looked hard at the phone before Li took it away.

"I can live without them," Hellen asserted.

"I can't," Shim muttered.

Li started laughing.

"What you want, woman?" Shim asked Li. "I'll set you up."

"Family discount," Core said.

"Obviously," Shim replied.

"*Yippeeeee*," Li cried as they moved away.

"Having a good day?" he asked Hellen.

"Totes," she said.

"Totes?" he teased.

She shrugged. "Li rubs off on me."

"We ending up at yours or mine?"

"Yours. I like how close we have to sleep when we're in my queen. I like how much area we have to play when we get down to business in your king."

His sentiments exactly. "You got it, sweetheart."

"You don't have to give her the family discount. She doesn't pay rent," she pointed out.

All he said to that was lifting his brows.

"Whatever," she muttered, but the smirk on her lips said she liked his response.

"You been in here at least five minutes and you haven't given me your mouth."

That was when she rounded the counter and curved her arms around his neck, pulling him down to her.

And there it was.

It had been pretty boring until that point.

But right then, he started having a great Saturday.

A COUPLE OF DAYS LATER, he was on his couch, feet up on the back of it, joint pinched between his fingers, a small fan he'd put away when he was done blowing the smoke out the windows he'd opened because Hellen didn't like the smell of pot.

She'd just come home and gone back to the bedroom to change out of her work clothes.

But right then, she returned, and she was holding a cardboard-brown box with fancy white writing on the top.

"Haley told me your size," he said, and squinted at her as he took a toke.

She stood there, holding the brand-new shoes she wanted but wouldn't let herself have.

She did this for two beats.

Then she dropped them on the chair and came his way.

He set the joint aside quickly, which was good, because she was on him, and he could tell right off the bat she was intent to share some serious gratitude.

He loved her always.

So he loved having sex with her always.

But there was something different, not better, but serious fucking nice about fucking when he was stoned.

Though there wasn't much fucking, since she sucked him off like she was gonna earn a ribbon for it (she got blue), and she was so turned on by having his dick in her mouth, she came on stroke seven when he finally drilled into her, and he came on stroke eight due to what she did with her mouth.

They were both still dressed, clothing fucked-up, when they were cuddling after, and she said quietly, "You didn't have to do that."

She meant the shoes.

"I know."

He felt her pull in a big breath.

She let it out saying, "I really, *really* love you."

He knew that too.

But she wasn't done.

"And it's not about the shoes. It's the attention and the follow through." A meaningful pause and then, "And it's the fan." She curled her hand around the side of his neck and finished, "I hope I give the same to you."

Fuck.

"You do," he grunted.

But Christ.

She needed to know. She deserved it. It was crucial she had it.

But he couldn't give it to her after he gave her a pair of eight-hundred-dollar shoes.

She was happy. She'd just come.

And it might seem like he was trying to buy his way out from under the shit he was going to land on her.

It wasn't the time.

He'd find the time.

Just not now.

But he'd do it.

Later.

19

YOU DIDN'T LIE

Hellen

I WAS at the office when she ambushed me.

It was late-ish.

Our receptionist was gone. Xanthia was gone. And I'd noticed in a vague way that Aayansh, one of the corner office guys, had just left for the evening.

I wasn't totally alone in the office.

Yvette was behind one of her three huge screens, designing swag for one of her clients (and I needed to get with her for a collab—swag design and fulfillment was one of the tiers I was going to add to my menu).

Other than that, it was just me.

I'd gotten a return text from Core after I told him I was heading home in a few minutes.

I'll get the steaks out, baby.

His text made me smile.

It was all about grilling from room temperature for him.

It was after six, I'd left the house that morning at seven, and he was at home, waiting to cook for me.

And this reminded me I had something to think about. He told me to take my time on a decision, but with what he'd put out there, I didn't think it was cool to make him wait.

He'd broached the "home" subject in all its fullness last night, as in pointing out I was at his place all the time, so the expense of keeping mine seemed imprudent (though, he didn't use the word "imprudent," he used the word "stupid").

It was nearly November.

We'd been together awhile.

I was ready.

And I wasn't ready.

We were in love. I was there all the time anyway. We got along great. My family liked him. His brothers dug me.

It was worth a repeat, we were in love.

And seriously, I spent the night at my place alone maybe once every two weeks (if that), and if I was there any other time, Core was with me. Most often, I hit my apartment to switch out clothes or because it was convenient to go there to get ready.

Core was right, keeping it seemed a waste of precious resources.

And I liked his house. It wasn't only bigger, his neighborhood was quieter, there were two parks close by where we could walk Nanook, and when they built my complex, they hadn't put much consideration into greenspace.

Further, I wouldn't have to give up any of my belongings, these being both hard-earned, and I liked them. My furniture would fit in his house and not only aesthetically. We could set up one of his empty bedrooms as a guest room, and fill his empty den with my living room furniture.

Huge bonus: due to Core being a strictly jeans-and-tee/Henley/thermal/sometimes when the occasion warranted it button down-type of guy, his huge walk-in closet was barely filled. My closet was overstuffed. My things would fit in there, *and* I'd have room to expand.

We'd double up on kitchen stuff, but other than that, like we had into each other's lives, I could slot right in.

Then there was the fact he had a garage.

He had a yard.

He had a dog.

He had a much bigger kitchen.

He had a pool table where we played, he regularly trounced me and I secretly loved it, because he was almost that teeny-weeniest bit of cute when he'd rub it in after he beat me.

The only con was that my office was about ten minutes farther from his place than the drive from my apartment.

Oh, and it was a big step.

Sure, we'd done a lot of the work of starting a relationship, getting into the deep stuff, mingling friends and families, fighting, making up.

But we hadn't talked kids. We hadn't talked future. We hadn't talked money in the sense of what his home expenditures were and what I'd contribute. We also hadn't talked money in the sense that I was already building a nest egg that would mean I'd live a very cushy, hopefully early retirement, and where he was with that kind of thing.

In thinking about it (which, since he suggested it, I'd done...a lot), I didn't care about giving up my space. Core had a three-bedroom house with a den and a big back patio. We didn't have to be up in each other's business every second we were together, we had places we could go.

Truth, in all the pros, outside the fact we had some deeper conversations to have, there really wasn't a single con.

Everything with us was so great, I didn't know what my hang-up was, except the fact I didn't want to fail. I didn't want to be one of those women who got all wrapped up in the first bloom of a relationship and made irrational decisions based on orgasms and male attention.

But this was not me.

Failing was part of living. I'd done it before and survived. And I couldn't imagine Core and I would fail.

We worked great together.

Further, I didn't care what anyone thought of me and my decisions.

Except Dad.

The thought hit me like a streak of lightning.

Because it was true.

Okay...

Well.

Shit.

But there it was.

My hang-up was all about the fact I didn't want it getting to Dad I'd met someone, and within a few months, moved in with him, and then it went to hell, and I had to start over again. I didn't want him to feel smug knowing I fucked up, and maybe, if I'd come to him for advice, or maybe, if I hadn't gotten in deep with a biker, but instead, set my sights to someone Dad deemed worthy, I'd be on the fast-track to the perfect life with a doctor or a lawyer or something.

And maybe, since this was true, the foundation of what was driving me in pretty much everything I did was the need to prove something to him too.

To prove I didn't need him anymore for the child support he held over Mom's head, or the college tuition he held over mine.

To prove I had it together. I wasn't just making it, I was killing it. I was twenty-three (nearly twenty-four), I had my own business, employed a member of staff, was expanding, and oh yeah, on top of all of that, I'd found the perfect guy who Dad would probably hate, but that guy was everything.

Okay.

Well...

Damn.

This was real.

This was who I was.

This ambition had been poured into the foundation that created me.

And seriously, what the hell was this nonsense?

So my dad being a dick made me want to make certain I was never just making it, I was killing it? So he had a part in giving me the drive not just to look after myself, but make something of myself? Giving me the strength to be independent and content to do my own thing?

Who cared?

Finally, I had something to thank him for (not that I'd do that).

I wanted to live with Core. Wake up and go to sleep beside him. Come home and eat his cooking. Go with him to his clubhouse for a drink with his brothers and their old ladies. Watch him, chilled out and stoned, his eyes to the TV, his fingers in my hair, settled and happy.

Fuck that noise. Fuck that damage.

And fuck my dad.

I wanted all I wanted, and I was going to get it.

And I wanted Core.

I nearly started laughing.

Because I couldn't deny it.

I wanted to be an old lady.

I was actually thrilled with the idea.

I was keen to get home then, having made the decision.

Get home and tell Core I'd made it.

Then celebrate, because Core was going to be ecstatic (and Core's version of ecstatic made *me* ecstatic).

After that, talk kids, and future, and money.

And all the things.

We had time, and we'd be living together so plenty of opportunity to do it.

Honestly?

I couldn't wait.

So I was closing down, feeling light and bubbly and excited and fluttery, and all those girlie things that I also no longer cared Core made me feel because they felt fucking *great*.

I had all that goodness taking my headspace when there came a knock on the doorframe.

I lifted my head, thinking it would be Yvette telling me she was leaving and I was going to be the last person in the office.

It wasn't Yvette.

Shock pulsed through me at who I saw standing there, but with one look at her, I had the weird feeling that my world was about to fall out from under me.

"Fancy digs," was my cousin Eleanor's greeting.

I sat arrested in the process of sliding my laptop in my briefcase.

My cousin strutted in.

She was pretty, I'd always thought that. She got good from Dad's side of the family, like Li and I did. She had obviously fake boobs, which normally would not cause me to jump to judgy, but the nasty look on her face and the triumph with which she wore it made me think those boobs made her look skanky.

She was younger than my mom, older than Core, dressed like Pamela Anderson in her glory days (another no-judge, except for Eleanor it wasn't a style, it was a weapon and that wasn't okay).

What Rush had heard all those months ago had been legit.

She'd come up to Denver. She'd scoped things out. She might have noticed we had people looking out for us and waited until the time where we didn't so she could strike without anyone ruining her thrill.

Like she'd waited for Aayansh to leave, knowing I was mostly alone, and as such, vulnerable.

But whatever thrill she was after, she was starting with me.

I gave her a chance not to be a bitch.

I finished shoving my laptop in my bag and asked, "I'm not sure if I should say 'good to see you.' You're not exactly giving that vibe. So I have to ask, is this a friendly visit, Eleanor?"

Without being invited, she sat her round ass in the chair across from me and answered, "Yes. Very."

I didn't believe her.

I kept giving her an opportunity anyway.

"You home to see your dad?"

Her face twisted and she didn't bother to right it.

"Hardly."

"Okay, I'm surprised to see you out of the blue at my office, and—"

"You are?" she cut me off. "You didn't know I was back and forth from the Valley these days?"

Oh yes.

She knew we'd been covered.

And now we were not.

"I'd heard—" I began.

"Of course you've heard, because you're fucking Hardcore."

I didn't know who she normally played with, but she wasn't going to play with me.

"Whatever you have planned—"

"Do you know who Rosalie Kavanagh is?"

"No, and I don't care who she is."

"Really? You don't care that she was Beck's woman, and she was informing on Beck's club to Chaos, and Beck found out? Now, I know you're new to the life, so take it from me, that's not a smart thing to do to an MC. Club business stays club business. No questions. None of those ifs ands or buts. But a rat?" She made a *shoo* noise. "A rat is dealt with like any rat should be."

She clapped her hands together loudly, and I jumped.

"Swiftly," she continued. "And that was what they did with Rosalie. Got her alone and beat that bitch down, she couldn't even fucking move when they were done with her. Bitch didn't walk away from that. Left her for dead. Beat her fucking bloody, just like she deserved. Beck did it. Spiderweb did it. Spartan did it. Rainman did it. Muzzle. Eightball."

I wasn't breathing.

Because, like I knew she was going to do while I listened to her taking aim, she pulled the trigger.

"And Hardcore," she finished.

And the bullet tore through me.

She lifted a hand with finger pointed my way and wagged it at me.

"That's your man. That's your man's club." She settled back, getting into her story. "I mean, Resurrection, girl? Woo, they... are...*busy*. Mercenary shit, *goddamn*. Bad...fucking...*ass*. Who knows what bitches with big mouths, or any bitch who's earned a smack-down, has gotten from those boys? It's impressive. I mean, the One Percenters are some scary dudes, but even some of those clubs are terrified of the Angels of Death. All that justice, clan, honor shit?" She shook her head. "The words they don't ink into their skin are '*no mercy*'."

Another finger wag.

And then she continued to flay me.

"You doubt me, you ask Rosalie. She's with a Chaos brother now. Those clubs mingle, because those MC boys don't put much stock into what their women think, but I bet she doesn't show at those hog roasts when Resurrection is around."

Oh my God.

Rosalie was *Rosie*. I didn't know her last name. She was married to Snapper, one of Jagger's Chaos brothers.

While I grappled with this revelation, and visions of that pretty, sweet woman beat bloody, Eleanor sat forward, and her expression turned pure evil.

"No, ask your sis. Archie. She's Chaos now. I bet she knows *all* the lore. She'll tell you. None of those Chaos bitches are down with the alliance between Chaos and Resurrection. They know. Their men just don't give a shit."

"Are you done?" I asked, my voice tight.

"Does your daddy know you're fucking a biker?"

"Dad and I don't talk anymore."

She nodded like she got me. "I shoulda done that. Woulda saved a lotta headache. Didn't. But whatever. Still, beware. You ever change your mind, knowing you're biker snatch now, nothing will ever change his."

"Okay, I don't care if you're done. I am. Can you please leave?"

"No, baby," she cooed. "One more thing. You ask around. You sit with your sis Archie. You ask her to tell you the story of poor old Benito Valenzuela. You ask her to share how Resurrection hounded that man until he lost everything. Until he was selling his own ass just to feed himself. Played with him so much for so long, he stopped being able to deal. Took his own life. But Resurrection, they don't always play with their mice that way. Sometimes they just need to get done so they"—she faked shooting a gun—"take care of business."

She then shot me a look that chilled me to the bone.

"But your girl got into some trouble, so you know that already, don't you, sweetie? You know what Resurrection is about. You know who you're fucking."

I said nothing.

She waited.

I remained silent.

She waited more.

"I guess we're done now," she decided.

"'Bye," I said shortly.

She smiled a smile spiked with malice, rose from my chair and looked down at me.

Her parting shot?

"Never knew how fun it was, visiting with family."

I didn't take my eyes from her as she strutted out.

I made sure she disappeared then I waited to make sure she didn't come back.

Only then did I snatch up my phone.

I didn't call Archie.

I called Jagger.

"Hey, what's up? Everything okay?" he sounded friendly but uncertain, and with reason.

I'd texted him in the past, but I'd never phoned.

"Did the Resurrection Motorcycle Club beat up Rosie?" I asked.

Utter, complete silence.

Oh my God.

Until then, I didn't believe Eleanor.

Or, I didn't *want* to believe.

It didn't make sense. It didn't fit who Core was. Or Beck. Web. Spartan.

Maybe Eight, he was edgy, still, he was mostly cool so it would be a push.

But it definitely, *definitely* didn't fit Core.

Now, I knew she spoke truth.

And it was then I remembered Core's words from months ago, when we first met, before we were us, when he first told me about the Angels of Death business, when he spoke about the dark path his club was on.

And then later, at his house, when he'd shared more.

Brother business is brother business, sweetheart.

They never open their mouths, not ever to anyone, even other brothers, about the club business they know.

Oh my God.

So this was how it felt to bleed internally.

"Listen," Jagger said urgently. "I'm going to call Dutch. And Rush. Where are you? They need to talk to you."

Archie owned her own store. Archie owned the whole building. It had apartments, so she was also a landlord. Archie was relatively newly married and setting up a life with her husband. And Archie was like Li, she worked to live. She traveled a lot. She took long weekends. She'd go up into the mountains on a whim. And now, Jagger went with her.

I'd never been tight with Archie, but I liked her. We'd been getting closer of late. That said, it honestly wasn't an unusual thing that months went by when I didn't see her, the same with us being in contact, because obviously, I was busy and had a life too.

So I didn't know if Andy said something (he probably did) or if it was a between-clubs thing (and it probably was).

But Jagger knew I was with Core.

And now he knew I knew.

I knew.

I knew what Eleanor said was true.

And it sounded like he was immediately instigating damage control.

God, Archie was married into this?

Apparently, that documentary about Chaos wasn't a documentary. It was propaganda (which of course it would be, the woman who directed it, Rebel, was married to Rush).

Now I knew something else too.

They weren't all about brotherhood and family. They didn't put it all on the line to get clean for their women and children.

They were just like all the other MCs.

They were about men and men only.

They were out there, in this modern world, living like it was the 1700s, where men were all-important and women were property.

"That's okay," I said softly in response to his offer.

"Listen to me, Hellen," he ordered firmly. "I don't know who talked to you—"

"I've gotta go," I mumbled.

"Hellen," he called.

I disconnected.

I also turned off the sound on my phone.

I'd have to deal with how I felt about Archie being in that, and what I might have to say to Andy about it later.

I also had to call my fucking dad and warn him about Eleanor, as well as tell Mom and Li.

But I had to do that later too.

I needed to deal with this now.

Then put it behind me.

I had my proof. I was never in love with Bryan, nowhere near it.

Because this?

What I was feeling right now?

This was *excruciating.*

My phone buzzed in my hand, so I looked down at it.

It was a call from Archie.

She was the single coolest chick I knew.

And she was brainwashed with this shit.

I got that.

Boy, did I.

They sucked you in with sweet talk and great sex, so by the time you realize you've agreed not to ask any questions about the shit they get up to with their brothers, realize you've thrown yourself into a life you don't know dick about, you're so addicted to that life, to *them,* you can't get loose.

I went to my car, and I'd give myself shit for this later, but I drove to Core's without taking a second to get my head together. I was in such a fog of pain and betrayal, I could have hurt myself or someone else.

But I made it.

I hit the garage door opener on my visor, and the act of doing that felt like a knife sinking into my flesh.

I parked, shut down my Mini, nabbed the opener and took a minute to take Core's key off my ring before I left my purse and briefcase where they were and went into the house.

The first thing I saw was that I had laundry folded on his dryer. I hadn't put it away yet.

My laundry folded and mingled with his.

Just like everything else between us, it had happened naturally.

He did the cooking, so he also did the grocery shopping.

Without a word, I'd started to do our laundry.

He had a cleaning service, so that wasn't a thing.

After he cooked, for the most part, we did the dishes together.

Sometimes, he'd be off doing something with his club (and at this point, I knew that "something" could be more *anything* than the *anything* I already knew it to be). If he was, I'd do the dishes. Sometimes, I'd be off for drinks with the girls or need to check a scheduled post went out, and track its progress, so he'd do them.

We'd just clicked in like we were meant to be.

In everything, we'd done that.

Clicked in like we were meant to be.

I made it to the kitchen and put the opener and his key on the island, seeing the steaks out, already seasoned.

There it was. Allowing them to come to room temperature.

He said it produced a better result.

He was right.

I saw movement and watched him walk in from the back, probably out checking the grill, and I did this having to completely ignore Nanook bounding in with him, coming straight to me. I needed to get this done, and I was broken, but taking a second to come to the understanding I was losing both my boys, that would shatter me.

And anyway, taking in Core was enough.

God, he was gorgeous, that tall, hard body. That hair. Those eyes.

That smile which started to falter after he caught sight of me and then processed the state of me.

"You ran late," he said guardedly.

"Did you and your brothers beat up Rosalie Kavanagh?"

I knew they did on the word "beat."

I knew it because he didn't turn awkward or defensive. He didn't shut down or appear wily.

His eyes went dead.

Completely *dead.*

Somewhere deep, deep down inside of me, I registered that look in his eyes with alarm.

However, the prevailing emotion was keeping my feet, due to the fact my heart had exploded.

My tone was suffocated when I pushed, "You, all of you, beat up a single woman?"

"Yes."

I stood there, silently dying as I stared at him, waiting for more.

But that was it.

Yes.

If that was true, then everything else Eleanor said was too.

No mercy.

"You told me you weren't good for me," I whispered.

He didn't wince, reach out to me, move my way.

He stood there, his lifeless eyes locked on me, and that was it.

"You didn't lie."

With one last look at him, I did the hardest thing I'd ever done in my life.

I turned my back on Dustin "Hardcore" Cutler and walked away.

20

HOURS

Hellen

WITHIN TWENTY-FOUR HOURS, I knew it wasn't a club, it also wasn't a gang.

It was a cult.

And cults never let you get away easy.

Archie texted seven times, and called three.

Jagger called twice.

Dutch and Rush both called once. They did this even though I'd never had any direct communication from them before. I only knew it was them because they identified themselves before I stopped listening and deleted their voicemails.

Janna, who I liked a whole lot, she seemed sweet, I was considering asking her if she wanted to hang with us during our Fortnum's Sundays, but we had yet to exchange that first phone communication, texted once and called twice.

She was the only one I responded to.

I didn't read her text, but I returned one, politely requesting that she communicate with Core then tell me when it would be a good time for me to go to his house and get my things, without him there.

I worked from home and spent an hour and a half drafting an email to Web about how I'd need to give them thirty days' notice because I was voiding our contract.

This was all the work I was capable of doing due to being glassy-eyed and exhausted from crying, emotion and no sleep.

I did not contact Marcy, Kyra or Li. I did not call my mom.

And I did not hear from Core.

WITHIN FORTY-EIGHT HOURS, I'd gone from heartshorn to pissed.

Because I'd spent an uncomfortable five minutes huddled in my fucking house, having to ignore Archie calling through the door.

But I was oh so much more pissed because I loved him enough to keep his secret.

And because he made me into the woman I never wanted to be.

Because I still hadn't called Marcy, Kyra or Li, but when I eventually did, I couldn't tell them the man Core was. I didn't have it in me to make them feel some of the heartbreak I felt in knowing the person they liked so much, the person they liked with me, was so insanely awful.

I couldn't tell my mom.

I certainly couldn't tell Andy.

I'd have to dodge and weave when the time came and I explained why we were through.

When I explained why Core and me, who were perfect together, suddenly were over.

It actually caused me real, physical pain to think of them knowing what I knew about Core, not the actual knowledge, but how they'd feel about him when they knew.

I loved him so much, even when we were done, I felt I had to protect him from people thinking he was an asshole.

Oh yeah.

That pissed...me...*off*.

And I had to keep this all to myself because I didn't want them to know how badly I'd been duped. I didn't want to come up against those questions about just *how* he took care of the Greeks. *How* I knew his club waded into shit like that. *How* they were not Angels of Death, nor Angels of Vengeance, they were *mercenaries*, and I'd bought into his, "Don't ask, baby, I can't share," line of bullshit.

I'd allowed myself to become that woman.

But he was the one who put me in the position of feeling ashamed and embarrassed.

I was Bree times a million.

Because he hadn't stolen my jewelry.

He'd stolen my heart.

WITHIN SIXTY HOURS, I was furious.

I was because I still hadn't told Marcy, Kyra or Li, and I was still working from home because, if I left my house, between here and there, I didn't want him to have the chance to ensnare me and use his biker charm and empty promises of *making it worth it* to try to get back in there with me.

I was furious because I was scared to leave my house because I loved him so much, I knew if he caught me, I could talk myself into believing. Turn the other cheek. Live my life and just be good, never share club business and never rat, and I'd be fine.

I was furious because I spent ages typing out angry messages to him on my phone, and then deleting them.

I was furious because I was powerless on another matter.

But what could I do?

Everyone in the family loved Jagger. How did I tell them he was probably just like Core? He knew what Core's club had done, and his first thought was to cover for him.

So eventually, I'd have to pretend to put up with Jagger, which meant in every meaningful sense I'd lost a man I really liked, and with him, probably Archie too.

All because of Core.

So yes, I was furious. Furious Archie, Jagger and Rush were still trying to contact me. They wouldn't leave me be (but thankfully, Archie hadn't come back to my door).

I was blind with rage.

All I could see were Core's dead eyes.

And all I could hear was him saying, "Yes."

Ninety-six hours later, I was enraged.

Because I worried about him.

Because I loved him.

And he loved me.

And I was here and he was there, and we would never be.

It had broken me.

And all I could think was...

How was *he* feeling?

Ninety-six and a half hours later, I was apoplectic.

Because I missed Nanook.

A hundred and eight hours later, I was lost.

Janna had texted. She said Eight was going to leave my things outside my door that evening. He'd hang to make sure they were safe, but could I please try to be home by six to take my belongings inside?

I was there by six.

I didn't look for Eight's truck to see if he kept his promise.

I just hauled the three boxes of stuff in, feeling extreme relief Eight didn't try to approach in order to state Core's case, and feeling heartbreaking sadness he didn't make an attempt to tap into that part of me who'd leap at any excuse to have my man back.

I took the boxes to my bedroom, because I knew it was mostly clothes and shoes and makeup.

When I opened them, I saw someone had packed them carefully.

There was respect in that packing.

There was love in it too.

I ignored how they were packed, but I unpacked them just as carefully and put everything away. But when I hit the Louboutins, I tucked them in their box on a top shelf and hid them with folded sweaters.

At the bottom of the last were two burgundy boxes.

That was when I started to fall part.

Those, I shoved in the bottom back of my T-shirt drawer, because it was fall, winter would be coming soon, and I wouldn't need tees for months.

I would deal with them then.

Then I sat, face to knees, having shoved myself in my too-full closet, and I sobbed for what seemed like an eternity.

No Core to hand me tissues.

No Core to clean them up after.

But Core was in every second, every tear, every hiccup, every hitched breath.

All I could think about were his hands on me. His wink. Him setting fence posts into holes with Andy. The mermaid over his heart. Him listening to something Marcy was saying with a smirk on his face. The way his cock felt inside me. The perfect crumble of his cornbread. The lazy look he'd get in those amazing blue eyes when he was high, and how that made me feel happy. Because in that state, he was exposed, and what he exposed was that he was content.

He seemed a man who was right where he wanted to be, and that was with me.

It felt like I cried through every moment with him, every nuance of him, every word he said, laugh we shared, every shout that exposed how much I meant to him from the very beginning.

When I was done, I curled up, mind hazy and adrift.

I was going through the motions.

We'd been together mere months, and I didn't know how to live without him being there at the end of my day.

I didn't know how to start another day without him either.

I curled up and slept there, in my closet.

But when I woke, I was back to fury because it was all Core's fault my body was full of kinks.

More.

I had to start another day without him.

And that was his fault too.

I'D DONE it because I had no choice. They were freaking out because I was ghosting them.

And yes, I'd had to be vague and cagey.

Which of course set off alarm bells.

But through a text, I told my girls Core and I were through.

They knew I thought I was going to spend the rest of my life with him so they'd freaked out.

But when I asked, since they loved me too, they gave me space. I knew it wouldn't last very long, but they gave it.

Which was the only beauty I'd experienced in a week.

And I hated it.

And I hated Core for making me hate it.

But no matter the hate and fury, no matter how hard I tried, what texts I typed to him I never sent, what number of tears I shed, what thoughts I had trying to convince myself it was lucky I found out before I was in too deep.

No matter what, I just couldn't stop loving him.

And I needed to figure out how to stop loving him.

Because I missed him so badly, I worried it was going to kill me.

21

SHADOWBOXING

Hellen

He came as a surprise.

I sensed it would eventually happen, but the top dog coming himself?

That threw me.

Still, even as I saw Beck lounged in the entryway by the door to my apartment, I didn't hesitate to pull in, park, shut down, grab my things, get out and walk right his way.

It had been two hundred and sixty-three hours since I ended things with Core.

And now it was time for it to be fully over. For me to assure the President of the Resurrection Motorcycle Club I'd keep my mouth shut about their activities, and we could all move on with our lives.

How I would do that, the moving on with my life part, I had no idea.

Things were not improving.

The girls had stopped giving me space, but I was still asking for it.

Kyra was getting increasingly upset.

Li was getting impatient.

Marcy was getting pissed.

Now Mom had started calling me.

Archie never stopped.

I still wasn't sleeping. I had so much concealer under my eyes to hide the shadows, I should invest in the company that made it so I might get some of my money back.

Xanthia was freaking out and perhaps wondering if she'd made the wrong decision to accept my offer, because she kept catching me in my office, staring off at nothing.

Food tasted like crap, so I didn't eat it.

I detested the sunrise.

I abhorred the sunset.

I woke up not knowing how to face the day, and I went to bed scared of another sleepless night.

I'd let it happen.

I'd lost myself to a man.

And I didn't know how to start the journey back to me again.

I pulled my focus from that to focus on Beck, and something that never occurred to me in the times I'd been around him before hit me.

He was a very handsome man, but he had a huge scar on his face. However, he got it, it was so big, it had to be traumatic.

It wasn't something you mentioned. Someone who endured something like that, unless they wanted to share, you simply let it be a part of who they were. I didn't even ask Core after it because it wasn't any of my business.

Now I wondered how he got that scar.

And I wondered if Janna knew what kind of man he was.

Beck's gaze on me was careful, but open, rather than scary and threatening, which I had to admit was a bit of shock.

When I got close, I also noticed he was carrying what looked like a binder, his fingers curled under it with it resting on his hip, like guys carried their books to class in high school.

"Hey, Hellen," he greeted.

"Beck," I returned tersely.

I moved right by him, opened the door, went in, but held it and stared at him to indicate he should come in.

There was a hint of surprise before he accepted my invitation.

I shut the door behind him, went to my couch and threw my bag and briefcase on it.

I turned his way and said, "You'll forgive me if I don't offer you refreshments."

"Hellen—"

I held up a hand.

"You have my promise, I won't tell anyone. I haven't even told my girls anything except Core and I are over. I tell them everything, but I won't tell them this. I mean, obviously, they know you all dealt with the Greeks. But they won't know what else I've learned. What little I know of your secrets are safe with me. Now you all can go your way, and I'll go mine."

"Can I ask who told you?"

"Why, so you can beat her down too?"

He flinched.

My body jerked.

Because there it was, easy to read.

Real pain.

No, *anguish.*

I stared.

He recovered and said, "So it was Nails."

Fucking *shit.*

I just had to open my big mouth, and now I had to control the damage.

She was a bitch, but she was my cousin after all.

"She wasn't nice about it, but she did me a favor. And since I'm not like all of you, she did you all a favor too. We're not good for each other. So in the end, it works for both of us."

"Do you think it's working for Core?"

As that blade sunk true and I mentally staggered under the pain, suddenly, I realized my error.

This was not a good man.

And I'd let him in my house.

I'd let the quiet, contemplative brother of Core in my house, the one who helped build fences, the one I knew.

I forgot he was someone else.

"Respectfully, can I ask you to leave?"

He drew in a big breath.

It seemed to take forever for him to let it go.

When he did, he didn't leave.

He said, "His father was a drunk."

So it was going to be this.

Damn.

Right, okay.

He felt the need to do this, I wouldn't fight it. I'd let him. I'd let him think I was hearing him out, so he could tell Core he did what he could, and more importantly for me, things right now wouldn't get testy.

I just had to make it through.

"He told me," I confirmed.

"The man abused Core's mother."

"He told me that too."

"Did he tell you his father beat her to death?"

Every muscle in my body hardened because no.

He did not tell me that.

She died an ugly death.

That was what he said.

But he didn't come close to telling me how ugly.

"When his old man surfaced from the place he was in his head to be able to do that to her, saw what he'd done, he got his gun, put it in his mouth and blew the back of his head off."

I staggered back, hit the arm of my couch, and sat on it.

"Core was out with buds when it happened. He was sixteen. He was the one who found them."

My brain screamed, *No!*

And my head turned sharply. I looked away, unable to hold his gaze at the same time deal with the pain that seared through me at his words.

"Core thinks his dad did it out of guilt, blowing his brains out. That's what he needs to believe. I think, from all the rest Core gave us about that fuckin' guy, he did it because he didn't want to get into trouble. He didn't want to go to jail. He didn't want to be someplace he couldn't have booze, which was more important to him than his woman and son. And he didn't want to be someplace where he couldn't bully and rape—"

My head shot up and the word escaped my mouth as a horrified gasp because my lungs had suddenly ceased working.

"Rape?"

Beck nodded once. "Yeah, rape. Sometimes, he coerced her to have sex with him in exchange for him not beating her up. Core would have to listen to that shit when he was a kid."

I had the strong feeling I was going to be sick.

"You ever know anyone in the foster system?" Beck asked.

Oh my *God.*

It just kept...getting...*worse.*

"There are really great people who take care of kids," he told me. "And then there are some who really suck at it. Core got those. In two years between the ages of sixteen and eighteen, he had three of them."

I tried to stand, I didn't know why, maybe to run away from all he was saying, but my legs were numb, as were my feet, so I couldn't move.

"He was searching for something, and he sure as fuck found it, hooking himself up with Bounty."

Wait.

What?

"Bounty?" I asked.

"Who we were before we became Resurrection. Who we were when we did that to Rosalie."

Man, Core and I didn't get into anything deep at all, did we?

I thought we had.

But we had not.

"He was fucked-up. He was searching. Found Bounty, and that was perfect. All we wanted to do was party and cause trouble, fight and piss in corners. Pretend we were outlaws and howl at the moon. Anything that would mask what we were really feeling. Anything that would shroud the path that is long and hard and terrifying, which we should have been walking. Take our anger out at anyone and on everybody. Nothing mattered. No person did either. All of that in the guise of brotherhood. We thought we had honor. We thought we understood the true meaning of family. All we did was get tangled up with a bunch of other fucked-up souls and dig the tunnel away from redemption all the deeper."

I said nothing.

He didn't either.

And then he did.

"Then came Rosie," he whispered, the sheer torment on his face hurting even me.

And I knew.

I knew Beck found a way to live with it.

But Core...

With what Core's father did...

Core had let it kill him.

I remembered his house when I first walked in.

I thought it was a life incomplete.

It wasn't.

It was a life being lived without the person in it actually *living*.

"We were shadowboxing," he said. "I'll tell you mine, and I gotta say, in hearing the others, it made me feel even weaker than I knew I already was, because mine was nowhere near as bad. Nowhere near as bad as Core's. But my mom didn't give a shit about me. I had an older brother. And she gave him everything. All her love. All her hope. All her devotion. I gave it to him too because he was that good of a guy. Golden. I loved him, fuck, only person on this earth who had that from me. He gave that love back. It meant everything to me. And then he was killed in Afghanistan. We both lost him, and she made clear I knew which one of us should have been under dirt."

He paused, and I had no idea what to say, though I felt for him, and I wanted to know what his dad did. I wanted to know if he had any love at all, outside his brother.

And I was even more grateful than ever that I had Mom and Liane and then came Andy.

"I acted out, looked for something that would work out that emotion in me," he continued. "Everything I did was such shit, such trash, it dug me in all the deeper, because my brother would have been disappointed in me. For some reason, though, I just couldn't stop."

It lay between us right then.

It hung like a spirit holding the Wheel of Fortune.

One turn, and things change.

What hung there were the two words that turned the wheel to bring change.

Until Rosalie.

"All of us got a story," he went on. "All of us were shadowboxing demons that life planted in us, way down deep. We were called Bounty, but we did not wake the fuck up and look around to see what bounty we actually had. Each of us was in a brotherhood, and we were all totally alone."

He shook his head.

And kept going.

"Now, this is no excuse, none of it is, but we had two men in our crew who were snakes in the grass. They injected poison, but only in the way they filled the syringe and handed it to us, and we sunk the needle in our own flesh. So what was bad got worse, and we were all in for that ride." His gaze bore into mine. "I can honest to God stand here, look you in the eye, and tell you that then, when it happened, when the decision was made, I was all for it. I jumped right in. She was mine, and I was the one to take the first swing, and I spat on her when it was over."

The wet came and spilled right over the edges of my eyes.

"I gotta live with that," he whispered.

"Beck," I whispered back.

He cleared his throat.

"If he wants, he can get into it. He can tell you the full story of what we were and what we became if you give him a shot. But you're sharp, you can put it together. There's a reason we're called Resurrection. We burned it to the ground. And so we could live with ourselves, we had to walk away from those ashes, go somewhere good and right, and do the work to build it back up."

He tossed the binder on my coffee table. It landed with a plop that felt like an explosion.

"That's our charter. Those are our rules and regs. No one but a brother has read those. But I'm giving them to you."

Holy shit.

Slowly, I shifted my gaze to the binder.

On the cover it said:

Iustitia
Tribus
Honoris
Fidelitas

And that was all.

Not the name of their club. Not an author of the document. Not the name of their officers.

Just those words.

"When we got our shit tight, we did the work," Beck said, regaining my attention. "We left our women and we hiked into the woods and we sat on rocks and built a fire and we didn't hike back out until it was all out there. Until everyone knew everything. It took over two weeks. It was hard as fuck to do it myself. But it was harder, watching my brothers reach into their own souls, pull those fuckers out and expose their demons for the other men to see. But we didn't know what brotherhood was about. We didn't know the shadows our brothers were fighting. We didn't know what brought us there. We didn't understand family. And not knowing, it took us to a place we didn't want to be, but in one way or other, we will never leave. Out in those woods, we became a family. And we took that home to our women."

Another tear slid down my cheek.

"Every man who comes to us and wants a part of who we are, what we do," he went on, "before we give them a patch, we take them to those woods. And I don't give a shit, Hellen, if they share they still feel like an asshole because the girl they liked in high school said no to a date, and that fucked them up. It means something to them. It lives in them. It festers in them. And me and Eight, and Muzzle, and Core and all the rest are there for them to help work that poison out."

After delivering that, he walked to the door.

I wanted to cry out because for some reason I didn't want him to leave.

But he didn't leave.

He turned back to me.

"We do not take payment for the services we render," he said quietly. "They come to us, and we do what's necessary, no matter what that means, to right the wrongs that were done to them. I can never wash my woman's blood off my hands. I get some abusive husband's blood. Or some rapist who got a slap on the wrist or got away altogether. Or some sociopathic geek who spends his time messing with girls online to the point they try to take their own lives. I got *that* blood on my hands, I got no problem with it."

Putting it that way, I didn't either.

He kept going.

"Also got no problem helping a man who doesn't pay child support see the light, pay his due, and ascertaining he won't lapse in that reasonability again, and do all of that by any means necessary. Or showing the righteous path to a high school softball coach who thinks he can touch his girls and watch them shower, sharing with him in a way he cannot mistake he needs to get on with a job that isn't around kids, or doesn't allow him to harass females of any age. Then keeping tabs to make sure he doesn't veer off that path. Got no problem with any of the things we do to help people who can't get anyone else to help them. Neither does Core or any brother. It's what we do. It's who we are. It's the vow we made to make amends for the shit we pulled, not only to Rosie, but any of it. And we are all gonna live that vow until the day we die."

Okay, so it seemed there was some truth to what Eleanor said.

But there were also some big, fat lies.

And forcing their way through the lifting haze of betrayal, longing and pain, more memories emerged of what Core said about his club that night he got so mad at me.

About penance.

And redemption.

Beck put his hand to the knob on my door.

But he wasn't done.

"He's a wreck."

I knew it.

I knew he was.

Because I was too.

But having it confirmed utterly destroyed me.

I dropped my head, and there was no hope in trying to stop my shoulders from shaking.

"Kiki left him when we beat down Rosie. He's not let himself have a woman since. I don't mean he hasn't seen to basic needs, I mean he's not let anyone close to his heart. In those woods, when he gave us what haunted him, I knew he'd suffer more than the others. He thinks he's his father. And you got every right, this seems like a guilt trip, but it's not, still, you leaving him, at least to him, proved that true."

I gulped down a sob, and embarrassingly, it was audible.

"I'm sorry, honey," Beck said gently. "I know this is a lot. But I gotta say one more thing before I leave. If what I shared moves you to give him a shot. If you sit down with him and listen. If in the end, you decide to let him make you happy, you won't have a single brother giving you any shit that this went down. Families have misunderstandings. And families get it. Then they get on with it. I came here to tell you, I like you, my woman likes you, we want you to be a part of our family. But mostly, I came here because I want my brother to be happy and he's completely in love with you, so right now he's completely lost without you."

And with that, I heard a whoosh, the chill from outside wafted over me, and after that, the door snicked shut.

22

RED

Core

Core was stoned and slightly drunk, flat out on his couch, with Nanook mostly on top of him, the TV on, the sound off.

This had been their state whenever he was at home since she left.

He got his shit done. He did his duty to the club. Saw to the stores. And he was sober when he did it.

He also didn't get totally wasted. He was a piece of shit, but he wasn't going to go there. He wasn't going to get messy and foul like his old man.

He'd smooth the edges, but he deserved what he was feeling.

He'd let down all three of the women he'd loved.

His mom, by not being there when she needed him.

Kiki, by becoming the man no woman needed.

And Hellen, by not giving her the information she needed.

Core had no clue if he would have been able to find the words to make her understand it felt like he'd lived two different lives. That the name "Resurrection" for him and his brothers had all kinds of meanings, but only one important one. That he'd buried the man he used to be in the woods. After that, he waited for her to show so she could breathe life back into him.

But he'd been weak, so someone got to her before he did.

Nanook's head came up from where it was resting on his paws on Core's chest, his eyes going to the front door.

Core tried to ignore it.

Since the door closed on Hellen, Nanook had been sticking close to his dad. He sensed where Core was at.

But his pup was feeling his own feelings.

So even though he didn't know every time he did it, it made Core feel like someone sunk a blade in his gut, whenever Nanook heard a car on the road, he came to attention, thinking it was her coming home.

His dog didn't know her clothes were gone. He didn't know her makeup wasn't rolling around in his bathroom drawers anymore. He didn't know her earrings weren't on her nightstand and her shoes weren't on the floor in the closet for either of them to trip on.

He didn't know the crystal butterflies she'd put on the shelves by the TV were packed up and had been sent away.

He didn't know she wasn't coming back.

He'd get used to it eventually.

"*Oof!*" Core grunted as Nanook planted his back paws in Core's thighs and leaped off.

He twisted his neck as Nanook started barking at the front door.

He came back to Core, then he raced again to the door, now not barking.

He was howling.

"Fuck," Core mumbled and threw his legs over the side of the couch.

He shouldn't do this. If it was Jehovah's Witnesses, he probably didn't have it in him to be cool.

But Nanook kept flipping his shit so Core walked to the door.

He got there just as the bell could be heard over his dog's racket.

He turned the lock, opened it, and stared at Hellen standing outside.

And that was when his chest caved in.

She looked beautiful, and she looked like shit.

She'd lost weight, her eyes were sunken in, her skin didn't look healthy.

He'd done that to her.

Fuck.

Nanook didn't see any of this. He went nuts, jumping on her and barking with excitement.

She bent to give him attention.

It was hoarse when he said, "Hellen."

She remained bent to his dog but tipped her head back to look up at him. "Can I come in?"

He had no idea what she was doing there, but it didn't matter. Whatever she had to deliver, he'd take, because whatever it was, all he knew was, he deserved it.

He stepped back.

She stepped in, Nanook dancing and twirling around her, so happy she was there he didn't give her any openings to get her hands on him when she stopped in the living room.

Core let this go on for a while, then he ordered, "Boy. Sit."

Nanook sat instantly by her leg, lifting his snout Core's way with a look on his face that said, *See Dad, Mom's home.*

And another blade in his gut.

Christ, was he going to be able to get through this?

She scratched the fur on top of Nanook's head, her eyes on Core.

"Did I miss packing something?" he asked.

For some reason, his question made her startle, a flicker shimmered in her eyes, there and gone.

"I'm here to return something," she replied.

"You can give my shit away," he muttered.

"You didn't leave anything at mine. We never really spent much time there."

Core had no idea what to say to that, but it made him wonder what she was returning if he didn't leave anything.

She didn't make him wait long.

She opened the big bag that was on her shoulder, reached in and pulled out a copy of Resurrection's bylaws.

What the fuck?

She held it out to him. "Beck gave it to me to read."

Woodenly, he took it, shocked as shit any brother, much less their president, handed their confidential rules and regs to someone outside the club.

He then tossed it in the chair, and tried to hide the pissed he was now feeling when he asked, "Beck spoke to you?"

"Yes."

"Sorry about that," he murmured. "I'll talk to him. Won't happen again."

"Why didn't you tell me your father killed your mother?"

Blindsided by that blow, he took a step back, didn't make himself, he just did it.

Nanook, feeling the abrupt charge hit the room, got on all four paws and let out a soft, uncertain woof.

"Why didn't you tell me?" she repeated.

"Same reason I didn't tell you we beat down Rosalie," he told her. "I'm weak."

"Really?" she asked dubiously.

"Yup," he answered.

She studied him.

He could see plain she didn't buy it, though what she thought he was selling, he had no clue.

"Listen—" he began.

"Beck told me everything."

"I'm getting that."

"Maybe not everything, everything. But he told me about your parents. And he told me about his brother and his mom."

Core did a slow blink.

Outside his club and his woman, Core didn't think Beck told that to anybody.

"Did you not think I'd...?" She flapped a hand beside her. "I don't know. Get it? Understand?"

"I thought you'd leave me."

"Not telling me accomplished that."

"Didn't miss that part, babe."

That time, her eyes straight up flashed, and his heart spiked, coming alive for the first time in a week and a half.

There was his girl.

Or...

Not his girl anymore.

His heart went dead again in his chest.

"Why didn't you tell me your dad did that to your mom?" she pushed. "We talked about them. Why didn't you give it all to me?"

His hands started shaking.

Fuck.

It was happening.

He ticked his head to chase it away.

She misinterpreted the movement.

"You're not going to explain now?" she asked.

"I'm not proud of it."

"What do you mean?"

"Not a lotta women love it when their man comes from stock where his daddy murdered his mom with his fists."

Her words were terse when she declared, "That doesn't have anything to do with you."

He felt red encroach at his eyes.

Red.

"It doesn't?" he bit off.

She lifted both hands, palms his way and modulated her tone. "No, no. I didn't mean it like that. I mean, you didn't do it."

"His blood is in me."

"You mentioned that. We talked about that. But you didn't give me the fullness of it."

"Hellen—"

"I get it was hard to share what you all did to Rosie. But your parents. We talked about that. Why didn't you tell me?"

"I've already explained."

"No, you haven't."

Red.

Damn.

So much *red.*

She took a step forward.

Reflexively, he backed up.

Her tone was different, Core just couldn't put his finger on how because he had other things happening to him, when she asked, "What's happening now, Core?"

"I wanna give you what you want," he said carefully.

Red.

"You deserve it," he went on.

Red.

"But I'm not sure what you want right now, Hellen."

"I want you to open up to me," she said gently.

She took another step forward.

He retreated.

"Why didn't you tell me?"

She continued to advance, Nanook now coming with her.

She tossed her bag on the chair as her movements forced him to where his pool table was sitting.

Core kept retreating.

"What'd you give your brothers in those woods, honey?" she asked.

He missed the "honey."

And he didn't have it in him to realize just how much Beck shared with the question she just asked.

Like they were working together, they separated.

Nanook moved to cut him off from the hall.

Hellen moved to cut him off from the garage.

Trapped.

Core heaved out an unsteady breath.

"Did you give them everything?" she pressed, watching him closely.

God.

Fuck.

Christ.

It was happening.

He had to move. He couldn't stand still.

Red.

So much fucking *red.*

He shifted along the pool table, Hellen adjusting position to keep him there and not give him access to the garage or back door. He went the other way, Nanook trotting to keep him from the hall and living room and the front door.

He retraced his steps.

She was there.

And returned.

His dog was there.

He had no idea he was prowling like a caged animal.

But goddammit, she was relentless.

"Okay, what *didn't* you give them?" she asked, worry stark in her tone now, easy to read, along with the fear threading through it.

"I gave it all," he muttered.

No he didn't.

Red.

She called him on it.

"No, you didn't. Beck said they were there. They were all there to help you through. You're going through something now. What didn't you tell me? What didn't you tell *them*?"

He kept prowling.

"Back off, Hellen."

"No."

"Back off."

"No."

He stopped when he was facing her and roared, "*Back off, Hellen!*"

"*No!*" she roared back.

Red.

Everywhere.

And in his mind's eye, he saw his mother's face.

That was all he could take.

"*If I'd been there, I would have saved her!*"

He watched pain suffuse her expression.

But Core was gone.

Lost to the gore that was his parents.

All that *red.*

"He was a waste of flesh. I'd beat his ass before. He knew not to come back. He knew not to come back." He pounded a fist against his chest. "*He knew not to come back unless I wasn't there!*"

"Honey," she whispered, coming to him.

"*Get the fuck away from me!*" he snarled.

She stopped dead, the color draining from her face.

Nanook came from the other direction.

He turned to him and shouted, "Back! Sit! Stay!"

Nanook whimpered as he backed off, sat down and stared at Core.

"You couldn't have—"

When she spoke again, he swung back to her. "No?" he asked snidely. "I couldn't have? You know? You know how it would have gone down? You know I couldn't save her?"

"It wasn't how it happened, baby," she said miserably.

"Nope, it sure as fuck wasn't," he clipped. "I mean him,"—he rolled his head on his neck—"who gives a fuck about him? But, Jesus Christ, I'm sixteen and I walk in to see my dad's brains all over the wall?"

She winced.

"Yeah, *nice*," he agreed. "Happy family memories. Shoulda taken a snapshot, baby. Put it in one of your frames. Dad with the back of his head all over the wall. Gotta hand it to the man, he didn't do half measures. He was a fall down, mean, nasty drunk, and he gave that his all. He was a lazy, unemployed, waste of space, and he gave that his all. He was a shit, motherfucking dick of a husband, and he gave that his all. He was useless as a father, and he gave that his all. And when he murdered his ex-wife, he *really* gave that his all. So, of course, when he ate a bullet, he didn't choose a .22 to do the job. He grabbed his .38 and gave *that* everything."

She was still pale, her eyes huge, as she suggested, "Let's sit down and—"

"What?" he demanded. "Talk? You wanna know all about it? You wanna know how, after I got over the state of him and first looked at her, I was confused as to who the fuck she was. I didn't fucking *recognize my mother*, Hellen. Her hair was matted with blood. Her face was beat to shit. If she wasn't wearing her waitress uniform from the truck stop with her nametag on it, I might not have known who the fuck she was until the cops figured it out. That was how bad he beat her. That was how far it went."

"But you'd defended her. You'd told him not to come back."

"Oh yeah I did. I mean, I learned when I was a little kid, if I tried to get in the middle, he'd knock the snot out of me. She told me," he set his voice higher, "'Dusty, baby, when Daddy's like that, you steer clear for Momma, okay? That's Momma's job, to make sure you steer clear.'"

Hellen was now crying.

He hated seeing that. It tore him up.

But he couldn't stop.

In his head, seeing his mother's face as she held him by his cheeks and asked him to do that for her.

Seeing her face after his father had beat it to a literal pulp.

"So I waited. I bided my time. And when she couldn't call me off and he couldn't beat me down, I took care of business. And then he's gone and I'm thinking we're good. I'm thinking we're golden. So I'm off with my goddamn buds, takin' in a fuckin' movie," he bit.

He moved then.

Went right to her.

Got right in her space.

Right in her face.

"Then what do I do, sweetheart?" he cooed. "I beat another defenseless woman to shit."

She lifted her hands toward his head, forcing out a heavy, "*Core.*"

But he stepped away. "Don't put your hands on me."

She came at him. "I have to."

He retreated again. "You need to get gone."

"You were allowed to be a kid."

"Get gone, Hellen."

"You were allowed to be with your buds."

"He waited. He knew I wasn't there to look after her."

"You were a kid, Core. You couldn't be with her every second. It isn't your fault."

His back hit wall.

Again, trapped.

"*Get gone,*" he snarled.

She bellied up to him.

"It isn't your fault."

"Get out of here."

"I'm not going."

"Get out."

"No."

"*Out!*" he shouted in her face.

"*No!*" she shouted back.

And then she kept going.

"I want two kids. I don't want to get married, though we can have a commitment party or something. I'm just not the white-dress kind of chick. But if we have a party, I don't want to spend a lot of money on that kind of thing because I could think of better uses for it, like a fabulous vacation at a beach somewhere."

He stared down at her, his chest heaving, hearing her words but not believing what he was hearing.

She continued chattering.

"And if we have two kids, we have to get a bigger house, because they might be a boy and a girl, which means they'll have to have their own rooms, and I want to have a house with a guest room. Though, I don't know anyone from out of town I'd let stay with me, but who knows where life will take us? We might meet people who will come visit us and we'll need a guest room."

He kept staring down at her.

She kept prattling.

"I also want a home office. And a den, because if the kids want to watch something we don't want to watch, they'll need their own space. But I don't want a TV in the bedroom. The bedroom is for sleeping and fucking."

She took in a huge breath.

And kept jabbering.

"So, the fence is gorgeous, but we shouldn't put too much more in this house. It's already been flipped. It's good as it is and it isn't our forever home. So, I figure, we're going to need at least four thousand square feet, maybe more. This means I hope you boys sell a lot of weed, though, I'll hold up my end. Oh, and I hope you're putting aside for retirement, because I figure I'll need a month for Italy alone, and this ass is nowhere near whatever sheets they put in two-star hotels in Rome...or *anywhere*."

He took hold of her then. He took hold of her hair on either side of her head.

He didn't go easy.

She didn't flinch. She held his eyes and held her ground and stood strong for him.

She stood strong for him.

That was his girl.

That was his Hellen.

His.

The words were as ragged sounding as they felt coming out of his mouth. "I didn't want you to think I was him."

"You're not him."

"She was beautiful."

"You're beautiful, so I believe that."

"When I thought he was gone, I got a job. I bought her a dress. It was the first brand-new thing either of us had in years."

The tears were coming again, and she was pressing against him as she moaned, "Oh, honey."

"I had dreams. Of getting us out. Getting her out of that trailer. Getting her far away from him. Two more years of high school, and then I was gonna take her and go."

Her hands were on him now, smoothing his cheeks, his forehead, his hair.

"She fought like a hellcat."

He felt her body shake with silent sobs.

"She lost," he whispered.

Hellen was done then, he knew when she wrapped her arms around his head and pulled it to her chest.

The weight of it was always too heavy to bear, and it was no different then.

So Core went down and she came with him, straddling his lap, holding him to her, rocking him as he locked his arms around her, Nanook snuffling his neck and whimpering, and one more time in his life, Core beat back the red.

He didn't cry, not that he was the type of man who thought that was weak. There'd been a lot of that going on up in their woods.

Just that he'd used up the tears he had for that mess years ago.

She cried though, so he let her hold him and he held her in return as she did it.

Finally, she pulled it together.

"You can't keep things from me," she sniffled into his hair.

"I won't," he grunted.

"Okay," she mumbled.

He pulled out of her headlock, but not out of her hold, when he tipped his head to look at her.

"I need to take care of you."

"How?" she asked.

"I don't know. I just need it."

"Okay," she repeated easily.

Jesus.

This woman.

"Okay," he muttered.

She started messing with his hair again, watching her hands as she pulled it away from his face.

"Babe."

She stopped doing that and her eyes came to him.

"Two kids is good, and I'm down with being a house dad so you can build your empire. I'm also down with having a guest room. But when the club has business to do, I'm with my brothers."

"I know. I'm glad. Beck told me what you guys do, and it's important. People who can't, need people who can, to make wrongs into rights."

He stared up at her.

She stared down at him.

At the same time, they realized where they were at.

She went after his jeans.

He went after hers.

"I got it," she said impatiently, rolling off to a hip, and taking care of business while Core unzipped and yanked his jeans and shorts over his ass.

She swung a leg over him and was back on.

He had knees up, cocooning her, when she sat on his dick.

"Fuck yes," he groaned.

She bounced, tagging his hair.

He watched, glorying in having her back, the sight of her, the feel of her, the smell of her.

And he kept watching until a week and a half without her caught up with him.

"Faster, baby," he encouraged.

"I love you," she gasped.

"Love you too. Now fuck me faster, baby."

She went at him harder and faster.

He went after her clit.

Her head fell back. "Oh my God."

He took a handful of her ass in his other hand.

The flush moved up her face.

"Pop," he grunted.

With a sweet buck and a cunt squeeze, she went for him.

He left her clit, took hold of her hips and pounded her down on him.

Then he blew for her.

She had her arms tight around his neck by the time he came down.

They had other things to talk about.

But only one they had to get to now.

"Do you forgive me?" he asked.

She slid her hands to his shoulders and looked at him.

"For what?"

"Rosie."

Her eyes grew soft and she cupped his face in both hands.

"That's not mine to give. And it's not yours to expect from her. So at this point, honey, the person you need forgiveness from is yourself."

"Must have fucked some wisdom in you along the way," he muttered, but his voice was heavy with the emotion her words caused.

Because she was right.

He didn't know if he'd get there.

He just knew she was right.

"Hardly, that was all me," she teased.

He looked into her eyes.

"Yeah, it was."

Her smile trembled.

It stopped doing that when she kissed him.

CORE SLID AWAY from Hellen in bed, took his feet, tugged on some jeans, pulled on a hoodie and yanked on some socks.

"Stay," he murmured when Nanook made moves to go with him.

Nanook did as told, concerned about his dad, but now she was back, still happy to stay with their woman.

He left the bedroom and tagged his phone.

It was dark, but not late.

He'd made sure she was fed because she needed to gain back that weight he took from her.

They'd talked.

She'd told him about Eleanor's visit.

He'd told her about how Bounty became Resurrection and answered her questions about Benito Valenzuela.

When she heard what he had to say about Valenzuela (and he'd given her the condensed version, but the guy had been a such piece of shit, that was enough), she got seriously pissed, because, although Nails spilled about Rosalie, most of the rest of what she said was shit.

They fucked again, and since she'd come twice, cried a lot, they'd worked it out and it had been emotional, not to mention, she told him she hadn't been sleeping great (he hadn't either), she'd been exhausted.

So she passed out.

But he had a call to make.

He stepped out on the patio and closed the door behind him.

He was lifting his phone to make the call when he stopped.

He stopped and looked around.

He saw the furniture and the rug, the toss pillows and the lanterns, the flagstone and the fireplace, the rusted outline of a motorcycle hanging.

He turned to look in the house.

He could see most everything because he had a lot of windows. French doors to the kitchen. A huge picture window by the pool table.

The under-cupboard lights in the kitchen were on, casting a shine on his blender and coffee maker, dimly illuminating the pool table that was set with balls ready to break.

He didn't live in a trailer.

He wasn't wearing secondhand clothes.

The woman in his bed would never take a fist to her flesh, and if by some slim chance she did, it would not be Core's, but the man who did it would not continue breathing.

She would forever be beautiful, nothing weighing down on that, no one stealing it away.

She was safe.

He was safe.

He'd found a family.

He'd made something of his life, fucking up royally along the way, but he still did it.

He'd made something of his life.

On that thought, he placed his call.

Beck picked up right away.

"Hey."

"She's home."

"Brother, man,"—that came out in a gush of breath—"*damn.* Happy for you."

"She brought the bylaws back."

Hesitation and then, "You pissed at me?"

"She's sleeping in my bed. She needs sleep. She needs to eat, get meat back on her bones. But she's in my bed. What do you think?"

Beck didn't respond to that.

"We need to go back into the woods," Core told him.

"Figured that," Beck muttered.

"You gotta get it, when I found her, I had to give it to her. She had to get it first."

"I know, brother. I been there before you, remember?"

Right.

"I'll call a meet," Beck said. "We'll find a time. Then we'll gear up and go into the mountains."

He heard the door open behind him, twisted, saw Hellen step out with Nanook, and lost his mind.

"Gotta go," he whispered, because if he talked louder, he would shout.

"Later," Beck replied.

Core just took his phone from his ear and stalked to her.

She was in another one of his hoodies, it fell over her ass, barely, and she had a pair of his socks on her feet.

That was it.

"Get your ass in the house. It's fucking freezing out here." He came up against her and stopped because she didn't move, except to wind her arms around him.

"What are you doing out here?" she asked.

Damn, he liked her hair like that, a mess from his hands having been in it.

He shook off thoughts of her hair.

"Get in the house."

"Were you talking to Beck?"

Fuck it, he'd answer her questions fast then get her into the house.

"Yes. We need to go back to the woods."

"Good," she mumbled.

"Babe—"

"You had to come out here to do that?"

Shit, she knew before he did why he came out there to make his call.

She could see down deep into him.

All the way to his...

Fuck him.

All the way to his core.

"I had to be in my space. Space I made."

"Okay."

"I didn't get it until you asked that."

"Okay," she repeated.

He slid his arms around her. "Maybe, I don't know, when she died, she probably wasn't thinking about anything but the pain she was feeling."

Hellen pressed closer, held tighter...

And listened.

"Or that she knew she was going to die."

She held on but said nothing.

"Tortured myself for years that what was in her head in those moments was that she worried about me. I got into trouble. Acted out. I worried that at her end, she thought she brought another man like him in the world. Worried that she died thinking that."

"I bet she was worried," she said.

A familiar current of rot charged through him.

"Worried about her boy," she went on. "And what he'd do when he got home and saw his mother that way, and knew, for years, maybe the rest of his life, he'd blame himself for not being there for her."

Core dropped his forehead to hers.

"She didn't think you were him, honey. She knew who you were. You proved it to her by making her safe. It didn't last as long as it should have, but that's what she had, that's what you gave her before he took her away."

"Yeah," he pushed out.

"So why are you out here?"

"Because I had to look at it. What I made with my own hands. And I wish she'd lived to see I got out and built something."

Hellen shoved her face in his neck.

"Found a family. Found a good woman."

She shoved her face in harder.

"And maybe got the chance to give what I found to her."

Hellen held on tight.

"You gonna get out of the fucking cold now?" he asked.

"Yeah," she answered.

He let her go and took her hand.

He led her inside.

He took her to his bedroom.

When he got in bed with her, her legs were freezing.

He knew it.

"Hellen," he growled.

"Make me warm," she whispered.

Well, shit.

He could do that.

So he did.

23

DONE

Hellen

THE NEXT MORNING, I sat at Core's kitchen table while he made eggs and bacon.

As for our pup, unless Core and I were in the same space, it was a difficult decision for Nanook to pick which one of us he wanted to be with.

Though, he had no issue with this when one of us was cooking, and definitely not when his dad was frying bacon, and he knew Core put in a couple of strips just for him because Core always cooked a treat for his boy.

Hence, Nanook was in the kitchen.

I'd texted Xanthia to tell her I'd be late into the office, and we needed to have a meeting so I could explain how some personal issues had been troubling me, but now were sorted.

It was going to be harder to send my next texts, but they had to be sent because people I loved were worried about me.

First, to a group that included Marcy, Kyra and Li.

Crisis averted. Core and I are back together. It's a long story, but everything is good now. Cocktails at my place on Friday, not only so I can explain everything, but also so we can officially bid adieu to my apartment since I'm moving in with Core.

I sent that bombshell, and while it exploded, I sent my next to Archie.

Core and I talked. We worked it out. I hope you understand how things went down and why I reacted the way I did. But I'd really like to chat with you when you have some time.

My phone blew up before I finished my text to Archie.

What?! Marcy.

Whoa! Wow! Are you okay? Kyra.

That's it? It was over, you go into seclusion, now it's back on and you're moving in? Marcy.

And is Core okay? Kyra.

And then just...Friday, cocktails? Seriously? Marcy

Before I could reply to them, I got from Archie, *Absolutely. Just say when.*

Thanks, I sent to Archie, then, *I'll get back to you. My phone is blowing up because I just told my friends we're back together.*

Then I sent to the girls, *It's a lot. It was emotional and I'm warning you, it's private for Core so I'm not certain how much he's okay with me sharing with you.*

Then, before they could reply to that, my thumbs flew over my screen in order to send my next.

It meant a lot to me you gave me space. I needed it. I couldn't have dealt with anyone being in my face, no matter how well-intentioned.

Off that went and then I sent, *But I'm okay. More than okay, I'm happy and relieved and Core and I are in a good place. And yes, Core is okay too. It's all good.*

While typing this, I got from Archie, *Not a surprise and cool. I'm just glad you took the time to listen to him. I know it was heavy. I get it. It was tough to wrap my head around too. I just had to get to the place where I paid attention to the men I knew, not what I knew about them. But we'll talk. Just let me know what time is good for you. xxoo.*

Reading her text, I felt like my heart let out a breath it had been holding for a week and a half.

Because there it was, in a text-based nutshell.

Paid attention to the men I knew, not what I knew about them.

That was exactly what I needed to hold on to.

While reading this, I received, *Okay. Friday. Love you and SFG you sound better*, Marcy.

For a second, I didn't know what "SFG" meant and thought I'd have to open Safari to find out, then I figured it out: *So fucking glad.*

I catalogued that to use it later.

So pleased for you and Core and can't wait to see you! Kyra.

And finally, Li, who we probably woke up from all our texting, *OMG! THIS MAKES ME SO HAPPY!*

I figured Li would tell Mom and Andy, but I also had to tell Mom and Andy.

Therefore, I texted Mom, *Everything is fine with Core. Back as it should be. Can I come over tonight for a glass of wine and explain?*

I immediately got back, *Yes, honey. I'm so relieved to hear you two have worked things out. I'd hoped you would. See you tonight. Can't wait.*

Simple. No pressure. Loving.

My mom knew me so well.

And my mom was the best.

I put my phone down and took a second with that because I had an appreciation for it then like I'd never had before.

I was interrupted in this warm thought when Core slid a plate in front of me.

I stared at it.

It wasn't eggs and bacon.

It was a homemade hash brown patty browned to perfection, on top of which were precisely sliced avocados, on top of which was a perfectly fried egg that appeared artistically dotted with pepper and sprinkled with minced chives. And to the side there were three rashers of crispy bacon.

It looked restaurant quality.

I turned my attention to him. "This says 'welcome back' almost better than the two orgasms you gave me."

He chuckled, dropped a kiss on the top of my hair and sat beside me in front of his own plate, reaching for the hot sauce to shake on his food.

My man liked his hot sauce. It was something I'd noticed, but never really paid attention to.

Being able to watch him spice up his food again felt weirdly profound.

"That was a lot of the Baby Yoda theme," he noted.

He meant the texts.

Prior to our big blowup, he'd asked about my ringtones because he'd never seen *The Mandalorian*, something I intended to rectify when winter hit, days were colder and shorter, and binge-watching became the meaning of life.

"I think that theme is Mando's," I told him.

"Whatever," he muttered, lips tipped up while shoveling food in his mouth.

I watched.

I missed those lips.

And that stubble.

He noticed me watching, put his fork down, reached a hand to me, curled his fingers under my jaw and rubbed his thumb along it, his beautiful blue eyes tender on me.

"Told the girls we're back together," I shared. "They're keen to know what happened, but they're happy for us. And I'm going to see Mom and Andy tonight. They'll be relieved too. I've been shutting them out. And they think the world of you."

"All right." He didn't move his hand and continued to hold my gaze.

"I won't share anything you don't want me to. What happened is private to you. They don't ever need to know."

He was still rubbing my jaw when he said, "Do they know Nails is active?"

Shit, I hadn't seen to that.

I mean, in my defense, I thought I was dying of a broken heart, so I had other things on my mind.

But still.

How had I forgotten to share about Eleanor?

"I'll get on it," I promised.

He nodded, then said, "It's up to you whether you tell them who I was and what I did. It's your family."

"Okay." Damn, this was harder. "But I think it's important they know your history about your mom and dad." Before he could argue, I went on, "I won't go into detail, but as hateful as it is, it's a part of what makes you, and if I'd known before I heard—"

He moved his hand to curl it around the side of my neck and cut me off.

"I'll rephrase. It's up to you *what* you tell them. But I'll say that I learned the hard way this kinda shit, if you don't share, finds a way to bite you in the ass."

He was right.

Paid attention to the men I knew, not what I knew about them.

On the reminder, I made a decision.

"I think they need to get to know you better. They need to know the man I know, not just the man they think is good for me." I softened my tone. "I'm going to tell them about your parents, but the rest can wait. For now or forever. We'll see."

His eyes flashed with relief, and I knew I'd made the right decision.

He'd been through a lot recently, reliving that with me. He was tall and strong, but he was still human. We got through it, but now he needed a break.

Thinking that, I continued to look into those beautiful eyes, right there beside me.

"Missed you," I whispered.

"Yeah, me too," he whispered back.

I turned my head and kissed his wrist.

After I did that, with one more swipe of his thumb against my jaw, his hand dropped away.

Okay, good.

Enough of the mushy, it reminded me of the pain.

"Everything's okay," I assured.

"Awesome," he muttered.

Yes. It was.

On that thought, sitting with my guy, we ate breakfast.

"So, Eleanor told me some stuff about Core's past when his club was under a different charter, and they got involved in some not-great things."

Ugh.

Understatement.

But I had to leave it at that and keep going.

"This led me to walking away from him, only to find out why he allowed himself to get messed up in a situation where he did those things. That being what I just told you about his mom and dad. Not to mention, some experiences in the foster care system, which Core and I haven't gotten into yet, because frankly, reliving the nightmare of when he found his mom and dad was enough for one night."

I was sitting, holding an untouched glass of wine, talking to Mom, Andy and Li.

I was tense because I'd just mentioned the not-great things, and even though it was an understatement, Core was a biker. They might not be able to guess it all, but they could read between the lines.

But I had to mention to them because they needed to know why I walked away, and should the time come when I told them the fullness of it, I'd need to lay the groundwork now.

It didn't seem like that mattered.

Mom was openly weeping.

Li was pale, and she had tears in her eyes.

Andy's face was red, and I could see he was torn between anger at another father somewhere down the line doing something so hideous to his wife and the mother of his child, not to mention his actual child, concern for me and the same for Core.

There it was.

Proof my family was the bomb.

And proof that understanding what made a person helped you understand that person, including the things they did.

Part of me wished I'd saved Core and I the wretchedness of the last week and a half and given him the chance to explain.

Part of me allowed myself the response I had after what I'd learned.

But all of me was beginning to realize I admired Core and his brothers for where they took their club.

You could wallow in the hurts done to you and use them as an excuse to live your life hurting other people. Or you could fight the cycle and find ways to do better.

It said a lot about them that they'd sunk so low, but they recognized how low they'd gotten and fought to find ways to do better.

Last, all of me was glad it was mostly over for him and me.

Once I told my girls, Core and I could just move on.

"It'd probably be good if you all kept your eyes peeled for Eleanor," I advised. "She seriously got off on killing my joy. And I don't think she's done."

At that, Mom was still weeping, but she also looked kinda ticked.

Liane looked very ticked.

And the red in Andy's face had a different meaning.

"Just to make certain you know, the club cleaned up and essentially rebranded," I continued. "Except a rebrand for them is something a whole lot deeper. I don't want to get into their past now, but Beck, their president, let me read their bylaws. I guess it isn't the done thing if you're not a member, but he wanted me to see what the club was about so I'd give Core a shot. Because"—I couldn't stop my lips curving—"Core loves me and he was as miserable without me as I was without him, and I guess he was that in such a way that Beck didn't miss it."

"He does love you," Mom sniffled. "He didn't hide that." She swiped her nose with a tissue and held my gaze. "And I'm glad I raised a daughter who knows what's important and takes the time to listen."

"Why is he not here with you now?" Andy asked.

This question startled me because I hadn't thought to bring him.

"I think he went through enough, sharing his truth with Hellen yesterday," Mom said. "And if we were going to be terrible and judgy, he shouldn't have to go through that."

Andy's eyes narrowed.

On me.

"Did you think we were going to be terrible and judgy?" he demanded.

"Well...no."

"He needs to come around. Break this seal so it doesn't get awkward," Andy proclaimed.

"Yes," Mom said fervently. "He needs to come around."

I took a hard look at my mother.

She wanted him around for a different reason, in other words, to be all Mom Unit and give him the good parts of family.

I took another hard look at Andy.

The red was going out of his face, and he was taking a pull from his beer.

Okay.

Um...

That was a lot easier than I thought it would be, and I had an idea I knew why.

Archie.

On that thought, I finally took a sip of my wine, realizing I'd been tense about this, but I shouldn't have.

Because that was what I had.

The good parts of family.

I CAME HOME that night with a suitcase full of clothes.

I was moving in, might as well start right away.

Core met me in the laundry room and took it from me but otherwise didn't move out of my way.

"Go good?" he asked, and I could hear the tightness in his voice.

My family liked him.

And he liked my family.

"Mom wants you over for dinner Sunday."

The relief he exposed was about a thousand times deeper than what I felt.

Yeah, he loved me.

And he liked my family.

He bent to give me a kiss.

Then he took my suitcase to the bedroom.

THAT SATURDAY, I opened my apartment door to my stepsister, Archie.

She was the coolest chick I knew.

She was also the most beautiful.

Andy's first wife, Bryn, had been Black. I'd seen pictures of her, she was gorgeous. Mom also made sure she was a part of our lives, so a couple of said pictures were in frames in our house, and she encouraged Andy and Archie to talk about her.

Thus, from what I'd heard, Archie's mom also seemed amazing, and although I loved Andy with my mom, I still was sorry Andy, Archie and Elijah lost her.

Elijah's issue with his dad was that Mom was white. He took that as a rejection of their Blackness.

Although on a certain level, I understood this, mostly, I never would because I wasn't Black.

Also, I never would because Andy gave no indication that he didn't love and adore his children, or his dead wife. So, to me, he gave no indication of this rejection Elijah was feeling.

But again, I wasn't Black. Elijah was daily experiencing things out in the world that I never did, nor ever would, so whatever he felt from his dad that exacerbated those things were things I'd never feel.

That was between Elijah and his dad.

What I wasn't down with was the fact he took it out on my mom, and by extension, Liane and me, and of course coming along with this was not only Andy, but Archie.

We were a family, whether he liked it or not, and even if he didn't like it, he should still treat people with respect.

As I mentioned, things had improved with Elijah, but mostly, I steered clear of him, not because I didn't want to give him a shot (though, as mentioned, I was still holding a *wee* grudge), just because he'd been such a prick in the past, I was conditioned to doing it.

Archie was another matter.

She wasn't sweet and gooey, like Kyra. She wasn't edgy and full of attitude, like Marcy. She wasn't hippie laid-back and mellow, like Li. She wasn't honest, loyal and ambitious like me.

She was kind of all that (save the sweet, gooey, hippie and attitude parts, though she could be boho if that struck her fancy) in a chill way that always impressed me.

Seeing her standing there, making herself available when I was ready to talk, I knew I needed to make more of an effort with my stepsister. You couldn't have too many sisters, but she *was* my sister, not by blood but definitely through family.

So I had to sort myself out.

"Hey," I greeted, stepping aside for her to come in.

"Hey," she replied, accepting my invitation.

"I'm packing some stuff in the bedroom," I shared. "You want something to drink? You can hang on my bed while I keep at it, and we can talk."

"Sounds good," she agreed.

I got us both bottles of Topo Chico, and we headed to my bedroom, which was rife with empty and partially filled boxes.

"Obviously, I'm moving in with Core," I stated.

Her eyes twinkled. "Dad mentioned that."

"Today's mission is packing my clothes, bathroom and vanity," I told her. "Core's doing something with the club now but coming later to load it up so we can take it to his place. I've got until the end of the month to move, so we have time. Though, I want to be with him, not here, and this is the important stuff."

"Want help?" she offered.

"Sure," I agreed.

She saw I was in the middle of dealing with my vanity, so she headed to the closet.

I felt uncomfortable and I worried she felt the same.

Time to get into it.

"What do you know about what happened?" I asked.

"I know your cousin doesn't seem like a very nice lady," she answered from the closet.

"Yeah," I agreed to that understatement.

She came out with arms full of my clothes on hangers and went to a wardrobe box I had set up in the corner.

"And Dad says you all talked," she went on.

I nodded, tucking my trays of makeup into another box.

I'd also shared with my girls last night.

They were my girls for a reason. As such, they didn't make a big deal of the breakup (though there was some weeping when I shared about Core's parents, and it wasn't just Kyra), but they did make a big celebration we were moving in together.

This was because they knew me. They knew I wasn't a chick who had her head turned by orgasms and male attention. They could tell by the extreme of the story of Core's parents that we'd been dealing with something extreme in our relationship, and they left it at that.

Even Marcy.

Which meant a lot to me.

I didn't have an issue with them not knowing the fullness of the story in the now, none of them. That wasn't theirs to have. It was mine.

Now I had it.

And Core and I were beyond it.

Done.

"Haley especially." Archie stopped on the way back to the closet. "I'm glad you two are going over for dinner. She's feeling very motherly."

I felt one side of my mouth curl up at that, but said, "She's not old enough to be his mother."

"You know what I mean," Archie replied, her lips also curled up as she disappeared into the closet.

I knew what she meant.

Hesitantly, I remarked, "Core told me a lot about his club's past, what things were like when they were Bounty. He also told me a little about Chaos."

She came out with more clothes. "If you're worried. Don't. Jagger's told me everything."

From what little Core told me, Chaos had a dodgier history than Bounty.

Back in the day, Bounty were wannabe outlaws.

Chaos straight-up *were* outlaws.

Now, neither of them was, but the path to legitimacy had been thorny for both clubs.

Jagger being forthcoming caused me to experience a wave of relief.

I tucked my makeup wipes in the box.

Archie came and sat on the corner of the bed closest to me, so I turned to her.

I got straight to the point.

"Did you talk to Mom and Andy about Bounty before I got to them?"

She nodded but said, "Actually, Jag did. He didn't get into specifics, he just shared they'd done some fucked-up shit they knew was fucked-up, but they're on a path to redemption, they're good men, and he hoped we could find a way to helping you realize that."

Well, there you go.

"But also," she continued, "Jag had already told Dad and Haley who Chaos used to be. The documentary touched on it, but he wanted it to be out in the open so they'd feel free to ask questions. He also wanted to make sure they knew where the club was now, and they've made oaths to each other as brothers they won't stray from that path. He did this because he didn't want them to have any worries about me, and by extension them, being part of the Chaos family."

I didn't know he'd done that.

"So, they had experience with this already," I remarked.

"Yeah."

Okay.

Now the tough stuff.

"Did you tell them about Rosie?"

She shook her head. "No." She looked at her lap then at me again, "Did you know that Resurrection lost a brother in the war Chaos was having with Benito Valenzuela?"

I felt my heart squeeze.

Core had given me the condensed version, and apparently it was very condensed.

"I...no. Lost, like, he *died*?"

She nodded. "They were all willing to go down so Chaos could be free of that situation. It was a pretty extreme act of penance. And Rosie didn't miss it."

Oh God.

I held my breath.

"It's not my place to speak for her," she carried on. "I just know there's no bad blood between Chaos and Resurrection, that died with Bounty, and I know the reason for that is Chaos took its cue direct from Rosie."

"Wow," I whispered. "Does Resurrection know this?"

Archie took in a deep breath and said, "That's the thing, Hellen, they have to, but it seems like they don't care. To them, the act was still committed and that was their flashpoint. Jagger thinks, and from what he says, I agree, your man's club does what they do in order to stay the course. It isn't about atonement anymore. It's making certain they don't go back. And I get that. If I'd done something like what they'd done, it'd scare the fuck out of me I might do it again. It's like fighting addiction, every day is a new day where you have to make the right choices. You find a touchstone to help you make the right choices. Rosalie is their touchstone."

So they understood in some way that Rosalie had moved on?

"That makes sense," I mumbled then asked, "But they know Rosie is..." I didn't know how to put it. "Okay with them?"

She tipped her head to the side. "I'm not sure she's gone to each and touched their head and formally absolved them, but the club Chaos is would never associate with them if that wasn't the case, and Resurrection knows it. And the club Resurrection is would never be in Chaos's space if they didn't know it too."

That also made sense because it was clear Core hadn't forgiven himself, and maybe none of them had, and they didn't because they needed that reminder to stay true to what they aspired to be.

"Now, to get to what I should have made time to tell you months ago," she began.

I lifted my chin, an invitation for her to go on.

"For me," she began, "Jag's history, what he came from, what he belongs to, is one of the reasons I love him so much. There's something really beautiful about being your own individual, but still understanding how important it is to be a part of something bigger. To demonstrate loyalty and put the work in to keep a family healthy, even as you're all giving each other the space to be just who you are."

She lifted a shoulder and hitched her lips before she carried on.

"I've never been a joiner, because most things you join, if you already aren't like them, they make you be like them. Think like them. Dress like them. Act like them. Honestly, I understand wanting to be a part of a community, but stuff like that worries me. Losing your identity, who you are to a collective whole."

I was with her on that.

"But I get what Chaos has," she went on. "It's kind of the same thing, still, it's also the antithesis. There's a sensibility they all share to be in that life, but other than that, anything goes. The joining for them is a celebration of differences, and it works. Like, there's Tyra in her high heels, and Lanie with her award-winning advertising firm, but also Rosalie, who's a biker babe down to her bones. Then, of course, me, who's not like any of them. I mean, really, *really* different women. On the face of it, not much in common. But I've never seen a stronger sisterhood than the one we share."

I thought about this. About how much I liked Janna, Peanut, Choppy and Ducks, but how completely different the last three were than Janna. Further, how I was different than all of them. But how lovely they were with Janna, accepting she preferred to be quiet and in the background while they were loud and rowdy, and how cool they were with me.

So what Archie said made me feel happy.

Because I knew I'd have in Resurrection what Archie had in Chaos.

She reached out, touched my knee and kept going.

"And we wouldn't have that sisterhood if they didn't have their brotherhood," she carried on.

Yes.

That.

Absolutely.

"They are not in Jag's and my business," she continued. "They're not a part of our day-to-day lives. At least, not mine. Jag works in the garage. Jag goes to meetings. Jag works with the club. What I'm saying is, there's no insidious 'you have to be this way, act this way, dress this way.' However, if we ever needed anything, if something happened, all of them would be at our backs."

"Yes," I said softly, feeling this down deep.

Like Janna texting me. And Eight returning my things. And Beck coming to visit me.

Something happened, and they were at Core's and my backs.

"We heard you were with Core, and we thought he'd tell you. Maybe not on your first date, but Jagger knows him. He respects him. They work together on occasion. I've met him. I liked him. If either of us thought you weren't safe with him. If we—"

I cut her off. "I know. I figured that out after the fact."

"I felt bad," she admitted. "Because I was so wrapped up in Jag, in the store, setting up our new house, I didn't find time to reach out to you. Kinda to welcome you to the new sisterhood we shared. And then your cousin did what she did, and you didn't have me to go to in order to ask questions I could have answered for you. I'd had months to become that person for you, and I blew it."

I forgot she and Jag bought that new house.

But as for Archie feeling bad...

"I didn't reach out to you either."

"We fall into that, you and me. It's a bad habit. And I have to say, I don't like it."

That made me smile straight out. "I don't either."

She smiled back, but got serious when she stated, "I love Haley. I love her with my dad. I love the life they share together. And I love you and Li too."

She didn't really make a secret of that, but, God, it was nice to hear said out loud.

"I know, I feel the same about you."

"Maybe I think I feel strange, like some of Elijah's damage

brushed off on me. I think I feel it." She hesitated. "Especially with you."

Well...

Shit.

"Okay, I'm holding a grudge," I admitted.

"I get that."

"I shouldn't do it."

"I still get it."

"But you aren't Elijah."

She held my gaze. "No, I'm not."

No. She wasn't.

I had work to do on my own self.

Time to do that too.

"So we both should have reached out," I began. "We didn't. You tried to rectify that when something unexpected happened. I wasn't in a place to receive it. Now, all that's done, and we're here. You're busy with your life and your man. I'm busy with my life and the new one I'm building with my man. But let's make a pact in the midst of the sacred act of a woman helping a woman box her most precious belongings, we'll find time. Even if it's just touching base by texting. Though, it'd be cool you guys show at dinner tomorrow night to start it off. Deal?"

"Is this where we hook pinkies or make up a secret handshake?" she asked.

I began laughing, but said, "How about we do this instead?"

I stood and opened my arms.

She stood and did the same.

We hugged.

"It's cool to have a big sister," I said in her ear.

"It's cool to get to be one," she said in mine.

We stopped hugging and got back to work.

Archie didn't give up until the whole bedroom was packed, and we'd stacked the boxes, and three suitcases, in my living room.

I then cracked open a bottle of wine.

Because, again, with something tough but right that had to happen…

Done.

THAT EVENING, Nanook and I wandered into the living room after I put away the last of my stuff.

Core, who was stretched on the couch reading the book on the history of Harley Davidson I bought him (I hadn't allowed him to pay me back for that), took one look at me, closed the book, set it aside and pushed up to his feet.

"Last boxes ready to break down?" he asked.

He couldn't help me unpack (correction: I didn't let him because it was easier to do it myself rather than undo what he might do), so his self-appointed task was box breakdown and removal to one of the empty bedrooms.

However, it felt weirdly like he was standing to attention, reporting for duty.

"They can wait," I pointed out.

"I'll get 'em."

He then walked by me, touching my hip, and considering what Core was going to be doing was more exciting than me taking a load off in the living room, Nanook went with him.

I turned and watched them disappear into the bedroom.

Because something wasn't right about that.

And I didn't like it.

But I was too exhausted to do anything about it.

As far as I was concerned, I was moved in. I had my clothes, shoes, accessories, makeup and hair stuff. I'd go back to the apartment here and there, when I had time, in order to pack for the big move that didn't have to happen for three weeks.

So I was, for all intents and purposes, sharing my home with my man.

We were getting back to us, so maybe things would be weird for a while.

If that didn't go away, then I'd get into it.

For now, I took what I had in my hands, walked to the media unit and placed my Baccarat butterflies where they belonged.

I then plopped on the couch, listened to Core and Nanook do their thing, and when he came back, I told him, "I'd kill for some Chinese."

He got right on his phone.

He then joined me on the couch.

I knew exactly when he saw the butterflies.

Because instead of hanging with me on the couch, we were making out on the couch.

After the food arrived, we ate Chinese in front of the TV, neither of us making a big thing I was there and had no reason to go back to my place except to pack.

That wasn't weird.

Core and me just being, but doing it together?

As usual, we slotted right in.

24

MOODY

Hellen

I WAS IN THE CLOSET, rushing through changing clothes because I was late getting home and Core and I were going over to dinner at Beck and Janna's that night.

We were supposed to be there in five minutes. I felt shit that I'd lost track of time before I left the office, because no way would we be there in five minutes.

And I was looking forward to this.

I was keen to get to know Janna better. I was also keen to meet their kids. I was further keen to get beyond the last convo I'd had with Beck and move into a much better place with him.

But things had been crazy since Core and I got back together.

I'd been spaced out, dealing with our breakup, so I'd let work slide, and I had to catch up on it.

Not to mention, Xanthia had her own connections, she'd worked them and brought in five new clients (I was *so* right to hire her, she was sharp, had hustle and went the extra mile—she was the bomb!). But even if this was great for income, it was quite a bit of work.

Topping that, another of my clients heard we were expanding services and asked us to take over their website, newsletter and affiliate maintenance.

Further, Xanthia and I agreed the menu we were going to roll out, so it was full steam ahead on the conference we'd decided to host in Sedona next February.

In sending out a save the date, we already had seventeen clients that expressed interest, and considering we were thinking it'd be around ten, that was very exciting.

In other words, it wasn't a great time for me to mentally check out due to having a situation with my boyfriend, and it meant a lot of work when I checked back in.

Because of this, I wasn't getting home until after seven every night (and sometimes it was closer to eight), and I was working weekends, so I didn't have time to swing by my place to do much packing.

I had the hall bathroom sorted and maybe a quarter of the kitchen. But the kitchen was always the biggest job.

Since Core didn't need me to deal with the heavy stuff, he, Beck, Eight, Muzzle and Shim had driven their trucks to my pad, and now we had a guest room and furnished den at Core's.

It was up to me to get the kitchen sorted and clean the unit, and I was facing the fact (and some panic) my once expansive three weeks to do this had now dwindled to only a few days.

I just didn't know how I was going to be able to carve out the time.

Last on my taking-up-time-and-headspace list, Liane had sent a two-word text while I was driving home: *Call me.*

I hadn't read the text until I got home.

This wasn't very Liane, and it concerned me, but I didn't have time to call her and change my clothes so we might be fashionably late, not offensively late.

I'd call her on the way over to their house.

On this thought, Core entered the closet and tripped over the shoes I'd just kicked off (and, truth be told, two other pairs I hadn't yet put away).

I stretched my lips down in an eek expression while his face tightened.

"Sorry, I'll put them away when we get home," I said.

"Not a problem," he grunted. "You close?" He then lifted his hand to show me his phone, and I took that as he wanted to call Beck to give them our ETA.

"Five minutes," I said, yanking a pair of jeans off the shelf.

"Five real minutes or five Hellen minutes?"

I turned back to him, my lips beginning to curve in a smile, thinking he was being funny, but the serious look on his face did not say he was amused.

"Are there Hellen minutes?" I asked cautiously.

"Babe, when are we gonna be in the truck?" he asked in return.

"Five real minutes," I said quietly.

He took off, head bent to his phone.

Nanook looked to me, to Core, experienced a moment of doggie indecision, then he followed Core.

I hurried in changing clothes, and to shave off time, made the very difficult decision not to switch my purse to one that matched my outfit (this was hard, but I told myself it was just two couples having dinner in a home, I wouldn't be rated on accessorizing). Then Core and I were in his truck, heading to Beck and Janna's.

He was quiet and it seemed a moody quiet.

"Are you mad at me?" I asked.

"Nope," he answered.

I didn't believe him.

"I know I've been getting home late. I'm sorry. I'm trying to catch up. But Xanthia's fully in the saddle, she's an amazing help, and it'll calm down soon."

He didn't reply.

For some reason, this made me start babbling, and this babbling included being too honest in the current atmosphere.

"Though, the conference is going to be a lot of work, and we have a lot of new clients. If the take-up in new services is healthy, I may need to hire someone else. Possibly part-time. I didn't expect Xanthia to have so many contacts and getting new clients rolling is always extra effort at first. But even though this is unplanned, it's a good problem to have. I just can't let our service slide in the meantime."

"So, it's not gonna calm down soon," he noted.

"Um..."

I was feeling anxious, and I didn't know why.

He'd been mad at me before, and we'd talked it out (okay, yelled it out).

Maybe it was that this was work. He knew how important that was to me. And if he was mad about work, that would not only be upsetting, it would also be troubling.

"It does get like this a lot," I warned.

"Why are we having this conversation?" he asked.

Considering the climate in that truck, I didn't understand the question.

Though I did my best to answer it.

"I'm trying to explain why I was running late."

"I know why you were running late."

"I don't want you to get upset because I work so much, seeing as I always work so much."

"I'm not upset you work so much."

"You seem to be in a mood."

"Yeah?"

"Uh, yeah."

"So when you asked, 'Are you mad at me,' you didn't hear my answer?"

All righty then.

"Is something else bothering you?" I pressed.

"Nope."

Hmm.

I wasn't a fan of that because it sure seemed something *was* bothering him, and if it was, we should talk about it.

But now was not the time to get into it.

I'd been looking forward to that evening since we'd planned it, and Beck was Core's best friend (with Eight and Muzzle close seconds), so I knew he was looking forward to it too.

Now was the time to enjoy the evening.

Thus, I let it go.

"Would you mind if I called Li? She texted me on the way home and I haven't had a chance to call her."

"Why would I mind if you call your sister?"

There seemed some attitude in that when he could have just said, *No*.

I didn't get into that.

I called Li.

"Hey, everything okay?" I asked when she answered.

"Are you at work?" she asked in return.

This didn't bode well for our conversation.

"No," I answered hesitantly.

"I didn't want to interrupt you at work with this," she said.

"With what? Are you okay?" I pressed.

"I got to feeling guilty," she told me. "So I called Grandma to feel her out about Granddad. And the truth, he does have diabetes and it's messing with him because diabetes does that. The lie, he might not be fit as a fiddle, but he isn't reaching to death's doorbell."

"So..." I couldn't finish it because I couldn't force my mouth to say the words.

Li could. "So Dad used that as a ploy to see his daughters. On the one hand, it indicates how much he missed us that he'd go to those lengths. On the other hand, that's super fucking shitty, and if he'd managed to reconcile with us, how would he explain he played us like that?"

I had no answer to this question.

It was Li's turn to ask, "You okay?"

I wasn't. You never got used to a controlling parent's ever-changing and sometimes escalating attempts at control.

I also was. Because I might not be close with my grandparents, but I didn't want them to die. And this was further indication that it was healthier not to have my father in my life.

"I am," I told her. "You?"

"It's entirely messed up, but at least Granddad isn't dying."

She was right there with me.

I told her Core and I were on our way to dinner, and she let me go.

I'd barely taken my phone from my ear when Core demanded, "What was that?"

"Granddad isn't dying," I began, then told him the rest.

Okay, so maybe there wasn't a mood coming from Core when we got in the truck, because now, there was definitely a mood.

"Honey, I'm used to this kind of thing," I placated him.

He reached for my hand.

I gave it to him.

He squeezed it, pulled it to his lips, kissed the back of it, and then let me go.

I smiled.

All righty then.

All around all better.

"Okay, I feel the need to apologize," I said to Janna.

We were in her kitchen.

She was doing something with corn in a skillet, I was placing biscuits on a baking sheet.

I'd discovered a bit earlier that Janna and Beck's kids were adorable, but very young (aged two and a half and a six-month-old baby). They had Beck's dark hair and Janna's dark eyes. I got to meet them, then they had to put them to bed.

Which made me feel even more crap I'd been late.

"No, you don't," she replied.

"We were late."

"Core said you own your own business. It probably gets hairy sometimes."

"It does."

"So that's understandable."

That was sweet.

Then again, Janna was sweet.

She moved to the oven and peered in.

I got to the heart of it.

"Okay, then I need to apologize about not taking the hand you were offering when Core and I had our thing."

She came to me, took the tray of biscuits and returned to the oven.

Opening it and sliding them in along with what appeared to be the most delicious stuffed pork chops known to personkind, she said, "Relationship stuff never needs an apology."

Again, sweet.

"I think it's an adjustment, being in the life," I remarked.

"What life?" she asked the oven she was closing.

"The biker life."

She turned to me, tipping her head to the side. "Do you think that?"

"Well...I..."

Shit, I'd put my foot right into my mouth.

She walked to me, leaned into a hip on the counter and placed a hand on it.

She then looked at me with an expression that was guarded, but also kind.

"You two are back together, so obviously you listened to Beck and made your decision. My opinion?" She touched her chest and offered a small smile. "The right one. I'd not known good until I met Beck and the club. What they were before, that doesn't matter to me. It didn't then, and I met Beck close to after it happened, and it doesn't now. I have two beautiful babies. I have a husband who loves me deeply and who has always treated me with almost excruciating care. And we never have to worry if we need a babysitter."

Three things struck me about that.

I filed away the babysitter information.

And I addressed the first.

"I'm sorry you've never known good."

"Until Beck," she corrected.

And that was the last thing that struck me.

Almost excruciating care.

"Until Beck," I murmured, not sure I knew her well enough to ask her to unpack that with me.

"But you know what he did. And I know what he did. And still, that's my reality."

"Yes," I agreed.

She touched my arm, dropped her hand and said, "It's simple. You're just a woman who met and fell in love with a man. People put labels on stuff. They do that so they can justify making decisions about things they don't know anything about, so they can't possibly understand them. Core's not your first boyfriend, am I right?"

I shook my head. "No, he's not."

She nodded once. "So it's that. You're learning to be with your boyfriend. He just happens to ride a bike and hang with other guys who ride bikes. Of course, the biker world might not be one that you're used to, but it's not that much different, unless you focus on the differences, instead of seeing they're just people."

"You think it's that simple?" I asked as she moved back to the corn.

She picked up a wooden spoon and started pushing it around.

"You might think I'm crazy, but I think people making blanket decisions about who people are is what complicates everything in this whole wide world. You don't know unless you know, and you can't possibly know every living being on this planet. So you can't possibly say, 'They're all like that,' and then treat them how you decide people 'like that' should be treated. Not one single person is just like another, no matter what traits or customs or inclinations they share. The biker life isn't an adjustment, it's just life to bikers. In other words, it's just life. It might be different than the life you live, but once you live with people who live that life, it becomes just life to you too."

"Okay, so maybe it is that simple," I mumbled, deciding that maybe I underestimated Janna.

Not that I didn't think she was smart.

Just that I didn't know she was sage.

"I'm not lecturing you," she replied gently. "I just wanted you to know that if you let it be easy, it's easy. If you make it hard, it'll be hard. And I'll go on to advise that it isn't hard, so don't make it hard."

"Yeah." I was again mumbling.

"Something else on your mind?" she asked, still stirring the corn.

I lifted a shoulder. "It's just that Core seemed in a mood earlier tonight and he didn't want to talk about it."

She laughed a pretty, quiet laugh, and when she was finished, she winked at me.

"Get used to that, sister. These boys have moods. Don't worry about it. If it's a situation that you need to know, he'll eventually let fly."

I hoped so. Letting things fester wasn't my favorite thing.

"But I have five years in with these guys. Actually, longer," Janna went on in a teasing lilt. "So if you need help adjusting to *that*, I'm your girl."

"I would expect that eventual call," I accepted her invitation, earning another one of her quiet laughs.

"What are you women talking about?" Beck asked as he strode in with Core.

"How moody you boys can be," Janna answered.

Oh shit.

Core's eyes cut to me.

Awesome.

"Absolutely," Beck agreed. "Need my woman's touch to snap me out of it."

"So that explains it," Janna said, making eyes at me. "It's a ploy for his woman's touch."

He slid his arm around her shoulders and murmured, "Everything is a ploy for your touch."

How cute.

I loved that Beck and Janna were cute, and I loved it especially for Janna.

She leaned back so she could again catch my gaze in order that I wouldn't miss her rolling her eyes.

I laughed, but I didn't commit fully to it.

Core said nothing, but he did come to lounge against the counter with me, gliding an arm around my waist.

So there was that.

Janna called all hands on deck to get dinner on the table, and we all moved to help, with her giving direction in her quiet way of who she wanted to do what.

I liked that. I liked it wasn't formal. She made it seem like family with all of us putting food in bowls or carrying it to the table.

I also liked Janna, and not only because she was wise, and she shared that awesomeness with me. But she did it honestly and kindly.

It always felt good when you knew you'd made a new friend.

And soon after we sat down, I learned her stuffed porkchops *were* the most delicious known to personkind.

On the way home, I addressed it.

"I'd just mentioned you were in a mood."

"Come again?"

"That's all I said. I wasn't talking about you to Janna. I'd just mentioned that you seemed to be in a mood."

"I lived with Kiki for three years."

I wasn't sure why he was repeating this information to me.

"Okay," I said slowly.

"I know women talk."

Ah.

"Okay," I muttered.

After that, the rest of the ride home was silent.

So yes.

Core wasn't a chatterbox, but he wasn't the quiet broody type.

This meant I was right.

Something was bothering him.

Hmm.

When we got home, we had sex I instigated that Core didn't shy away from in the slightest, and after, he cuddled me close just like usual and fell asleep.

However, I lay awake thinking that something was playing on his mind. The work he did with the club was heavy. And maybe he'd give it to me when he was ready.

The sex had been no less intimate and intense. The cuddle no less loving.

People had moods. Core was human (regardless that he sometimes seemed godlike when he was fucking me), of course he'd have them too.

I just needed to give him space to have them and patience until he was ready to share the reasons for them with me.

On that thought, I fell asleep.

25

EXCRUCIATING CARE

Hellen

It all went down three weeks later.

I was exhausted.

I was because, in assessing what might contribute to Core's mood the night we went to dinner with Beck and Janna, I decided to alleviate what I thought might be a part of it.

In other words, in order to give Core more of my time, finish up the move, slide through the first family Thanksgiving with Core (which went great, obviously, because Core was awesome and my family was amazing), and get work done, I was getting up at four thirty rather than my normal six.

Also, to get to work even sooner, I shaved off time in the morning by picking an outfit and switching purses the night before. I was further in the throes of training my hair to take a once-every-two days wash, rather than every other day, to save the half an hour of a blowout two days in a row.

All of this because I made it my personal goal to leave the office no later than six (drop dead, six twenty) so I could get home to Core.

Sometimes I snuck in some work when Core was off doing things with the club. Or when we were hanging in front of the TV, Core with a joint and chilled mood, watching something he dug that I had no interest in, so I'd grab my laptop.

Sometimes he went to bed without me so I could spend an hour or so on my computer getting a jumpstart on the next day.

I was doing this for him, but things for me were rough.

The conference was more work than I expected. Christmas was approaching and I had at least a dozen new people to buy for. I'd called an all hands on deck with my girls to do a fast pack and clean of my old apartment, they'd pitched in and we'd gotten it done. But I hadn't yet had the time to work with Core to decide what stuff of mine we could use in our kitchen and what could be stored.

This meant those boxes, as well as other detritus from my apartment, were stacked at the front of where I parked my Mini in the garage. This was annoying to face every day, those boxes taunting me that they needed to be gone through. But also, they were in my way.

We couldn't put them in front of Core's huge-ass truck. That barely fit in the garage as it was.

They needed to be sorted, and stuff we weren't going to use put up in his attic to get those boxes out of the way.

So yes, I was exhausted and there seemed to be a mile-long work and life to-do list I faced every day.

And okay, maybe I was a little crotchety because of all of this when it all kicked off.

But who wouldn't be?

It began before we left the house.

We were going Christmas shopping, something I usually loved to do.

What was more, Core had no decorations at all, and mine were meagre, so we were off to augment that and Christmas-ify the house.

I should be in a great mood. I loved Christmas, and the little decorating we'd already done—putting up my tree—had been awesome (because we'd had sex under it after it was up but only halfway through adding the decorations).

I was in the closet again, finishing up getting ready.

Core was in the bathroom.

I heard him curse and Nanook gave a muted howl.

I was about to go see what was happening when Core walked into the closet holding up my tube of mascara.

"Is this important?" he asked.

"It's my mascara," I answered.

"Should I take that as a yes?"

I walked to him. "Yes, it's a yes." I reached and took the mascara from him. "Why do you have it?"

"Because I stepped on it and nearly broke my neck in the bathroom."

Oh shit.

"Maybe I didn't put it away," I stated the obvious.

"Yeah," he said, then, before I could apologize, he turned and prowled out.

However, it must be noted he glanced along the floor, all the way to the corner where our hamper was *before* he prowled out.

I glanced at the floor too. And yes, it was true, my shoes were everywhere. So were a couple of pairs of my jeans, a few sweaters, a skirt, a bra and the laundry hamper was overflowing because I hadn't had time to do the laundry in a few weeks.

This was when I started to get annoyed.

Because, okay, if he didn't realize I was burning the candle at both ends, doing this so I could have time to be with him, then he really wasn't paying attention.

And it wasn't like he didn't have five hundred pairs of faded jeans and eight hundred tees/Henleys/thermals, not to mention his thousand pairs of underwear (okay, exaggeration, but he had a lot of those things).

He was a bachelor before me, and as such, he packed the closet so he'd have to do laundry as little as possible.

He wasn't hurting for things to wear.

And if he was, he could do a couple of loads of the laundry his own damned self.

I mean, they had staff for the dispensaries, so outside of the brothers keeping an eye on them, it wasn't like Core's day job was super taxing. And his pro bono vigilante work happened night or day, but it was his choice to put that time in.

If this was House Dad material for when that time came, it was for the birds.

I walked into the bathroom to grab the lip gloss I wanted, and to put my mascara back, and...

Right.

I had to admit, the dry shampoo can was out, so was my brush, and I hadn't put away my blush, highlighter, foundation or any of the brushes or sponges I used to apply them.

He had a great bathroom. The flippers that had rehabbed his house had gone the extra mile in there with white tile laid in a herringbone pattern with black grout, a soaking tub as well as a big shower, and a long, black vanity with double sinks, which were kick-ass white bowls sitting on the counter.

There were also illuminated mirrors, which were perfect for doing makeup.

He had his space at the basins, and I had mine.

But it couldn't be denied, not only was I was encroaching on his, his side was very tidy and mine was...not. Not just the makeup and hair stuff, but the dust from the makeup was sprinkled on the white counter and some of it had smudged.

It looked like shit.

It also looked like Oscar and Felix were sharing a bathroom.

In fact, Core was generally tidy, not leaving his keys and phone just anywhere. When he grabbed the mail (and Core always grabbed the mail), he sorted through it, his correspondence whisked away to wherever he tucked his paperwork. When I got home from work, I'd see my mail stacked in a neat pile on the little built-in desk that sat in the corner of the kitchen by the door to the laundry room (and, truth, I hadn't touched that growing pile in days).

He had cleaning people come every two weeks.

But although I'd never seen him do it, we had a dog that was hella fluffy, yet the dog hair did not overwhelm us between these visits. I knew this was because, before I'd even moved in, Core had one of those expensive rechargeable, cordless vacs that were superpowered so they sucked up dog hair.

He had to run it, almost daily.

I thought this because I hadn't run it, ever.

Evidence was suggesting my man was a neat freak, and I was not super messy, but if I got caught up in work and life, I could let things get out of hand, and maybe that was bothering him.

However, he was a grown-ass man, so if it was, he could use his words.

But in the meantime, at the very least, I needed to remember to put my mascara away because I wasn't super hip on the idea that he might break his neck tripping on it in the bathroom.

Quickly, I tucked everything where it was supposed to be and wiped up the makeup sprinkles with a hand towel. I put out a new towel (our last clean one, eek!), took the dirty one with me, tossed it on the hamper (it rolled off and onto the floor...mental note: do a couple of loads of laundry tomorrow) and headed out to Core.

"Ready to go?" I asked.

"Yup," he answered, hitting the remote to turn off the Christmas tree lights and then heading to the garage.

I'd done preliminary research, and considering the aesthetic we seemed to share, assessed that CB2 and West Elm were our primary targets for Christmas décor. Therefore, Core headed us to Cherry Creek.

"I'm sorry about the mascara," I said.

"Not a big deal," he replied.

"I'll do better at putting away my makeup," I told him.

"Again, not a big deal."

"Things have just been busy. I'm usually a lot neater than this."

"Doesn't matter, babe."

He sounded like it didn't matter, but I looked at him anyway.

He looked like Core driving, not Core driving while he was ticked.

Okay, so maybe I read into that glance in the closet. I, too, would be ticked if I tripped on something he left out and it rolled onto the floor.

Then I'd get over it.

He reached a hand my way.

I put mine in his, he squeezed it, tucked it to his chest for a second and then let it go.

Yes, I'd read into it wrongly.

He was cool.

We were in CB2, and I was trying to talk Core into buying a trio of white, fluffy (as in, they were made of feathers) baby Christmas trees for table décor.

He was not feeling it.

And as such, right in that moment said, "No."

Or I should say he repeated the word no, since he'd already said it once.

I grinned at him. "It's perfect for a festive arrangement on the kitchen island. Maybe we could buy some candles and those little snowmen over there."

I pointed to the snowman figurines that would go perfectly, nestled among the fluffy trees.

He looked that way and said nothing.

I leaned into his side, grabbing his hand in both of mine. "Trust me, I have a vision."

It was then I caught the expression on his face and the fact he seemed frozen.

I turned that direction, and this time, I didn't see the snowmen figurines.

I saw a very pretty woman, her gaze darting up and down between Core and me, and she was walking our way.

I knew who she was before she got to us and Core greeted, "Kiki."

"Hey," she pushed out breathily, gazing up at him like she'd been dieting all year long in order to let loose during the holiday season, and he was a life-size chocolate Santa.

Core took his hand from mine but only to slide his arm around my shoulders, holding me right where I was pressed to his side.

"This is Hellen," he introduced.

She tore her gaze from him and looked at me.

One could say, he had a type.

She had ass, she was brunette, she was average height, but her eyes were dark brown. She was either only a few years older than me, which would be impossible if they broke up five years ago and he was with her for three, or she took care of herself. She looked twenty-five but was probably closer to thirty or even older.

Oh, and it was worth a repeat, she was really, very pretty, which would stand to reason because Core was gorgeous.

Still.

"Hi," I said.

"Hi," she replied, cutting that short word off so it sounded like a clipped "hiyee."

I didn't get ugly vibes, I got pained ones.

"You doing good?" she asked Core.

He lifted up the basket that held precisely four baubles we'd agreed on, and that was it.

"Getting ready for Christmas," he told her.

He wasn't rubbing it in, he was being informative.

Even so, I feared those baubles would sprout wings like a golden snitch cursed by a Slytherin and attack her, such was the way she was staring at them.

I nearly reached across Core to make him lower his arm.

"Uh, great, uh...yeah. Christmas," she stammered.

"You good?" Core asked, finally dropping the basket.

"Yes, uh..." She pulled herself together. "Yes. Real good."

Core's eyes moved over her head through the store. "Where's your man?"

In a small voice, she said, "We broke up."

Oh boy.

This was around the time I kicked him with the toe of my boot, just a tap, but he needed to get with the program.

She was rethinking her decision of letting him go.

I wondered if she'd heard the direction the club went after what happened, and now she wished she'd stuck it out.

I wondered if he just gave good boyfriend, like he did with me, and she missed him, regardless.

I'd never know, and I was grateful for that.

"Well, I should get to it. Lots of presents to buy," she said.

"Nice to meet you, Kiki," I put in quickly, trying to sound low-key and genuine, not snarky.

"You too," she replied to me, then up to Core. "Good to see you..." She swallowed. "Good to see you happy, Dusty."

Oh man.

She called him Dusty.

Dusty, straight up, was a cool name. It was kind of cute, kind of cowboy, the first Core was only rarely (such as, when he was winning at pool), the last he just was a modern version of, considering his bike riding and vigilante ways.

I realized in that moment that I'd unconsciously vowed to myself never to use it because his mom called him that.

However, right then, I got peeved because now I couldn't use it since that was what Kiki had called him.

"You too," Core said.

You too?

She didn't look happy.

I didn't indicate that to Core in any way.

I pasted a smile on my face when she glanced at me before she walked away.

Core turned back to the fluffy Christmas trees.

He then repeated, "No," took my hand and started to guide me to another display.

"Are you okay?" I asked, watching him closely.

"Sure," he answered.

"I...well, when you first saw her, you looked stunned."

"Haven't seen her in a while, used to see her every day. She kicked me when I was down, even if I deserved it, it still hurt. So, yeah, I was stunned."

He stopped us, let me go, and picked up a little polar bear who would look adorable wandering through some fluffy trees and snowmen.

"Do you want to go get a coffee and talk?" I offered. "Or maybe bag this and come back out tomorrow?"

He ignored my questions completely.

"Not the feather trees, the white cone ones, the snowmen, and these," he put the polar bear in our basket, grabbed another, smaller one (momma and baby, perfect!), and finished, "And some candles."

He had an eye for Christmas décor. That would work, it was both of us, unlike those fluffy trees, which were just me.

I was impressed.

It was hard to focus on the impressed even as he dragged me to the snowmen.

"Core," I called.

He looked down at me.

And growled, "Babe, let it go."

Okeydokey.

I didn't like that much, but I wasn't going to cause a scene in CB2. Furthermore, CB2 was not the place to have this conversation.

Core grabbed the snowmen, pulled me to the trees, picked three of varying sizes (and threw a clear one in with the white, which was rad, since they were hollow and I could put a string of those tiny LED lights in it and the whole arrangement would sparkle), and then off we went, him leading, me following, so he could add some black candlestick holders and white taper candles.

It was going to be a sweet arrangement.

I no sooner had this thought when we were off to the cashier.

So I guess we were done at CB2.

He paid.

So I guess he was buying.

We went out to the truck and got in.

"Where's this other place?" he asked.

"How about we grab an early lunch?"

He turned to me, forearm draped over the steering wheel. "You hungry?"

No, I was feeling weird.

"I just think that—"

"Christ, Hellen," he bit off. "Kiki and I are over. I was surprised to see her. Don't make something that's not a thing, into a fucking thing. It's you. I'm living with you. I'm fucking you. I'm in love with you."

"I never doubted that."

Or, at least I didn't until he got pissed about talking about Kiki.

"So let it go and tell me where this other place is."

We could walk there, but I didn't say that, and anyway, it was best the bags were stowed in case we went crazy in West Elm and had to drag a whole bunch back.

I directed him where to go.

We got some lighted swags to drape around the media center, plus Christmas stockings for him, me and Nanook, and we did this trudging through West Elm like strangers forced to shop together.

When we got back in the truck, Core made an effort.

His voice was soft and even sweet when he asked, "Now, you want to get some lunch?"

I wasn't feeling soft and sweet.

I was dwelling on Kiki.

"I'd just like to go home," I told the windshield.

"And she hasn't let it go," he muttered irritably, soft and sweet a memory. He started up the truck and headed us home. He was driving for five minutes before he modulated his tone again and noted, "You wanted to get some presents."

"I'll shop online."

"You wanted to go to physical stores because you don't want them to disappear, because everyone shops online and something about how all the packing materials are gonna fuck up the environment," he told me something I'd told him.

"I can do curbside pickup."

He said no more.

When we got home, he pulled into the garage and did his usual, not letting me carry anything in. Truth told, it wasn't that much. Not the massive, festive Christmas haul I'd fantasized about when thinking of shopping with him, bringing it home, unpacking it and putting it around the house. Then maybe doing something Christmas-y, like baking cookies or wrapping presents at the kitchen island.

It ended up being absolutely nothing like my Core-and-Me-Christmas Fantasy, seeing as I laid the polar bear/snowman arrangement on the kitchen island, he draped the swag, it took maybe five minutes for us both and we were in two separate rooms while we did it.

When I was done, I moved toward the hall on my way to grab some laundry and heard him remark, "So, that was fun."

Okay.

No.

I whirled on him and declared, "You have a problem."

"Just because you think I have a problem doesn't mean I actually have a problem," Core fired back.

"No," I contradicted. "You have a problem."

"So what's my problem, Hellen?" he asked, putting his fists to his lean hips. "That my ex is hot, and you got a good look at her, and it's flipping your shit?"

Oh my God!

"No," I snapped. "Though, you keep saying things like that, I'll start thinking on them."

"Is that a threat?"

I threw my hands out to the sides. "What's the matter with you?"

"Generally?" he asked, then waved a hand between us. "Or in the context of this shit?"

"Is it the laundry?"

"What?"

"The laundry. Me not doing the laundry?"

He appeared genuinely confused. "The laundry?"

"I haven't done it in a couple of weeks."

"Do you need laundry done?"

Was I going insane, or was this an extremely frustrating conversation?

No, an extremely frustrating *day*.

"Not really, but it's overflowing."

"You need the laundry done, I'll do it. I steer clear because you got nicer clothes than I do so I don't wanna fuck anything up. But if that's your damage, when I hit something I don't know what to do with it, I'll ask."

I crossed my arms on my chest. "I don't want you to do laundry."

"Then why are you talking about the laundry?"

I sought patience. "I'm asking if you're pissed at me that I haven't done laundry."

"It'd be nice there wasn't a mountain of dirty clothes in the corner of the closet, but—"

He cut himself off.

"But what?" I prompted.

He shook his head, not in a negative, as if he was clearing it.

Then he said, "Nothing. You want the laundry done, just take anything out that needs dry cleaned. I'll drop it off and do the rest."

Okay, wait.

What was happening?

I didn't know, but I sensed something was very wrong because I was not insane, this conversation *was* frustrating, I just was no longer certain why it was.

"I do the laundry," I pointed out carefully. "You do the cooking."

"That's the way it was, but if you need me to get on it, just tell me."

"I'm not saying I need you to get on it."

He didn't respond. Instead, he pulled in a big breath, tipped his head back and looked at the ceiling.

I tried something new.

"Are you mad about the mascara?"

"Jesus, fuck, someone kill me," he said to the ceiling.

"Core," I called.

He looked at me. "Please do not tell me we're gonna talk about your goddamn mascara again."

Right, that didn't work.

"I'm getting a weird vibe from you."

"And I'm telling you, you're feeling what you're feeling, and that isn't coming from me."

He was so wrong, and I was not a fan of being gaslit.

"It *is* coming from you," I asserted.

"Okay, good, great, it's coming from me," he gave in. "Sorry, babe. We done with this now?"

Oh no.

Not okay.

"Don't be a dick," I groused.

"How am I being a dick when you're up in my shit about something I do not get?"

I tried his tack. "Right, fine, everything's cool. I'm getting up an hour and a half earlier so I can get work done and be home to have time with you. I'm busting my ass at the office and squeezing work in so you know you're a priority to me. You're neat, I've let some things slide, mostly because I'm busy, it's the holiday season so it's even busier, so I don't put my mascara away—"

"I didn't ask you to get up early so you can get home earlier."

"You were in a mood because I made us late to Beck and Janna's."

His brows shot up and his vibe plummeted into the hellfire zone.

As such, his tone was sizzling when he asked, "Are you fucking shitting me?"

"No. You were," I stressed.

His voice was rumbly, and not the good kind, when he stated, "I do not need one of those bitches in my life who sits on shit for days, weeks, fuckin' months, then throws it in my face."

My voice was rising. "I'm not throwing anything in your face! And don't call me a bitch!"

"Then don't sit on shit you need to talk out and lay it on me after you've let it gnaw at you so I gotta deal with the fallout. I do not care if you're late. You got a job you dig, you were clear that comes with the territory, so I'll repeat and hope it sinks in. I...do...not...care...if you're late."

"Okay, so obviously everything's awesome between us," I said sarcastically.

"Everything is totally awesome between us," he agreed snidely.

"And I'm perfect, you're living with me, you're fucking me, you love me, and I can do no wrong, even if I work late and you trip on my mascara."

"And now you're back to Kiki," he griped, getting it right because I harked back to his words when we were discussing her.

"I don't need to worry about Kiki," I retorted. "I'm perfect. Right? You're perfect. We're perfect. You don't mind if I work all the time. Oh no, it wouldn't be *you* that's sitting on your mood so it can gnaw at you, and later, I have to deal with the fallout," I drawled sarcastically.

"I'm not sitting on a mood," he growled.

"I know, baby, didn't I just say that?" I replied fake sweetly.

"*Jesus Christ!*" he exploded. "It's your goddamn shoes."

I stood unmoving, staring at him.

"And it's not a big fucking deal," he shared.

"Then why did you just shout at me?"

"Because you're right, I'm a dick."

But looking at the expression now on his face, unease mixed with guilt, it hit me like a shot.

I need to take care of you.

He had to navigate my shoes, my clothes, my runaway makeup.

I need to take care of you.

He piled my mail, vacuumed, chilled out and watched TV I wasn't interested in so I could work.

Always treated me with almost excruciating care.

Oh my God.

This was excruciating care.

Core came to me, took my hands in both of his and dropped his forehead to mine.

"We're good, baby, all right?" he placated me. "I'm good. It's all good. It sucks today went off the rails, but we'll chill and go back out tomorrow."

"I'll put my shoes away," I said to him.

He squeezed my hands and lifted his head. "Promise. It's okay."

"You're allowed to find me annoying, Core. I'm actually not perfect."

He gave me a crooked smile. "Damned close to it."

Oh God, I loved this man.

But this was not okay. This was not the way forward.

This was the way to head right to an eventual end.

And it was something deeper for Core that I had to help him let go.

I squeezed his hands and didn't stop squeezing. "I need to know if I do something that bothers you."

"You don't," he said swiftly.

I pulled our hands between us and pressed them to his chest.

"Stop this," I whispered.

"Stop what?" he asked.

I looked around then back at him. "Are you neat?"

"What?"

"Do you run the cordless every day?"

"Nanook sheds."

I tried to remember before I moved in officially, and yes, there was shedding. It wasn't out of control, but it wasn't neat as a pin every day.

And he'd throw his phone and keys on the kitchen island. Maybe not every time, say, when they were in his pockets, or he was home in order to stay home and he didn't leave them lying around.

But it happened.

"Core," I called.

"Right here," he said.

"Everything doesn't have to be perfect for me."

"You got nice clothes. You don't need dog hair on your clothes."

I let his hands go and framed his face.

He put his hands on my hips.

But he appeared uncomfortable.

"You know I'm in love with you," I said gently.

Another crooked grin, his fingers dug into my flesh, and he replied, "Yeah."

"And I agreed to you taking care of me, but do you understand I need to take care of you too?"

"Sure."

He said it, but his expression said something else.

"I mean that, Core. Say, I leave my shoes out and you trip on them, and it ticks you off, you need to tell me."

"It isn't that big of a deal."

"I know when things don't seem like that big of a deal, until they happen over and over again, and the person who's supposed to love you constantly does little things that lack the most common of courtesy, and it doesn't feel very good. Do the shoes bug you?"

He tried to pass it off by joking, "I'm getting used to dodging them."

They bugged him.

"I'll make a point to put them away. And clear my basin when

I'm done. But I can't guess at stuff that might bother you. You have to tell me."

"Babe, this is—"

I pressed in with my hands as well as my body.

"No, Core, I *need* you to tell me. And if you want to vacuum Nanook's fur every day, I'm not going to stop you. But I don't *need* that. My clothes will be fine and that's why we have lint rollers."

He opened his mouth, but said nothing, though his brows slammed down over his eyes, and he twisted toward the door because someone was hammering on it.

Loudly.

"Stay right there," he growled, snapped his fingers, pointed at the floor by my feet, and Nanook came right to me and sat in front of me.

I leaned to the left so I could see around the wall that made the small foyer at the front door and felt my body jolt with shock at what I saw when Core opened it and demanded, "What's your fucking problem?"

"*Nice*," my dad spat, giving Core a derisive up and down. "Jesus Christ, look at you."

He then, in pure Dad style, being a man Core had never met, tried to bowl Core over at Core's own front door. How he thought he'd manage that, I did not know, and unsurprisingly, it didn't go well for him.

Core's arm shot up to his side, Dad ran into it and fell back like he'd run into a tree.

It would have been funny if I wasn't outrageously pissed he was there at all.

First Kiki.

And now Dad.

Could this day get any more fucked up?

What happened to holiday cheer?

Core didn't move his arm, effectively caging Dad on the other side of the threshold.

"What the fuck?" Core bit out.

"Would you mind I talk to my daughter?" Dad asked.

Core, realizing he'd just met my father, turned his head to me.

I stepped deeper into the living room, Nanook crowding me, and called, "What are you doing here, Dad?"

Dad glared at Core, but my man was still looking at me.

"It's okay," I said, even if I was uncertain if it was.

Core dropped his arm and walked directly to me, positioning at my back so close, I felt his heat.

Dad came in behind him and was looking around, attempting to find fault in our home, and I suddenly wished I'd held my shit so we bought more Christmas stuff to deck the place out.

And then I thought, fuck that and fuck him.

Our home was awesome, and it didn't matter what he thought.

"Dad, what are you doing here? And how do you know where I live?" I asked.

He shifted his focus to me. "Imagine being me and hearing your child demand to know how you knew where she lived."

"The question remains," I prompted.

"Eleanor paid me a visit."

Well, shit.

"She told me you've moved in with a man you barely knew, but you did know he had an unsavory past," he carried on.

I felt something unpleasant beating off Core into my back.

"And I would like to know, Hellen," Dad continued, "what the hell you think you're doing?"

"I've moved in with the man I love," I replied.

"This man?" Dad asked scornfully, flinging a hand up at Core.

"Yes." I leaned back so I was touching him. "This man."

"Hellen—"

For so many reasons, I wasn't doing this.

"Dad." I sighed. "I can't even begin to understand why you think you have some right to come banging at my door to demand I explain the decisions I make in my life. From your own actions, you've made it so you don't know me. You don't know the person

I've become. You don't know that I'm not impetuous. You don't know that I am ambitious. You don't know that I'm a risktaker. And you don't know that even if that's the case, I don't take stupid risks. You also don't know this man at my back. You don't know that he's tender and sweet and protective. You don't know that he's the best dog dad ever. You don't know that he's a rare breed who gives me space to be who I need to be and doesn't make everything about him all the time. You don't know that he's so intent on taking care of me, he vacuums every day so I won't get dog hair on my clothes."

Dad was staring up at Core.

I took a breath and kept going.

"What you *do* know is Eleanor. You know she didn't come to you out of concern for me. She came to you so you'd do what you're doing right now so it would upset you, Core and me. And you fell for it. You came here, upset, and you upset Core and me."

"You can't possibly know—" Dad tried.

I didn't let him continue.

"I can, but you don't know that either. Now, my man and I were having an important conversation when you started banging on the door. And I may be wrong about you because I don't know you very well either, which I'll point out, is not my burden. It's yours. Because you were never around to allow me to get to know you unless you were ready to be around. And those times were rarely pleasant because you were controlling and demanding of our time when you invaded a life we lived mostly without you in it. You did this instead of fitting into our lives and making the time we had with you something nurturing for all of us. So my take on this is that I don't think you're here for my own good. I think, as usual, you're here to demand attention and to make a scene."

"I—" he tried again.

I cut him off again.

"You could have called, or texted, set up a time to sit down and have coffee, discuss what Eleanor said to you, so I could explain. I could tell you the man my boyfriend is so you could be happy that I found him, like Mom is. Like Andy is. Like Li is."

His face grew hard at those last three mentions.

Mostly Andy.

I ignored this and kept talking.

"You didn't do that. And I don't feel like having a scene with you, Dad, not in my own living room that you practically forced your way into, not anywhere at any time. I feel like making hot chocolate, putting on Christmas music and baking cookies. And I'm sorry, I don't want you around when I do that."

"It would seem we have deeper issues to discuss," Dad got out, looking and sounding like the words pained him.

We did indeed.

At this juncture, I could get into his Granddad ruse.

I didn't pick that one.

Because it wasn't our deepest issue.

"Where did you take Tigger?" I asked.

Red started climbing up Dad's neck.

Core, who I had not yet gotten into the whole Tigger heartbreak with, sensed the turn of the conversation. I knew it when I felt his hand flatten at the small of my back.

"Where, Dad?" I pushed.

"I dropped him at a shelter," he forced out.

My body went solid.

My father dropped the beloved family dog at a shelter because he was pitching a fit.

"A kill shelter?" The words were strangled, and I felt the pads of Core's fingers press in.

"I don't know," he muttered.

Lord God, I hoped it wasn't, and if it was, then someone adopted and went on to love and adore my baby at least as much as I did.

He must have been so confused, in a loving home with his three girls devoted to him one second, and in a cage the next.

I couldn't dwell on it. I'd dwelled on every version I could conjure about it for years, and each one always tore me apart. Now knowing what befell him didn't make it better in the slightest.

"You know," I said quietly, and hearing my tone, Core pressed in fully at his hand at my back, but also, I felt Dad's sudden hyper focus on me. "I've thought about it a lot. And I loved my dog. I loved him and he loved me. But it wasn't just losing Tigger that hurt so goddamned much. It was you taking him away from me being the beginning of me losing you too. It was you doing something so selfish and cruel because you weren't getting the attention you wanted when you finally deigned to spend time with your family. And this made me start falling out of love with my own dad. And since then, that never stopped happening."

His neck was fully red now, and he looked genuinely wounded.

But, too little, too late.

"Hellen—" Dad started.

However now, Core was having none of it.

"You done?" Core grunted his question at me.

"Yes," I replied.

Core walked around me.

Dad was looking at me, but his attention quickly went to Core.

I watched, impressed, as Core used everything but his hands to herd Dad to the door while Dad exclaimed, "Don't touch me!" and "Stay back!" and "I'm not done talking to my daughter!"

He I'm-not-doned himself out the door, after which Core shut it in his face and locked it.

He waited.

I waited.

No banging, no shouting.

I should have known.

Dad was not one to fight for his kids. He'd just been embarrassed because, in his mind, he'd just been unmanned. He would go lick his wounds and then one day (maybe) try again with his shenanigans.

My man turned to me.

"*That*," I jabbed my finger at the door. "*That* is how you take care of me. And you're really fucking good at it."

And then I started crying.

Shit!

When did I become a crier?

Suddenly, I was in Core's arms and also in his lap in the armchair.

He rubbed my back and fussed with my hair and didn't once shush me or make me talk to try to release the pain.

When I was wiping my face, I realized the weight on my thigh wasn't Core's other hand.

It was Nanook's jaw.

Man, I was so damned lucky.

I reached out and covered Core's hand that was resting on our pup's head.

"The best dog dad ever?" Core teased.

"It bodes well for our future," I sniffled.

Taking my hand with it, he gave Nanook a rub then he dislodged us so he could wrap both arms around me.

"Your shit all over the floor in the closet bugs me," he said softly into my hair. "The mess you leave in the bathroom is not my favorite thing. I don't mind clothes in the hamper, but I don't like to look at them spilling all over the floor. I've learned a Hellen minute is three actual minutes so if you say ten, you mean thirty, and that can get aggravating. And I don't like to go to bed alone. I wouldn't mind it if it was once in a while, but it happens a lot."

I took in a shaky breath and lifted my head to look at him.

When I did, he went on, "But I honest as fuck don't mind you working late. If it's tough for you to get up early, don't. Do what you do. That's the woman I fell in love with."

And here was the man I fell in love with.

"I'll pick up the closet," I told him. "And I honestly didn't realize I did that with time."

"You tell me what you think I want to hear, not the way it is."

I had no idea I did that, but I didn't doubt I did.

"I'll have a mind to that too."

"Okay, baby," he murmured, moving in to touch his lips to mine.

When he pulled away, I promised, "I'll also have a mind to my stuff in the bathroom and not working too often when it's time to go to bed."

"Appreciated."

"But you cook and grocery shop, so I do laundry," I continued. "It's not quite an equitable distribution of chores, but it makes me feel better because I'm doing something."

His lips hitched up. "I like to cook, I hate laundry, so that works for me."

I put a hand at his throat and stroked there. "You don't need to clean up after Nanook every day."

"Sweetheart, growing up, I didn't have nice *anything*. We had a shit couch in a shit trailer in a shitty trailer park. I got nice things now. I take care of them. Yeah, I went into overdrive because you got pretty clothes and I didn't want Nanook all over them. But you and your girls gave me an awesome crib. It means something to me. What doesn't mean anything to me is taking ten minutes to run the sweeper every day."

And there it was again.

I was going to start crying.

"Hey," he whispered, cupping my face. "None of that. Not for me. Look at what I got." He gave me a squeeze with his arm around me and then dipped his chin to where Nanook was sitting. "I'm not there anymore. I'm here. Every day, I'm grateful. Because I learned not to live in the past. I wake up with you in my life and stay the course and it's all good."

"Okay," I mumbled. "I'm glad. And you can vacuum all you want."

He chuckled.

That sound died as he swept his thumb along my cheek and said, "I'm sorry about Tigger."

"Me too."

"And I'm sorry your dad is such a dick."

I felt my lips quirk. "Me too."

"You wanna talk about your pup?"

God, he was so amazing.

I shook my head but said, "It happened just like that. He came home after a long business trip, and he wanted us to dance attendance. I was playing with Tigger, and he got enraged that I was more into my dog than my dad coming home. So he grabbed him and took off and then..."

I didn't finish because I couldn't finish.

"Yeah, a fuckin' dick," Core snarled.

"Well now, I wake up with you and Nanook in my life every day, so it's all good."

He stopped looking pissed.

"Right," he said, "Now he's gone, and we don't have hot chocolate and I don't know what cookies you wanna bake so I gotta go to the store. And I'd love it if you went with me."

That was when I felt my lips curve fully because my day turned on his words.

"That sounds perfect."

It would be later, when Core got a text and said he had to take off for half an hour, which he did, I called her.

Janna picked up right away.

I didn't beat around the bush.

"I get excruciating care too," I told her.

She already knew.

"Mm-hm."

"I don't want him to think he has to do that."

"Hon, you just gotta keep a finger on the pulse. When is it him doing what he needs to do? When is it going too far? When it's too far, talk to him. One thing these boys have learned is how to listen and *hear*."

That was very true.

"Do you want to meet up with me and my girls at Fortnum's for coffee sometime?"

It was her turn not to beat around the bush.

"I'd love to."

Core

They met where they often met, in the parking lot of the grocery store.

Core was waiting for him, and Beck approached on his bike from the front and stopped to Core's side, so they were facing.

Beck cut power and looked at Core.

"We got a problem with Eleanor Moynihan," Core announced.

Beck's lips thinned.

Then he nodded.

EPILOGUE

THE MAN HE NEEDED TO BE

Hellen

"I FEEL the need to have a thing," Janna announced. "And I think I should kick it off with a New Year's Party, but I don't know what that thing should be."

It was the Sunday before Christmas and the new girl gang was at Fortnum's, that gang including Marcy, Kyra, Janna, me and my two sisters, Li and Archie.

We were hanging on the couches and armchairs at the window and were deep into coffee number two.

"A thing?" Marcy asked.

"Like Chaos has hog roasts, Resurrection needs a thing," Janna answered. "The guys, they get together. The whole club, women, kids, we sometimes do, but mostly it's whoever is hanging in the clubhouse at any given time. We don't have our *thing*. A bonding thing that we can invite our friends to and just let loose, be together and make memories. We need a *thing*."

Chaos's hog roasts were the bomb, so I thought Janna was right.

Resurrection needed a *thing*.

It came to me.

"Smoke," I declared.

Li perked up. "A weed fest?"

"Jag and I would be all over that," Archie joked.

I shook my head, laughing. "No." I turned to Janna. "Beck loves to smoke meat. You told me you got him that smoker a couple of years ago, and now he smokes his own meat all the time. When we were over for dinner the other night, he smoked that pulled pork for us. It was *amazing*. The club needs to buy a big smoker and have smokes."

"Oh my God, that's the perfect idea," Janna breathed.

"I'd be all the way down to attend a smoke," Marcy said. "And as an aside, calling it a 'smoke' rather than a 'barbeque' is badass."

I smiled proudly because I thought so too.

"You could have all sorts of yummy sides. It can be potluck. Everyone can bring something."

"A New Year's Smoke. I dig it," Li agreed.

"Resurrection's *First Annual* New Year's Smoke," Janna corrected. "Sisters, you're in on it. We're making it a tradition." She was already on her phone. "I'm going to text the women, get it on their calendars right now. New Year's is just around the corner. We're a family." Her eyes moved to rest on me. "Our family is expanding. We should have family gatherings."

Her gaze coming to me, making it official, at least from the old lady perspective that I was Resurrection, felt super good.

And no one could argue what she said.

So no one did.

Core

Rush Allen brought three of his brothers to the meet: Shy Cage, and Dutch and Jagger Black.

Resurrection pulled up some chairs at the table for them.

They were gathered.

Beck started it by saying, "Core's gonna run shit down."

Beck looked at him, so Core ran everything down.

When he was done explaining what Nails had been up to, he pointed out the obvious.

"She knows a lot about me. She knows a lot about Hellen. She knows a lot about the history and activities of our club. Too much. She's from Denver, but she's lived in Phoenix the past twenty years. People talk, but not to her. What she did to the brothers of Aces High, she's known and she's an outcast from most clubs. She's also not a supersleuth. She's a biker bunny. This isn't a black sheep taking her daddy issues out on members of her family. This is something more."

"She's being fed info," Rush said, then added. "Which means you're being watched."

Core nodded. "And we're being investigated. It isn't just the present she's raking up, it's the past."

The Chaos brothers looked as happy about this as Resurrection.

"Distraction?" Rush suggested to Beck.

"My guess was the same," Beck replied.

"From what?" Dutch asked.

Beck looked to Dutch.

"That's what we gotta find out."

Hellen

I walked in through the garage door after coffee with the girls and called out, "Baby, I'm home."

Nanook heard me come in and was there to greet me. I returned the sentiment with a rubdown, then I threw my keys in the tray on the desk area in the kitchen where they landed next to Core's.

We had new additions on that desk. Core bought them.

Seriously, he was getting into this settling down thing.

And I was really loving he was.

The tray was new. As was a charging station that hid cords for our phones. An attractive desk caddy, which held pens and scissors and stuff. And a letter holder with different sections, front for my stuff, middle for Core's (always empty), back for bills and other we-type things (which he mostly dealt with, but he kept them there until he filed them away so I could see them and arrange to pay my half).

I couldn't say I went through my section daily (as in, I didn't check it yesterday), but I didn't allow it to get out of hand.

Since Christmas was close, I had to go through it more often because of Christmas cards.

And front and center in the letter holder, there was what I knew was a Christmas card that had a forwarding label from my old apartment.

I recognized the handwriting.

I nabbed it, grabbed the letter opener from the caddy and slit it open.

I was tense because I thought I might see a perfect-couple picture collage of Bree with Bryan.

I didn't, but apparently, Bree took a vacation to the Grand Canyon since we parted ways.

A folded piece of paper had come out with the notecard depicting a selfie of Bree against the backdrop of one of the great natural wonders of the world with SEASON'S GREETINGS, XO BREE printed at the bottom.

With trepidation, I unfolded the paper.

I was about to read what was on it when Core greeted, "Hey."

I turned my head to watch him walking toward me, appreciating the movement of his slim hips in his faded jeans and the stretch of the thermal across his chest.

Most especially, I appreciated the tender look in his beautiful blue eyes that were resting on me.

"Hey," I replied.

He arrived, put a hand on my hip and gave me a kiss.

"Good time with the girls?" he asked.

"Yes. We're having a New Year's Day Smoke at the clubhouse. A big thing, kids, extended family and friends invited."

He smiled. "Sounds ace. What's a smoke?"

"You and Beck are in charge of smoking a lot of meat to feed the throng."

His smile got bigger.

My man liked to feed people.

I waved the paper I held in the air. "A letter from Bree. It came with her Christmas card."

His smile died and was replaced with a stormy expression. "That bitch sent a Christmas card?"

"I may be reading into things, but it seems she's spending her friendless hours taking solo vacations."

He cared nothing for that, I knew, when he asked, "What's the letter say?"

"I haven't read it yet."

He raised his brows and dipped his chin to the letter to indicate I needed to get on that.

So I got on it.

Hellen,

I don't know how to start this. I miss you and have been wanting to reach out to you, but I didn't know how.

I thought Christmas was the perfect excuse.

We have a lot of history and so many great memories. I consider myself lucky you were assigned to be my roommate our first year in college. I'm not lying when I say I knew right away that we were going to be friends forever.

Because of all of that, I want you to know that I'm open to hearing your apology...

"Say what?" I snapped at the paper.

"What?" Core rumbled.

I kept reading.

...I know your pride might make that hard to do, which is why you haven't reached out.

But I care about you, I love you, I miss you, and I'll forgive you.

You were with another guy, it was serious. I hear it's even more serious now. That you'd be with someone new and break Bryan and I up out of spite isn't...

I didn't finish it.

I looked to Core. "She's on about me breaking her and Bryan up out of spite and wants an apology."

My wise Core translated: "In other words, so she can live with the shit she pulled, she's twisted how things actually went to a version that makes her the victim."

"In other words, yes."

It was an awful thing to realize about a person, especially one you cared about, but it seemed Bree had a penchant for finding ways to be the victim.

There were red flags with Christos, of course.

And if I dug deeper into our history, examining her bad breakups with guys that were always filled with drama, I would see it wasn't the growing pains of a young woman finding her way in relationships.

It was Bree.

"Official," Core stated. "We're putting that jewelry to better use. We know people who struggle to get shit they need, like food and money to pay rent. Turn that jewelry into cash, we can do some good with it."

Bree had never contacted Kyra to look at the pieces Core nabbed for her. Since they held meaning, I'd set them aside because, regardless how she'd behaved, I believed she should have them back.

Now, Core wasn't asking for my support of his plan.

Even so, I said, "Agreed."

Without hesitation, he took the letter I was holding, along with the card still in my hand, and being his usual thorough, he nabbed the envelope I'd tossed on the desk.

He walked them to and through the French doors, Nanook following, maybe because he was curious what Dad was doing out in the cold, probably because it had snowed and Denver showed signs of being Nanook's natural habitat.

I was right. Nanook ran straight into the yard and started frolicking.

Core, though, went right to the grill, opened it, pulled his lighter out of his pocket, and lit Bree's version of Christmas cheer on fire, every vestige of it.

He dropped it on the grill and stared at it until it flamed out.

He then closed the grill and came inside, whistling for Nanook to come with him.

Nanook quit frolicking and trailed snow into the house on his paws and fur.

Core closed the door behind them and looked at me.

"You hungry?" he asked.

I wanted to laugh.

I didn't.

I said, "I love you."

"Love you too," he replied. "Now, you hungry? 'Cause I could eat."

And there was Core taking care of me again because that was precisely as much headspace as Bree deserved.

"Yeah, I'm hungry, honey."

"Cool," he muttered, starting to get to work. "We're having lasagna."

"Awesome," I replied because he gave good lasagna.

Then again, he gave good everything.

I started to move to take my boots off and put them away when Core reminded me, "Empty bedroom is still off limits."

So I was smiling as I walked to our closet, because the empty bedroom had been off limits for a week. He was hiding my presents in there, I knew, because he'd gone so far as to lock it (I'd tested it, not to spoil his surprise, just to see how far he'd go to keep his secret).

I had no idea what he might get me as a present.

But if he wanted to go all out for it to be a surprise, I wasn't about to kill my man's joy.

I WAS knees to the bed, ass in his hands, face in the covers, moaning and taking Core's cock.

He suddenly smacked my outer thigh, wrapped an arm around my ribs and pulled me up.

I was close to coming, the smack nearly sent me over the edge, being yanked up to sit on his dick edged me even closer, but then he pulled me off that big dick.

"Wait!" I cried.

He fell to his ass, back to the headboard, and positioned me facing and straddling him.

Okay then.

I took hold of his cock and impaled myself.

I bounced.

He slid his hand along my neck and fisted it in my hair.

I watched the dark heat in his eyes intensify as he watched me fuck him, and I bounced harder.

He took a handful of my breast and tweaked the nipple.

I bounced even harder.

He pulled me down to him and kissed me, deep and wet.

I whimpered into his mouth.

"Pop," he whispered against my lips.

I came.

He moved to his knees, deposited me on my back, then angled in a power position with his hands in the bed beside me, arms straight. He watched me as he fucked me through my orgasm, then I watched him as he fucked me to his.

He then collapsed on me, and I smoothed his neck, his hair, his shoulders, down his back, and what I could reach of his ass.

He rolled so we were on our sides, tangled in each other.

He kissed me sweet, broke the kiss and whispered even sweeter, "Merry Christmas."

He could say that again.

I smiled at him and whispered back, "Merry Christmas."

He touched his lips to mine, and then said, "C'mon."

I was given no choice but to "c'mon."

I was out of bed, on my feet, and he was tossing me his tee.

I put it on and thought we'd go to the bathroom and begin to face the day then make coffee, put on Christmas music, open presents, and after, shower and get ready. After that, as planned, we'd go over to Mom and Andy's, where we would open more presents and share the rest of the holiday with my family.

But when I had his tee on, and he'd yanked on a pair of jeans commando, we did not go to the bathroom.

He took my hand and guided me to the empty bedroom with Nanook dancing beside us (not with his need for breakfast or to be let out, I knew, because I felt Core leave me to take care of these things before he came back and woke me for our Christmas fuck).

There was a big red bow tied to the door handle of the empty room.

"Open it," he said.

Okay, this meant he wasn't hiding my presents in there, it meant my present was big.

I was trying to figure out what it would be, and decided it was the rug that I ran into while Christmas shopping. A rug I thought would be perfect under our bed, so I showed it to Core. Core didn't jump on buying it like he did everything else because I told him not to. I said I'd find something similar, since that rug was made of silk, and it cost far, far more than any rug should.

Still, it was the bomb.

And I knew it was in that room.

It was crazy-generous, but sweet, and totally would bring the room together, which was why I was grinning at him when I opened the door.

It was early, still dark outside, so he reached in and flipped the light switch.

Nanook ran in, howling with excitement, then came to me, still howling.

I stood statue still in the doorway.

Core didn't buy me the rug.

"You said you wanted a home office."

I did.

And there it was.

Set to the side so I wouldn't have the window at my back, there was an attractive large black table desk facing two comfortable chairs, all of this on top of a kickass zebra-print rug. The desk chair was black leather and chrome, and the desk lamp was also chrome.

Behind the desk was a long, black credenza that ran the length of the room and was topped with some decorative vases.

And on the wall above the credenza were six large black-and-white pictures framed in black with a wide white matte. They were set three and three in two rows.

Top left: Me and Liane as little girls, hugging in front of Li's birthday cake with five lit candles on it.

Top middle: Mom, Andy, Archie, Elijah, Li and me, a formal portrait taken on Mom and Andy's wedding day.

Top right: Mom, Li and me not too long ago, hanging in Mom's she shed.

Bottom left: Marcy, Kyra and I drinking shots at a party during college.

Bottom right: Me working at my desk at the office (Xanthia must have taken it).

And bottom center: Core and me walking Nanook in the park (he must have arranged for Kyra or Marcy to stalk us, because it was a candid, and I had no idea it existed until that moment).

It wasn't overly decorated, so I could put my stamp on it.

What it was, was beautiful.

"There's a printer hidden in the cabinet," Core was saying.

Dazed, I looked up at him.

He was gazing down at me. "Kyra helped me."

I said nothing.

He started to look uneasy.

"Do you like it?" he asked.

"I love it," I said softly.

He smiled.

"I don't...I don't..." I stammered. "Sometimes I don't know what to do with how much I love you."

He stopped smiling.

Nanook woofed.

And then I was on a biker's shoulder, this right before I was on my back in our bed and that biker was on me.

I was all for round two, but I grabbed his face and called, "Core."

"Later," he growled.

And it was going to be later because he kissed me.

IT WAS LATER and I was tangled naked with my man.

I studied his face as I stroked his cheekbone, his jaw, sifted my fingers in his hair, and I confessed, "My feelings are so big right now, I don't have words."

"I just paid for it," he shrugged it off verbally. "Kyra designed it."

"I love her for that, but you know." I flattened my hand to the side of his head and pressed gently. "*You know* what that means to me."

"I know," he murmured.

Excruciating care.

"I worry that I don't give you as much as you give me," I admitted.

His lips curved. "Baby, you'll be rolling in the dough before either of us can blink."

"I don't mean that way," I replied.

He took my hand from his head, curled his fingers around it and pressed both to his throat.

None of this prepared me for what would come next. Not even

the expression he was wearing. My feelings were too big to fully process anything.

Even if I had processed it, I wouldn't have been prepared.

"I had one foster dad who thought my ass was his for fucking because he put a roof over my head and food in my stomach, both of which he was being paid to do."

My mouth filled with saliva.

"I got moved from that house after I not only fucked him up when he tried that shit with me, I fucked him up more when he tried that shit with another kid that was there with me. They investigated, I didn't get into trouble, but I got rehomed with a lady who took the state's money but fed us nothing but generic Cheerios and chicken noodle soup. Like, breakfast and dinner every day for weeks. Lunch too on weekends. We didn't eat at school because she didn't give us the money to do it. The two months I lived with her, I lost twenty pounds."

My chest caved in.

"Core—"

"Do you think once, even fucking *once* in the life I lived that I thought I'd ever wake on Christmas to fuck my woman's sweet pussy and give her what she asked for, knowing I'm gonna go to her family's house later. And knowing, once we get there, there's gonna be nothing but love and laughter and good food and good memories?"

No. It gutted me, but I knew he didn't think even once that he'd have any of that.

Core wasn't finished.

"Do you have any clue what it feels like to walk into my house when you're not even home from work yet, hit the remote, and the Christmas tree lights come on with presents under the tree and it smells like pine needles from the candles you burn all the time? It smells like that but feels like home. It feels like I walked right into love because you give that to me. Woman, I'll trip on your shoes every fucking day of my life, if it means you're in my life."

"I'm still going to put away my shoes," I said, my voice husky, my words lame because I was again at a loss for what to say.

"I know, baby, because you love me. Do you think ever in the life I led that I thought I'd win a woman like you?"

"I'm just a woman."

"No, Hellen, you're amazing."

He was killing me.

I swallowed and said, "You are too."

"And do you think I ever dreamed I'd hear a woman like you say that to me?"

"Stop it, Core," I forced out.

"What I'm saying is, you don't have to worry, sweetheart. You give me exactly what I need."

I pulled our hands down so I could shove my face in his throat and concentrate on not crying.

"I'm happy," he said into my hair. "I'm happy because I love you and you love me. I'm happy because I never thought I'd earn the love of a good woman, because I didn't deserve it after what I'd done. I'm happy because I know my mom would be happy if she knew this was the life I have. I'm just happy, baby. You give me that. So no more tears from you."

"Okay," I croaked against his skin.

He cupped my jaw and pulled my face out of his throat so he could look down at me.

"Coffee, and I got this French toast bake I wanna try out on you."

Of course, he did.

"And your presents," I whispered.

"And presents," he replied.

We kissed. We got out of bed. We did our morning thing and I turned on Christmas music and made coffee while Core whisked eggs. I then left him to it while I stuffed his and Nanook's stockings.

While the breakfast he made was baking, we took our coffee to the living room to start the official proceedings, and I saw Core's consternation that he didn't stuff my stocking.

I didn't say anything, but I knew he filed that away for next year.

I didn't do anything as spectacular as give him a room furnished to his heart's delight. But he laughed out loud at the TODAY I FEEL tee I got him with nine pictures of Grogu on it and options such as sleepy, confused, cute and hungry (yes, I introduced him to *The Mandalorian*, and yes, he fell in love with The Child just like anyone who had a pulse did).

And Core really loved the gold Zippo I gave him that I'd had inscribed with *IUSTITIA, TRIBUS, HONORIS, FIDELITAS* on the front and DJ"HC"C (Dustin James "Hardcore" Cutler) on the back.

His eggy, gooey (but crispy-edged), brown-sugary, cinnamony French toast bake was a winner, so after we took a shower together and got ready, we packed up the leftovers, the wrapped presents for my family, our pup...

And headed over to Mom and Andy's to finish out Christmas with our family.

By the way, I knew how much he loved me (and The Child) because Core wore his Grogu tee.

Core

After Christmas dinner, Core was out on Andy and Haley's back porch with Nanook in the yard when Jag joined him.

Jag stopped at his side, watched Core's dog wander the snow, sniffing, and then he asked, "You wanna talk about it?"

Jagger and Archie came over at around one after spending the morning with Jag's family. Once they and Elijah arrived, they did a massive present gig, and after, they had dinner.

Hellen had given Arch and Jag presents from her and Core, and it was just a few hours ago, but considering the orgy of gift-giving they'd survived, Core didn't remember what they were (Haley either really liked shopping, wrapping, or her family because she went over the deep end—Core had two new Henleys, a new hoodie, a knife block filled with top-of-the-line knives, and a new set of kickass grilling tools).

Core had doubled up on Jag's present, giving him the same as he gave Li.

A pound of premium grass.

Jag had been less outwardly appreciative than Liane had (she'd let out a scream and declared Core had "mad gift-giving skills," though he sensed this had more to do with her sister's new office, something Hellen wouldn't stop talking about and showing everyone pictures of), but Jag hadn't hidden he liked the gift.

"Not sure what to do," he grunted in reply.

"About Haley giving Hellen and Liane the gifts from their dad?"

About exactly that.

Core grunted again, but this one was a sound and not words.

Jagger spoke.

"Archie's dad is Andy, salt of the earth, good human being, and my dad is Hound, who'd take a bullet for me and Dutch. I'm telling you what you know to point out I got no experience dealing with my woman's father who happens to be an asshole. Also got no experience dealing with a mom who knows that, but wants her kids to have a decent dad, so she keeps herself open to be the conduit to give that asshole chances. What I do know is that you can't get pissed at Haley for doing what she thinks is right and hoping that one day her girls will have what they deserve. You just gotta be there for Hellen with whatever the fallout is."

"I looked it up on my phone, that bracelet he gave her cost ten K," Core said.

"Shit, really?" Jag sounded shook.

"He didn't pay a dime for her college."

Now Jag sounded understanding. "So that's why she looked like she wanted to throw it in the garbage when she opened it."

"She knows labels, and apparently, Bulgari is a thing. She knew and she didn't have to look it up."

"They're not twelve and ten, Core," Jag reminded him. "And

warning, Haley's an optimist. This means, her daughters at the ages they are, and she's still hoping, she's not gonna give up on that anytime soon."

In other words, suck it up, don't get pissed and just take Hellen's back.

Jag sensed Core made his decision to do that, so he changed the subject.

"What's your take on Elijah?"

Archie's brother showed half an hour after Archie and Jagger did. It was the first time Core had met him. What he'd been doing to celebrate his Christmas until the time he showed had not been asked after, nor had the information been offered by Elijah. Though his ploy was not hidden, that for whatever reason, he needed to be sure Archie was there as a buffer before he turned up.

He was a good-looking guy. Clearly sharp. Even though he was still young, he was an accomplished attorney who'd started his own firm with a couple of buds, and according to Andy's puffed-chest pride in the telling of it, they were killing it.

Elijah wasn't an asshole. He was polite. He brought gifts for everyone, including Jagger and Core (the dude got him a gift card at Lowe's, which was cool). He clearly loved his sister, there was also love for his dad, and he showed respect to Haley, Hellen and Liane.

Still.

"Guy's got a chip on his shoulder."

"Yup," Jagger agreed, sounding mildly ticked.

"Hellen says there's unhappy history."

"It upsets Archie."

Core did not repeat what Jagger just told him.

He said, "I got experience losing my mom at a young age, and boys and their moms..."

He said no more, but he felt the intensity of Jagger's gaze on his profile.

He also felt it when it clicked for Jagger.

Jag and Dutch were tight with their mom. It was lore how close-knit that family was, including Hound's place in it.

This was because Jag's dad had been murdered when Jagger was just a baby.

Jag knew loss. He'd lived with it his whole life.

So he got Core's message to cut Elijah some slack. The man was his wife's brother, and Jag had to give it space, lend support when necessary and take Archie's back.

Jagger sighed, and Core knew he accepted his limitations, just as Core had.

They heard the door open behind them, they twisted, and saw Archie had her head stuck out.

"We're talking board game," she declared. "And I don't want to assume, so I'm here confirming that you two are out."

"Totally," Jag said.

Over which Core said, "Absolutely."

Archie smiled her cool chick smile and disappeared behind the door.

"Board games," Jag muttered, a chuckle in his tone.

Core had never played a board game in his life. He loved the fact Hellen and her family did, but it wasn't one of the innumerable things in his childhood he felt was missing.

"Yeah," he agreed.

Then both men stood in the cold watching a dog amuse himself in the snow, and after sharing a moment of solidarity in the new brotherhood they'd formed, they shared another through laughter.

THEY WERE in his truck on the way home.

It was late. Haley didn't skimp on the holiday food. Andy stocked good beer. Li was generous with the pot Core had given her, and he gave no fucks he had to smoke it sitting on a flower-covered pad on a girlie-ass chair in a she shed.

He was full. He was mellow. His woman was happy. And Core was looking forward to getting home, having a quick, solid fuck and passing out.

The music her phone made when she got a text sounded, and the screen illuminated the cab as she looked at it.

She made a strange noise.

"What?" he asked.

"Uh...Bryan," she said. "Wishing me a Merry Christmas and hoping I'm happy."

Core didn't say anything for a beat, before he asked, "You gonna reply?"

"I don't know. I don't hate him. It's kinda nice he reached out in a non-stalkery way to say he's thinking about me during a big holiday."

"So reply," Core urged.

He heard the ticks and the swoop of her sending a text back.

He then heard the return swoop.

"I said, 'same back at you,' and he replied with smiley face," she told him.

"Good?"

"Good," she answered.

"You cool?" he asked.

"I'm cool, honey," she murmured, and her tone sounded just like his mood—mellow, happy and ready to fuck and pass out.

So Core let that go and concentrated on getting his woman home and putting the finishing touches on the best damned Christmas he'd ever had.

This wasn't hard, except he had to drum up some energy once he got her into their room and she saw the rug Eight and Muzzle had come over sometime that day to put under their bed.

So the quick solid fuck lasted a lot longer before they passed out.

So yeah.

Best damned Christmas he'd ever had.

On New Year's Day, Core walked through the clubhouse, watching Linus behind the bar pop a bottle of beer open. He slid it down the bar to where Hound caught it. Hound gave it to his wife, Keely, and turned back just in time to catch the second one Linus sent flying.

That one was for Hound, Core knew, because after he caught it, he chugged half of it.

Core was walking by him when he dropped the beer, caught Core's eyes and said, "Bro, that brisket, fuckin' A."

Core grinned to Hound, dipped his chin to Keely, and buried the knowledge that not too long ago, it was Hound's blade that carved into Beck's face after what they did to Rosalie.

He then disappeared into their kitchen, moved through it and out the side door where they now had a long, black, industrial-sized smoker battened to a concrete slab.

Beck was working it, Shim and Eight with him, all of them had beers.

Core moved to the big cooler they had out there and got his own beer.

After popping the cap, he asked, "You talking business?"

"Yup," Beck answered.

Core tipped the neck of his beer at his brother, his request to be filled in.

"Holidays got in the way, we still need to go up the mountain," Beck said. "We're thinking it's time for Linus to be patched in. So we wanna knock that out while we're up there."

Core swallowed the pull he took on his beer while Beck was talking and said, "Makes sense, needs a vote."

"You agree Linus is ready?" Eight asked, sounding skeptical.

"He's young,"—and he was, he was only twenty-two—"but he's been prospect for over a year. He's loyal. He doesn't bitch. He's good to dig in. And he's got mad skills with anything that has wires."

Eight didn't reply.

"You got reservations?" Core asked.

"Same as I said when we took him as prospect," Eight replied. "I think you should be old enough to be able to rent a car before you decide to commit your entire life to a mission. He's too fucking young."

"You want him to prospect for another three years?" Shim asked.

Eight shook his head but answered, "I want him to have some life under his belt before he's too far down it to realize he'd made a commitment to something he was too young to devote his life to. We put ourselves out there. Our biggest expense is our lawyer because we get arrested to take heat off cop allies and Chaos brothers, covering for them when they're doing the work. We do shit that cannot be undone. It all seems good-guy outlaw when you're twenty-two, but later, you realize, even if you're the good guy, you're still a fuckin' outlaw."

This was something to consider.

"We'll take it to the table," Beck decided.

And that was it because it couldn't be decided anywhere else.

"Hup," Eight warned and Core turned to the door.

Hellen was doing her cute-drunk gallop his way.

When she made it to him, she latched onto his Henley with her fists and leaned into him.

And there was more cute.

He put his hands to her hips and smiled down at her.

"Dutch and Georgie have challenged us to a game of pool," she announced.

Core knew one thing, they were going down. He knew this because Dutch could shoot a solid game of pool. He had no idea what skill level Georgie had, but whatever it was, it had to be better than how shit Hellen was at it. Core knew how to shoot pool, but she was so bad, he couldn't carry them both.

"I take it you're in," he muttered.

She smiled.

"Right," he said, unlatched one of her hands from his Henley, and with juts of his chin at his brothers, holding her hand, he walked his woman inside.

Classic rock was playing, which meant Web had taken control of the jukebox.

There was a long table covered in homemade sides and bowls of chips, and plates stacked with desserts that had mostly been decimated, even if the eat-a-thon was going to continue throughout the day. This was because the party had no end time, you came, you went, you came back if you wanted to.

Every chair, couch and stool had someone's ass on it.

Conversations were a low hum.

Laughter rang out often.

Haley and Andy were there.

Marcy and Kyra were there.

Core's eyes narrowed when he saw Liane huddled in a corner with Saddle, a Chaos brother.

But he didn't have time to go big brother on her, and more importantly, give Saddle the heads up she had a big brother. He had a pool cue in his hand because Hellen had shoved it there.

Dutch was racking them up.

It was about fifteen minutes later when he felt it.

He had his arm slung around Hellen's shoulders, holding her to him, and he'd just lifted his head from watching her laugh out loud after he'd given her shit for a miffed shot that was so bad, he was wondering if she was purposefully bad because he got such a kick out of giving her shit, and she got off on making him happy.

He felt it, and seeing as he was so happy, he didn't think when he looked in the direction it was coming.

And he locked eyes with Rosalie.

He couldn't say he'd been in her presence often since that night. He could say he hadn't looked at her once when he was, and he, like all his brothers, had been careful to give her a wide berth of safe space.

The fact she and her man Snapper showed had caused a ripple

that no one said dick about so neither of them would feel uncomfortable.

Nevertheless, them being there made a statement.

Looking straight at the pretty woman he'd once thought of as a kind of sister, who he liked a lot, who Kiki had loved, who he'd left lying broken on a floor, he felt his insides freeze solid.

She tipped her head and her face got soft.

She didn't smile at him.

She didn't lift her beer his way or come over and say hi.

Core gave her the respect of his gaze until she was ready to let it go.

She did.

He twisted his neck because it had gotten tight, and Hellen was right there.

She caught the underside of his jaw in a firm grip and the lock she had on his gaze was unbreakable.

She'd noted the look he exchanged and who it was with.

You have to forgive yourself.

He couldn't.

No, he wouldn't. He couldn't be the man he needed to be if he did.

"Love you," Hellen said, steel and emotion heavy in those two words.

Yes, he wouldn't.

Because he wouldn't be the man Hellen needed him to be if he did.

"Love you too, baby," he whispered in return.

She kept hold of his face, his gaze, and when his woman knew her man was all right, she let him go and leaned into his side.

"Sentimental Lady" came on the jukebox and Core looked that way to see Web leaning against it, staring at him.

Motherfucker.

The song played.

Core's throat closed.

He caught Web's smile before the man looked to his feet and wandered toward the bar.

Someone laughed.

Beck's baby girl screeched.

Hellen's weight warmed his side.

The memory of his mom twirling in her new dress after she tried it on hit his brain.

Christ.

He had not remembered that twirl, or the smile she'd had on her face, not once. Not in twenty years.

But there she was in his head, twirling.

Core tucked Hellen closer.

And he sighed.

The End

The next story of the Wild West MC series will return to Chaos.

DISCUSSION & REFLECTION QUESTIONS

Smoke and Steel

1. Hellen and Bryan have been in a relationship for a year. Bryan was definitely raised with a "boys will be boys" attitude, and he expects Hellen to fall in line with that. However, if she did, this would give him the opportunity to shirk accountability for bad behavior, finding another mother to take care of him, instead of a partner with whom to share his life.

Were you surprised by Hellen's tone when she ended things with Bryan? Did you feel she was being too hard on him? Or did Hellen's issues feel familiar to you?

2. In this book, Kristen is focusing on the fact that, in recent years, women—especially younger women—have become more vocal about their agency.

Why do you think that is? What do you think will become of this? How do you think men will respond to this demand for change?

Do you think men will change? How will that happen or how would you like to see that happen?

3. The dating world has changed considerably with smartphones, apps, and social media. This can be fun and a cool way to meet people you'd never run into, but like anything, it holds dangers.

The kernel that was planted that bloomed into this book was Kristen having a conversation with a friend about *The Tinder Swindler* documentary, and how a little support (and perhaps some meddling) from friends or family might have gone a long way to save those women from the heartbreak and financial hardships they faced.

Have you used a dating app? If not, and you're unattached, would you? If you have, have you run into a scam artist/catfisher? What did you do?

And how would/do you protect yourself or friends and family from the scam artists and other unsavory folks who populate those apps?

4. Repeating the sins of a parent is a prevalent concern for both Core and Hellen. Core is afraid of the violence learned by his abusive father infiltrating his behaviors, and Hellen and Liane are both averse to the idea of marriage based on their relationship with their father.

Were you surprised to learn Core's tragic backstory? Does it surprise you that Hellen and Liane are not "white dress" type of women, even after watching their mother and Andy's love story?

5. No matter how hard they may wish to try, there are no perfect parents or parental decisions. Obviously, some instances are

more traumatic than others, for example, the history of Core's parents and the fallout and trauma Core experienced because of that.

How do you navigate coming to terms with these less-than-great parenting adventures? Have you or someone you love entered into therapy of any sort as a result of childhood drama? Have you found yourself in a relationship with someone with unhealed childhood wounds? What do you think is the best way to exist in a relationship when one or both of you has unresolved trauma that affects their relationship or bonding styles?

6. Traditionally, women are expected to slot themselves into a man's life. What are your thoughts on that? If you have a daughter, have you discussed this with her? Did it seem unnatural to you that Core was willing to navigate their togetherness the other way around, living his life around Hellen's work, goals and ambitions? Were you relieved when Hellen made the effort to confront Core about this and balance their lives so that Core was not losing himself in the relationship?

7. As Hellen suffered in this book (Bree vs. Bryan), is it your experience that the loss of a friendship is sometimes harder than the loss of a romantic partner?

8. After reading *Smoke and Steel*, do you have a favorite part? A most relatable character? A favorite secondary character you'd like to see get an HEA?

9. The Wild West MC series is heading back to Chaos next, who do you think will be the main character?

ACKNOWLEDGMENTS

I have to shout out to my girl Malia Anderson for our text discussion on *The Tinder Swindler*. Specifically, her comment about how the women he'd swindled needed a good friend or an auntie to step in and tell them what's what. Her wisdom led to that plotline for Hellen and Core, and since it was the impetus for them to get together, I'm grateful for it.

Many thanks to Donna and Liz for reading along, and to Jillian for being excited about all that was Hellen, which made me fall in love with her even more.

Also, thanks to my girl Hellen Fernandez for having a kickass name I could steal and give to a heroine.

And more thanks to Donna, as well as Kelly Brown, Lillie Applegarth and Amanda Simpson at Pixel Mischief for keeping my shit tight and making me look good.

Last, as ever and always, much love and gratitude to all my readers whose support and loyalty allows me to continue to do the best job in the world.

ACKNOWLEDGMENTS

[illegible]

Head to the Chaos Compound!

Read the first in the Chaos Series,

Own the Wind.

HEAD BACK TO THE CHAOS COMPOUND

Own the Wind
Chaos Series #1

Tabitha Allen grew up in the thick of Chaos—the Chaos Motorcycle Club, that is. Her father is Chaos's leader, and the club has always had her back. But one rider was different from the start. When Tabby was running wild, Shy Cage was there. When tragedy tore her life apart, he helped her piece it back together. And now Tabby's thinking about so much more than friendship.

Tabby is everything Shy's ever wanted, but everything he thinks he can't have. She's beautiful, smart, and as his friend's daughter, untouchable. Shy never expected more than friendship, so when Tabby indicates she wants more—*much* more—he feels like the luckiest man alive. But even lucky men can crash and burn...

Keep going to read a tease of *Own the Wind.*

OWN THE WIND

You Don't Know Me

...Parker Cage only felt right on his bike.

It started with the dirt bike he got when he was fourteen, and it never stopped.

Five years ago, on his thirdhand Harley, he'd cruised by Ride Custom Cars and Bikes, a massive auto supply store that was attached to a garage in the back that built custom cars and bikes. He'd heard of it, hell, everyone had. The Chaos MC owned and ran it, and the garage was famous, built cars for movies and millionaires.

But it was the flag that flew under the American flag on top of the store that caught his attention. Until that day, he'd never looked up to see it. It was white and had the Chaos Motorcycle Club emblem on it with the words "Fire" and "Wind" on one side and "Ride" and "Free" on the other.

The second his eyes hit that flag, he felt his life take shape.

Nothing, not anything in his life until that time, except the first time he took off on a bike, had spoken to him like that flag. He didn't get why and he didn't spend time trying. It just spoke to him. So strong, it pulled him straight into the parking lot and set his boots to walking into the store.

Within months, he was a recruit for Chaos.

Now, he was a brother.

Outside his apartment, he parked his bike and moved from it to his truck. If she was in a state, Tabitha Allen wouldn't be able to hold on to him on a bike. If she was feeling sassy, which was usually the case, she'd put up a fight he couldn't win with her on a bike. So he hauled his ass into his beat up, old, white Ford truck, started it up and took off in the direction of the address on the text Hop sent.

As he drove, that fire in his gut intensified.

She was in college now, supposedly studying to be a nurse. Cherry, the Office Manager at the garage who also happened to be Tack's old lady and Tabby's stepmother, bragged about her grades and how good she was doing in school. Shy had no clue how Tab could pull off good grades when she was out fucking around all the time. He couldn't say one of the brothers got a Tabby Callout every night but it was far from infrequent.

The girl liked to party.

This wasn't surprising. She was nineteen. When he was nineteen, he'd liked to party too. Fuck, he was twenty-four and he still liked to party in a way he knew he'd never quit.

But he wasn't Tabby Allen.

He was a biker who worked in a garage and auto supply store, oftentimes raised hell and kicked ass when needed.

She was studying to be a freaking nurse with her dad footing that bill, so she needed to calm her ass down.

This didn't even get into the fact that it wasn't a new thing she liked to party *and* take a walk on the wild side. Three years ago, on his first Tabby Callout, she'd been sixteen and her twenty-three-year-old boyfriend had roughed her up because she wouldn't put out. That was the situation where Cherry nearly got her head caved in with a baseball bat, and it happened right in front of Shy. It was a miracle of quick reflexes that didn't end in disaster. Shy liked Cherry, everyone did, the woman was the shit; funny, pretty, sexy, smart, strong, and good for Tack in every way she could be.

If you could pick the perfect old lady, Tyra "Cherry" Allen would be it. She had sass but with class, dressed great, didn't let Tack roll all over her but did it in a way she didn't bust his balls. She was hilarious. She was sweet. She was a member of a biker family while still holding on to the woman she always was. And, honest to Christ, he'd never seen a man laugh and smile as often as Kane Allen. He had a good life, and it wasn't lost on a single member of the Club that Cherry made it that way.

So, during Tabby's first callout, it would have sucked if Cherry was made a vegetable or worse because of Tab's shit. Not to mention, if Shy had to explain why he was at Cherry's back, watching her head get caved in with a bat, instead of taking the lead and protecting her from that eventuality, Tack was so into his old lady it was highly likely Shy would no longer be breathing.

How the fuck Tabby hadn't learned her lesson after that mess, he had no clue, and as he drove it came crystal that she needed to get one.

And he was so pissed, he decided he was going to be the one to give it to her.

Tonight.

Own the Wind is available now.

ABOUT THE AUTHOR

Kristen Ashley is the *New York Times* bestselling author of over eighty romance novels including the *Rock Chick, Colorado Mountain, Dream Man, Chaos, Unfinished Heroes, The 'Burg, Magdalene, Fantasyland, The Three, Ghost and Reincarnation, The Rising, Dream Team* and *Honey* series along with several standalone novels. She's a hybrid author, publishing titles both independently and traditionally, her books have been translated in fourteen languages and she's sold over five million books.

Kristen's novel, *Law Man*, won the *RT Book Reviews* Reviewer's Choice Award for best Romantic Suspense, her independently published title *Hold On* was nominated for *RT Book Reviews* best Independent Contemporary Romance and her traditionally published title *Breathe* was nominated for best Contemporary Romance. Kristen's titles *Motorcycle Man, The Will*, and *Ride Steady* (which won the Reader's Choice award from *Romance Reviews*) all made the final rounds for Goodreads Choice Awards in the Romance category.

Kristen, born in Gary and raised in Brownsburg, Indiana, was a fourth-generation graduate of Purdue University. Since, she has lived in Denver, the West Country of England, and she now resides in Phoenix. She worked as a charity executive for eighteen years prior to beginning her independent publishing career. She now writes full-time.

Although romance is her genre, the prevailing themes running through all of Kristen's novels are friendship, family and a strong sisterhood. To this end, and as a way to thank her readers for their support, Kristen has created the Rock Chick Nation, a series of programs that are designed to give back to her readers and promote a strong female community.

The mission of the Rock Chick Nation is to live your best life, be true to your true self, recognize your beauty, and last but definitely not least, take your sister's back whether they're at your side as friends and family or if they're thousands of miles away and you don't know who they are.

The programs of the RC Nation include Rock Chick Rendezvous, weekends Kristen organizes full of parties and get-togethers to bring the sisterhood together, Rock Chick Recharges, evenings Kristen arranges for women who have been nominated to receive a special night, and Rock Chick Rewards, an ongoing program that raises funds for nonprofit women's organizations Kristen's readers nominate. Kristen's Rock Chick Rewards have donated hundreds of thousands of dollars to charity and this number continues to rise.

You can read more about Kristen, her titles and the Rock Chick Nation at KristenAshley.net.

facebook.com/kristenashleybooks
twitter.com/KristenAshley68
instagram.com/kristenashleybooks
pinterest.com/KristenAshleyBooks
goodreads.com/kristenashleybooks
bookbub.com/authors/kristen-ashley

ALSO BY KRISTEN ASHLEY

Rock Chick Series:

Rock Chick

Rock Chick Rescue

Rock Chick Redemption

Rock Chick Renegade

Rock Chick Revenge

Rock Chick Reckoning

Rock Chick Regret

Rock Chick Revolution

Rock Chick Reawakening

Rock Chick Reborn

The 'Burg Series:

For You

At Peace

Golden Trail

Games of the Heart

The Promise

Hold On

The Chaos Series:

Own the Wind

Fire Inside

Ride Steady

Walk Through Fire

A Christmas to Remember

Rough Ride

Wild Like the Wind

Free

Wild Fire

Wild Wind

The Colorado Mountain Series:

The Gamble

Sweet Dreams

Lady Luck

Breathe

Jagged

Kaleidoscope

Bounty

Dream Man Series:

Mystery Man

Wild Man

Law Man

Motorcycle Man

Quiet Man

Dream Team Series:

Dream Maker

Dream Chaser

Dream Bites Cookbook

Dream Spinner

Dream Keeper

The Fantasyland Series:

Wildest Dreams

The Golden Dynasty

Fantastical

Broken Dove

Midnight Soul

Gossamer in the Darkness

Ghosts and Reincarnation Series:

Sommersgate House

Lacybourne Manor

Penmort Castle

Fairytale Come Alive

Lucky Stars

The Honey Series:

The Deep End

The Farthest Edge

The Greatest Risk

The Magdalene Series:

The Will

Soaring

The Time in Between

Mathilda, SuperWitch:

Mathilda's Book of Shadows

Mathilda The Rise of the Dark Lord

Misted Pines Series

The Girl in the Mist

The Girl in the Woods

Moonlight and Motor Oil Series:

The Hookup

The Slow Burn

The Rising Series:

The Beginning of Everything

The Plan Commences

The Dawn of the End

The Rising

The River Rain Series:

After the Climb

After the Climb Special Edition

Chasing Serenity

Taking the Leap

Making the Match

The Three Series:

Until the Sun Falls from the Sky

With Everything I Am

Wild and Free

The Unfinished Hero Series:

Knight

Creed

Raid

Deacon

Sebring

Wild West MC Series:

Still Standing

Smoke and Steel

Other Titles by Kristen Ashley:

Heaven and Hell

Play It Safe

Three Wishes

Complicated

Loose Ends

Fast Lane

Perfect Together (*Summer* 2023)

Printed in the USA
CPSIA information can be obtained
at www.ICGtesting.com
LVHW040344230724
786164LV00001B/44

9 781954 680180